ALSO BY ROXIE NOIR

The Loveless Brothers

Enemies With Benefits

Best Fake Fiancé

Break the Rules

The Hookup Equation

One Last Time

Wildwood Society

The One Month Boyfriend

The Two Week Roommate

The Three Night Stand

The Four Year Crush

Dirtshine Series

Never Enough

Always You

Ever After

Standalone Romances

Ride

Reign

Torch

Safekeeping

The Savage Wild

Convict

ROXIE NOIR

AUTHOR'S NOTE

I made up almost all the geography in this book: towns, national forests, rivers, mountains, etc. They're loosely based on real places, but not too closely.

I'm also nearly certain I got some aspects of wildlands firefighting wrong. I've never done it before, and no amount of research is a substitute for experience, so apologies for anything I screwed up.

But otherwise… enjoy the ride.

ONE

CLEMENTINE

The white-haired man at the front of the line grabs the salad tongs for the third time. He's still holding his paper plate in his left hand and trying to hold *both* tongs in his right, which is his first mistake.

Mr. Jessop's second mistake is trying to grab the salad like a claw in one of those stuffed animal machines. The right move is to scoop it with the bottom tong and use the top one to keep the salad in place.

Listen, when you go to enough spaghetti dinners hosted by the Ladies' Auxiliary to the Lodgepole Rotary Club, you learn a thing or two.

He's got salad in the tongs. He's moving his arm slowly from his shoulder, maneuvering the mass of green closer to his paper plate. *Everyone* behind him in line is watching, sweating in this non-air-conditioned basement, and praying that this attempt works.

Move your plate closer to the salad bowl, I think. *You have two hands, use them both.*

Closer. Closer.

Then, an inch away from his plate, a tomato slice falls to the floor.

"Dang it," Mr. Jessop says.

"Whoops!" says Katie Parker, the rotund, cheerful woman serving meatballs. "Don't worry about it, Mr. Jessop, we'll get it in a minute."

Mr. Jessop just shakes his head, smiling.

"I've got butterfingers these days," he says.

Please let this line move forward, I think. Mr. Jessop is a sweet old man who owns the tiny grocery in town, and we all love him, but right now we just want this buffet line to move, because I can *feel* the sweat trickling down my spine.

Not that my seat is much cooler, but at least I won't be standing in heels that I last wore three years ago. I've only been upright for ten minutes, but I swear my feet are about to develop gangrene and fall off.

"Great spread as always," Mr. Jessop says. "I keep comin' back for the great food and the pretty ladies serving it."

He's nearly ninety, so it's charming instead of creepy when he flirts with a woman in her mid-twenties.

"Enjoy!" Katie says brightly, and Mr. Jessop moves toward his table.

The rest of the line takes a deep breath of relief, all at once. From there it moves more or less smoothly: we pick up plates and forks and knives and napkins. Nancy Turner gives me a regulation amount of spaghetti noodles, and Katie Parker gives me three meatballs and one spoonful of sauce.

Say what you want about the Ladies' Auxiliary, but they know what they're doing when it comes to feeding a crowd. Every plate of spaghetti is perfectly uniform, and I've got no doubt whatsoever that the last plate they serve will look exactly the same as the first.

These ladies do *not* run out of food early.

I put my plate down on the buffet, serve myself salad with

a tong in each hand, take a glass of non-alcoholic punch, and finally make my way back to my uncomfortable folding chair next to Jennifer, my boss.

"They ought to clear up that bottleneck at the salad," she says as I sit down, carefully folding my skirt under myself and lowering my butt toward my chair like a person used to wearing heels.

"It's the tongs," I say. "They'd be better off with the plastic ones you squeeze, but they always use those fancy wooden ones that the Boy Scouts gifted them a couple years ago."

Jennifer just shakes her head, then points to my plate and hers.

"Look at this. I bet if we were to get out a scale, we'd have exactly the same amount of spaghetti, sauce, and meatballs. They've got military precision with meatballs, but they can't control their salad?"

She's mostly kidding. Like, eighty percent kidding. The other twenty percent of Jennifer *loves* efficiency and is obsessed with finding solutions to inefficient problems.

Why she decided to work for the U.S. Forest Service, which isn't exactly a model of efficiency, is beyond me.

I sit down, cut a meatball in half, and wind some spaghetti around my fork.

"Are *you* gonna go tell Nancy how to make her buffet dinner better?" I ask, grinning at Jennifer.

Jennifer just laughs and winds spaghetti around her own fork.

"Please, my reputation in town is already bad enough after the Gertrude incident last week," she says. "I don't need to *also* be the woman who thought she could tell Nancy how to do something better."

Gertrude is a poorly-behaved husky who loves two things: escaping Jennifer's yard, and stealing ladies' undergarments from clotheslines. She's a sweet dog, but it's not a great combination of interests.

"Yeah, you should probably lay low for a while," I say. "Your invitation to the annual Pumpkin Festival Celebration Dinner is probably hanging in the balance."

Jennifer snorts, looking quickly behind her, as if to make sure that Nancy's not listening in somehow.

"If *that's* the threat, maybe I should actually—"

On the table, her phone starts buzzing, and a picture of her thirteen-year-old daughter Jessie pops up on the screen. Jennifer doesn't finish her sentence, just sighs.

"I'll bet you five bucks she can't find the microwave popcorn in the pantry," she says, picking up her phone. "Hi, sweetie."

I can hear Jessie's high-pitched voice from where I'm sitting, and Jennifer's eyebrows both go up at once. She stands.

"You've gotta slow down, sweetheart, I can't understand a word you're saying," she says into the phone, mouthing *sorry* at me as she walks away from our table.

"That girl was always a little high-strung," says Mrs. Flughorn, seated across the long wooden table from me. "I wouldn't have left her home alone tonight."

"She's thirteen," I say, already defensive of Jennifer. "I stayed home alone every day when I was thirteen."

"Some kids can handle it," Mrs. Flughorn says, looking through her glasses at me. She's got a helmet of gray hair that I've never seen move, no matter the weather.

"Jessie has to learn sometime," I say, even though I don't know why I'm arguing about this. Mrs. Flughorn is exactly the kind of stern-but-secretly-kind small-town old lady who'll probably die without ever changing her mind.

I mean, I have no idea what her first name is. Everyone just knows her as Mrs. Flughorn. She just shakes her head and takes a dainty-yet-authoritative bite of her salad as Jennifer comes back.

"A raccoon got in the house," she says without preamble, and leans over her chair, still standing as she shoves half a meatball into her mouth from her plate.

"Again?" I ask.

Jennifer nods, her mouth full.

"You *have* to do something about that dog door," I say. "Or at least teach the raccoons that it goes both ways."

Jennifer shakes her head and swallows.

"Every one of those fuckers is probably rabid," she says, then looks at Mrs. Flughorn. "Sorry."

She leans over again, stabbing another meatball with her fork.

"I gotta go, can you present the plaque?" she asks casually, stuffing the meatball into her mouth.

My heart plummets, and suddenly I feel like something's squeezing all my organs together, and it's not my pencil skirt.

I just stare up at Jennifer, my mouth slightly open.

"Peez?" she says around a mouthful of meatball.

My mouth's gone dry, and I glance at the microphone in the front of the room. There's probably a hundred and fifty, *maybe* two hundred people in here, and half of them I don't even know. My palms start sweating, my toes curl inside my shoes, and the spaghetti inside my stomach starts writhing dangerously.

"Can't, uh…" I trail off, looking for *anyone* else here who can represent the Forest Service. "Can't Bryce do it?"

Jennifer glances over at our summer intern. He's nineteen and currently being grilled about his future by Jane Widman, the high school's college counselor. I can *see* him sweating.

"No," Jennifer says. "Clementine, you're the Communications Ranger, just go up, say this is a token of our thanks for your hard work in containing the Elkhorn fire, hand it over, you're done."

I feel like she may as well be asking me to juggle flaming torches while walking a tightrope across the Grand Canyon.

"I'm only the *temporary* Communications Ranger because Becky got that job at Yellowstone!" I say.

Jennifer puts on her jacket, and I can tell that the conversation is almost over.

"Clementine, please?" she says. "You gave a talk to three hundred middle-schoolers last week, this is way less people than that."

But these are adults who will be looking at me, and thinking about what I'm saying, and noticing how sweaty I am....

My heart is beating out of control, and I have to force myself to keep breathing normally. Jennifer puts one hand on my shoulder and leans in.

"I wouldn't ask if I thought you wouldn't do a perfectly great job," she says, and pushes the plaque in front of my plate. "Just pretend they're a bunch of kindergarteners and you'll be fine, I promise. You've gotta get over this public speaking thing sooner or later."

I just nod. My hair is sticking to the sweat on the back of my neck. Jennifer squeezes my shoulder.

"The stakes will never be lower, I promise," she says. "You'll be fine. I gotta go trap a raccoon."

"Good luck," I say, though my voice sounds far away, even to me.

Jennifer gives me one final pat and then walks away, through the double doors that lead out of the church basement. For a moment or two, I imagine that she'll come back and say *False alarm, I can present the plaque*, but she doesn't.

I look down at it. It's your standard commemorative plaque, maybe six inches high and ten long, a metal plate on wood.

This plaque presented to the
Canyon Country Hotshot Crew
by the
United States Forest Service
Big Sky National Forest, Copper Creek Ranger Division
With gratitude for your hard work and dedication
in containing the Elkhorn Fire
Fighters for Life

I know perfectly well that this shouldn't be a big deal. No one in the audience is even going to remember what I say — I'm just the person presenting some plaque, between the performance by Twinkle Toes Tap Dance and *America, the Beautiful* sung by the high school chorus.

But I can't help it. The thought of saying two sentences in front of this many adults panics me like nothing else. At least Mrs. Flughorn, across the table from me, is telling someone else where they're going wrong in disciplining their two-year-old and she's stopped looking at me.

I don't eat the rest of my meatballs. After a few minutes, the mayor of Lodgepole, Barry Vashton, steps up to the microphone and starts in with his small-town, folksy act, introducing the sixteen-year-old who's won an essay contest and is going to read a few pages on "What Service to My Country Means to Me."

The sixteen-year-old looks considerably less nervous than I feel. He does fine, then walks away from the microphone to polite applause. Barry comes back. There's a kid reading her poem, a high school student singing a song he wrote himself, a group of little kids presenting their drawings to the firefighters.

It's all your standard, small-town, thanks-for-saving-our-asses stuff. I'm at the back of the room, so I can't see the firefighters' faces, but I imagine they see this sort of thing a lot. Hopefully they still find it charming, at least.

Finally, Barry announces the Twinkle Toes. I feel as if someone's kneading my stomach like bread dough, but I take a deep breath and rehearse what I'm going to say.

On behalf of the Copper Creek Ranger Division, I'd like to present this plaque...

Does that sound dumb? That definitely sounds dumb.

I hereby present this plaque of thanks to the Canyon Country Hotshot Crew...

Oh my God, that's worse. The Twinkle Toes are tapping away at the front of the room, seven or eight elementary school kids with enormous smiles plastered on their faces, *almost* in sync. I take deep breaths and try to concentrate on just watching them, telling myself that the right words will just magically come to mind when it's time for me to get up there.

The song wraps up. Sweat trickles down the back of my neck, and I force myself to clap along with everyone else in the room, even though I'm trying to keep my hands from shaking. Barry walks back to the microphone.

"Weren't they wonderful, folks?" he says, grinning widely. "Let's hear it again for the Twinkle Toes!"

We clap again.

Maybe he'll misread the program, forget the plaque, and I won't have to present it, I think.

Maybe the earth will open, swallow me whole, and I won't have to do this.

"Next, I'd like to give the floor to the senior ranger from the Copper Creek Division, Jennifer Tetson. Jennifer?"

Oh God, he doesn't even know that she's not here. Now I have to say that, too, along with some variation on, "Here's a plaque, thanks for keeping things from burning down."

I've got the plaque in a death grip, but I stand. I swear I can *feel* a hundred and fifty or two hundred eyes on me, and I somehow navigate stepping away from the table and walking toward the microphone in my high heels.

You can do this, McKinnon, I think. *The stakes are never gonna be lower.*

My heels click across the tile floor. I hear the soft sounds of people whispering to each other, the scrape of plastic forks against paper plates, napkins rustling. Then I'm at the microphone, I'm clearing my throat, my hand is reaching out to adjust it in the stand.

"Thanks, Barry," I hear myself saying. My voice is higher pitched than normal, but it's not even shaking.

It's a fucking miracle.

"Unfortunately, Jennifer was called away at the last minute," I say, and pause.

Do I tell them another raccoon got into her house and she has to trap it? I think wildly. *Do they need to know that?*

I laugh nervously into the microphone and decide to cut it as short as possible.

"But, on her behalf, and on the behalf of everyone — of the whole Copper Creek Ranger Division, which I'm part of, actually, I'm also a forest ranger —"

This is going off the rails. *Fuck.* I take a deep breath.

Suddenly, a piece of public speaking advice comes back to me: *Pick one person in the crowd and pretend that you're talking just to them.* I glance over the tables in front of me, but they're all fire-fighters I don't know, and their faces just make me more nervous.

"In thanks for your hard work fighting the Elkhorn fire, which I'm sure everyone here knows is one hundred percent contained and actually almost out since we've had those big rainstorms rolling through..."

I stop.

I've landed on a pair of deep blue eyes. They're the color of a glacial melt lake in the spring. The color of a snowy hill-side in deep shadow.

I didn't make that up just now. I once waxed poetic for two

whole pages in my diary about these eyes, and even though I don't remember half the ridiculous things I wrote back then, I sure as *hell* recognize them.

Hunter Casden is staring right back at me.

I didn't even know he was here, in this church basement, let *alone* in the town of Lodgepole.

I wasn't even sure he was in Montana, honestly.

"Uh," I say.

My brain's frozen. I think I'd be less surprised if JFK or Elvis were sitting there. At least, I'd be less gobsmacked.

I didn't lose my virginity to Elvis. When I was eighteen, I wasn't *completely certain* I was going to marry JFK.

I swallow and manage to close my mouth. My brain is going a million miles a second, thinking a stream of nonsense like *holy shit is that Hunter yes that's him wait are you sure what if it's just — no, I'm really really sure that is him sitting right there, yes, oh my god, how long has it even been does he recognize me?*

Then, the worst thing happens.

Hunter smiles at me, and suddenly, I'm not here in front of practically everyone I know. I'm in the front seat of his truck after school, just the two of us, and he's looking at me like *that.*

I force myself to look away. I pick a spot on the wall and stare at it, even though I don't have the slightest clue where I was in my little speech.

"On behalf of the Forest Service and the Copper Creek Ranger Division, I'd like to present the Canyon Country Hotshot crew with this commemorative plaque of thanks, from us to you!" I say, the words tumbling over each other, like they can't wait to be out of my mouth.

A second later, I hold the plaque up in front of myself. I look everywhere but at Hunter.

People applaud politely. A middle-aged man stands from a table, walks up to me, and holds out one hand. I shake it. I hand over the plaque as a few flashes go off, and then he gestures at the microphone.

I'm more than happy to step back.

"I'd like to say a warm thanks to the people of Lodgepole for this beautiful plaque, and for opening your hearts and your homes to us like you have..."

He goes on for a few more sentences, but I'm not listening, because *Hunter Casden is sitting fifteen feet away and I didn't know we were in the same state.*

The man holds up the plaque. He looks at me. People applaud again. I smile mechanically, because this seems like the sort of occasion where people smile, even though I feel like every nerve in my body is vibrating so fast I might catch fire.

Barry comes back. The guy I gave the plaque to heads to his seat, and I walk back to mine, heels clicking on the floor, beads of sweat sliding behind my ears.

I don't look at Hunter again, but after I'm back at my seat, I stare at the back of his head and don't hear a single word anyone else says for the rest of the night.

My mind is swirling. I used to think about this moment all the time, about what I'd say to him if I ever saw him again. I'd imagined that I'd be happily married, hot husband on my arm, glamorous and confident, not stumbling my way through a simple speech in a church basement.

I didn't think I'd feel this deep, weird stab of *familiarity*. I didn't think I'd still recognize the look on his face. I didn't think it would feel like I'd just seen him yesterday, not eight years ago.

And I didn't think my brain would insist on repeating the last thing he ever said to me: *I never loved you anyway.*

TWO

HUNTER

From across the table, my Captain is glaring daggers, but I have no fucking idea why. I just stare back, wondering what his problem is *this* time.

I showed up to this dumb spaghetti dinner, even though I'd rather be with that cute waitress from the barbecue joint, showing her some fire hose techniques, if you know what I mean. Though from the way she winked at me and wrote her number on my receipt, I have the feeling she already knows her way around one.

Porter's still glaring, and now his jaw flexes a little, the way it does when he's *really* annoyed, but I still don't know why. I wore my only button-down shirt, a tie, and khaki slacks, so I look like a twenty-year-old interviewing to be the bag boy at the grocery store.

I'm not really paying attention to the tap dancing kids or the high schoolers reciting poetry, but come the fuck on. None of us are. This is the boring part of the job, the part where the people whose towns didn't get burned down tell us how glad they are about it.

Sure, it's nice of them. But I'd rather be doing pretty much anything else right now. Hell, I'd rather be digging a fire break in ninety-degree heat, watching smoke rise from trees a quarter-mile away. At least *that's* exciting.

The kids up front stop tap-dancing, and everyone applauds. I put down my plastic fork and join in, and even Porter looks away from me for a moment.

Then the guy with the gray hair — I think he's the mayor or something, if this town is even big enough for a mayor — comes back and starts saying something. I glance down at my plate, and suddenly, I realize what Ryan was so annoyed about.

My plastic silverware is in a pile on my plate, broken into tiny pieces. It's topped by my napkin, also torn into tiny shreds.

I've never been able to sit still. I need *action*, I need *things to do*, or I start getting a little stir crazy. That's when I do shit like tear napkins into tiny pieces. Porter once compared me to a dog who tears the house up out of boredom when the owners were gone, and even though I wasn't crazy about the comparison, he had a point.

I sit back in my chair and cross my arms in front of my chest, giving Porter a *happy now?* look. He turns away, and I wonder how much longer I have to sit here.

I don't do this job for the thanks, or to save lives, or any of that heroic shit. I do this because it's exciting. It's thrilling. It's the only thing that comes close to being in a war zone.

The mayor-or-whatever is still talking, but at least he's wrapping it up.

"Next, I'd like to give the floor to the senior ranger from the Copper Creek Division, Jennifer Tetson. Jennifer?"

A chair somewhere behind me scrapes against the tile, and as heels click toward the front of the room, I pray that this endless dinner is nearly over.

Then Jennifer Tetson comes into view, her back to me, and I sit up a little straighter.

Her ass in that skirt might make up for the last hour I've

spent listening to kids sing off-key. Hell, that ass might be worth *another* hour of sappy patriotic songs and bad poetry.

She threads her way past a few more tables, my eyes *glued* to her. I feel Captain Porter glaring at me again, but it's way beyond my power to stop watching the way her hips move under her professional-but-tight skirt.

Plus, there's something *familiar* about her that I can't put my finger on.

It's just déjà vu, I think. *How many times have you watched a hot girl walk across a room?*

I'm not convincing, even to myself.

Jennifer, I think, trying to jog my memory. The name doesn't ring a bell, but it's not like I can remember every woman's name, and I've *met* plenty of forest rangers in my line of work.

Then she reaches the microphone, says something to the mayor, and turns around.

My mouth *actually* drops open.

Holy shit, it's Clementine.

For a moment I just blink at her. My mind goes blank with surprise. Then I manage to pull my mouth shut and start spinning through possibilities.

Did she change her name? I think. *Does she have a twin? Separated at birth? What's she doing here? She's a forest ranger?*

I'm fucking baffled. Not that she's a forest ranger — that actually makes total sense — but I had no idea she was *here*. I had no idea her name was Jennifer now.

But I'm totally sure of one thing: that's *her*. I know it with a bone-deep certainty that I can't even explain, like the last eight years just peeled away and I'm about to walk her to class again.

She clears her throat and adjusts the microphone. Even from here I can tell she's nervous. I guess she never got over her dislike of speaking in front of more than four people.

"Thanks, Barry," she says, her voice high-pitched and tight, but the same as I remember. "Unfortunately, Jennifer was called away at the last minute, but I'm here on her behalf…"

Well, that explains that, at least.

Clementine goes on in her nervous voice, her light hazel eyes darting around the crowd. She's saying something to us, but all I can think is: she got *hot*.

That's not even accurate.

She got *hotter*.

Clementine was always hot, but she used to be secretly hot, her body hidden under a layer of sweaters and baggy cargo jeans. I could always tell how sexy she was — it's a talent — but now it's definitely *not* a secret. Not if her ass looks like *that* in a skirt, and not with the way she's looking out at the crowd with moss-colored eyes under deep brown bangs, even if she's nervous.

She rambles a little, fiddling with the plaque in her hands, scanning the crowd. I may be twenty-six, and may not have seen her in almost a decade, but I feel like I've been knocked back to seventeen again, fucking around in chemistry class, trying to get the cute nerd to notice me.

I've gotten *much* better at women, by the way. I haven't broken a beaker just so a girl would look at me in ages.

Her eyes sweep the crowd again, and suddenly she's locked on to me. She trails off for a moment, and even though her face stays perfectly still, two things are obvious right away.

One, she recognizes me.

And two, she had *no* idea I was here.

She swallows once, and I have to fight the urge to start laughing, because this feels so strange, and weird, and more than anything *familiar*.

I can't help but smile at her. For a second, I'm certain she's going to smile back, but then she snaps out of it, brushes her bangs out of her eyes, and starts talking again, even faster than before.

In a blur, she gives Porter the plaque. He says something nice. I can't tear my eyes away from Clementine. People clap.

They both walk away, and even though I shouldn't, I crane my head after her.

She doesn't look back at me.

Some high school girls come up and sing *America, the Beautiful*, but I can't even pretend I'm listening. I haven't even talked to Clementine in eight years. When we broke up, she practically fell off the face of the earth.

I feel like I'm seeing a ghost, except I'm pretty sure she's real.

The mayor comes back and talks more. I think about Clementine, years ago, the first time we fooled around in her parents' basement. On that ugly green couch with yellow flowers, my hands under her sweater.

The *noise* she made when I unhooked her bra and pinched her nipples. I was a little more experienced than her, but not much. I swear that noise was a revelation.

The next time we were on that couch, when I got my hands under her sweater, she wasn't wearing a bra at all. I still remember exactly the way she smiled when my fingers found nothing but skin.

Everyone around me applauds, and then they start standing. Someone's calling my name, but it's background noise. I stand and turn away from the table, already scanning the crowd over everyone's heads, but I don't see her at the table where she was sitting.

I don't see her *anywhere*.

Shit.

I pick up the pace, dodging around old ladies who are slow to stand up, nearly tripping over some kids who dart right in front of me. A mom gives me a dirty look but I ignore it, glancing over her head, looking for Clementine's dark hair and hazel eyes.

Nothing.

Did she run away from me? I wonder, and my heart sinks. I know our breakup was ugly — hell, I was there too — but I didn't think it was avoid-me-eight-years-later ugly. For fuck's sake, we were teenagers, and now we're adults.

She can't even say hi?

"*Excuse* me," a very prim voice says, and I snap out of it to find a middle-aged woman in a button-down denim dress, sneakers, and a stern expression standing there, staring at me.

"Yes ma'am," I say, and smile at her.

"The rest of your team is helping the Ladies' Auxiliary clear the tables and chairs," she says, pointing, but her voice has lost the grating quality it had before.

Even if she won't come out and directly *ask*, I know exactly what she wants. I'm not stupid.

"Just one minute, ma'am," I say, still smiling. Then I walk off before she can say anything else, her withering glare following me across the room.

She can glare 'til the cows come home for all I care.

I shoulder my way through the exit, still looking around at the people milling around the foyer, heading up the stairs to the cool night. No Clementine, but I'm not that surprised.

Back when I knew her, when she was upset, other people were the last thing she wanted to deal with. If she was angry, or embarrassed, half the time I'd find her alone in a dark room, sitting on the floor, staring out a window, and she'd tell me she just needed *space*.

So I look for space. I walk down a hall, away from the throng of people, away from the ladies who want me to put away tables and away from the teenaged singers and the dads who smell like spaghetti. I turn a corner into a darker part of the church basement.

Near the end, there's a closed door, light leaking out from underneath it. Behind me, a couple of the crew burst into laughter, and just from the sound, I can tell they've spiked their fruit punch. After this they're heading to the Rusty Beaver, the only bar in town, and they'll probably all go home with the town's three eligible women.

I step forward into the dark hallway. I don't know why I'm so sure, but I *know* Clementine's in there, that she escaped here for a minute alone after her presentation.

Halfway down, I pause for a second and listen. There's the hubbub of the crowd behind me, but there's a sound from behind the closed door, too, and suddenly I pause.

It's Clementine.

And I'm almost positive she's *sobbing*.

She doesn't want to see you, I think. *She always hated it when people saw her cry.*

I walk to the door anyway, drawn in, a moth to the light.

Inside, there's a long, drawn out gasp, like she's having trouble breathing, and I frown, my heart clenching.

"Clem?" I call, one hand on the door frame.

There's no answer, just a muffled sound from inside, and I realize I was wrong: she's not sobbing, she's *choking*.

I try the doorknob, but it's locked. Probably a bathroom.

I slam my shoulder against the door, and it shudders but doesn't budge.

From inside the room, I just hear another wheeze, the sound of someone struggling for breath.

"Get away from the door!" I shout, and take a step back, readying myself.

I pause a moment, gathering myself. I find the best spot on the door: right above the knob, the most likely to pop the lock.

Then I kick it in with as much force as I can muster.

THREE

CLEMENTINE

I put both hands on the edge of the sink and grip the porcelain so hard my fingertips go white. Then I force myself to stop coughing for just long enough to finally take a real breath.

Hunter's outside. I don't know how the hell he found me down here, but he's shouting my name. I can't even answer without coughing harder.

God, don't let me be the first person to die from inhaling fruit punch while her ex-boyfriend pounds on the bathroom door, I think. *How did this even happen?*

"Move back!" Hunter shouts, and at that moment, I start coughing hard again, tears running down my face, bent over the sink.

I wave one hand at the door helplessly, like *that* will somehow keep him from doing whatever he's about to do.

It doesn't.

A second later there's a crash and the door flies open, the doorknob slamming into the wall. I bury my face in my elbow, still coughing hard, as Hunter rushes toward me.

All I can do is hold up my other hand and shake my head,

hoping to communicate *please don't try the Heimlich and break my ribs or something.*

"Clem," he says, but he stops just short of me, hovering both hands near my shoulder.

I shake my head harder, then grip the sink again and take another long, shaky inhale.

"What happened?" he asks, still sounding concerned.

His voice still sounds almost the same. He's got the same slow, twangy cadence that he used to have, the one he learned growing up on his parents' cattle ranch. I think he's a little raspier now, maybe a little deeper, and his words might be a little more clipped, but he's unmistakably *familiar.*

As an answer I just point at my half-full glass of punch, sitting on the sink, and start coughing again. This time he puts on big hand on my back, right between my shoulder blades, and even though I'm still gasping and hacking, it's warm and comforting.

"I'm fine," I finally manage to gasp. A tear runs down my bright red face.

"This is fine?" he asks, letting his fingers rub a small circle on my upper spine.

I'm still coughing and just nod, meeting his gaze in the mirror. He doesn't look worried any more. If anything, he looks slightly amused.

"Because it *seems* like you took your drink into the bathroom with you and now you're choking half to death," Hunter says, his hand still circling my back.

I inhale again, clear my throat, and manage to not start coughing.

"Appearances," I start.

I cough again, but get it under control.

"Can be deceiving," I say, then cough again.

He just chuckles, his deep blue eyes sparkling at me.

"Also, shut up," I gasp.

Now he's laughing, and even though I'm still panting for breath and leaning over the sink, I can't help but laugh along with him at this *incredibly* dumb situation. I could never help but laugh along with Hunter.

Then, for a second, it feels *normal* that he's standing there, rubbing my back, teasing me for doing something dumb like choking on fruit punch. It doesn't feel like I haven't even heard from him in nearly a decade, or like we had a horrible breakup, or like I cut the varsity letter jacket he gave me into shreds and threw it away.

I do regret that last thing, for the record. That was a little too far.

I wipe the tears off my face, and Hunter takes his hand off my back to grab some toilet paper, handing it to me.

"You sure you're okay?" he asks as I wipe my eyes.

"Is someone down there?" I hear a man's voice call from outside the bathroom.

"Shit," I say, and even that makes me cough softly, twice.

Hunter glances at the broken door and makes a face. I grab my plastic punch cup, dump the pink liquid down the drain, and toss the cup in the trash just as Phil Herman appears in the doorway, his plump face in a permanent frown.

"Is everything all right?" he asks, even though from the look on his face, if I say *yes* he's going to disagree.

I clear my throat again and suppress a cough.

"I got some water down the wrong pipe," I say, my voice weak and raspy. "Guess I've got a drinking problem."

Phil doesn't smile. He just blinks. Hunter puts his hand on my back again, and this time, I shiver a little bit.

"I apologize," he says, and he sounds surprisingly authoritative. "I thought she was having an emergency."

"I'm fine," I offer.

Phil nods, completely unamused, his mouth a near-perfect

straight line. We stare at each other, and I wipe one more tear from my eye, clearing my throat.

"I see," he says.

"I'll get the door fixed," I say quickly.

"It's my fault, sir," Hunter says, and I can hear the smile in his voice. "I thought she was choking and overreacted. I'll fix that door first thing tomorrow."

Phil looks at the door, then at Hunter, and finally at me.

"Glad you're okay," he says, still without cracking a smile. Then he disappears, and I can hear his fading voice call, "It's fine, Clementine inhaled water and one of the firemen thought she was choking to death..."

And just like that, we're alone in a bathroom.

"At least he didn't find out that you choked because you took your drink into the bathroom with you," Hunter finally says, and I look at him in the mirror. His eyes are crinkling around the corners, and though some of the lines are new, the expression isn't.

He's behind me, looking over my shoulder. To summarize: he's the hot, handsome, rugged picture of masculinity; I'm bright pink, eyes red and still watering.

I turn away and lean against the sink, cross my arms over my chest, and sigh.

"It's a small town and word travels fast," I say. "I can't have people thinking I'm the kind of girl who takes food into the ladies' room."

"Even though you are?" he teases.

"I did it once," I say.

"Right."

My throat is still scratchy, and I clear it again.

"You know the joke about the bridge-builder, right?" I ask.

Hunter shakes his head.

"Well, I forget the setup, actually, but the punchline is, you can build a thousand bridges, but fuck one sheep and no one ever says, *here comes the bridge-builder,*" I say.

Hunter just raises his eyebrows, leaning back against the wall.

"Because they're all saying *here comes the sheep-fucker,*" I explain. "Because that's the thing—"

Hunter laughs.

"I got it, Clem," he says. "And you don't want people saying *here comes drink-in-the-bathroom girl.*"

"Right," I say.

Then there's a long moment where we just look at each other and I have no idea what to say. A thousand things are rushing through my head, like *Hey! It's been a while!* or *So you're a firefighter now?* or *How long have you been back from Afghanistan* or even *How's your mom, who hates me?*

They all seem like dumb things to say, so I don't say any of them.

"You'd just have to do something even more newsworthy," he says.

I raise one eyebrow.

"I'm not fucking a sheep," I say. "Or any farm animal, for that matter."

"That actually wasn't going to be my first suggestion," he says. "I was just going say dye your hair pink or something."

I laugh.

"Fucking a barnyard animal was at least number four or five on my list," he says.

"Pink hair might be more newsworthy around here," I say, still laughing. "Lots of lonely men on ranches, you know."

"Well, there's one way to find out," Hunter says, his blue eyes dancing in his head. "I'll dye my hair, you fuck a sheep, and we'll compare notes later."

"I have to fuck the sheep?"

"You're the one who came up with that *immediately*," he teases. "Almost like you had it waiting in the wings."

"I haven't gotten *that* kinky," I say without thinking.

Then I realize what I just said out loud, and my mouth snaps shut, my face getting hot.

Hunter laughs again, and I swallow, blushing and smiling. I'm not generally in the habit of joking about bestiality or how kinky I may or may not be, but something about talking to Hunter feels so natural and comfortable that I completely forget to censor myself.

It feels like it used to, is what I'm saying.

"I won't ask how kinky you've gotten," he asks, his voice slow and laconic. I laugh awkwardly again, and push myself off the sink.

"We should get out of here," I say. "Now that I've embarrassed myself twice in this room."

"You're blaming the room?"

"Easier than blaming myself," I say. "Also, there are better places to stand than a bathroom."

I walk for the door and Hunter follows, hitting the light switch on the way out.

We walk into the hallway, and we're plunged into near-darkness, the only light the fluorescents from the other end of the hall.

For the first time, I wonder *why* he was outside the bathroom door, at the end of this dark hallway. There are plenty of other bathrooms in the church basement. I don't ask, though.

"Sorry about the door," he says as we turn the corner, the lights washing over us. "Sometimes the training kicks in."

"Pun unintended?" I say, grinning at him.

Hunter chuckles and shakes his head.

"I guess that hasn't changed either," he says.

We walk up the stairs to street-level, where plenty of people are still milling around the Methodist Church's small front yard, some kids playing on the fenced-in swing set. My ankles wobble a little in my heels on the grass, but I stay upright.

As soon as Hunter steps toward the crowd, I *swear* every head turns, and it catches me by surprise.

Old ladies who'll barely give me the time of day light up like gray-haired Christmas trees. The high school cheerleaders whisper to each other and giggle. Thirty-something moms holding babies give him a long, slow once-over while ignoring their husbands.

He's a firefighter who just saved the town, I remind myself. *The point of this whole dinner was to says thanks to his squadron. Of course people are staring.*

Then Nancy Turner, the plump, iron-haired lady who was in charge of giving everyone *exactly* the same amount of spaghetti, waves him over toward her. Hunter looks down at me.

"I wouldn't refuse if I were you," I say, even though I'm a little disappointed, and drop my voice to a murmur. "The Ladies' Auxiliary can cause you pain in ways you've never even *imagined*."

"I've seen hell, and it's an endless spaghetti dinner," he mutters back, waving at Nancy.

She makes an even more emphatic *come over here* gesture, and Hunter glances down at me.

"Back me up, will you?" he asks.

Then he starts walking for Nancy without waiting for me to answer.

For a split second, I'm annoyed, irritation flaring through me like gasoline catching fire in a rush.

I guess he still does this too, I think. *Just walking into something and expecting me to follow.*

But then it fades almost instantly, and I realize I just got annoyed about something that happened eight years ago.

Just pretend this is all brand-new, I tell myself. *At least pretend you're just old friends seeing each other after a while.*

Not everything he does is about you. It never was.

I follow Hunter to the throng of ladies, where Nancy already has one hand on his arm and is gushing about him to her friends, *all* of whom are actually smiling real smiles.

I sure don't get real smiles from this crowd.

"The fire came within a few miles of Trudy's house," Nancy is saying. "She told me she nearly had to evacuate. Had her bags packed and *everything*."

"Thank the Lord she didn't," says another woman — Shelly? — who's got her hand over her heart.

"All those mementos she has," pipes up another woman. "She's been collecting those spoons for almost forty years."

Everyone nods somberly. Then they look at me like they're noticing my presence for the first time.

"I didn't know you two were acquainted," Nancy says, her voice cooling a little. She's never been a big fan of me, though I'm not sure why. Maybe just because her personality sucks.

Hunter and I look at each other for a moment, then back at the ladies.

"We're old friends," he says.

"We went to high school together," I say. "Over in Ashlake."

"Oh, my sister lives there," one of the ladies says, but I barely hear her.

Old friends.

It feels weirdly good to put a label on what we are, and it feels weirdly good that the label is *old friends*, like we really are past our dumb breakup bullshit. Like finally, at least, we've talked again and we're cool.

"Go fighting bison!" Hunter says, holding up one fist, and the ladies all titter-laugh.

"We want to hear *all* about firefighting," one of them says. "Isn't it scary?"

"Actually, I said I'd see Clementine home," Hunter says, and looks over at me.

I'm about to say *no, you didn't*, when I remember his request for backup.

Well, his *demand*, but that's not a fight old friends have. Instead, I fake a huge yawn that turns into a real one.

"Yeah, I have to get up bright and early tomorrow," I say.

"It's sweet of you to walk a lady home," one of the ladies says.

Nancy nods, but the look she gives me isn't quite as positive. She lets his arm go.

"Come into Ellie's Bakery sometime," a woman says as we turn away. "Free cookies for firefighters!"

"I'd be delighted," Hunter says, and then we're walking away from the knot, across the lawn, and onto the sidewalk.

We walk in silence for half a block, cross a street, and then he speaks up again.

"Thanks for the rescue," he says.

"It's your hide when they find you later," I say. "And make no mistake, they *will* find you."

"I can only take so much goddamn fake nice in one day," he says. "Tonight they're grateful their houses didn't burn down, but give them a week and they'll be writing letters to the editor about how today's misspent youth will never amount to anything and we should all be drafted."

I laugh out loud.

"Miss small-town life yet?" I ask.

"I don't have to miss it," he says. "I still live in Ashlake. In the winter, anyway."

Ashlake is an hour away as the crow flies. Three hours if you're a human and have to drive around the mountain.

"I didn't know that," I say.

"You would if you had Facebook, or Twitter, or went to our five-year reunion," he says. "I was starting to wonder if you were dead."

I make a face, but deep inside, I think: *he looked for me.*

"I spend half my time in the woods, digging holes to poop into and not showering a whole lot," I say. "And I didn't really want to re-live high school."

"You're the only one," he says, as we cross another street and I lead us left. "I'm pretty sure most everyone we went to high school with peaked at about age seventeen."

I glance over at him. Even if he looks a little uptight right now, in a button-down shirt and khakis, I can tell that at least he didn't peak *physically* at seventeen. Not that he was bad then. Not at *all*.

A quick shiver runs through me, and I tear my eyes away.

Old friends, I think.

"You don't think you peaked at seventeen?" I ask.

"I sure as hell hope not," he says, and smiles his most charming smile at me. "You think I did?"

"I don't think I'm in a position to judge," I say. "I don't know what you've been up to."

He gives me a long look. We turn right, onto my block, and I start to feel like I'm under a microscope. I keep my eyes straight ahead, suddenly too nervous to look over at him.

"I did two more tours after the last time we talked," he says. "And you know how I always said I was gonna go to college after?"

I just nod.

"I lasted less than a semester," he says. "Then I applied for the Hotshots, went to training, and here I am. Summers, I dig fire breaks and set controlled burns. Winters, I stay with my parents and I work on their dude ranch."

"You're a firefighter half the time and a cowboy half the time?" I ask.

"It sounds better when you put it that way," he says.

"You're half the Village People all by yourself."

"That'll look good on my resume," he says.

We're almost to the house I share with two other forest rangers. It's big, creaky, and could use some fresh paint, but the rent is cheap since it's owned by the forest service, and it's in a good location, right on the edge of town.

Besides, I spend half my time out in the woods, doing my job. I don't need all that much house.

I stop in front of it, and Hunter looks up at it, then at me.

"This is you?" he asks.

"This is me," I say, rummaging in my purse for my keys.

He laughs, and I look up. Hunter jerks his thumb over his shoulder.

"They put us in the old bunk house," he says.

I blink. Then I turn and look at the house next to mine. I know it used to be some sort of lodging, and it's owned by the Forest Service too, but I didn't know they were having people stay there.

"We just got in this afternoon," Hunter goes on.

"How long?" I ask, finally pulling my keys out.

He's next door? I think. *I'm going to see him all the time, whether I like it or not.*

"Probably four, five days," he says. "Just enough time to rest up before something else catches on fire. Don't worry, you'll be rid of us soon."

I make a face at him.

"That's not what I meant," I say.

"I know," Hunter says.

I don't know what to say to that. I can't find the words for *I like that you know* or *this is more okay than I thought it would be,* so I just look at him for a long moment, his deep blue eyes nearly black in the dark.

"You look good," Hunter finally says, his deep, raspy voice softer now. "And you seem happy."

"You look the same," I say, because he does. He looks a little older, maybe his face looks a little leaner, his hair a little shorter, but all that's minor. In all the ways that count, he's still the handsome, all-American jock who got assigned to be my lab partner in eleventh grade.

"I'll take that as a compliment," he says, smiling.

"You would," I tease, and we both laugh.

"I'll see you around?" he asks.

I swallow, because I'm suddenly nervous that he's leaving. I wanted more than *see you around*. I don't know what, because I don't really understand what we are to each other.

I don't have a map for *this* relationship. But this kind of casual *later, dude*, isn't quite it.

Old friends, I remind myself.

"Yeah," I say, ignoring the sudden butterflies in my stomach. "You're just next door."

His gaze flicks from my eyes to my lips and back, so fast I nearly miss it.

Kiss me, my subconscious whispers, and I hold my breath in sudden alarm.

DO NOT KISS ME, I think. *I definitely don't want that, not even a little.*

Then he nods once, still smiling, and turns around. I don't exhale until he's walking away.

FOUR

HUNTER

"**S**leep well, Casden?" Porter barks.

I'm still standing in the doorway of the kitchen, wearing nothing but boxers, still half-asleep. Normally I'm not this groggy, but I got ten hours of sleep in a real bed last night, and my body's not used to it.

"I slept fine," I say, already feeling defensive. As out of it as I am, I can just fucking *tell* he's spoiling for a fight.

"Good," he says, and shovels a spoonful of cereal and milk into his mouth. "You've got a door to fix down at the Methodist church."

I clench my jaw and open the fridge too forcefully, getting out the milk. I don't respond to Porter just yet, because if being in the Marines taught me one thing, it was how to fucking bite my tongue when I needed to.

"You hear me?" he asks.

"Yeah," I say, pouring myself a cup of coffee and adding the milk. Coffee's a rare luxury for me during the summers — anything not strictly necessary doesn't usually make it into a fire camp — and Ryan goddamn Porter is ruining it.

It's not even that he wants me to fix the door. *Obviously* I need to fix the door that I kicked in. It's the asshole way he says it, like I'm a child who needs to be kept in line. I like my job, but I'm not sure how much longer I can deal with having him as a boss, because sooner or later, I'm going to stop being able to keep my mouth shut.

"You gonna fix that door?" he goes on.

I take a long, long gulp of coffee and look out the kitchen window, forcing myself not to say anything until I'm good and ready.

It takes a little while.

"I'm heading over there right after breakfast," I finally say, the words clipped and brusque, not that I give a shit whether Porter knows I'm annoyed.

"Good," he says, scooping another spoon into his mouth. "Try not to kick in any more doors to get to the pussy behind it, all right, Casanova?"

I put my coffee mug down too hard and it slams onto the counter, the coffee sloshing out and over my hand. My anger flares, hot and bright, at someone calling Clementine *the pussy*.

"I thought she was choking," I say, my voice tight and short. "I misread the situation. I made the wrong call. I'll fix it."

Porter just levels his gaze at me, chewing his cereal.

"Casden, don't go thinking I don't know what motivates you," he says mildly. "I don't care who or what you stick your dick in as long as it doesn't reflect poorly on Canyon Country. And broken doors reflect pretty goddamn poorly."

I pour more coffee but skip the milk this time, because I need to leave this kitchen before I make the situation worse.

"Understood," I say, then leave the room before Porter can respond.

Back in the dorm room I'm sharing with three other guys, I consider not fixing the door at all, just to prove to Porter that he can't force me to do anything. When I was twenty, I'd probably have done just that.

It's a *wonder* I made it out of the military with an honorable discharge.

I pull on clothes, gulping down my coffee. No matter what Porter thinks, I *am* actually mature enough to know what needs to be done, and I'm grown enough to fucking do it without being told.

I leave the house through the side door so I don't have to see his face again.

———

Forty-five minutes later, I'm standing in front of the busted door frame with Phil. He's balding, double-chinned, and might be the slowest talker I've ever met.

I grew up on a ranch. I've known some slow, serious talkers, but none of them ever managed to *annoy* me like this guy does, standing there with his hands on his hips, his unsmiling face looking at the door.

"Well," he says, for at least the fourth time. "You sure did do quite the number on this here frame."

"Sorry about that," I say, doing my best to sound sincere and not irritated.

"Cracked the wood right off there," he says.

Then he pauses.

"Yup. Clean off."

I take a deep breath.

"I'll probably need to replace the whole jamb," I say, running one hand up the inside of the door. "I could glue it back together, but that wouldn't—"

"Yeah, I wouldn't glue it if I were you," Phil says, interrupting me.

I just fucking said that, I think.

"I don't think that would be very sturdy at all," he goes on. "Not. At. *All.*"

"No. That's why I'd prefer to replace to whole jamb," I say, starting to feel like I'm talking in circles.

He nods.

"You ought to replace the whole door jamb," he says, like he thought of it himself.

I don't answer, because clearly, it's pointless.

"There's a hardware store a little ways down Fishfawn Road," he says. "A little closer to the interstate, but before you get to Goldfield Crossroads. It's right across from the McDonald's where that little bar-bee-cue joint used to be..."

He gives me long directions to the hardware store, based mostly on landmarks that used to be there. Slowly, he shows me to a closet that's got some tools in it, also in the basement of the Methodist church. He reiterates his opinion that I should replace the whole doorjamb, instead of gluing it back together. He gives me more directions.

By the end, I'm beginning to worry that Phil has brain damage or something. At last, he walks off to go talk slowly at someone else, and I take a deep breath of relief.

Then I go borrow a truck and head to the hardware store. The one across from where the barbecue joint used to be.

———

THE GOOD THING about listening to Phil's endless slow talk was that it kept me from thinking about Clem. But now, driving this borrowed truck down the winding, two-lane road, there's not a lot *else* to think about.

Here's the thing: I've thought about what would happen if I saw her again. I've thought about it a *lot*; I still live part-time in the town where we grew up, where I think her parents still live. I went to our high school reunion three years ago, because it happened to be between tours of Afghanistan.

I keep thinking I'm going to see her, but I don't. I kept looking for her, out of curiosity if nothing else, but she's not even on Facebook.

And then she showed up in a little town, presenting a plaque, and it was nothing like I thought it'd be. I'd imagined it being strange and awkward. I imagined her being engaged or married.

Once I had a dream where she was pregnant, and I was unsettled all day.

I thought we'd fight. We sure as hell fought the last time I talked to her, and the time before that, and the time before that. I can still remember her, the video connection between Missoula and Afghanistan crackling apart, shouting *I don't fucking care if you come home.*

Not that I was a saint either. I said some shit I sure regretted later.

But it wasn't like that. It wasn't awkward, and it was only weird that it *wasn't* weird. It felt like we'd talked last week, like we'd stayed in touch all these years. Like all that time didn't matter.

It feels like it used to, and I have no fucking idea what to think about that.

I turn a corner in the truck and suddenly there's a river on one side of the road, beautiful and blue, rushing through a stone canyon. That's why I love Montana, why I'm not sure I could ever really leave: this is just *here*. For me to find when I come around a bend in the road. The whole place is so beautiful that this is nothing special.

At last, I find Goodman's Hardware. It's across from a Wendy's, not a McDonald's, and I have no idea what it used to be. The guys who work there are pleasant enough, and I'm out of there with what I need in no time at all.

I spend the drive back thinking about Clementine again, no matter how much I try not to.

————

PHIL LOOKS over my handiwork like he's appraising a diamond ring, not checking over a doorframe in a church basement that was shitty to begin with. Once I had the supplies, it didn't take too long, and he seems vaguely surprised that I knew what I was doing.

Not that it kept him from checking on me every five minutes.

He lets me go at last with a handshake, a clap on the shoulder, and an offer to call me if they have any other things that need fixing around the church. I laugh and thank him, even though I have *no* intention whatsoever of actually taking him up on that.

When I get back to the bunk house, I fall onto an ancient armchair in the living room and just stare at the wall in front of me. For the past ten days at least, I haven't had a moment of quiet between being in the fire camp, working eighteen-hour days, and then coming back here and being treated to a circus of a spaghetti dinner right away.

That's not even *counting* Clementine.

I don't know where the other guys on my squad are, but they're not here, so I take the silence as a gift.

I'm not there for three minutes when there's a thump on the door, like someone's trying to open it with their hands full. Before I can even sit up, there's another thump, then another.

I've just gotten on my feet when the door creaks open and a yellow-and-white snout pokes through, followed by the rest of a *very* furry dog.

I guess that door doesn't latch too well, I think, then walk to the door and pull it open.

There's no one there. The dog walks into the living room and looks around expectantly, like it owns the place, and I raise my eyebrows.

"Okay, c'mere," I say, and it turns around obediently, bumping its head into my hands. I scratch it behind the ears, and the dog starts wagging its tail and pushing its body against my legs, tongue lolling.

God, I miss dogs.

Before I know it I'm on the floor, play-wrestling and letting it lick my face, scratching that spot right above the tail that makes it hop a little in the air, it's so excited. I *think* it's a female dog, though I haven't gotten quite well enough acquainted to check.

Finally, I grab the collar and look at the nametag: TROUT.

"You're Trout?" I ask.

Trout licks my face.

"Atta girl," I say.

She licks me again, and I laugh.

"Trout, where are your people?" I ask, but she just pants in my face.

I flip the tag over to find a phone number. Scratching under her chin, I pull out my phone and dial it.

"Someone's probably worried about you," I say, and Trout lays on the floor and rolls over, requesting a belly rub.

As I sink my hand into her shaggy fur, I hear something I haven't heard since cell phones became common: a busy signal. I look at my phone in confusion for a moment, then shrug and put it back.

"Guess you're mine now," I say to Trout.

FIVE

CLEMENTINE

When I get home at four, I can already hear the partying next door. It sounds like they're playing horseshoes or something, and — by the sounds of it — having at least a couple of beers.

I try to see into their backyard, but there's a big wooden fence around it, so I don't have any luck.

Go over later and introduce yourself, I think, even though the thought of just showing up to a party makes my heart beat a little faster.

Show them some Lodgepole, Montana hospitality. I'm sure they'll appreciate it.

Oh, hell, I don't even believe *myself.* Hunter's over there, having a grand old time with a bunch of dudes and *probably* some girls, and I want to see him again.

Which is fine and normal and okay. We're old friends. Old friends hang out when they run into each other, and it definitely doesn't mean that anything is getting rekindled in either party.

I've gotta go back to work tonight, because I'm giving a stargazing talk for kids, but I've got a couple hours before it gets dark, so I toss my stuff into my room and rummage through the fridge. I've just barely grabbed cheese, jam, and crackers when the phone rings.

I know who it is without even looking at the caller ID. My mom's the only one who calls our land line, because she claims that the static on cell phones gives her a headache. I love her, but she can be a little dramatic sometimes.

No one else is home, and I don't answer the phone, because I'm not sure I can handle my mom right now. Besides, she's called me nearly every day for the past six months, ever since my dad suddenly asked her for a divorce, and I feel a little like I'm starting to crack under the pressure.

The phone stops ringing. I chew cheese, cracker, and jam, and hold my breath. Sure enough, it starts again.

If she calls back a third time, I'll answer, I think.

It stops. I cross my fingers.

Silence.

Come on, don't ring, I think.

It rings. I sigh. Then I walk over, take a deep breath, and answer.

"Oh, Clem, I thought you weren't going to answer," she says, already sounding upset with me.

I ball one hand into a fist.

"Sorry, I was in the bathroom," I say.

Not staring at the phone from the kitchen, hoping you'd stop calling.

"The *neighbor*," she says dramatically.

I sit on the couch.

"The neighbor?"

Neighbor is a generous term for the people that live closest to my parents, since they're each about a half-mile away.

"You know those new neighbors that moved in last October, the man who wore all those bolo ties and that blond woman with the ostrich skin cowboy boots?" she asks.

I think I met them once and they were perfectly nice. My

mom just didn't approve, probably because they clearly had more money than my parents.

"Yeah," I say.

"Clem," my mother says, then pauses for effect. I stay quiet. "I think it was *her*."

I stand up and start pacing. I wish I'd let the phone ring a thousand more times, because I don't want to have this conversation with my mom right now.

"Okay," I say. "What does that change?"

There's silence on the other end of the line.

"Don't you think the timing works out?" she says, sounding taken aback. She doesn't answer my question, because the correct answer is that it doesn't change anything.

"They moved here in October, he *demanded* a divorce in February, and I haven't seen them once since April!"

"Maybe they're summering somewhere else," I say. "That's their second home, isn't it?"

"I know I'm right," she says. "An affair with the *neighbor*. Right under my nose, Clem, how could he?"

I walk up to a wall and lean my forehead against it without answering her. Ever since my dad presented her with the request, she's been bound and determined that he's been having an affair. Sometimes, in her mind, it's a torrid one-night stand, sometimes it's been going on for decades, but she's got a different suspect every single time.

Then she calls me and tells me the awful things that my dad is doing, the women she sees him with, how he's *demanding* half of their assets after he *did this to her*.

I hate it.

She's trying to turn me against my dad. I know what she's doing, and even though I feel terrible for her — after twenty-five years of marriage, a divorce? — I don't want to hear any of this.

I'm almost certain he didn't have an affair. He says he

didn't, and there's no evidence otherwise. Besides, for most of my life, they've alternated between fighting constantly and almost never speaking, so it's not like they had a great relationship to ruin.

I'm almost relieved that they're divorcing, to be honest. They both deserve to be happy, and they sure weren't when they were together.

I just wish they could do it without putting me in the middle.

I open my eyes, staring into the blank white wall, and realize my mom is talking.

"—And he wants the quilt, Clem, after I birthed and raised his children, he wants the *quilt* we slept under—"

"His mother made that quilt," I say, then immediately bite my lip, because I *know* better than to let myself get sucked into an argument. It's completely pointless, because she's not really upset about the quilt, she's upset about *everything*.

And I get it. I'd be upset. But there's a limit to how much of this I can take, for my own sanity, no matter how terrible I feel for my parents.

"But we *slept* under it," she says, sounding taken aback.

"Mom, I gotta go," I say.

"What are you doing?"

Nothing, actually.

"I've gotta go to a thing. I'll talk to you later, okay?" I say.

"Clem, I just don't know why you—"

"See you this weekend," I say, and hang up the phone, even though I know she's still talking.

It's unkind of me, and I *know* that. But I also know that I need my sanity, and frankly, I need my sanity more than I need to be nice right now.

Almost immediately, the phone starts ringing again. I ball my hand into a fist again and answer.

"Mom, I really don't want to talk about this right now, okay?" I say, sounding more pissy than I mean to.

There's a pause on the other end.

"Clem?" Hunter's voice says.

I take the phone away from my face and look at the caller ID. Nope, not my mom. I clear my throat.

"Hey, what's up?" I ask, sounding as casual as I possibly can.

"You know anyone named Trout?" he asks.

I narrow my eyes and look toward the window.

"You have Trout?"

"Yup. I'll keep her if you don't want her anymore," he says, and I think he's laughing.

"She's a terror," I say. "I'll be over in a second."

————

THE GUYS WAVE me into the backyard instead of the house, and sure enough, there's Trout, basking in the attention from half a dozen firemen.

Shirtless firemen. Trout's a lucky girl.

"Hey, I'm sorry about her," I call.

"Aww, she's no problem," says her current human. "You're not a problem, are you girl?"

Trout blinks at me, tongue lolling, like she agrees that she's not a problem.

The fireman tosses a stick across the yard and she bolts after it.

"I'm Silas," he says, and holds out one hand. I shake it.

"Clementine," I say.

Yes, he's hot. Not *quite* as hot as Hunter, but I'd take it.

"You presented the plaque the other night," he says, smiling. "I remember."

I laugh and tuck my hair behind my ear, a nervous tic

because I'm not really sure what to say when a cute fireman says he remembers me.

"Thanks," I say.

Trout comes back with the stick, briefly saving me.

"Okay, Houdini," I say to her. "Ready to go home?"

"We're just hanging out back here, drinking some beers," Silas says. "You're welcome to stay."

Just as I reach down to take the stick out of Trout's mouth, the back door opens and Hunter walks out. Wearing a shirt.

Maybe it's my imagination, but I think he pauses for half a second in the doorway, looking from me to Silas and back, but then he keeps walking. Trout drops the stick before I can grab it, then trots over to Hunter.

"Traitor," I mutter, and Silas smiles.

"Watch out, I might steal her," Hunter calls. He roughs her up for a few moments before she leaves and walks over to the firemen playing baggo at the end of the yard, and he walks over to us.

"Want a beer?" he asks.

I *was* going to do laundry and make chili for next week before I went back to work, but standing between two hot firemen, suddenly those things don't seem like much of a priority.

"Come on," Silas adds. "It's Friday."

"We've got a whole case of Pabst," Hunter says, like that'll entice me. "Or, if you're gonna be discerning, Fat Tire."

I blow my bangs out of my face.

"I'll take a Fat Tire," I finally say, sneaking a glance around the yard.

I'd be an *idiot* to say no, after all. Someday, I'll be telling my granddaughters about the afternoon I spent surrounded by shirtless firemen.

Hunter heads back inside. A shout goes up from the other end of the yard as a game of baggo ends and someone wins.

"Wanna play?" Silas asks.

I honestly can't tell if he's flirting or just being friendly.

But is either one that bad? I think. *Nothing is going to happen with Hunter because there's never been a worse idea in human history, and a little flirting never hurt anyone. Nothing's gonna happen.*

"Sure," I say.

SIX

HUNTER

I grab two beers from the fridge, and as I open them, I glance through the kitchen window. Silas and Clementine are walking together toward the baggo boards, and as I watch, he smiles at her and she laughs at something he said.

My stomach knots.

Quit it, I think. *There's no damn reason at all to get upset. You two are done as hell. Silas is a good guy.*

It doesn't make me feel better. I walk back outside, give Clementine the beer, and play a game of baggo with them and Daniel, another one of the guys. She and I are standing opposite each other, maybe twenty feet apart, but she's next to Silas even though they're on different teams.

I make myself act normal, but every time she smiles at something he says, my stomach knots a little harder. I fucking *hate* not being the guy she's laughing with.

Finally, Clementine and I win. She sticks her tongue out at Silas, who says something back.

"Rematch?" Daniel calls.

We play again, and I have to watch them enjoy each other's company for even longer.

———

As the afternoon wears on, more of my squad shows up, along with Clementine's roommates and some people I don't even know. But we've got beer, a cute dog, and plenty of outdoor games, so let the good times roll.

I try to ignore whatever Clementine's doing, or who she's talking to, because it's none of my goddamn business. We're just two people who knew each other in high school, who used to date a long time ago, and none of that *matters* any more.

I fail. After playing two rounds of baggo with Silas, she plays one with me and then one with Daniel. Some more guys come in and she tries to teach Jordan and Rupert how to lawn bowl. I toss some horseshoes and try to pretend that she's not sitting on the lawn furniture, drinking beers and chatting with Mandy, one of her roommates, along with Silas and Daniel.

When I walk to the cooler for another beer, Mandy calls out to me.

"Hunter!" she says. "Daniel says you had an encounter with an owl."

I grab a beer from the cooler and open it, grinning.

"This asshole said that?" I say.

Mandy reaches out and pulls a plastic chair up next to her, smiling back at me. Maybe I'm imagining it, but Clementine's face freezes, her eyes flicking away.

"Come on," she says. "Owl."

I sigh and pretend to be slightly annoyed.

"This was about a year ago," I say. "The thing you gotta know is that, when we're on the job, we're lucky if we get five hours of bad sleep per night. More often it's four hours, maybe even three, and half the time we're just sleeping wherever we can stretch out."

Clementine tucks one leg under herself and takes a sip of

beer, and I can't help but watch the cords in her throat as she swallows.

"Excuses," says Daniel, but he's laughing.

"I'm just setting the scene," I say. "Because one night, I walk a little ways away from the camp to take a piss, and I hear this weird *noise*. It's this low, melancholy *ooooooo*, like nothing I've ever heard in the woods before."

Everyone's looking at me. I'm looking at Clementine.

"So I follow it," I say. "I'm sleep deprived as hell, and my first thought is, *that's the most beautiful sound I've ever heard*. I think it's angels or something, like maybe I died and didn't know it. And I go around this big tree, and suddenly, I swear to God, I see an *alien*."

Daniel's laughing softly already, and Silas is grinning. They know the story. Clementine at least looks amused.

"It's this big, white, imposing, majestic *being*, and it's got a tiny mouth and big eyes, and I swear to God, it was *glowing*," I say. "I have no idea what to do. I think, *they're here to take me away*, and I know that I should run or something, but I'm pretty sure the alien is controlling my mind already, so I just drop to my knees in front of it instead."

Mandy's giggling behind her hand, and Clementine is biting her lip, trying not to laugh.

"I'm on my knees, with the alien, for a *long* time. A couple minutes, at least, and it's staring at me, looking around making these weird, soft, strange, *peaceful* noises. I start thinking, *maybe it won't be so bad. It seems like a nice alien*."

I pause for another moment. Silas snorts.

"Then, from behind me, a voice shouts, 'Casden, what in *God's* name are you doing?'"

Now everyone is laughing.

"I'm so surprised that I nearly fall over, and right at that second, the alien spreads its wings and flies right at my head. I screamed like a little girl," I finish.

I felt like a total idiot when this happened, but it's a good story now.

"Porter wasn't impressed," Silas says.

"He never is," says Daniel.

"Especially not with me," I say.

"You sure you were sleep deprived and not drunk?" Mandy asks. She's got one leg up on the chair, her elbow resting on her knee as she plays with her hair.

She's cute. She's not the make-your-mouth-go-dry knockout that Clementine is, but I'd pick her up in a bar. I bet she's a fun time when she's had a couple of drinks.

"I don't drink on the job," I say, leaning back in my plastic chair. "*That's* a good way to get yourself killed."

"We make up for it on our time off," Daniel says, and he and Silas clink their beer bottles together.

"We've been invited on a historic pub crawl tonight," Silas says. "Organized by... who was it?"

"The Homebrewers Club of Lodgepole," Daniel says.

"Better than a spaghetti dinner," I say, then glance at Mandy and Clementine, who looks faintly amused. "Sorry."

"Does a pub crawl mean you're going to *both* bars?" Clementine asks.

"Isn't the Harried Bear closed right now?" Mandy asks.

"I thought it reopened last week," Clementine says.

"It looked closed when I drove past the other day," she says, and shrugs.

Both girls look at us, then laugh.

"Sorry," Clementine says. "You might be going on a crawl of exactly one historic pub."

"Want to come with us?" Silas asks her.

For a second, they look at each other, and I feel like my blood stops pumping because *I think he just asked her out.*

Then I breathe again and hope no one noticed, because I don't fucking care if Silas asks her out. I don't care if they go on a date, I don't care if they go home together, and I don't care if they fuck and she whispers his name into his ear—

"I can't," Clementine says. "I have to go back to work, I'm hosting a stargazing session for kids up at the mountaintop visitor's center."

I realize my hand's gripped tightly on the arm of my plastic chair, and I let it go.

"That sounds cool," Daniel offers.

"You could come up if you wanted," she says. "We usually go pretty late, until eleven or so. Less alcohol, though."

Maybe it's my imagination, but I think she glances at me.

Clementine can do whatever she wants. We tried having a relationship. It didn't work, and I'm smart enough to know that people don't change, not really. Just because we're older now doesn't mean we won't have the exact same problems.

I'm also pretty sure you can't casually hook up with someone you once swore you'd love forever, even if you were young and dumb when you swore that.

Move on, I think.

"You around tonight for this one-bar pub crawl?" I ask Mandy.

"Sure!" she says brightly.

———

The Harried Bear *is* open, in an old hotel in Lodgepole's historic downtown. It's got a huge, beautiful, polished wood bar with a mirror behind it, booths lining the walls, and black-and-white photos of Lodgepole's mining town past all over the place.

To someone who spends a lot of his time in former mining towns deep in the mountains, this kind of bar feels like home. There's something particularly western about it, like at any moment Billy the Kid could come through the doors, guns blazing.

"I just work in the office, actually," Mandy says. The bar is pretty full and pretty loud, so she's leaning in toward me, her hair tickling my neck so I can hear her.

"You don't spend three weeks a month out in the wilderness?" I ask.

She laughs, putting one hand over her mouth.

"God, no," she says. "I don't know *how* they do that. I feel gross if I go a whole day without showering."

I said that once, but it was before I went to basic training and then spent months in the dust and dirt halfway across the world. After that, a few weeks without a shower wasn't a big deal at all. I can't imagine I smell good when I come in from the field, but I never notice.

"You get used to it," I say, and take a drink of my beer.

Mandy's nice. She's cute. She's into me, even if she's not the most forward girl. Any other night she'd already be sitting in my lap, giggling, and in ten minutes we'd either be making out in the bathroom or going back to her place.

But tonight, I'm fighting the urge to ask her how Clementine is. What she's been up to. What her favorite movie is these days. Dumb shit like that.

Mandy looks down at her drink, like it'll tell her what to say next.

"So, is firefighting a full-time job year-round, or do you..."

The rest of her sentence gets lost as another woman bumps into me by accident, then turns and puts her hand on my arm.

"Sorry," she says.

Then she does a double take, tilting her head a little to one side, her red lips just barely parting.

"Are you one of the Canyon Country Hotshots?" she asks, her voice suddenly getting lower, almost a purr.

She's wearing a tight white t-shirt, tight jeans, high-heeled cowboy boots, and has *hottest girl in a small town* written all over her.

"Yes ma'am," I say, turning on the charm without meaning to.

She laughs.

"God, don't call me ma'am, you're making me feel like my mother," she says. "I'm Jean."

Her hand is still on my shoulder. Mandy is just looking at her like she's been betrayed.

"Hunter," I say. "Nice to meet you."

"Let me buy you a drink as thanks," Jean says. She's acting like Mandy's not even there, and from the corner of my eye, I can see Mandy look away.

If I wanted, I'm almost positive I could have a threesome tonight. Jean's ready to go, and Mandy might take another drink, but I bet she'd be down for a night of fun.

Instead, I wonder what Clementine is doing. I imagine her, lying in a field, surrounded by a bunch of kids, all on their backs, as she tells them about the constellations.

Fuck this, I think.

"Thanks, but I've actually gotta go take care of something," I say.

Jean's mouth droops a little at the corners, and she looks taken aback, suddenly unsure of herself.

"Thanks for hanging out with me," I tell Mandy, which is a fucking lame thing to say, but I can't think of anything better.

Then I grab my jacket and head out the door of the Harried Bear, turn left, and walk for the mountain.

SEVEN

CLEMENTINE

"Okay," I call out. "Has everyone got their star maps?"

A chorus of small voices all say "Yes," with varying degrees of enthusiasm. Most of them are into it, though there are always a few whose parents dragged them out here when they'd rather be watching TV.

"Great!" I say. "Now, who can find Mars?"

I like to give them a pretty easy one first. If I ask where the moon is right away, everyone over the age of about seven rolls their eyes and thinks this is kid stuff. But Mars is easy enough to find that they can do it, and hard enough that they don't think I'm making fools of them.

A whole bunch of fingers point in the general direction of Mars.

"Exactly!" I say. "If you look a little to the left and up, now that your eyes are adjusted you can *really* see the Milky Way."

I sweep my arm up and over my head, indicating the broad swath of stars that speckle the black sky. This is one of the best places in the country for stargazing — the closest city is Missoula, which isn't very big *or* very close. Other than that, it's small towns like this one and nothing but wide open sky, with hardly any light pollution for miles.

Especially on a clear night, like tonight, with just a sliver of a moon, it feels like you can see the whole universe from here.

Sometimes, I really understand how people used to think the earth was the center of the universe. It sure feels that way.

"...So when we look at the Milky Way, we're actually seeing the flattened disc of our own galaxy," I'm saying, the words pretty much on autopilot. "Like being in the center of a frisbee and looking out toward the edge."

Lots of small, thoughtful faces look upward, craning their necks.

"Now," I say. "Can anyone tell me which way is north?"

A bunch of hands point. Several of them are even pointing north, but something's caught my eye: a figure, walking through the parking lot and toward the field where we're all standing.

It's Hunter. I can barely see his outline, and I can't see his face at all, but there's something familiar in the way he walks, his hands in the pockets of his jacket. I can't help but smile.

"That's right!" I say.

I keep talking about the north star and the big dipper, but I'm not really paying attention. I've got this on autopilot. Instead I'm watching Hunter walk up and stand way, way in the back of a group of kids. In another minute he's following along as I talk about the constellations — Orion, Sagittarius, the Pleiades — and I just think, *he came.*

At the end of the naked-eye portion of the evening, I clap my hands together and then rub them.

"Who's ready for telescopes?" I ask.

A couple of kids run for the telescopes set up at the opposite end of the field, each manned by a volunteer. Most of the kids just walk. It's probably not very cool to get excited for telescopes.

Hunter waits until they're gone, hands in the pockets of his Carhartt jacket, then walks to meet me.

"You picked stars over beers?" I ask.

"I can drink beers anywhere," he says. "I don't get many stargazing invitations."

"You could just look up."

He smiles.

"Smartass," he says. "Fine. I see too much of those guys and figured I'd spend time with an old friend instead. Happy now?"

There it is again: *old friend*. He came all the way here, away from a pub crawl to see me. An old friend.

"Cool!" I hear a *really* enthusiastic kid shout.

"Happy that I dragged the truth out of you?" I tease.

"Kicking and screaming," he says.

Be sincere for one second, I think. I swallow and look straight into his eyes.

"Thanks," I say. "It's good to see you again."

"It's good to see you too," he says softly.

I can't help but smile. I almost say *I didn't think it would be*, because the last time we talked, over video chat, I alternated between sobbing and shouting for two hours.

But there's no point bringing that up now: he's here for a couple of days, and it's nice to see him again. As friends. The past is past.

"I've gotta go monitor the telescope situation," I say, nodding my head toward the circle where people are gathered. "But you're welcome to hang out if you want."

"I CAN SEE THE RINGS!" shouts the same kid, who sounds almost *too* excited.

"That *is* why I came," Hunter says, his drawl dusky, his blue eyes sparkling even in the dark.

"C'mon," I say. "I'll show you some cool planets," I say.

Instantly, Hunter grins a huge, shit-eating grin, and I sigh. I know what he's going to say. I roll my eyes.

"Don't," I say, trying not to laugh.

"Don't what?"

"Don't say the thing you're about to say."

His eyes glitter.

"Am I gonna get to see..." he says, still grinning. "...*Uranus?*"

He looks so pleased with himself that I have to bite my lips together so I don't laugh.

———

"WHAT IS it I'm looking at again?" Hunter says, looking carefully through the telescope. It's set up for someone about two-thirds his height, so he's crouched down and looking up, which is a pretty awkward position.

"The bright blob with stuff around it," I say. "If you really look close, you can make out the rings, though not the individual ones."

It's an hour later, and most of the kids are gone. Just a few are left, including the eleven-year-old who got *so* excited about Saturn's rings. He's been quizzing one of the volunteers about the asteroid belt for about ten minutes now, and before that, he talked my ear off about the differences between Mars's two moons. His dad is standing nearby, looking tired and ready to leave.

Hunter's quiet for a long time, peering into the telescope. Then he backs away, blinks and shakes his head.

"Maybe I should look at another planet so I can see the difference," he says.

"That one's got Jupiter," I say, pointing at a different setup.

Hunter walks to another huge telescope, crouches down, and looks up.

"Which one is it?" he asks.

"The big, bright one," I say.

"There's two of those."

"Let me look," I tell him, and he steps aside, but not quite far enough. I bump into him as I crouch and look up through the telescope, and I can almost feel the warmth from his hard, solid body through both our heavy jackets.

I have to fight the urge to reach out and put one hand on him to steady myself. My body refuses to listen to my brain when I'm around him, because I keep telling my body *it's over and it's been over for ages*, but I still have the urge to reach out and hold his hand, touch his arm, lean into him.

I know better than to kiss him, but all those little, intimate touches between couples? Those are what I can barely keep myself from doing out of sheer habit.

It doesn't help that I've got a very, *very* clear memory of everything else we did. Half-clothed fooling around in the back seat of a car? Check. Getting eaten out in the basement of my parents' house while they were watching TV upstairs, holding a pillow over my own face so I wouldn't scream? Check.

Fucking in the back of his pickup truck, parked behind the barn, underneath the stars on a warm summer night, my nails raking down his back? Definitely check.

Sudden arousal prickles through me at *those* memories, and I wonder if I remember a little too well. Obviously I'm just remembering my first through rose-colored glasses, right?

"You can't tell either, huh?" Hunter says, his slow voice coming from above me.

Right. Jupiter.

"It's on the left," I say, and stand.

As I do I can feel his hand brush my back, his fingertips running from my shoulder to my hip. It's casual, almost automatic, and I wonder if he even meant to do it.

Hunter bends down and looks back through the telescope

again. I shove my hands into the pockets of my jacket and step away so I'm not tempted to touch him again.

"Okay, got it," he says, after a moment. Then he walks to the other telescope and looks up.

The excitable kid is finally being walked off by his dad, even though I can still hear his excited yelping from where I stand. I wave to Albert, the last volunteer who's still around.

"You want help putting the telescopes back?" he calls.

I glance at Hunter, still folded in half and staring up through the telescope.

"Go home," I call back. "We've got it."

"See you around," he calls, and walks toward the parking lot.

Just like that, it's me and Hunter alone in a circle of big, powerful telescopes. I wander back to where he is and look up at the stars, mentally ticking through the constellations.

"I think I can see them," he says. "They're real faint, but there they are."

He stands up straight and then squints at the sky.

"You can't see them without the telescope," I say.

Hunter just looks at me with a *no shit, Sherlock* look on his face, and I laugh.

"Sorry," I say. "I explain a lot of things to eight-year-olds."

"I assumed that was *why* I was looking through a telescope," he says, a smile in his voice.

He's standing up straight, his hands in his pockets, gazing intently at the horizon. After a while he points.

"It's one of those, right?" he says.

He's pointing at a sky full of stars on a dark night. It's hard to tell *which* one he thinks it is.

"It's sort of down there," I say. "See Mars?"

I point. He moves in, closer to me. My stomach flips and I swallow.

"It's the one that's a little bit red," I say. "Right near the horizon, right above the branches of that tall tree that got struck by lightning a couple years ago."

"Because I know which tree got struck by lightning."

"It's the one without leaves on top," I tease. "I thought one of the Canyon Country Hotshots might know what a struck tree looked like."

"It's full dark with no moon, you know," he says.

He moves closer, standing behind me. We're not touching, but it's just a technicality, because he's leaning over my shoulder and so close I can feel his body heat.

Then, after a moment: "Okay, I think I've got it. That one?"

He reaches over my other shoulder and points right at Mars. We're still not touching, but my heart is beating about a thousand times a minute, because my dumb body remembers *everything* and it wants me to put my cheek against his, lean back against his chest.

"Now, look a little down and to the right," I say. "That's Antares, another bright star."

He points at the wrong thing, and I grab his forearm, gently point him at the right one.

"Okay," Hunter says. He's so close I can feel the vibrations of his voice.

"Now, go up a little, and see the third star kinda making a triangle?"

I move his arm again, until he's pointing to Saturn.

"That's it," I say.

There's a long moment where we both just look at the two planets and the star, right above the horizon. He moves his arm, and for a moment I think he's going to drape it over my shoulder, because that's what he *would* have done, back then.

He puts it back in his pocket instead. I try not to be disappointed.

"Can I tell you something?" he asks.

"Of course," I say. My stomach twists, and I rock a little on my heels, fighting my urge to lean back against him, let him wrap his arms around me.

"When I got back from the desert, I was surprised that we've got the same stars," he says.

The desert is Afghanistan. He was calling it that before we ever broke up.

"Not exactly," I say.

"I was surprised we've *mostly* got the same stars, then," he says. "I didn't know the sky depended on latitude, not longitude."

"You learn something new every day," I say, because I have no idea what else to say.

There's a long pause.

"When did you get back?" I ask.

"Two years ago."

I do some quick math.

"You signed up for another tour."

"Sure did," he says. "Semper Fi and all that."

"You didn't want to be career military?"

I'm not sure why we're talking like this, side-by-side, pretending to look at the stars instead of face-to-face, but I'm too nervous to move. I'm afraid if I do, I'll *somehow* end up with my lips on his, and he'll pull back and laugh and tell me that he hasn't thought of me that way in years.

"I'm not cut out for it," he says. "I... didn't always have the level of respect for my superiors that they preferred."

"But you signed up for another two years of active duty," I press.

It's dumb because it doesn't *matter*, but somehow, it feels like another betrayal. We were together when he signed up in the first place: four years of active duty, four years of being in the reserves. His father had been in the Marines, his grandfather, most of his uncles. *All* Marines.

So when I had a complete and total meltdown, he didn't understand. But I didn't want him going away for four years, to somewhere dangerous and scary, somewhere that I wouldn't see him and he might die. I was seventeen, insecure, selfish, and fucking *terrified*.

It was our first big fight. I didn't want him going at all, and I made him swear up and down that when his four years was up he wouldn't sign up for another tour.

"I signed up the week after you dumped me," he admits.

I blink. I was pretty sure *he* dumped *me*, but I don't say anything.

"I ended up wishing I hadn't, to be honest," he goes on. "But it was the only thing I could think of to do that would really show you I didn't give a shit about you anymore."

He's straightened up now, his head somewhere above mine, still standing behind me. I'm frozen, looking at the stars and not seeing any of them.

He stayed in a war zone just so I'd know he didn't care about me any more, I think.

That's not what someone who *actually* doesn't care does, and we both know it.

"Except I think you just found out for the first time, so the joke's on me," he says, a chuckle in his voice. "I'm sure you're *really* hurt about something I did years and years ago. I sure showed you."

I don't say anything. I wouldn't say I'm *really* hurt, but I don't feel nothing. I wish I did.

"Clem?" he says.

"Sorry," I say. "I didn't know you were..."

I let my voice trail off, because I'm not really sure what to say.

"I didn't even know you stayed in the military that long," I say instead.

I didn't know it would still kind of hurt my feelings, I think.

"Are you okay?" he asks, because of *course* he can still tell when I'm upset.

"Yeah," I say.

"Clem."

I stare resolutely at the horizon.

"Clem, c'mon. Turn around."

He takes me by the shoulder, and I let him spin me in a circle until I'm eye-level with the collar of his jacket. I look at it, the stretchy brown material that edges the dark green canvas, because I don't know how to look him in the eye right now.

"It worked," I finally blurt out, then look up at him.

He looks confused.

"What worked?"

"You signing up for another tour," I say.

There's a long, long pause. My hands are fists in my pockets. I don't think I can explain *why* my feelings are still hurt, because I don't understand myself. It doesn't make any sense, and I know it.

"I didn't want it to," Hunter says softly. "Not any more. Not for years now."

"I know," I say.

"I didn't think I could come back and see you," he goes on. "Even the thought of living in the same town with you three years later seemed unbearable."

His hand is still on my shoulder, warm and strong and oddly comforting. I try to laugh.

"I'm that bad, huh?"

"Yeah, you've got this weird smell," he teases. "It *definitely* wasn't because I was afraid to see you with someone else."

I give in. I lean forward and put my head on his shoulder. Even through his jacket it feels familiar, and a tremor runs through me as he puts his arms around me, my hands still in my pockets.

Friends hug, I think. *It's fine.*

"Think we can wipe the slate?" I say. "Just start over, like all that didn't happen?"

I feel a gentle tug on my scalp, and I realize he's playing with my hair, absentmindedly winding a strand of it around his finger over and over again. Like he used to.

"I don't think *that's* possible," he says, and I feel his voice rumbling out of his chest. "But I think we can accept that it happened a long time ago when we were different people."

"I'll take it," I say.

I believe it for exactly one second, and then there's another light tug on my scalp, because he can age and he can come back from the military and he can be more mature and he can change, on the surface, but he's still playing with my hair the same way he did at seventeen.

I take my hands out of my pockets and put my arms around him, and he holds me a little tighter, my head burrowed against his chest. I don't know what I'm doing. I'm not sure that people can change, or at least, I'm not sure I believe that they can change *enough*.

I never loved you anyway, he said. I don't think he meant it. I haven't thought that for years, but he still said it and that's what counts, right?

"Can I tell you something?" I ask.

"No," he says.

I roll my eyes, even though he can't see. Then I take a deep breath.

"I missed you," I say.

"You missed me?" he says, and he sounds genuinely surprised. "You were at college. There were tons of people around."

I shrug against him.

"After a while it was just little things," I say. "I'd see a really great dog or something, and I'd think, *I have to tell Hunter about that dog* and then remember that I... couldn't."

"Tell me now," he says. "Clean-ish slate. All that is just background noise."

I laugh, and he adjusts his stance a little bit, pulling me even closer. I hope none of the volunteers come back and find me just standing here, in a weird hug with some guy, but I don't really care that much. I'm an adult. I can hug whoever I want.

"Start with Trout," he suggests.

"I'll make you a deal," I say. "Help me put these telescopes away, and I'll tell you about eight years' worth of notable dogs."

I pull back and look up at him, my hands still on his sides.

"You remember all eight years?" he asks.

"I can always invent dogs you'll like," I say.

I'm about to say something else, but Hunter's looking down at me, our eyes locked, and it flies right out of my brain.

He's going to kiss me, I realize. *He's going to kiss me and I'm not going to do anything to stop it.*

Hunter inclines his head toward me, just a little, like he's bending down with a secret.

"I bet I can tell the made up dogs from the real ones," he says.

I tilt my face up so our noses are almost touching. My heart feels like it might beat out of my chest. I let my eyes slide closed, because I know what happens now.

And, if I'm being honest: this is what I want to happen. I don't give a shit how I feel about it tomorrow.

"No way," I say.

I'm on autopilot, guided by pure instinct. I put my hand on his neck, run my fingertips along his skin and I hear a faint, deep rumble from his chest. Our noses bump.

"Try me," he says, and his lips just barely brush mine.

I pause another instant, because if I back out now I won't have kissed him again, but instead of making a good decision I press forward and suddenly our lips are touching again, and he's warm and rough and familiar, all at once.

For a moment we're both frozen, lips pressed together, and then I pull back a fraction of an inch. My fingertips drift over his neck, and I can feel his pulse racing, maybe as fast as mine.

Then Hunter kisses me again, and he's got one hand on my lower back and he's pulling me in toward him. I push my fingers through his hair and even though I have the wild urge to crush him against me, as hard as I can, I don't.

Instead I move my mouth against his. I feel the tip of his tongue against my lip and I meet it with my own, still breathless with anticipation. Still half-convinced, despite all evidence, that I'm reading this situation wrong, that any second now he's going to push me away and say he just doesn't think of me this way any more.

Hunter pushes his tongue further into my mouth and now we're winding them together, like we're desperate to explore each other. He's got one hand on my neck, pulling me toward him.

We kiss like that, long and slow, for what seems like minutes until we both pull away. Hunter leans his forehead against mine, and I think he's about to say something, but he doesn't. He's just quiet, breathing hard, holding me in this empty field dotted with telescopes.

I might regret it tomorrow, but fuck *that*.

I need a minute to catch my breath. I need a moment to let my brain catch up with this, to make myself slow down, to process. I lean our foreheads together and let my thumb wander along Clementine's jawline. I think I might be trembling, and I take a deep breath, force myself to stop.

Before I know it I'm kissing her again, because I feel like I can't restrain myself. My tongue is in her mouth and hers is in mine, and it feels right and perfect and great, and this is what I've wanted from the minute I saw her again.

She snakes her fingers through my hair, pulling me even closer, and I think, *I've wanted this for longer than that.* I'm hard, and as Clementine rocks her body against mine, I *know* she can tell, heavy jackets be damned. I have to fight the urge to slide my hand under her jacket and feel the warm, soft skin of her back, run my fingers over the notches in her spine.

Suddenly, Clementine pulls away. She whips her head around.

Then she gasps.

"Hey!" she shouts and then she's out of my arms, practically running across the field.

There's a kid at one of the telescopes, standing on his tiptoes and messing with it, his face intent.

"DON'T TOUCH THAT!" Clementine shouts, and the kid looks over, suddenly freezing. "Those are *very* expensive and also *very* breakable!"

The poor kid looks terrified, and he backs away, his sad eyes looking up at her.

"I wanted to look at Andromeda," he says. "This one was positioned the closest, and you looked busy, so I just thought..."

I walk over as Clementine checks the telescope quickly, then heaves a sigh of relief.

"What's your name?" she asks.

"Aidan," he says.

"Aidan, I know you're just interested, but these are *very* delicate and you need special training to use them without breaking them, okay?" she says.

"Sorry," he says, looking a little like he might cry.

I feel bad for the little guy. He's obviously just over-eager and let his excitement get the better of him. Apparently satisfied that the telescope is fine, Clementine looks at the kid, then looks around.

"Where are your parents?" she asks.

He looks a little guilty.

"In the camper," he says.

We all pause a moment.

"Asleep," he goes on.

Clementine sighs.

"Okay, we're going to walk you back there now," she says.

"But can I just—"

"No," she says, and points in the direction of the campground. "Move it."

The three of us start walking, Aidan between the two of us. He sighs *very* dramatically for an eleven-year-old, and I almost feel bad.

"Where *is* Andromeda?" I ask, trying to get his mind off of this.

He looks up at me, suddenly excited.

"It's next to the constellation Andromeda," he says.

"I thought we were talking about the constellation," I say.

"*That's* perfectly visible to the naked eye," he says, as though he's explaining this to an even younger child. "I wanted to look at the Andromeda *galaxy.* It's the spiral galaxy closest to the Milky Way, and you need a telescope to really see—"

"Aidan!" a voice shouts.

We stop and squint into the darkness on the road. A moment later, a man appears, running in sweatpants, a t-shirt, and unlaced hiking boots.

"What the hell do you think you're doing?" the man yells. "I woke up and you were just *gone*, you scared the shit out of your mom and me. I had no idea where you were. You can't *do* that."

When he gets closer, he looks at Clementine and me. His hair's wild and he's breathing hard, completely freaked out.

"I'm sorry," he says. "I had no idea he was gone, thank you so much for finding him..."

"No problem," Clementine says. "He just wanted more telescope time."

The man gets on one knee and looks Aidan in the face.

"You *cannot* just disappear like that," he says.

"I'm sorry," says Aidan, looking at the ground. "I just wanted..."

The man pulls Aidan in for a long, tight hug, practically squeezing the air out of the kid.

"You're still grounded," he says. "*God*, are you grounded."

Clem glances at me, obviously trying not to laugh.

"Thank you," the guy says to us again, then stands. "I nearly had a heart attack when I woke up and he was gone."

"I'm just glad he didn't get eaten by bears," Clementine says, half smiling.

Aidan's eyes go wide.

"Don't worry, we only lose a couple kids a year that way," she says.

Aidan's dad mouths *thank you* over Aidan's head

Then the two of them turn and walk away, the dad still lecturing Aidan on all the reasons not to wander off in the middle of the night. Clementine and I turn back and start walking to the telescopes.

"We should put those away," she says, her hands jammed into her pockets. "It's not good to leave them out for very long."

"Sure," I say.

She makes sure they're turned off, lens caps on, legs folded up, and in their cases. It's my job to carry them to the Forest Service SUV, because each case is about four feet long and *heavy*. When we finish, we drive them to the visitor center, and Clementine locks them away in the store room.

I watch her lock the door, leaning against the wall. I want to push her up against it and kiss her again, her mouth under mine. I want to lift her up so she can wrap her legs around me and feel the way her hips move when she rubs herself against me.

I don't. If I'd just made out with *any* other girl I'd have already done it. We'd probably be naked in the back of the truck right now, and then tomorrow morning I'd have forgotten her name already.

Not Clementine. I *tried* to forget her name and couldn't, and I know I won't tomorrow, either. So instead of pushing her against the wall I slide a hand around her hip and pull her in toward me.

I know it could end badly. I know *how* badly, but I want what I want, and I want Clementine more than enough to throw caution to the wind. I've never been good at denying myself, at least where women are concerned.

"It's been a while since we made out in a car," I say, pushing my thumb beneath her shirt, stroking the soft, warm skin on her side.

She leans against the building too, the faint light from the moon and stars glowing dully on her dark hair.

"You want to go park it behind the old middle school?" she teases.

There weren't a whole lot of places in Ashlake dark and quiet enough to park and fool around.

"Hey, we're adults now," I say, moving my hand to the small of her back, still against her skin. "What's wrong with right here?"

"Do we have to get in the car?" she asks, a smile crinkling the corners of her eyes.

I kiss her again, her lips warm and inviting and yielding, her hand on the back of my neck, pulling me in toward her. I lick her lower lip again and she opens her mouth, her tongue against mine, and I hear someone growl quietly.

Me. It's me.

This time I'm already rock-hard and I *know* she knows, just from the way she's pressing her hips against mine, just barely shifting back and forth, the pressure driving me crazy. I pull away, gasping for breath, our foreheads together and she puts her hand on my face, her eyes closed.

"Is this stupid?" she whispers.

I don't know the answer. Somewhere, deep in my subconscious, I've been wondering that myself.

"It could be," I say. "But I don't fucking care."

She kisses me, long and slow, pulls back again.

"That means yes," she says.

Kiss.

"Stupid's not the same as wrong," I murmur.

Kiss.

"I know it's not *wrong*," she says. "That wasn't the question."

Kiss.

"I have a question, then," I say. "Your place or mine?"

Her back muscles stiffen below my hand, instantly, but I don't take the hint.

"I vote your place," I murmur. "I've got three roommates."

I kiss her again, and she kisses me back but it's almost like she's not present any more, and I pull away.

Clementine is already shaking her head.

"I have to get up early tomorrow morning," she says.

I know an excuse when I hear one, and I just stay silent. We look at each other for a long, long moment. She finally swallows and looks away.

"And I don't want to sleep with you," she says, her voice just above a whisper.

I almost say *yes, you do, I fucking know you do* but I know better.

"No?" I say.

She flicks me an *are you kidding me* glance, but it doesn't stick.

"No," she says. "Not—"

Clementine takes a deep breath and pushes her hand through her hair, tucking it behind her ear.

"Not tonight," she says, her voice softer. "Blank slate or not, I can't just pretend this is all brand new."

I don't want to pretend that, I think. *Not exactly.*

I nod, trying to ignore my hard-on.

"I get it," I say.

She finally looks at me again.

"Sorry," she says, softly. "You want a ride back to your bunkhouse?"

SLOWLY, as we drive back to town, things get back to normal between us. Or, the normal of the past two days. If we even have a normal.

Clementine tells me about Trout the dog, how she got her name when they found her in a burlap sack next to a trout pond. She was probably the runt of her litter, probably part husky, part golden retriever, plus a hodgepodge of other dogs that Clementine can't identify.

I tell her about the Elkhorn fire, the one that recently got put out, the one she gave us a plaque for. I tell her about the frustration of spending days digging a firebreak — a wide strip of bare earth that a fire can't cross easily — only for the wind to change direction and the firebreak to be useless.

When we pull up in the driveway of her house, I can hear that the party has moved back to the dorm. From the sounds of the merriment, it's co-ed, and there *might* even be more women than men in the back yard right now.

"Want to come over for a drink?" I ask.

Clementine kills the engine and shakes her head.

"I really am getting up early," she says. "I've gotta drive to Ashlake and help my dad move."

"Where are your parents moving to?" I ask.

She looks out the windshield and blows her bangs out of her face, her hand still on the keys in the ignition.

"Not my parents, just my dad," she says. "They're getting divorced."

I blink in surprise. I can't *imagine* my parents getting divorced.

"Shit, Clem, I'm sorry," I say.

"Thanks," she says, and then there's a long pause.

"It's been rough, but I think it's for the best, long-term," she goes on, though it doesn't quite sound like she believes herself.

She doesn't make a move to get out of the car, so neither do I.

"They were never really happy together," she says quietly, still looking out the windshield. "I don't know. Maybe they'll be happier apart."

I put my arm around her and pull her close. She presses her face into my neck, and I take a deep breath of her hair — lemon and pine needles — and force myself not to do anything but give her this friendly, chaste hug.

I want her. I want her like *crazy*, because I absolutely remember how *incredible* everything we did was. But I know better than to think I'll get her by pushing, because Clementine's also fucking stubborn.

"Thanks," she mumbles into my neck, and I can feel her lips move, her voice vibrate. It sends a tremor through me, and I clench my jaw against it.

I don't say anything, and we stay like that for a while, in the front seat of the Forest Service SUV. Quietly, slowly, I press my lips against her dark hair, hoping she doesn't notice.

"I gotta get to bed," she says, and sits upright.

Then she turns her head to look at me.

"I'm sorry," she says. "It's just... I need to think."

"Don't think," I say, and give her my most charming, rakish smile. "Give me a night and I can change your mind."

Clementine makes an annoyed face.

"Is that what you think is gonna happen?" she says. "That's what clean slate means?"

Shit.

"Clem," I say.

She just shakes her head again.

"Just give me a couple days," she says, and gets out of the car.

———

I HAVE a couple beers at the party. I talk to Mandy, her roommate, for a while, along with a few other girls from town. The other guys are all pretty drunk, and I mostly sit back and watch. Normally I'd be right in there, but I feel a little like I've been capsized, like everything I thought I knew is upside-down.

The waitress from the barbecue joint is there, the one who wrote her number on my receipt. She flirts with me, and I try to flirt back — it's harmless, and besides, Clementine just turned me down — but my heart isn't in it, and after a few minutes she goes off to find someone else.

I finish my beer and go to bed, muttering something to Daniel about not feeling too great. Once I'm there, I lie awake on the too-soft mattress, and wonder if I'm an idiot.

I shouldn't have told her why I signed up for another tour of duty. I shouldn't have told her that I didn't think I could handle seeing her with anyone else, even a year after we split up. I wish I didn't know she missed me afterwards.

For a long time after the break up, I was pretty sure she'd cheated on me. I never had any proof, but I was wildly, *insanely*, incurably jealous. We'd video chat sometimes when she got home from a night out, and it would be three in the morning for her, early afternoon for me. I was with a bunch of other guys in a dusty hellhole, and she was getting drunk and going to parties.

She made friends. She had homework, and study groups, and a social life, and suddenly it seemed like she was *popular*, miles different from the nerdy, kind-of-shy girl I'd fallen in love with the year before. We talked less and less, and I thought more and more that I was the former, forgotten boyfriend on the side, the guy she thought she couldn't break up with because he was serving in the military.

I have no idea if she really did cheat on me. She swore up and down that she didn't, even when she was sobbing in her dorm room and shouting at me over a staticky connection. In the end it didn't matter because we broke up anyway, and then I re-enlisted, even though I was three years away from finishing the term I was already on.

I went halfway around the world, and I ended up in the same tiny town with her anyway. If I believed in fate, I'd think this was it, but I don't. I'm stuck thinking this is just cold, unfeeling coincidence, and I'm not sure which is worse.

I fall asleep to the sound of drunk horseshoes, thinking about Clementine's lips on mine with the stars above.

NINE

CLEMENTINE

When I drive up to my parents' house, there's already a ton of furniture on the front lawn. My dad is sitting in an armchair, just looking at it. He waves when I get out of the car, and even from thirty feet away, I can tell that he's trying to be cheerful but failing miserably.

"Hey, Dad," I say. "What's going on?"

He gets out of the chair with a grunt — one of his knees isn't what it once was — and looks around, surveying the scene.

"She wanted my things out of the house," he says, his tone carefully neutral.

I glance at the front door.

"She's not there," he says. "She rode her broomstick off earlier this morning. Something about a 'much-deserved girls' day out.'"

I'm here for two days. Today is Dad's day. Tomorrow is Mom's day. I'm staying with my sister, who's at least a neutral party, since I'm afraid that staying with either parent will make the other angry at me.

I try to ignore the broomstick comment. Neither of them is

exactly handling this well, and I'm still trying to be supportive and understanding, yet stay out of it.

"Will she mind if I go get a glass of water and pee?" I ask.

"Go for it," he says.

Inside, the house looks weirdly half-empty as I fill a glass and drink it slowly. Things that I wouldn't have thought were my dad's are gone — the old cuckoo clock that used to be in the foyer, for example. I always just assumed it had been my mom's idea, but now it's not there.

I finish my water, stare at the spot where it used to be, and wonder how well I know my parents as *people*. I know that they have lives that extend before and beyond my time on earth, but it's hard to think of them as *Martha and Rick* and not *Mom and Dad*.

Sometimes, I wonder if they were ever in love, like really in love. I know they got married quickly, and that I was born about a year and a half after the wedding. Maybe they felt like they were already stuck by the time they realized they weren't right for each other.

Maybe they were right for each other, though, I think. *And they couldn't make it work anyway. I'm sure it happens, people who love each other but just can't be together.*

I force myself to think about anything but Hunter, last night. I finish my water, pee, and go back outside, where my dad is lounging on a couch, waiting for the movers.

———

I'M REALLY JUST THERE for moral support, because three burly men come and move all his furniture and possessions into a moving truck, then from the moving truck into his new apartment, in an old building across town. It's not a particularly nice place, but it's perfectly fine. There's nothing wrong with it.

"I don't think I'm gonna be here for long," he says, flipping on the lights. "Just until I figure out what I want to do next. I've been thinking of moving to Mesa, it's a nice place, got that cute downtown, and the commute to Ashlake wouldn't be a problem..."

We arrange his furniture and start unpacking. He's got boxes and boxes from Target: four plates, four bowls, four sets of silverware, a microwave. He tells me that all my parents' flatware was from their wedding registry, and that when my mom wanted to keep it, he let her out of spite.

"Let *her* remember that she married me every time she eats yogurt," he says, tearing into another box.

Then he looks over at me.

"Sorry, sweetheart," he says.

I never ask him *why* he wants a divorce. Honestly, I don't really want to know the details, because I think I understand the larger picture pretty well.

It's close to eleven when I say goodbye. He hugs me tight, for a long time, so long I almost start to worry that he won't be okay.

"Thanks for helping your old man out," he says. "I know this hasn't been easy on you."

I don't say anything.

When I get to Jane's apartment, she opens the door, and without speaking, points to her couch.

"Sit," she says, and goes into her kitchen. "Wine or whiskey?" she hollers.

"Whiskey," I holler back, practically flopping onto her couch.

"Straight or sour?"

I think about it for a moment, but it's not hard. Jane bartended her way through college — a better choice than working in the library, which is what I did — and makes *great* whiskey sours.

"Sour," I call.

A few minutes later, she kicks my legs unceremoniously off the couch, hands me a drink, and sits down.

"Here's to growing old with cats and spiders and definitely not men," she says, clinking her glass against mine. "And for the record, if I were a man or a lesbian I'd say definitely not women, because the enemy here is marriage and not one sex or the other."

I laugh and take a drink. It's delicious, because Jane knows how to make a fucking *drink*.

"How was he today?" she asks.

I look into my glass and shrug.

"He seemed... more good than bad," I say. "He managed to only say a couple of bad things about Mom, so I guess that's progress."

Jane just shakes her head. She's two years younger than me, but we've had an inverted relationship since we were teenagers: she's louder, more outspoken, a little pushier. I've always been shier than her, and because of that, sometimes I think she feels the need to protect me.

I keep telling her I don't need protecting, I'm just quiet. I'm not sure she believes me.

"I'm glad he's finally getting his stuff out of there and into his own place," she says. "Uncle Brandon's guest room is *not* a long-term plan."

"I don't get why he even asked for a divorce if he didn't have a better plan," I say, leaning my forehead against my hand and my elbow against the back of the couch. "Why not wait a week, until you've found an apartment or something?"

Weirdly, dissecting the logistics of my parents' divorce makes it easier to deal with. Emotions are tricky and slippery. Apartment leases are not.

Jane just looks at me, and instantly, I know there's something she's not saying.

"What?" I ask.

She looks away.

"*Jane*," I say.

Jane squeezes her eyes shut, her whole face scrunching up. I wait.

"She cheated on him with a guy she works with at the hospital," she says, the words coming out in a rush.

My mouth falls open, and I stare at her. She cracks one eye open.

"I'm sorry," she says.

All those phone calls, accusing my dad of cheating? All those crazy guesses about the neighbors? It was her, the *entire fucking time*?

"Why are you sorry?" I ask, because I'm still processing the rest.

"I wasn't supposed to tell you," she says. "I mean, I wasn't supposed to *know*, but I was over there having dinner before they announced it, and I guess they were in counseling at the time, and it just... came out."

I take a long, long drink.

"And, I've only gleaned this in bits and pieces, but I *think* they were trying to work through it, and then she did it again, and he just asked for a divorce on the spot," Jane goes on. "So he didn't really have a plan."

I stare into my whiskey sour. I don't even know if I'm surprised, because of course my mom would go on the offensive about something like this, try to get suspicion off of herself.

I love my mother, but that doesn't mean she always handles situations well. She's only human.

Jane stands and points at my glass.

"Finish your last sip," she orders me. "You need another one."

I obey, because she's right.

————

Two whiskey sours later, we're still on the couch. It's late, and we're *this* close to Really Drunk, but not quite there. I feel like it's justified, though. She's just finished telling me about the fight she and my dad got in. It was over a dresser, but as she's telling it, I can tell it's *really* because he felt like she was picking our mom over him, and I tell her that.

She's quiet a minute.

"Yeah," she says, and kicks her feet onto the coffee table. "Fights are never about what they're about, huh?"

"You should make that into a poster," I say, leaning my head back against the back of the couch. "You know those, like, cutesy posters of cheesy sayings that people hang over their bed? 'Always kiss me goodnight' and shit? Make one that says *fights are never about what they're about.*"

"For people to hang in their bedrooms?" she asks.

"For people to hang wherever they have their fights," I say. "Last dude I dated, it was his car. Dude before that, the kitchen."

"Hmm," she says.

We're both quiet for a moment, and of course I think back to Hunter. Jesus, we had some fights, and Jane was right about those, too: they were never about what I thought they were. Not in retrospect.

Really, they all boiled down to the same thing. For me, anyway. I was just afraid that I loved him more than he loved me.

Fuck, was it really that simple?

I sigh and look at Jane's ceiling.

"I know, right?" Jane agrees.

I have the urge to tell her about Hunter, that he's back and still *very* hot and actually seems to have matured, and I have too, but I don't. Dealing with our parents is more than enough.

"I'm with Mom tomorrow," I say, instead of telling her about Hunter. "Any advice?"

"Don't fucking tell her I told you she cheated," Jane says.

"Duh," I say.

"She just started watching *Game of Thrones*," Jane says. "Talk to her about that."

"I've never seen it," I say.

"It's the middle ages, a brother and sister fuck, and a bunch of people die while fighting to be King," Jane says. "That's about it. Oh, and there are lots of naked titties on TV, and she does *not* approve."

"Thanks," I say.

After a long silence, Jane stands and takes our glasses to the kitchen.

"I should get to bed," she says. "I'm working in the morning. You want help pulling out the sofa?"

I consider the couch for a moment, but I don't think I've ever wanted to do anything less than pull out a sofa bed right now.

"I'll just sleep on it," I say.

"Cool," she says, and points at a chair. "Sheets and shit. Night, Minty."

"Night, Shay-shay."

When she was little, she couldn't say her own name, and it stuck. She sticks her tongue out at me, then heads into her bedroom.

I manage to brush my teeth and wash my face like an adult human before collapsing back onto the sofa, haphazardly wrapping myself in sheets and rolling onto my side. Then I try to fall asleep, but I can't.

My parents' divorce makes everything feel like it's turned upside-down. Suddenly, I'm the adult here, the one who's handling things maturely, and it's bizarre. When you're a kid, it's normal to see your parents as a unit, so suddenly seeing them separate is strange, to say the least.

Especially when you're an adult yourself. Once you're past a certain age, you just assume your parents are stuck together. And then, one day, they're not.

Maybe nothing lasts, I think, feeling very dramatic. *Maybe there's no real love. Maybe everyone winds up alone and miserable either way, married or divorced or whatever.*

I burrow harder into the couch, trying to make myself fall asleep.

Just bang Hunter, I think, half-asleep and drunk. *You want to. If it goes bad it can't be worse than last time, right?*

Drunk me has a point.

———

MY MOM and I go shopping for stuff to replace everything my dad took. There aren't all that many stores in Ashlake, so I don't *think* it's going to take all that long, but I'd forgotten that my mom is legendarily indecisive.

Somehow, we debate between two different plate sets for twenty minutes. That's not that bad, except they're both white, and the patterns are barely different.

"I just wonder if it won't be unpleasant to scrape a fork along this one," she says, rubbing the slightly raised design with one finger. "Don't you think it'll be a little weird, Minty?"

"Get the other one, then," I say, my patience wearing thin.

"But I do like this pattern," she says. "I think it's really nice, and it's kind of a contrast to the pieces we already have."

"I don't think the fork scraping is a big deal," I say.

She just looks at the plates again.

I'm getting annoyed, and I have to fight the urge to say *is your lover gonna be eating off these or something?* but I know better.

Lord, do I ever know better.

I know her choices have nothing to do with me, and I don't want to be mad at her. I'm pretty sure people can be complex enough to cheat on their spouses and still love their kids.

But I definitely feel some kind of way about it, and I'm having a hard time acting normal around her, knowing what I know. Knowing that she was married for almost thirty years, and then she just *did* that.

I guess no one's ever safe, I think. *You think things are fine, and then bam.*

My mom takes a couple steps away and starts looking at different plates.

"These blue ones do add an exciting pop of color," she says.

I grit my teeth and follow her.

TEN

HUNTER

I open the cupboard and stare into it. Two days ago, we were fully stocked with every cereal under the sun, but today, we're down to Grape Nuts and Raisin Bran. I want to be annoyed at the other guys for eating the Lucky Charms like a bunch of children, but that's what I wanted to eat, so I don't have a leg to stand on.

I grab the Raisin Bran, pour some into a bowl, put milk in, then grab my coffee and head into the living room. There are guys sitting in almost every seat, all watching something on the TV, empty cereal bowls and mugs on the coffee table and the floor.

It feels like a frat house in here. At least, this is what I assume a frat house feels like. We're older, probably a little less hungover, and quieter, but we're still wearing nothing but boxers and openly scratching our balls.

I sit on an easy chair with my cereal, balance my cup of coffee on the floor, and take a bite of raisin bran. It's gross, but I'm hungry, and to be honest, I eat worse most of the time.

We don't talk much, but only because there's nothing to say. I'm with these guys pretty much 24/7 for six months, so it's not as if there's a lot of new information for anyone to impart. Someone gets the hiccups, farts, or sneezes, everyone knows.

I'm just assuming they know something is up with me and Clementine, even though I'm not exactly sure there is. Not that we talk much about relationships.

There's some movie on TV. Something with a lot of explosions, and one guy in particular seems to always be running away from them, then getting thrown forward dramatically. Every time he does, a couple of the guys in the room chuckle.

Explosions don't work that way at *all*. Not even close. Take it from a bunch of guys who've seen it.

I try to concentrate on the movie, but it's hard. Clementine gets back from Ashlake today, and I haven't heard from her for two days, even though I almost texted her a thousand times.

She wanted a couple of days. I gave her a couple of days, even though I hate feeling like this, like I'm sitting around, waiting for someone to decide about me.

It's not what I do. It's not how I operate: I decide on a girl, and I *get* her. I don't wait around, hoping she'll decide she likes me.

Except, apparently, I do. For Clementine, I do.

Shit.

After a while, Silas comes in. He's fully dressed, and stands in the doorway, arms crossed over his chest. We all look over at him.

"Utah's on fire," he says. "Might be big."

"What part?"

"North of Salt Lake City, close to Idaho," he says, and points at the TV. "Look at the Weather Channel, they've got it."

Whoever has the remote flips the channel, but it's on commercial.

"Where are we now?" someone else asks.

It sounds like a dumb question, but we've been traveling all summer from one place to another, and they start to look alike after a little while. Hell, in June I thought we were in Idaho for an entire week when we were actually in Oregon.

"Montana," I say.

"Does that border Utah?" he asks.

"Nah, Wyoming's in between," I say.

"Right," he says. "I thought there was something."

The weather news comes back up, and we sit through the forecast to hear about the fire. We *could* go get our phones and look it up, but when we're not working eighteen-hour days, we tend to be pretty lazy.

At last, they talk about the Wasatch fire. Started sometime yesterday, northeast of Salt Lake City, already thirty thousand acres. Zero percent contained.

Shit. I guess I know where we're headed next, unless a miracle happens.

I've only been doing this for two fire seasons, but I keep hearing that this is the worst anyone can remember. The western United States, and especially California, has been in a serious drought for ages, so the forests are pretty dried up. There are places where you could drop a match and a thousand acres would be gone an hour later.

That's probably what happened here, actually. Something like ninety percent of forest fires are started by humans. People who drop cigarettes, who leave campfires burning, that kind of shit. I wish they wouldn't, but then I'd just be working at my parents' ranch year round, and I *like* this job.

"We going?" I ask.

"Porter says not yet, but get ready," Silas says. "A couple closer crews are working it, but it's still up in the air."

I look at the map of Utah on the TV. They've marked a bright orange splotch where the fire's burning. I get a weird, bad feeling just looking at it.

Utah. That's two states away, and Clementine is *here*. I just found her again, and even though I understand that this is my job, it's my duty, and it's fucking *important*, I don't want to go to Utah.

I want to stay here. With her. As long as she wants me, anyway.

God, I hate uncertainty.

"Better be ready to move," says Jeremy Dashell, Porter's second-in-command who's much cooler than Porter. "Looks like that thing could break bad any minute now."

Everyone groans, but we get up. We take dishes to the kitchen, we take showers, we get dressed, and two hours later, there's fire gear all over the living room, the kitchen, and the back yard.

I get my own kit together pretty quickly, because it's not like I leave it unpacked. Sometimes we leave with twenty, thirty minutes of warning, so it pays to be ready.

Once that's done, I head down to the kitchen, grab a checklist, and start going through boxes of camp stove fuel, MREs, and freeze-dried rations. In the backyard, I can see Silas and Daniel with a tent set up, examining a patch, arguing over whether it needs to be redone.

I'd re-do it, I think. *You never know when your next chance to fix something is gonna be.*

Something bangs through the open door, and I turn as Dashell walks into the kitchen, carrying a heavy-duty plastic box.

"Got the new fire shelters," he says.

I look up from the checklist.

"I thought we weren't getting those until next season," I say.

He puts the box down on the table and cracks his knuckles, looking at it.

"After Kaibab, apparently the Department of the Interior decided better shelters were a priority," he says.

We're both silent for a moment, just looking at the thick plastic box on the table. I've been trying not to think too much about Kaibab ever since it happened a month ago. At least, I've been trying not to think about the details. I think about twelve dead firefighters plenty.

"These are better than the old ones?" I ask.

Dashell half nods, half shrugs.

"That's what they say," he tells me. "Apparently some kid at MIT invented an adhesive that can withstand up to seven-fifty degrees, and that's what's holding these together."

"That's better," I say.

The adhesive is always the weak point on fire shelters. The combination of aluminum, silica and fiberglass can protect you up to a thousand degrees or so, but the glue only goes up to five hundred degrees. Or, seven-fifty, now. Allegedly.

"Yeah," he says, grabbing the box by the handles, yanking it from the table with a grunt. "It's a nice gesture. Seven-fifty wasn't gonna save the guys at Kaibab either."

Dashell leaves the kitchen with the box, and I go back to my checklist, even though my mind is elsewhere.

The Kaibab fire is named after Kaibab, Arizona, where it started. It's hot and dry in the summer, and this summer, it's been hotter and drier than normal. *Way* hotter and drier, which means that fires catch faster, they heat up faster, and they *move* faster.

To make a long story short, a dozen men were on a ridge line when the wind suddenly changed direction, and they were trapped.

They deployed their shelters, but they didn't make it. An hour later, another crew finally got there and found twelve bodies wrapped in scorched aluminum foil.

I go down the list mechanically: provisions, check; batteries, check; flashlights, check. I try to keep myself from thinking about what it must have been like in one of those shelters: your body flat on the ground, breathing in dirt, heat pressing in. How loud the fire must have been.

How it must feel to know you're trapped.

I shake my head and look out the window. There are some nasty clouds in the distance, but Silas and Daniel are still discussing whether or not to re-patch the tent, even though they could have done it twice since they started this argument.

Most people who do this go twenty years without ever using a shelter, I remind myself. *Kaibab was a freak accident.*

I'm not afraid of dying. I spent too long fighting in the desert to be afraid of that. But the idea of being trapped, helpless, in a tiny confined space as a wildfire bears down, with nothing I can do?

That makes me a little uneasy.

———

BY LATE THAT afternoon we're back to doing nothing. It doesn't take us very long to get prepared, and everything is packed, sitting around the house in crates. We could be out of here and on the road in ten minutes, *maybe* even five.

It's my fourth day in a row off, and I'm starting to get antsy. One day off is great. Two is fun, three starts to get boring, but by now I'm about ready to climb the walls.

Plus, no Clementine. I'm trying to be patient, but it doesn't come naturally. She can't keep me on the hook like this forever.

If she doesn't want me, that sucks, but I'll live. But she's gotta fucking *tell* me that.

I try to read a book for a while, some murder mystery that I found on a bookshelf downstairs, but I can't concentrate for more than a page or two at a time, so I wander back into the kitchen to the sound of a girl laughing.

It's not Clementine, but it's Mandy, her roommate, plus another girl I don't recognize. They're sitting at the kitchen table with Silas, playing some board game. Mandy sits up straighter when I walk in.

"Hey, Hunter," she says, tucking one foot underneath her. "How's it going?"

I give her a quick glance as I open the cabinet to get a water glass.

"Well, Utah's on fire, so I've still got a job," I say, mostly kidding. "How are you?"

She laughs, a nice, bubbly sound. Mandy's no knockout, but she's cute, and she seems nice.

"Oh, you know," she says, shrugging, her hands clasped on the table. "The usual. Kids go back to school next week, so this week we're flooded with everyone who suddenly remembered to get their vacation activities done before that."

She told me Saturday that she works at the Visitor Center for the Big Sky National Forest, though she's not a ranger like Clementine is, just an employee. I want to ask her whether Clementine is back yet, but I don't.

I walk to the table, and I'm about to say something else, but then I look down at the game they're playing and realize I recognize it.

"You guys are playing Candyland?" I ask.

The girls both laugh. The one who isn't Mandy takes a long drink from a bottle of beer, blushing.

"We already played Chutes and Ladders, so it was this or Monopoly," Mandy admits. "This is my other roommate Lucy, by the way."

Lucy and I shake hands. She's cute too, even though she's not bubbly like Mandy. Silas is already making subtle faces at me, trying to get my attention, like we're gonna split the girls up right now and each take one.

I'm beyond uninterested.

"Wanna play?" Lucy asks, her voice quiet and dry. "If you can pull cards off a deck, you'll be great at it."

I look at it. The box says it's for kids three years old and up, and technically, that *does* include me. Plus, I have no idea what the fuck else I'm gonna do besides mope around, not get laid, and see if Clementine calls.

God, I feel like an idiot, just *waiting*.

"Sure," I say. "How?"

Mandy moves all the cardboard pieces back to the beginning.

"Hey!" says Silas. "I was winning."

"I believe in you," Lucy says to him, sounding slightly sarcastic, leaning on one hand. "I bet you can do it again."

"It's just luck," Silas says. "I can believe in myself until the cows come home and it won't help."

Lucy just laughs, pats his arm, and puts another piece on the board.

"Okay, here are the rules," Mandy says. "You draw a card, then you move to the next space of that color. The end. You don't even have to know how to read."

I nod, looking at the board seriously.

"Ready to get your asses kicked?" I ask.

The girls both laugh. Silas and I smile.

ELEVEN

CLEMENTINE

I've got a pen between my fingers, and I tap it against the desk in my cubicle over and over again, staring at the gray wall without seeing it. I should be thinking about work, because God knows there's enough to do, but I'm thinking of what I'm gonna say to Hunter when I go over there tonight.

Okay, let's do it doesn't quite seem to capture the gravity of the situation, and neither does *I considered this and I think having sex would be fine and not too damaging*, or *this can't go worse than last time, so let's get it on!*

I think I might be bad at this, and I'm still wondering what the hell I *do* when Jennifer's head appears around the cubicle, and she smiles a dangerous smile at me.

"You're making me crazy," she says through her teeth.

I stop tapping.

"Sorry," I say.

"How's that budget going?" she asks, glancing at my computer screen.

I haven't used it in so long that the monitor went to sleep.

"It's going great?" I say, jiggling the mouse and praying

that a spreadsheet pops up on the screen, not something else. Jennifer glances at it.

It's the spreadsheet. It's half-done, but at least it's not something else.

"I'm sorry," I say. "I'll get it done in time, I just…"

My ex-boyfriend showed up again, my parents are getting divorced, and I just found out that my mom cheated on my dad and it feels a little like my whole world is inside a kaleidoscope, rearranging itself as some asshole kid turns it around.

"I've had a lot on my plate the last few days," I say, finding a more professional phrase.

Jennifer just nods.

"I know," she says. "Clementine, let me know if you're feeling overloaded, okay? I can have someone else do some of the grunt work."

"Thanks," I say. "I'll be fine."

It's nearly September, and for some reason, a lot of federal and state grant applications are due September first. That means we're rushing to put together proposals and budgets, dreaming up ways that renovating the picnic pavilion at the Alpine Lakes campground promotes diversity among the youth who visit the park.

I quit staring at the wall, and for the next ninety minutes, I stare at a spreadsheet. By the end of the day I've managed to make a graph, even if my mind keeps wandering to *very* different pursuits.

The cubicles are buried in the center of the administrative building, in a mostly-windowless room, so when I walk past a window to the bathroom, I'm surprised to see that it's raining hard. I stop and watch for a moment, and the sky blinks white with lightning, followed a few seconds later by thunder.

I'm glad it's not my week outside, backpacking and repairing trails. As much as I like nature, being indoors *sure* is nice sometimes.

When I get back to my desk, Jennifer is looking at my chair.

"Oh, there you are," she says.

"I went to the bathroom," I say, like I need to explain where I was or something. She just waves a hand.

"I was actually wondering whether you'd mind driving some stuff over to the firefighters in the dorm," she says. "Mike's worried that the power's gonna go out, and we took all the emergency supplies out when we renovated, and they got here before we put them back. It's just flashlights, lanterns, that kind of stuff."

Mike's the Head Ranger here, Jennifer's boss.

I almost say *sure, I was going over there anyway*, but then I realize I don't really want to have a conversation about *why* I'm going over there, because it's not like that's simple.

"Sure, no problem," is what I say.

"Thanks," Jennifer says. "He'll help you carry the stuff out."

By the time I get to the firefighters' dorm, next to my house, the storm is going full force. I can't drive much more than twenty-five miles an hour, rain sheeting over the windshield, lightning flashing through the sky every couple of seconds.

I like storms, but this is a big one. Mike's right — there's no way the power isn't going to go out when the wind blows a dead tree over onto the power lines or something. I don't envy the guys who get to fix *that*.

I park the SUV, pull the hood of my raincoat over my head, then take a deep breath.

Flashlights first, then talk to Hunter, I think. My stomach flips over inside me, but I grit my teeth, grab the keys, open the door, and then run like hell to the dorm.

No one answers the front door, but the rain is so loud on the tin roof of the front porch that they probably can't hear it. I just push it open and go inside.

The front door opens onto the living room, where a couple guys watching TV look up at me in surprise. Hunter's not one of them.

"Hey," says Daniel, one of the guys I played baggo with on Saturday.

"I knocked, but the rain's too loud," I say. "I brought your emergency supplies. Flashlights and candles and stuff."

"You need help bringing it in?" another guy, this one a little older, asks. He stands from the couch, and so do all the rest.

Shit. I'm pretty sure I met him briefly when I was here before, and I'm also pretty sure I don't remember his name.

"There's only a couple of boxes," I say. "I just need one or two people to help."

There's four of them, and they're all already putting on shoes and raincoats while I stand there. One of them, the older guy, winks at me.

"We need something to do," he says. "Even if it's just carrying some heavy things in the rain."

I laugh, because even if I don't *need* that much help, I'm not gonna turn down a bunch of burly firemen who want to lift heavy things for me.

"Thanks," I say.

I just stand on the dry-ish porch, unlock the SUV with the remote key fob, let the guys grab the heavy plastic bins, and lock it again when the doors are closed.

"Just take these on through to the other common area," the older guy says. "We'll dry 'em off and go through them there."

We file back inside, the guys carrying the big plastic bins. I push the hood of my raincoat back and unzip it, turning to the guy whose name I've forgotten.

"Thanks for the help," I say. "Is Hunter around?"

"Last I saw, Casden was playing board games in the kitchen," he says. "You're welcome to check."

I hang my wet jacket up next to the door, take off my shoes, and walk through the house. I'm hyper-aware of every movement I make, and hyper-aware that my hair is up in an ugly ponytail and rain-frizzed, that I'm wearing work pants, a cardigan, and polka-dot socks. It's not the most enticing outfit, but what am I gonna do, go put on a sundress before I say hello to Hunter?

As I come up on the kitchen door, I hear a girl shriek, then a giggle. It sounds like Mandy, and suddenly, I remember the way she laughed at his jokes on Saturday, the way she touched Hunter's arm, and something inside me freezes.

Calm down, I tell myself. *She's allowed to laugh.*

Then I walk through the doorway and stop.

Opposite me, Hunter is standing in front of an open closet, his back to me, and Mandy is on his shoulders, holding a board game in one hand. She laughs again.

"I got it, I got it, you can put me down," she says.

"That's easier said than done," Hunter says, a smile in his voice.

I'm frozen in the doorway, just looking at them. He's got his hands on her thighs, holding her steady as she wobbles a little, riding his shoulders.

I told you, a nasty voice in the back of my head whispers. *And you thought people changed.*

"Hey," says Silas, sitting at the table. "You're just in time to play Clue with us."

"Hey," I say, still staring at Hunter and Mandy.

They both turn their heads. Mandy's smiling, but the moment Hunter sees me, his face falls.

Yeah, no one likes getting caught, that same voice whispers.

I clear my throat and force myself to take a deep breath, even though I feel like all the air's been sucked out of the room.

"I brought over the emergency supplies you guys were missing," I say, my voice sounding hollow to my own ears.

Outside the window, there's a white flash as lightning goes off, then a boom so loud it rattles the dishes in the cabinets. The lights flicker.

"Just in time, seems like," Silas says.

"There's candles and flashlights and stuff in the other room," I go on. I can't take my eyes off of Hunter, Mandy on his shoulders, his hands on her knees, keeping her steady. "Just wanted to let you guys know."

I feel like someone's stuck a kitchen mixer into my stomach and turned it on. Part of me knows I'm being stupid, probably overreacting, but all I can think is *this is exactly what it felt like before.*

History's repeating itself, just like you fucking knew it would.

"Stay for Clue!" Mandy says brightly, holding it up. "We just found it buried on the top shelf."

I shake my head, doing my best to act normal.

"I can't," I say, already stepping backward. "I gotta go take care of some stuff at home, you know, laundry and Trout's been there all day, and... water the plant... stuff."

Mandy frowns, but I turn anyway.

"Clem," Hunter says.

I just walk. I need to be somewhere else *now*, I need to be alone and not surrounded by people I barely know, in a house that's not mine. If there were a hole I could crawl into I would, because I just want to be by myself, in the dark, where no one can watch me melt down.

I hear a soft thump, and then Mandy's voice asking, "Is something wrong?"

"Clem!" Hunter says again, closer this time.

I ignore it. I hurry to the living room, but he's right behind me in the hall, and he puts one hand on my shoulder.

"Clem, *wait*," he says. He sounds half-worried and half-annoyed.

"No," I say.

"For fuck's sake," he hisses, trying to keep his voice down.

Suddenly, there's a crackle just outside, like the air itself is splitting apart, followed by a boom that shakes the floor.

The lights go out, and in an instant, it's dead quiet, the electronic hum of everyday life gone. We both stop and look around.

"Well, we've got flashlights," one of the guys in the living room says. I can hear him get off the couch and walk into another room.

Hunter's hand is still on my shoulder, and I shake it off.

"Look at me," he says. "You can't just go silent and storm off."

I whirl around.

"Yes, I can," I say. "Watch me."

"Are you fucking serious right now?" he whispers, his voice slowly getting louder. "You don't even *text* me for two days and now you're just stomping off again?"

"I told you I needed space," I say. "I don't have to tell you what I'm doing every second."

How the hell did I get on the defensive?

"I don't want to know what you're doing every second," he says. "I just wanted *Hi, I'm fine, I think about you sometimes, I didn't forget you.*"

"You didn't say you wanted me to text you," I say, my voice rising too. I can hear people walking around upstairs, and I glance behind me. One of the firemen is padding through the living room, very carefully not looking at us.

The blood has rushed to my face, and I know I'm bright

red, my eyes quickly filling with tears, my throat closing. Right now I'd give a pinkie to be *anywhere* else.

"I thought maybe you'd *want* to text me, or call me, or fuck, *something*," he says. "I guess I should have known."

The hell does that mean?

"Like I guess I should have known I'd come back to find your head between someone else's legs?" I hiss. I'm clenching my jaw so hard it hurts, doing my absolute damnedest to hold back tears.

"That's fucking unfair," he says. "I didn't know you were coming over, I wouldn't have—"

"So it's fine that you were flirting with someone else until you got caught," I say.

One tear spills down my face and I brush it off furiously. My jaw is trembling, and it's taking everything I have not to lose my shit.

"That's not what I meant and you know it," he says.

Another tear.

"I'm not doing this here, in front of goddamn everyone," I say, holding up both hands. "We can talk about this—"

Hunter snorts. Then he walks past me, opens a door, glances inside, and enters.

"Come on," he says.

I walk into the bathroom, close the door behind myself, and turn to face him.

"I just *told* you, I don't fucking want to—"

"Yeah, well, I do, since apparently I don't know when I'm going to hear from you again," he says, his voice bitter.

"I'm not sure why I should call if I'm just going to find you putting the moves on my *roommate*," I say.

Lightning flashes again, outside the tiny bathroom window.

"I wasn't *putting the moves* on your roommate," he says. "You can't decide whether you want me or not, and in the meantime, I can't talk to other girls?"

I roll my eyes and snort.

"That was not *talking*," I say. "She was on your shoulders, for fuck's sake."

"She needed to reach the top shelf."

"There were no chairs to stand on?" I ask. "The first thing you thought was hey, let me lift you up on my shoulders?"

Hunter glares at me, clenching his jaw. He turns away, shoves his hands through his hair, and turns back. There's more lightning, close by, and we both turn to look at the window for a moment.

"It didn't mean anything," he says at last. "She suggested it, and I just got caught up."

I can't look at him, so I look away, at the ugly tile wall of the shower. There's tears running down my face now, my throat nearly closed off, and I have to force myself not to start sobbing, because holy shit does *this* feel familiar.

It's always been like this with us. He was the quarterback, the prom king, and I had to stand there in my fancy dress and watch him dance with Ashley Fucking Newman, who was blond and blue-eyed and a cheerleader and everything that I wasn't.

Hunter's handsome. He's charming. He's a fucking *fireman*, and worse, all that shit comes naturally to him. There's no reason at all that he should be with some quiet nerd, and I've *always* known it.

The only question is when *he'll* finally figure it out and leave me.

"I can't," I say, my voice coming out a strangled whisper.

He looks at me, his face flat and unreadable.

"Can't what?" he says.

"I can't do this with you," I say, a single sob escaping me. "People don't change. I should have known better to think you did."

"*I* haven't changed?" he says, incredulously. "You ignore

me for days and now we're fighting in a bathroom and *I'm* the one who hasn't changed?"

"I haven't fucking changed either, then!" I say. I'm trying to keep my voice down, but I think I might be bordering on hysterical. "I'm the same and you're the same and let's just skip the part where we have fun together because I already know how this ends, so let's just get it over with."

Better now than thirty years from now, I think, even as I'm trying so hard not to cry that I'm shaking.

Hunter's just staring at me, his mouth slightly open, like he's not quite sure what just happened. I push past him, wipe my face furiously, and leave the bathroom. Everyone is looking at me as I put on my things and then rush out of the house.

Lightning flashes overhead as I run the fifty feet to my own front door, even though I think the rain is starting to slack off. Trout greets me inside, happy as ever, and I throw my stuff on the floor and head upstairs immediately, flopping miserably onto my bed.

Then I lie there and cry. I cry until I've got the hiccups and I can't cry anymore, because I can't believe this happened *again*, with the same person, and I can't believe I didn't handle it better this time, I can't believe my parents are getting divorced. I can't believe my mom cheated on my dad.

The worst part is how it hurts *again*, the same way it did when he went off to Afghanistan, so pumped and excited to be in the Marines, doing something for his country, while I was trying to get through my first couple weeks of college. Every time we talked he was all smiles, friends with everyone else there, while I was usually alone in my dorm room, pretty sure that everyone I knew was at a cool party I hadn't been invited to.

Back then I thought he cheated on me. Not that I ever had any evidence, but the women in his unit all seemed to really *like* him. He was halfway around the world, how would I ever find out?

I'm not sure I think that any more, but it's better to just nip this in the bud than have months of drama play out again.

I stay there, on my bed in the dark, for a long time and just feel sorry for myself. It feels like nothing is stable, like I can't take anything for granted. Like I'm crossing a rickety bridge and don't know what's on the other side.

Someone knocks softly on my bedroom door, but I don't answer it. They knock again, and then I hear Mandy's voice quietly calling my name, but I still don't get up, because I'm not sure I can explain what just happened. Finally, I hear her footsteps heading back down the hallway, and I heave a sigh of relief.

After a long time, I get up. The lights are back on, so I heat leftovers, watch dumb TV. I go to bed at eight, because I don't want to be awake any more.

I feel like an empty, hollow shell, but a dumb one who can't learn from her mistakes. At least I fall asleep fast.

TWELVE

HUNTER

I watch Clementine leave, and I don't follow her, even though part of me wants to. But what the fuck am I going to say? Am I going to stand there, get soaking wet, and beg her to forgive me?

And for what, the *horrible* crime of touching another girl? Clementine and I aren't together. She made *damn* sure I knew that before she left for a couple of days, but now she's acting like I've betrayed her somehow.

The guys in the living room glance at me quickly, then go back to pretending they can't see me and didn't overhear the giant fight we got into. I turn around and head back through the kitchen, to the screened-in back porch, where I stand and watch the storm.

She says *I* haven't changed, but she's the one who saw me with another girl and went fucking *nuclear*. She's the one who kept me at arm's distance for two full days. I know two days isn't that much.

If we'd just met, I wouldn't care, but there's a long pattern here. Before we broke up, for *days* I'd call her and she wouldn't answer, she wouldn't email back, until finally she'd call at three in the morning her time, drunk, and want to talk.

You know what it feels like to be eighteen, in a war zone, half-thinking you'll get blown up any second, and your girlfriend won't even take your calls?

Shitty. That's how.

We never even *technically* broke up. Neither of us ever said *we should break up* to the other. True, our last fight was pretty spectacular, and I said a *lot* of things I didn't mean. But it was only our last because Clementine suddenly went totally silent on me.

She didn't answer my calls, didn't answer my emails, nothing. After a week I stopped, decided we'd broken up, and signed up for another tour just to get back at her.

I stand on the back porch for a long, long time. Flecks of rain fly in through the screen, so I'm covered in a fine sheet of water, but I don't move. Mandy and Lucy both leave, I think, or at least I hear them saying goodbye to Silas.

The storm slows, moving away, and eventually the rain stops. I glance at the house next door, where Clementine lives. There's a gnawing feeling in my gut, knowing that *this* time she's right there.

I could go over there. We could talk this over, like the adults we've become. But it's not what she fucking wants, so history's gonna repeat itself.

I head inside at last. The guys are all looking at me, but I don't say anything. I can't even explain this shit to *myself*, I'm not gonna try it out loud. I just take a long, hot shower, eat dinner, and go to bed.

———

I FEEL a little better the next morning. I remember that from before, too: sleeping always helped.

At breakfast, everything is tense. Not because of me. It's not like I'm the first guy who's had a huge fight in front of everyone. We're together all day, every day. Shit happens.

It's because we could be leaving for Utah any minute. The Wasatch fire is still borderline, so we're all checking updates, trying to get ourselves mentally prepared. It's toward the end of fire season, and we're all tired. The men with spouses and kids want to go home, and the rest of us aren't looking forward to sleeping on the ground.

I'm just afraid I'll leave and not get to say goodbye to Clementine. Even if it didn't work between us again, I at least want that.

I'm still brooding over that when Porter walks into the kitchen and stands in the doorway between it and the living room.

"Is everyone here?" he asks.

We all look around, tense, and shrug.

I guess we're heading to Utah, I think.

"I need a couple of volunteers to hike to some fire lookouts," he says. "There were a number of lightning strikes in the national forest last night, and there have been a number of smoke reports."

"Fire lookouts?" someone asks.

"That's correct," Porter says, speaking like there's a stick up his ass, per usual.

"There's no satellite or helicopter?" the guy asks again.

Porter runs one hand through his hair, then crosses his arms.

"This has been a very long, trying fire season," he says, and for once, his voice softens. "It's the biggest on record, and it's not even September yet. Every crew has been running ragged for months. We lost twelve men at Kaibab."

We're all silent, waiting for him to explain why there's no helicopters.

"Frankly, this season has been longer, hotter, and bigger than anyone anticipated," he goes on. "We're running on empty, resource-wise, and there's not much to spare to look for *more* fires. All that equipment is monitoring current, active fires, so we're gonna have to do this the old-fashioned way."

Heads nod, somberly. Everyone looks at their hands, because Porter is right: it's been a long, tough season, and it's not even over yet.

Porter takes a deep breath, straightens, and apparently jams the stick back up his butt.

"Each volunteer will be accompanying a forest ranger to an existing lookout tower in the Big Sky National Forest," he says. "The rangers know the forest, and from there, you can help them assess any possible ignition points. They're long hikes, but there's a bed and shelter at the end, so at least there's that."

I stopped listening at *accompanying a forest ranger*. My stupid heart leaps, even though it shouldn't.

"Volunteers?" he asks.

My hand shoots up, along with a few other guys. Porter pulls out a notepad and looks carefully around the room, giving each volunteer a good long look, then nodding.

"Miller," he says, writing the name down. "Dewar. Lawson. Snyder."

He pauses, glancing past me, like he's trying to see if there's anyone else.

"I'll volunteer," I say. I have the urge to wave my hand in the air like a school kid, but I resist.

He gives me a long, hard look. He glances around again. No other takers.

Come the fuck on, I think. *You'll get rid of me for a couple days. What more could you want?*

Finally, he gives a short sigh.

"Casden," he says, and writes my name down.

Within thirty minutes I'm standing next to a truck behind the visitor center, next to the other four guys. It's not even eight in the morning yet, but we've been given maps, been briefed, and now we're just waiting for the forest rangers to come out and meet us.

It feels strangely like I'm in middle school, waiting to be chosen for dodgeball. On the way over, it occurred to me that she might not even be one of the rangers hiking up to a lookout point. I might be making *sure* I don't see her again before my unit leaves town, which I didn't even think about in my eagerness.

All I can do is cross my fingers and pray.

At last, I see five figures walking toward us, and my heart squeezes as I scan over them.

She's not — wait, yes she is. She's slightly behind someone else, her frame pack is changing the way she walks, and she's wearing a huge hat, but it's her.

I feel like I might melt with relief.

Clementine's not more than halfway to where we're standing when she sees me, her mouth flattening just a little. She doesn't look surprised, though.

Mike, the guy in charge of this whole Forest division, claps his hands together and rubs them.

"Thanks to everyone for being available on such short notice," he says. "I'm sorry for the haste and lack of preparation, but we're stretched pretty thin right now, and as you know, lightning strikes represent a serious danger to several mountain communities, particularly with the dryness of the season."

He talks like a brochure or something, I think.

"You've all been briefed, so, any questions?" he asks.

We all look around, then shrug. It seems pretty simple: hike a long-ass way, sleep in a glass cabin on top of a mountain, see if there's a fire, come back.

Mike shrugs.

"Well, then, everyone pick your hiking buddy and let's get this show on the road."

Everyone else starts mingling. Some introductions are made, and Silas and Daniel both glance at me, then at Clementine, but they heard pretty much everything last night and have obviously decided to steer clear.

I look at her.

She looks at me. Then she looks away. Then she looks back. Finally, she steps forward.

"Hiking buddies?" she asks quietly.

———

WE TOSS our packs into the back of a Forest Service pickup and drive to the access point of a fire road, forty-five minutes away. It's blazingly sunny today, and everything has that shiny, painful brightness that happens after a hard rain sometimes, like the world's been scrubbed a little too vigorously.

Neither of us says much. She drives, country western on the radio, and I follow along on the detailed topo maps we have, though it's more so I know where we are than to give her directions. Clementine seems to know where she's going, and she doesn't ask for my input.

I don't mind the quiet. I don't think she's mad at me, or at least, she doesn't seem like it. Clementine is just quiet sometimes, usually when she's trying to work something out with herself.

When we were together, I couldn't *stand* that about her. She'd go quiet like this, and I'd needle her, trying to get her to talk to me, and then we'd fight.

But now, in the car, I don't say anything. I just enjoy the

scenery. We've got at least a day and a half together. She can have some time to figure out what she wants to say.

Clementine parks at the rutted dirt entrance point to a fire road, just outside a gate, and turns off the truck. For a moment she looks out the windshield at the woods, then over at me, her eyes somber.

"Ready for a hike?" she says.

"Wait, we have to *hike* up there?" I tease.

She looks *pissed*.

"Kidding," I say, feeling lame that my joke didn't land. "I volunteered for a hike."

"Oh," she says, relief in her voice. "Okay, good."

We get our stuff from the back, spend a few minutes adjusting hats and putting on sunscreen, and then we set out. Even though it's technically called a fire road, the path is both too narrow and way, way too rocky for any vehicles to get up here. Maybe once upon a time, but not now.

Thirty minutes pass. Then forty-five. I start wondering whether I'm right about her silence, or whether I really *should* say something.

We stop to drink some water, and I turn around to look at the road below us. I'm always amazed at how quickly I climb when I'm hiking, because it feels slow, but when I look, it's been so far.

Down below, there's almost nothing but forest. In the far distance I can barely make out a town — not Lodgepole, we're not facing that direction — and beyond that, a long grassy stretch, but even that's hard to see.

Nope. From here, it's just trees, birds chirping, the sound of the breeze. Clementine screws the lid back on her water bottle and hooks it back to her frame pack. Then she looks back at the vista.

There's a long moment where neither of us says anything,

and we just look out at the scenery. Then, at last, Clementine speaks.

"Did you hear Judson Hollins from high school is running for state senate?" she asks.

I glance at her, but she's looking out at the view, not at me. I'm relieved all the same.

"That's old news," I say. "You didn't hear the rest of the story?"

Clementine looks up at me. For a moment, her eyes are serious, but then she raises one eyebrow.

"I guess not," she says.

"He got a stripper pregnant," I tell her. "He's not running any more."

Clementine's eyes go wide.

"*Judson* did?" she says, and then presses her lips together like she's trying to suppress a smile. "That pompous, preachy, holier-than-thou asshole got a stripper pregnant?"

"Clem, you *have* to get on the internet more," I say.

"That poor girl," she says. "Did Charity stay with him?"

"She did," I say. "So far, anyway. We'll see what happens if he gets caught again."

"Shit," she whispers.

We start hiking again, and for a few moments, Clementine is quiet again, thinking over this new information.

Clementine couldn't *stand* Charity in high school, because not only was Charity the picture of the prim, proper nice girl, she looked down on anyone who wasn't as prissy as her.

"What's that word for kind of enjoying someone else's misfortune?" I ask. "I think that's what you're doing right now."

"*Schadenfreude*," Clementine says. "And yes. Yes, I am currently having some *schadenfreude*, Hunter."

I duck under a branch, then hold it out of the way for her.

"Though I prefer karma, because she was *such a bitch*,"

Clementine goes on. "Remember when she caught us making out in the equipment room after school one day and then, every time I saw her for the next month, she told me she'd pray for my impure, sinning soul?"

I don't remember that time exactly, but only because we made out in there a *lot*. I was twenty-three before the smell of used sporting equipment stopped giving me a hard-on.

"I didn't know she did *that*," I say. "That's…"

I trail off, not sure I have the right word for it, exactly.

"Fucked up? Not very Christian? Yeah," Clementine says. "And now her husband knocked up a stripper."

She takes a deep breath.

"Sorry," she says. "That wasn't very nice of me. But she was just the *worst*."

"My lips are sealed," I say.

Clementine looks over at me, and finally, there's a smile on her face.

"Thanks," she says. "I'm sure she could still fuck up my reputation if she wanted."

I grin back. This feels good, talking like old friends while we hike.

"Maybe she'll spread rumors that you tried pot once while you were in college," I tease.

"Once?" Clementine says.

It's not perfect. It's not what I wanted. What I *wanted* — hell, what I still want — is Clementine's nails raking down my back while she moans my name. Right now, even though she's wearing ugly hiking pants, a shapeless shirt, and an enormous hat, just the way she *looks* at me makes me think about what she looks like naked.

She looks *good* naked, by the way.

"Careful who you tell that to," I say. "Next thing you know, you'll be fresh out of rehab, according to Charity."

"If I hear that rumor, I'll know it was you," she says. "And you're not gonna turn me in to the moral police, right?"

"Not when I was your downfall in the first place," I say, grinning at her.

Clementine makes a noise, somewhere between a snort and a laugh and a guffaw.

"*You* were *my* downfall?" she says, laughing. "I'm pretty sure I remember *dragging* you down into my parents' basement and pretty much throwing myself on you."

I'm pretty sure I remember that too, and so does my dick, half-rising to the occasion.

"That was the first time I met your parents," I say. "I was raised to be a nice country boy, you know, not fool around with someone's daughter on a couch in the basement."

"I'm pretty sure I also talked you into sneaking behind the barn in your truck that first time," Clementine says.

She's talking about the first time we ever had sex. For just a moment, the memory takes my breath away, because even though it was a little awkward and in the back of a pickup truck, I'm never going to forget the way the stars reflected off the rear window or the way she bit her lip the first time I entered her.

"Just because you suggested it first doesn't mean you talked me into it," I say. "I was pretty goddamn willing."

Clementine looks over at me, her eyes laughing. It's hard to tell under the shadow of her hat, but I *think* she might be blushing.

"I'm just saying, you don't get to take credit for my current fallen state," she says. "I was a *very* active participant."

We come around a bend, and in front of us, there's a creek going across the trail, rocks poking out of it at intervals. At the edge of the water we both stop and look at it for a moment, planning a way across. I go first, treading from rock to rock.

It's trickier with my heavy pack on, and at the end I have to make a big jump, but I get across fine.

I turn and watch Clementine. She takes a different route across the rocks, longer but without that jump at the end.

She's nearly across when she puts her weight on a rock and it wobbles. She gasps, throwing her arms out.

Without thinking I step into the creek and hold my hand out toward her, and she grabs it.

Right away she relaxes, getting her balance back. In two steps she's on dry land and I step out of the creek, her hand still on mine.

"Thanks," she says. "That didn't feel unstable when I first stepped on it."

She hasn't let my hand go.

"That's what hiking buddies are for," I say.

"You got your feet wet."

"It's hot out, they'll dry," I say, shrugging. "It's kind of nice, actually."

"I probably should have just walked through the water," she says.

We look at each other for a moment. Then she lets my hand go, drops her eyes, and looks at the trail ahead. Her throat moves as she swallows.

"We're halfway there," she says, and starts hiking. "We should make it before sundown."

"Lead the way," I say, and we set off down the trail together.

THIRTEEN

CLEMENTINE

I t's another four hours to the lookout tower, nine miles in total, but it feels faster than that. Earlier today, I came *this* close to going with one of the other firefighters, because after our fight yesterday, I wasn't sure I could deal with talking to Hunter again.

And, honestly, it would be a hundred times easier to ignore him for another day or two until his crew is out of Lodgepole, and then pretend that nothing ever happened. It's not that I can't face my problems. Generally, in life, I face my problems just fine.

Just not *this* problem, because this one feels like a giant spider web that's also been doused in honey and then also in superglue, and then there's *another* spider web behind it waiting to catch me if I somehow get through the first one. It's sticky and tangled, is what I'm saying, and it's worse because every-thing hinges on old, half-buried, faded and questionable emotions that I can barely identify, let alone understand.

But here we are. Talking, like friends, like people who can work through problems. I know we're probably going to have it out again before this little adventure is over. I'm dreading it. I feel like an adult, though, like maybe I've finally made a mature decision about Hunter.

That's not happening yet, though. Now we're hiking through the sun-dappled woods. We gossip about people from high school. He tells me about being in the Marines, about living with constant dust and roadside bombs.

About how he slowly realized that it wasn't for him, even as he watched his comrades rise in the ranks, leaving him behind. He tells me about his first Fourth of July back in the United States, when he had to hide in his parents' basement from the sound of fireworks.

I walk next to him and think, *this is someone I don't know.* It feels strange, but good.

I tell him about being in college, about how unsettling it can be to go from a town of five thousand people to a dorm with almost that many. I tell him that when I first got there I felt like a back country hick in the big city for the first time, that I once got drunk and threw up on an ornamental statue, and that I finally figured the whole thing out and graduated magna cum laude in biology.

Before I know it, we're at a fork in the trail. I point left, and half a mile later, I can see the Spruce Mountain Fire Lookout poking above the trees.

"You know, I've never been to one of these," Hunter says, trudging up the trail next to me.

"That's because you don't get involved until the fire's already found," I say. "I've only been to this one once, when I was the lucky lady who got chosen to give it its annual cleaning."

Hunter laughs.

"That often?"

"On the good years," I say. "Though I only went because someone found out a family of squirrels had burrowed into one of the bunk bed mattresses."

"Maybe I'll sleep outside," Hunter says.

I look at the tower as I walk up to it. It's not big, maybe twelve feet square, but it's got broad windows on every side, and the whole thing is on twenty-foot stilts. If there was a way to it besides hiking nine miles, it'd be a great vacation spot.

"It's not so bad," I say, neck craned up. "Kinda—"

Suddenly my ankle buckles under me and I fly sideways, slamming into the ground. It happens so fast I don't even make a noise, just an *oof* when I land.

"Clem?" says Hunter, half alarmed and half confused.

My knee and elbow hit hardest, and I gasp as pain spikes through them. I don't dare move for long seconds, afraid I'll just hurt myself worse.

Hunter's on his knees next to me, his pack off, and he's saying something but I'm not paying attention. I just focus on breathing, flexing my fingers, and slowly the pain fades.

"Shit," I say.

Hunter reaches over and unbuckles my pack, letting it fall off my back.

"Did you hit your head?" he asks, and I realize it's the second or third time he's asked that.

"I don't think so," I say, blinking.

He takes my jaw in his hand and leans in, bringing his face inches from mine.

I hold my breath. My knee throbs. I wonder if I *did* hit my head and I'm about to hallucinate some weird romantic scenario.

"Your pupils look okay," he finally says, and I exhale. He lets my face go.

Right.

"What the hell happened?" he says.

I sit up slowly, bending my elbow, flexing my knee back and forth. It still hurts pretty bad, but I don't think it's broken, just badly bruised.

"I think I tripped," I say. "Or I stepped wrong, or something."

I straighten my leg, bend it, straighten. Hunter is hovering, kneeling next to me, frowning.

"I'm fine," I tell him.

He gets to his feet and offers me one hand. I take it, and he pulls me off the ground like he's lifting a stuffed animal, the muscles in his forearm bunching.

I'm suddenly reminded that we're going to be spending at least one night together in a twelve-by-twelve cabin, alone, and complicated feelings or not he's still *super* hot.

Maybe I should have picked a different hiking buddy after all.

"At least you chose the right place to take a dive," he says, nodding his head at the cabin behind him.

I laugh, and take a step toward my pack to pick it up again.

"Yeah, I — *shit*," I yelp, pain shooting through my right ankle.

I nearly go over again. The only reason I don't is because Hunter grabs me as I stand on my left leg, hopping a little, flailing my arms around.

"Your knee?" he asks.

I shake my head and take a deep breath.

"Ankle," I say. "Fuck. *Fuck.*"

This is bad. Immediately, I start running through disaster scenarios: it's broken. I won't be able to walk, and I'll have to get helicoptered down, all because I didn't look where I was walking. Or, there won't be any helicopters available, and I'll have to wait a week.

I feel like the world's biggest asshole.

"Okay," says Hunter, his hand on my back. "First thing, I'm gonna get you and our stuff into the cabin, and then we'll see what's going on with your ankle. You probably just turned it and all you need is ice."

I look over at him, a little surprised at how perfectly calm he is, and how fast he took charge of the situation.

"What?" he asks, giving me a funny look.

"Listen to you, mister calm-instruction-giver," I say. It's not clever, but my ankle fucking hurts.

Hunter laughs.

"You know it's my *job* to remain calm in emergencies, right?" he asks. "This is kid stuff. Where's the key to the cabin?"

He has a point.

"That funny little outside pocket on the waistband," I say. He bends over. Despite my injuries, I check out his ass, just a little. "The other one, and it's the thing with the Yellowstone keychain... yeah."

He holds up the key to the lookout cabin. Then he gives me a long, appraising look as I wobble a little on my left foot.

"If I can kinda lean on you, I'm fine to—"

I'm still talking as Hunter crouches down, puts one shoulder at my hip, and slings me over his back before standing. I yelp yet again.

"I'm fine," I protest. He grabs my arm to keep my steady.

"Is that what you call not being able to put weight on that ankle?" he says coolly, walking toward the stairs to the lookout cabin.

"I could have gotten myself up there," I grumble.

I don't really mind. I feel kind of silly, because I'm upside down and my ass is in the air, but if I'm being really, really honest? It's kind of hot to just be picked up like it's nothing.

Awkward position aside, I can feel the muscles in Hunter's shoulders move and flex under my stomach, even though I'm trying to ignore it. I don't hate it.

"No, you were gonna insist that you could get up a flight of stairs on one leg, and then get pissed when I carried you anyway," he says.

He reaches the bottom of the stairs and adjusts me a little before heading up.

"I feel like one of those sickly noblewomen who got carried around by servants or something," I say as we climb.

Hunter looks over at me, from the corner of his eye, as he unlocks the door.

"You hiked nine miles with a forty-pound pack on, now you're being lugged around like a sack of potatoes, and you feel like a noblewoman?" he teases.

He opens the door and turns sideways so I don't hit my head.

"I feel helpless like that, I mean," I say.

Hunter puts me down on one of the bare cots.

"I think you meant *thanks for the ride, I like your muscles,*" he says, darting a look at me.

I laugh and feel myself blush.

"Thanks for the ride," I say.

"And?"

"And... you're very good at carrying things?" I say, still laughing.

"C'mon, Clem," he says, his blue eyes dancing as he stands in front of me. "I *carried* you up all those stairs. On my *back*. It's one simple phrase."

I sigh dramatically, for show.

"If I say it will you stop harassing me like this?" I tease.

"One way to find out," he says. "Say it."

Hunter pulls his t-shirt sleeve up, revealing his right bicep. Then he flexes, and the muscle practically jumps up.

I feel my face go *bright* red, because holy shit, yes, I *do* like his muscles. It feels silly, but just watching that makes my body react without my brain's permission.

I clear my throat.

"Fine," I say, trying to sound casual. "Hunter, I like your muscles."

"Was that so hard?" he says, grinning as he grabs a chair and brings it over. I lift my foot onto it.

"There are worse payments for getting carried around," I say.

I lean forward, untie my hiking boot, and pull it off slowly, followed by my sock.

My ankle is swollen, but not purple or anything. I can wiggle my toes just fine. Right now, when I'm not putting weight on it, it barely hurts at all.

Hunter touches my ankle, his fingertips skipping along the pebbled indentations from my hiking socks. It sends a quick shiver up my spine.

"I'm pretty sure it's not broken," I offer.

"Where's the first aid kit in here?" he asks, looking around.

I pause, boot in hand, and look around as well. The cabin has a narrow balcony that wraps all the way around, and all the walls are plate glass windows. For a second I forget the question as I take in the spectacular three-sixty view.

Inside, there are two narrow cots, perpendicular to each other in one corner, a propane-powered stove in the other corner, a kitchen table in the middle, and the chest-height fire-finder table. Besides a couple of storage trunks and some cabinets, that's it.

"I don't think I need first aid," I finally say.

"It'll have those instant ice packs in it," Hunter says. "Since it's not like there's a freezer up here."

He finds the first aid supplies, breaks the capsule inside the packs, and stacks a couple around my ankle.

"Try not to hurt yourself again for a couple minutes," he teases. "I'm gonna go grab our bags."

He disappears down the stairs, and I lean my head back against the plate glass window, feeling like an idiot. I've only led about a thousand group hikes for kids, and even though they're on easy terrain, I *always* drive home that you should look where you're walking, or you could seriously hurt yourself.

Nine miles from help. In a fire lookout tower. With your ex-boyfriend. Whose muscles you like.

A minute later Hunter is back, carrying eighty pounds' worth of backpacks up the stairs like it's nothing. I try and fail not to notice his muscles as he sets them by the door, then looks around.

"Wow," he says.

I just laugh.

"Welcome to the Spruce Mountain Lookout Cabin," I say. "Spectacular views in every direction and only one invalid."

Hunter doesn't respond right away, just crosses his arms and looks out the windows. We both do, just sharing the silence comfortably.

I wiggle the toes on my foot, the skin on my ankle numb from the ice packs. Hunter walks to another window, and I watch him out of the corner of my eye, even as I pretend to rearrange the ice.

I'm slowly realizing something, and it feels strange and uncertain and *new*, but it's true.

I think I'd like him anyway.

Even if he wasn't the ex who broke my heart. Even if we'd never met before last week.

I keep watching him as he shrugs his shoulders a couple of times, then swings his arms around, loosening up from hiking nine miles with a heavy pack. The back of his t-shirt is damp with sweat, but I don't mind the way it sticks to him. I don't mind at all.

And that's the problem: if Hunter had just been a stranger in the fire crew who walked me home and called me about my dog and came to my stargazing talk, *I think I'd like him.*

I have no idea what the fuck to do with *that.*

FOURTEEN

HUNTER

Dinner is twenty-cent ramen followed by freeze-dried backpacking food. All it involves is boiling water, and I do that while Clementine sits on a cot, ankle wrapped in instant ice packs, scanning the horizon with a pair of binoculars.

"Anything?" I ask.

We both changed out of our sweaty hiking clothes. I'm wearing super-lightweight "lounge" pants — okay, they're basically *really thin* sweatpants — and tomorrow's shirt. Clem has on leggings and a long-sleeve t-shirt with no bra on underneath.

The no-bra thing is making it kind of hard to focus.

"Not yet," she says. "There's a couple of clouds that kind of look like smoke, but I'm pretty sure they're just clouds."

"Want the expert to take a look?" I ask.

"You're not the expert on fire *spotting*," she says. "You just put them out."

"Really, I'm the expert at making boundaries that fires can't cross, if you want to get technical about it," I say.

Clementine doesn't answer, and the cabin goes quiet. I

don't mind. The silence now is different from the loaded silence this morning in the car. That one felt like an anvil was swinging over my head, ready to fall, but this one is oddly comfortable. Companionable.

Sometimes you run out of things to say to another person, especially if you've been together for twelve hours already, and it's fine. It feels like putting on a pair of worn-in shoes.

Not that Clementine is a pair of old shoes.

The water on the stove boils, and I pour it into the laminated bags of freeze-dried spaghetti, close them, and wait. I'm not exactly a gourmet chef, but we won't starve.

"Hey, c'mere," Clementine says.

I walk to the cot where she's sitting and stand behind her. She looks back and hands me the binoculars, then points.

"That's a cloud, right?" she asks.

"I thought I wasn't an expert," I say, lifting them to my eyes.

"I didn't say you were," she teases. "I just need a second opinion."

I adjust the lenses and the faint white column she's pointing at comes into view. I stare at it for a long time.

"Huh," I finally say. I examine it harder, because while it *does* look like a pillar, it doesn't seem to be growing. It doesn't seem to be emanating from one spot, like smoke would be.

I *think* it's just a weird spot of half-fog half-cloud, though it's hard to tell. Plus, the sun is setting, and that makes it even harder to tell.

"We'll see if it's there in the morning," I say. "If it is, we should call it in, but if it's anything at all it's just a lightning strike. Most of those go out pretty fast."

As many wildfires as there are in the west, there are way, *way* more trees struck by lightning. Most of them smolder for a little while, then go out, and nothing around them even catches fire. Sometimes, some of the brush around them will catch, a few of the drier trees, but those usually put themselves out too. Even in a drought, live trees don't catch fire very easily.

It really takes a bad combination for a lightning strike to turn into a wildfire: dry, dead trees, lots of underbrush, dense foliage that hasn't gotten rain in too long. We're here because conditions in Big Sky National Forest *could* be right. They're probably not, but they *could* be.

Clementine just nods.

"Dinner?" I ask.

I pour the spaghetti onto tin plates, and we eat with sporks, sitting on one of the cots, watching the sunset. I don't say anything, and it's partly because I'm eating, but partly because I can't think of anything to say as the clouds above turn from pink to orange to purple, striping the sky with colors I wouldn't believe if I weren't sitting here, looking at them.

Then, when the last rays of the run disappear below the horizon, it's suddenly dark. The whole cabin is swathed in shades of purple and everything seems to go perfectly still, even the air. I hold my breath, afraid to ruin it.

I want to reach out, put my arms around Clementine, rest my chin on her head as she relaxes against me. It feels unnatural to be sitting here, her so close, and *not* do that. But she's been pretty clear: this, sitting and watching the sunset together, is gonna have to be good enough.

It isn't, but I've been disappointed before. I'll survive.

"This might sound weird," Clementine says, her voice slow in the stillness, "but this kind of feels like college."

I look around.

"Being in a lookout cabin on top of a mountain with a busted ankle feels like college?" I ask.

She brushes her bangs off her forehead, still looking out the window at the spot on the horizon where the sun went down, smiling.

"Not that part," she says. "But sitting on a tiny bed and eating in the dark does."

I grab our plates and stand, walking them to the basin. There's no real sink, but there's a big bucket and a tank of water for dishes.

"I thought you went to class and shit," I say.

She laughs.

"That too," she says. "But while I was living in the dorms, the only place to sit in anyone's room was the bed. So I ate a lot of cereal there, or if people wanted to watch a movie or something, we'd all have to sit on the bed. And now, anytime I'm on a twin bed doing something besides sleeping, it feels like college."

I sit down next to her again, leaning against a window so now we're facing each other. A small, mean part of me wants to ask what *else* she did on her bed in college, and who she did it with, but I don't.

"Sounds like I missed out," I say.

Clementine shrugs.

"Not really," she says. "Unless you really *like* sleeping on spilled coffee because you were too lazy to change the sheets."

I've done that anyway, but I don't tell her that.

"What else did I miss by not going to college?" I ask.

"What do you mean?"

She's sitting cross-legged next to me, and she scoots a little, turning so she's facing me instead of the window.

"I didn't know about the bed thing," I say. "I mean, I knew about classes and frat parties and tests and papers and all that, but what don't I know I missed?"

That isn't my real question, but I don't know how to ask my real question. I want to know what *she* was doing while I was sleeping on a cot in a dusty tent, or in a tank for twelve hours, or busting down doors only to find frightened women and children.

"You're thinking about this the wrong way, you know," she says, tipping her head against the window to her right and looking at me, her hazel eyes deep in the dark.

"What's the right way?"

"You were in the Marines," she says. "Just because you weren't in college doesn't mean you weren't doing something, you know, noble and important."

I raise my eyebrows.

"Can I get that in writing?" I ask.

Clementine kind of laughs, then looks out the window again, at the thin strip of light at the horizon.

"You're not the only one who managed to grow up *some* in eight years," she says. "I was kind of a dick about you going into the military."

I don't say anything. I'm too surprised for a moment, and I don't quite know how to respond.

She's completely right. She was a *total* dick about it, from the moment I casually mentioned I was meeting with a recruiter to the moment I shipped off to basic training.

It baffled me. Other guys who were joining up, and there were plenty at our high school, had girlfriends who were proud of them, who got t-shirts that said shit like "proud Army girl-friend" and bragged about it. But any time I so much as mentioned the Marines around Clementine, she'd go totally silent.

In retrospect, it was a huge, flashing neon warning sign. But at the time I was so head-over-heels that I ignored it.

"Yeah, kind of," I say, trying to keep my voice neutral.

She looks at me and starts laughing, the corners of her eyes crinkling. I can't help but smile.

"No, I was awful," she says. "I..."

She trails off, pushing her hair behind her ear, and looks out the window again.

"I was really jealous because I felt like you loved the Marines more than me, and I know that sounds dumb, but back then I felt like you *wanted* to be halfway across the world instead of where I was and I couldn't understand how you could say you loved me but want *that*," she says, the words tumbling out of her in a rush.

"That wasn't it at all," I say.

"I know that *now*," she says. "*Now* I understand that you can love a person and still want to do something else important, and it doesn't diminish anything. But I didn't then, and I couldn't stand the idea of you liking anything better than you liked me."

She laughs a little, shaking her head.

"God, that sounds dumb when I say it out loud," she says.

"Is it my turn to confess?" I ask.

"Go for it," Clementine says.

I pull one knee closer to my chest and drape my wrist onto it, staring at the dark windows across the cabin.

"I picked all those fights with you because I was jealous," I say.

My heart tightens in my chest, just admitting this to her. It took me ages to admit it to myself, even, and here I am, saying it out loud.

"You were jealous?" she asks, frowning.

I just look at her.

"I was *insanely* jealous," I say. "You were off at college, meeting all these new people and learning new things and moving on with your life, and meanwhile someone was still shouting at me to get up in the morning, telling me when I could eat, when I could shit, where to go, what to do."

I swallow. Clementine just blinks, like this has never occurred to her before.

"And I felt *dumb*," I say. "I was totally sure that you were meeting all these smart, interesting people and any minute you'd realize you were still dating some small-town moron from high school and you'd dump me. So I picked fights with you."

"Because that's a great way to keep a girlfriend around," she murmurs, teasing me.

"I didn't say it was smart," I say. "I said it was what I did."

"Well, thank God *now* we're mature, grown adults who can discuss their feelings calmly and rationally," she says.

I can tell there's more, so I stay quiet.

"I'm sorry about yesterday," Clementine finally says. "I should have... I don't know. Not freaked out."

"I shouldn't have put Mandy on my shoulders to reach that shelf," I say. "I wasn't trying to hit on her, but she sort of suggested it, and then was teasing me that I couldn't, and..."

Clementine just looks at me.

"And you had to prove yourself to a cute girl, even if you weren't interested?" she says.

"You called her that, not me," I say.

Clementine laughs.

"Mandy is totally cute," she says. "And I fucked up, too, because I don't think she'd have gone after you if I'd told her about us."

She shifts again, stretching her leg out onto the cot. I watch as she flexes her toes backward, then rotates her ankle and makes a face.

"Still hurt?" I ask.

"Not too much," she says. "A lot less than before."

I grab her calf and put her foot on my lap, then feel gently along the bones and tendons in her ankle.

"It's still a little swollen, but the ice definitely helped," I say.

"I'm sorry I didn't text you while I was gone," she says. "I almost did a couple times, but I didn't want to seem clingy or something."

"I promise that you're the opposite of clingy," I say.

I press my fingers into a soft part of her ankle and she makes a face.

"That hurt?" I ask.

"A little."

"I was afraid you'd disappear again," I say. "Like you did when you dumped me."

"That's the second time you've said I dumped you," Clementine said.

Now I'm just rubbing her ankle in small circles with the pad of my thumb.

"You stopped answering my calls," I say.

"You told me you'd never loved me in the first place," Clementine says.

My breath catches in my throat, and for a moment, I feel nauseous. I wish I'd never said it, and I wish she didn't remember it.

"I figured we were over once you said that," she says. "I didn't really want to get my heart stomped on more, so I didn't answer."

I take a deep breath.

"I didn't mean it."

"I know."

It seems so simple, *now*, so long after the fact. I don't know what to say, and I don't know that there's anything I *can* say, so I move my hands up to her knee and run my thumb over her kneecap.

"This still hurt?" I ask.

She leans over and pulls her leggings up, revealing a deep purple bruise that covers half the side of her knee.

"Yikes," she says. "That got nasty."

"Can you move it okay?" I ask.

She straightens her leg, then bends it, depositing her foot back in my lap.

"It's a little tweaky but fine," she says. "I just banged it pretty hard."

I run my thumb over the bruise again, and for a moment, we're quiet again as the darkness deepens in the cabin.

"You broke my heart back then," she finally says. "And yesterday, I'd just spent two days watching my parents call each other names, so when I saw you and Mandy, all I could think was that you were going to do it again."

She sighs, leans her head back against the glass, and closes her eyes.

"I mean, what kind of dumbass goes back for a *second* helping of that?" she says.

"And this whole time, I thought you broke mine," I say, running my thumb gently over the ridge of her kneecap.

"God, we fucked up," she says. "It's almost impressive how *much* we fucked that up."

"We were teenagers," I say. "If dealing with new Marine recruits taught me one thing, it was that eighteen-year-olds are kind of dumb."

"Yeah, but I was twenty-six yesterday," she says. "Apparently I haven't changed all that much."

She opens her eyes and looks at me sideways, the corners just barely crinkling.

"Didn't you *just* shout that at me in the bathroom?" I ask, half-teasing, even though it feels dangerous.

"Look, I already *said* I was sorry about that," she says, but she's laughing. "Don't make me say it again, once was bad enough."

"So you're also still bad at apologizing."

"And you still needle me until I'm about ready to kill you," she teases.

We look at each other in the dark, her eyes deep pools, her face dark blue and white. The sliver of the moon is somewhere overhead, and it's casting white light on the forests around us.

You're still so beautiful it aches, I think. *I still want to kiss you more than I've ever wanted anything.*

FIFTEEN

CLEMENTINE

We both go quiet again for a moment. Hunter's thumb runs along my knee, barely a whisper against my skin. I don't think he even knows he's doing it, because it has that familiar, habitual, time-worn rhythm to it.

It still feels the same, I'm thinking. *Like it did when we were good, before all this shit went down.*

I want to kiss him again. Well, I want more than that, *way* more, but I feel like an asshole. First, I tell him I need a couple days of time, then I decide to go for it, *then* I change my mind, cry in a bathroom, and yell at him.

I realize that heading to Hunter's as soon as I got back from two days of dealing with my parents' divorce probably wasn't a great call. Learning that someone you've known your whole life, who you've *trusted* your whole life, cheated on your other parent and has been doing her best to act like everything is his fault? It doesn't really put one in a very good place for dealing rationally with relationships.

It's still an excuse, though. A pretty good one, but an excuse.

And, for fuck's sake, he followed me up a mountain. I can do better.

I take a deep breath, because I'm about to act like a grown-ass woman.

"I actually came over yesterday, you know, before I freaked out, to say I think we should…"

I swallow.

Have sex, and see what happens then, but definitely have sex, I think.

"…give this a shot," I finish lamely, my face bright red.

I'm so nervous it feels like there's ropes tied around my stomach, because I *hate* saying stuff like this out loud. Admitting I have feelings? And especially that I have squishy, mushy ones? Ew.

Hunter's running one finger under my leggings where I pushed them over my knee, and that alone is making my body do *things*.

"What about now?" he asks. His voice has gone a little low and raspy, and I glance down at his lap.

Even though it's dark, his pants aren't hiding a goddamn thing. Hunter's pitching a *massive* tent, and a sudden thrill runs through me. For the first time in a long time, I let myself remember just *how* great some aspects of our relationship were.

We were both virgins at first, but let's just say that Hunter was a *very* quick study.

"I think I was right the first time," I say, my stomach in knots. "If you can kind of ignore the part where I yelled at you in—"

I don't get to finish the sentence because Hunter leans over and kisses me, his lips hard against mine, my head pinned against the window. I make a surprised *mmph* noise into his mouth.

He makes an *mmm* noise back, almost like he's teasing me,

but he opens his lips against mine and his tongue winds into my mouth. I curl mine against it as I put one hand on his shoulder, gripping the hard muscles there.

My heart is pounding through my entire body, so hard I swear I can feel it in my toes, and every beat is saying *fuck yes, fuck yes, fuck yes.* I grab the front of his t-shirt in a fist and pull, not that I could budge Hunter if he didn't want to be budged.

He does. Hunter pulls back a little. I bite his bottom lip and he chuckles, sliding his hand up the inside of my thigh. His hand just barely brushes over my lips and clit, touching me through my leggings, but my toes curl with anticipation and I gasp.

He grins.

"You used to do this *all* the time," he says.

I swallow.

"Make out with you? Yeah, I know," I say.

He shifts on the cot, pulling my right leg around him so he's on his knees between my legs. I'm still leaning back against the window, and he flicks both thumbnails over my nipples, through my t-shirt.

I make a *noise* and tighten my legs around him, my feet just under his ass.

"No, you used to go braless when you knew it would drive me *fucking crazy*," he says. "Remember the time we went to the county fair?"

He squeezes my nipples between his first and second fingers and flicks his thumbnail over them again. I gasp and squirm, digging my hands into his knees.

"I wore a bra and acted like a lady?" I ask.

He pinches a little harder, still through my shirt, then leans over and bites my ear.

"Not quite," he says. "I don't remember a goddamn thing about the fair besides the way your tits bounced and I stared at your nipples *all day*."

I half laugh and half moan.

"I might have a dim recollection of that," I say, breathless.

"I walked around with a hard on for hours and had to keep myself from punching anyone *else* who looked at you," he goes on. "Which was a whole lot of people, Clem."

I'm blushing at the memory, because I can't *believe* I wore a t-shirt with nothing underneath to a crowded county fair, just to titillate Hunter.

"I had the idea that I'd give you a blowjob in the Hall of Mirrors, but when we got there it was full of kids," I murmur. "It's almost like I was eighteen and a hopeless bundle of hormones who didn't think things through."

I run my hands down his torso, over his shirt, and swallow. I can feel the muscles rippling underneath, and it sends a bolt of heat rushing down through my body. Hunter lets my nipples go, only to grab my hips as he slides his knees further under me so now I'm sitting on him, his erection *right* between my legs, nothing more than two very thin layers of cloth between us.

I pull his shirt toward me again and we kiss, hard. I move my hips, rubbing myself along Hunter's length, and he *grunts*, his hands under my shirt. His rough fingertips find my nipples and tweak them, gently at first and then harder. I arch my back, my head against the glass.

Hunter pulls my shirt off over my head and bends down, his lips on my neck. It tickles, and I laugh but it turns into a moan as his lips keep moving down. He finds one nipple and swirls his tongue around it, sucking gently.

I gasp, and my hand tightens on his side, under his shirt. *That* move is new. He does it again, then does it to my other nipple and this time I moan, my fingers digging into the hard muscles around his waist, my hips rocking against him, his bulge still pressing against me deliciously.

Finally, he stops and I tug his shirt over his head. Hunter

throws it somewhere behind him as I grab the back of his neck, then pull him in toward me, kissing him desperately, my tongue searching out his.

I let my other hand drift down his torso, over the ripples of his hard muscles, until I've got my fingers on the head of his cock, sliding over the ridge of the crown.

Hunter growls and grabs my ass, his fingers digging in as he pulls me against him, so I wrap my hand around the shaft, through his pants, and squeeze.

He breaks the kiss, gasping.

"Don't make me come in my pants," he says, breathing into my ear.

I laugh and squeeze again, moving my hand down the length of his thick shaft. He groans.

"C'mon, Clem," he says, his mouth against my neck as he pushes his length into my fist. "Getting my only pair of comfy pants dirty is just *cruel*."

I kiss him again, slowly.

"That much of a hair trigger?" I ask.

"Not usually," he murmurs. "Just right now."

I squeeze his cock again, because I like the way he fills my hand, and I'm breathless with anticipation for what's about to happen.

Hunter groans again, then straightens his back and slides his hand into my leggings, the material giving way easily as his fingers find my clit instantly. I exhale hard and my eyes close. I turn my head to one side as he rubs me in slow circles, and I can feel his eyes searching my face.

"I find it?" he murmurs.

I just nod breathlessly. The first several times we did this, there was a lot more fumbling, but like I said: he's a quick study.

"It's like riding a bicycle," he says, his slick fingers still moving on me.

I swallow, then take a breath.

"I'm not a bicycle," I murmur.

I give his cock another squeeze, then grab the waistband of his pants and pull them down his thighs until his cock springs free.

I spend a moment just looking at it, because I'm going to be honest: it's fucking *magnificent*. I've been with other men in the past eight years, and some of them were pretty good lovers, but Hunter's *still* got the nicest cock I've ever encountered.

Honestly, it's kind of a bummer when the first dick you ever see ends up being the best. Well, it was a bummer until now. I wrap my hand around it, stroking him slowly from root to tip.

"I'm gonna give you a good, hard ride anyway," Hunter growls, and slides his fingers down and into my entrance, the heel of his hand still against my clit.

"*Shit*," I whisper as he crooks his fingers inside me, his hand still rubbing my clit. My hips buck on their own, and the glass behind me rattles in the pane. I don't even have time to be surprised that he said he'd ride me, just insanely turned on.

He keeps going, and I grip his cock harder in my fist. He's practically leaking precum, the head slick with it, and I rub my fingers over him as he growls softly.

I'm already getting close, my core tensing as his fingers keep moving insistently, my breath coming in gasps as his cock pulses in my fist, so rock-hard I think he also might be about to come.

"Jesus, Hunter," I whisper. He crooks his fingers again and I bite my lip so hard I think I nearly draw blood. I arch my back, my hips moving practically on their own, like I can make him do this harder or faster.

He's just watching me, a look of total concentration on his face. My eyelids flutter open and I look at him.

He grins, and I feel like everything is going a little blurry around the edges.

"I *did* miss watching you lose control like this," he murmurs.

I just whimper, because I think I'm about to come, and I feel totally helpless against it. His fingers move again, and I can feel myself on the brink, ready to fall over it.

"Oh *fu*—"

Hunter pulls his hand away, letting his fingers drag quickly over my clit. My body jolts but I don't come, and then I'm just sitting there, mouth open, staring at him. He's *grinning*.

"What the fuck?" I ask, trying to catch my breath. "Go back, I didn't finish."

"I also missed how bossy you are when you're horny," he says.

I take my hand off his cock, but Hunter just grabs me by the hips and rocks me against his naked erection. I move slow, my legs wrapped around him, our foreheads touching.

"You like torturing me?" I murmur.

"Yes," he says.

"Jerk," I whisper. "You promised me a ride, you know, and dry humping is getting old real fast."

"Where's the romance, Clem?" he teases. "A guy can't have a little foreplay?"

I reach down between my legs and stick a couple fingers inside myself. Then I pull them out and smear my hand down Hunter's cock, stroking him hard and fast as we kiss again.

Suddenly he puts his hand over mine and holds it still. He takes his lips off mine and nuzzles my neck slowly, his shaft throbbing in my hand. Then he scoots off the cot and leaves me sitting there, legs akimbo, trying to catch my breath.

"Get these off," he says, leaning over me and snapping the waistband of my leggings.

I lift my hips, watching Hunter watch me. It's hard to take

leggings off and look sexy. I don't think I make it work, but he strips too, never taking his eyes from me.

Then he turns and rummages through his pack for a moment. I touch myself, leaning against the window, waiting for him to turn around. When he does, I see the dim flash of a foil package in his hand, and then he's unrolling something onto his cock.

Right. A condom. Duh. I'm on the pill, but *Hey, when did you last get tested?* is kind of a boner-killer.

I just watch him unroll it onto himself, a big hand on a big cock, his torso tensing and flexing as he strokes himself a few times before looking up at me. I'm still touching myself, sliding my fingers up and down between my lips, across my clit.

"I like how dirty you got," he says.

I raise my eyebrows.

"This is dirty?" I ask, pushing two fingers inside myself.

"It's a start," he teases, and then he's on the bed, kneeling between my legs. He grabs my hand and sticks my fingers into his mouth, sucking them slowly.

He never did *that* before either, but it's fucking hot.

Hunter grabs me and then scoots me sideways, dragging me until my back is against the solid wood window frame instead of the pane. He pushes me up against it, his cock against my lower belly, his lips on my neck, biting my collarbone.

I cannot fucking wait any longer, and I arch my back and lift myself until the tip of his cock is at my entrance. I'm practically vibrating with anticipation, but I force myself to go slow, because it's been a while since I was with anyone this.... *endowed.*

About eight years, actually.

And *Jesus,* I'd almost forgotten what it feels like. My body practically goes limp as I lower myself onto Hunter's cock, my eyes sliding closed, my head back against the wall of the lookout tower. I hear someone moan and it takes me a second to realize it's *me*.

"Oh my fucking God, Clem, Jesus," Hunter whispers, his head on my shoulder, his fingers sinking hard into my hips. "I swear I almost just fucking came watching you sit on my cock like that."

I grab his shoulders in my hands and move my hips, just enough to slide him out a little before taking him again, and I exhale hard as pleasure sparks through my brain.

Hunter groans and thrusts just enough that our hips come flush with a light slap. I make a noise I barely recognize as human, and Hunter pulls back, gently.

"That was a good noise, right?" he asks, his voice low and dusky.

I just nod, swallowing hard.

"Do it again," I say.

He does, and this time when he drives himself deep I arch myself into him and he hits every pleasure center I have. White spots dance in front of my eyes, and I feel like all my bones might be melting.

"There it is," Hunter growls.

He does it again and again, slowly pushing me harder and harder into the window frame, fucking me as I arch into him.

"There's what?" I ask, my voice barely a whisper.

"The spot that makes you come like a freight train," he says.

Then he drives himself home again, but this time he grabs me and keeps me there, shifting my hips back and forth with his hands, filling me with his cock and just moving inside me.

"Oh, fuck, Hunter," I whimper. I've got one hand in his hair and one grabbing his shoulder as hard as I can. "That feels so fucking good, don't stop don't you dare fucking stop..."

I come like a freight train. For a moment the darkness explodes around me and then it's just the two of us, rocking back and forth in sheer bliss. I'm coming so hard I'm just gasping and whimpering, bolt after bolt of pure pleasure rocketing through me.

Hunter's saying something. I'm drifting back down to earth, feeling almost hazy, like I'm barely in my own body, but I've still got my legs wrapped around him and I realize we're fucking hard again, my back against the wall, leftover pleasure jolting through me with every stroke.

"—so fucking *good* when you come that hard," he's saying.

"You're the one who made me come like that," I murmur into his ear, rolling my hips against him. "I almost forgot how much I like it when you fuck me hard."

Hunter thrusts as hard as he can. He growls and bites my shoulder as his cock throbs inside me and we rock together like somehow he can get deeper.

I think he might come forever. I think he might break the skin on my shoulder, and it hurts a little but in a strange way I don't mind. I kind of like that I just made him come *this* hard.

Finally, he stops. He takes his mouth off me, then kisses the spot where he bit me and leans his head against my neck. Every couple of seconds he kisses the hollow of my throat, then nuzzles me again, and I wind my hands through his hair.

We breathe hard, like we're sharing one set of lungs. After a long time, Hunter takes a deep breath and finally speaks.

"I don't think I can move," he says.

"Have you tried?" I ask, stroking his hair.

"I just don't think it's gonna work," he says, his lips against my neck. "I came too hard."

I laugh, because it tickles.

"Well, I'm trapped until you move, and I've got shit to do, so you should probably give it a shot," I say.

"What shit do you have to do?"

"I have to look for forest fires, for starters."

"Not *now* you don't," he says. "It's dark."

"Just give it a shot," I say. "I believe in you."

He sighs. Then he grumbles.

Then, before I know what's happening, we're both falling over sideways onto the tiny Forest Service cot, and I yelp as we bounce.

"Thanks for believing in me," he says, laughing.

I wriggle further down on the bed until we're face-to-face, and I give him a long, slow kiss. He takes my hand in his and curls our fingers together.

We stay that way for a long time. At first I wonder if I should say something, but I have no idea what. Besides, I'm out of words, and all I want right now is to be here, with Hunter in my bed and no one else around for miles and miles.

W e lie there for a long, long time. My mind is almost perfectly blank, just a navy-blue haze of happiness and warmth that matches the darkness around us. Clementine's hand is in mine. Our legs are intertwined. I can feel her breathe.

I just have one small latex problem, and after a while, I can't ignore it any more. I sigh.

"So... there's no bathroom up here," I say.

"There's an outhouse on the ground," she says without opening her eyes.

I gather all my will, release her hand, and sit up on the cot. Then I stand.

I seem to be managing this okay.

"Be right back," I say, walking for the door, still completely naked. Who's gonna see me, raccoons?

"Don't throw the condom in there," she says, looking over at me.

I look down at my now-flaccid dick, the used condom drooping sadly off of it.

"Where do I put it?" I ask. My brain is still working half-speed, and I look around the lookout tower, vaguely wondering if it goes down the sink or something.

Clementine just starts laughing and rolls onto her back, still totally naked in the dark.

"I thought you spent six months a year camping in the wilderness," she says. "What do you do with *anything*?"

I look down again and sigh.

"Right," I say. "Leave no trace."

"There should be ziploc bags in one of the cabinets," she says, still laughing.

I find them, then take off the used condom, tie a knot in it, and deposit it in the baggie, sealing it. The moon has circled the sky and come around to the north-facing windows, and now it's cutting bright white shapes across the room.

"You look like you're in a movie where Humphrey Bogart plays a detective, except you're holding a baggie with an old condom," Clementine volunteers.

"And I need to pee."

"Even really good private investigators have to pee sometimes," she reassures me, her voice lazy but teasing. "They just don't show it in the movies."

I look over at her. The moonlight is just above her head, and she's flopped one hand up and into it, the rest of her still dark. I drop the baggie on the floor near my backpack, then lean over and kiss Clementine.

"Take a flashlight," she says.

I shove my feet into hiking boots and head down. The moon is bright enough that I don't need the flashlight, but I'm glad I brought it. When I finish my business, Clementine is there, waiting fifty feet away, looking up at the stars.

Fuck, she's beautiful. Especially like this, naked except boots and careless in the middle of nowhere, laughing and relaxed and not giving a shit.

"Did you hop down the stairs?" I ask, frowning.

"My ankle's not that bad anymore," she says. "It hurts a little, but honestly, I think it's fine."

"It's because I fixed it with my dick," I say, walking toward her.

"I don't think your dick even touched my ankle," she says.

"Close enough," I say. "You have any other ailments, come to me. I'll fix you *right* up."

Clementine laughs. I kiss her as I walk past, heading back to the lookout tower so she can use the outhouse.

As I walk away, she smacks my ass. Then she laughs.

Back in the tower, I go ahead and get our sleeping bags out of our packs and spread them on the two cots. Then I flop on the one where we just had sex and stare out the window.

I know this is the easy part. Being alone together for a night, with nothing and no one else to complicate things? It's a piece of fucking cake.

It's when we get back, to Clementine's divorcing parents and me fighting fires for weeks on end, to the real world where shit happens. That's the hard part.

Everything she said in that bathroom was true. I was flirting with Mandy, not because I particularly like her, but because it's habit. Two days after asking Clementine if she wanted to try again, I had another girl on my shoulders, giggling.

I'm also afraid I know how this ends. And I don't want to be stupid, but when I'm with Clementine — when we're hiking nine miles or, hell, when I'm talking to a group of old ladies and trying to get out of it — it feels *right*, like there's no other way I could imagine being. Like puzzle pieces that fit together.

I hear Clementine coming up the stairs in her heavy hiking boots, and then the door opens.

"Bleh," she says, and goes to the basin to wash her hands.

"Isn't this your job?" I ask.

"Peeing in outhouses?" she says.

"Peeing outdoors."

She shakes her hands, looks around, then finds her shirt and dries them there.

"My job is actually trail marking, trail maintenance, setting up wildlife cameras, surveying, and that sort of thing," she says, and walks over to me, flopping next to me on the cot. "The peeing outdoors is incidental. Scoot over."

"I can't," I say. "I'm already up against the glass."

Clementine solves the problem by getting half on top of me, her right arm flopped over my chest, her head on my shoulder.

"These things are too small," she says sleepily.

I stroke my fingers up and down her back. Her body against mine like this makes my dick twitch, but I hiked nine miles with seventy pounds on my back. I don't think I can move anything *else*. Round two is gonna have to wait.

"It's almost like they're not made for two people," I say.

"Smartass," she mutters.

"You wouldn't like me if I wasn't."

"You mean if you were a nice person who didn't tease me all the time?" she asks, tilting her face up.

I grin, looking down at her.

"If I were a nice guy who didn't challenge you sometimes you'd get bored and eat me *alive*," I say.

She taps her fingers on my chest, like she's thinking.

"I like nice guys," she says after a while, though she doesn't sound like she believes it.

"I'm nice," I say. "I was *real* nice earlier."

She laughs, then snuggles against me a little more. We both look out the window, at the horizon. I'm starting to doze off when she speaks.

"That's Saturn again," she says, pointing.

I follow her finger, remembering the directions from the other night: Mars, over to Antares, up to Saturn.

"Can you see the rings with binoculars?" I ask.

"You could barely see them with a big-ass telescope," she says.

Right.

"You know what planet I can see right now with the naked eye?" I ask.

Clementine looks at me again.

"If you say *Uranus* I swear I'm leaving and hiking nine miles back to civilization *right now*," she says, but there's laughter in her voice.

"I was gonna say Mars," I say, pretending to be offended. "I'm not thirteen."

I was absolutely going to say Uranus. It's always funny.

"Sure," she says, putting her head back.

There's another silence, and I look at the stars hovering near the horizon.

"This is different," she says.

"It is?" I ask.

It doesn't really feel different. It feels like we could be in the back of my pickup truck, or in her basement, or in my bedroom after my parents went to sleep and she sneaked over.

"No one's gonna catch us," she says. "And if they do, it doesn't matter."

I've started playing with her hair without noticing what I was doing, the slippery dark strands coiling through my fingers.

"Does that make it less exciting?" I ask. "Are you saying you miss the *thrill*?"

She laughs.

"The thrill of nearly getting busted by the cops that one time?" she says. "Or of Mrs. Hudgins finding us on what was *technically* her property and reaming us out?"

"Did she have a shotgun, or did I make that up?" I ask.

"I think it was a BB gun," Clementine says.

"I'd rather her shoot me than tell my parents," I say. "A couple years ago, I sort of let it slip that I wasn't exactly *saving* myself anymore, and I don't think my mom's forgiven me yet."

"But you live with them?"

"I stay in the guest house for half the year," I correct her. "And I don't... entertain guests there."

In high school, Clementine and I were in a slightly weird situation. I heard plenty of stories about dads in Ashlake, Montana answering the door holding a shotgun, threatening boyfriends who'd *dare* to touch their daughters.

But Clementine's parents were relatively cool. I mean, they weren't nearly as permissive as we'd have liked, but they never threatened me with a shotgun. It was *my* parents who were the strict ones, who were vigorously opposed to us ever being alone together, lest we be tempted by *sin*.

It didn't work. Not by a long shot. Sin won, hard. And fast. And deep. And as often as we could possibly manage.

"This is nice, though," she murmurs.

"Yeah, it is," I agree.

In a few more minutes, she's asleep on me. I'm tired as hell, but there's no way I can fall asleep sharing this two-foot-wide cot with her, so I stay awake for a little while. I listen to her breathing. I slide my fingers through her hair.

I think that maybe, *maybe*, this time will work out differently.

After a while I'm beyond sleepy and also beyond uncomfortable, so I gently get out from under Clementine, then climb gingerly over her until I'm off the cot.

She wakes up when I try to roll her onto her sleeping bag.

"You leaving?" she asks, barely awake.

"I'm leaving to there," I say, pointing at the other cot.

She closes her eyes again, snuggling into her sleeping bag.

"Fine," she says, and then she's asleep again.

I have a feeling she won't remember this conversation in the morning. I get into my own sleeping bag, in the cot perpendicular to hers.

I'm asleep in seconds.

———

I WAKE up to the sun slicing through the windows, the hard yellow rays hitting the ceiling of the lookout and illuminating everything inside. It takes me a minute to remember where I am, but I wake up in strange places a *lot*. Usually a strange tent, sometimes a strange motel, sometimes a strange bunkhouse.

I've never woken up in a strange fire lookout before, though given my job, it's weird that I haven't.

Then I think the same thing I always think.

Is something on fire?

No.

It used to be *am I in a red zone*, but two years of firefighting has at least changed *that* habit, even though I still wake up the same way: instantly, and all at once.

I stretch and look at the cot perpendicular to mine, but Clementine isn't in it.

"There you are," she says.

I look down. She's sitting, cross-legged, on a big wooden trunk, binoculars in her hands. All she's wearing is a shirt and underpants, though I'm not really sure why she's even wearing that.

"You need those to watch me sleep?" I ask, my voice still rough.

"Yeah, I really enjoy examining your individual pores," she teases.

I lay back, hands behind my head. I kicked my sleeping

bag mostly off during the night, because they're usually too warm, but it's still strategically covering my junk.

"Good, because I'm on the cover of the *Hot Firemen Pores 2017* calendar," I say.

"Hunter, wake up before you try to make jokes," Clementine says.

She checks me out anyway, and I just enjoy it. I get checked out a *lot*, and though I don't usually mind that much, I *like* it when she's the one doing it.

"You want me to move the bag?" I ask, still sounding blurry.

She glances down at my morning wood tenting up the sleeping bag, as if she hadn't already noticed.

"Actually, I want you to look at that white column," she says, and leans toward me, handing over the binoculars.

It's less exciting than showing her my dick, but it *is* why we're here, so I take the binoculars and look at the white column. It's the same one she showed me yesterday, but this morning it *looks* a little bigger, and it's definitely rising upward.

"It's smoke," I say, half a second later.

"I thought so," she says.

I keep looking at it, and a knot tightens in my stomach. It's not big. The smoke's not billowing upward, like it would if this were a serious fire, but something about it looks like it *might* be worse than just a lightning strike.

But it is definitely, absolutely a column of smoke. Clouds don't have that slightly tan tinge to them that smoke from burning wood does.

I take the binoculars down, and Clementine is still looking at me, though now she's not checking me out. Now she looks a little worried.

"Can you tell if it's just a lightning strike?" she asks.

"Not from here," I say.

"I'm gonna put on pants and radio it in," she says, hopping off the crate.

I turn and watch her walk across the lookout, blatantly checking out her ass.

"Why would you put on pants?" I ask. "They can't *see* you."

"I'll know," she says, laughing. "I don't want to talk to my boss without pants on. It's weird."

My boss has seen me naked more than once, but when you camp with two dozen guys for half the year, privacy is one of the first things to go.

"Suit yourself," I say, and finally get out of bed.

SEVENTEEN
CLEMENTINE

I put my pants on. I know perfectly well that Mike and Jennifer, or whoever's manning the radio this morning can't see me, but it feels unprofessional to call in a forest fire with nothing on but underwear.

Hunter gets up and starts making instant coffee still buck-ass naked, standing in front of the propane stove with his arms crossed while he waits for the water to boil.

"You want some?" he asks.

I just hold up the mug I made while he was still asleep, and he nods. I take a sip and walk to the Osborne Firefinder. It's a circular, spinning map in the center of the lookout, mounted on a chest-height table. I haven't used one in a couple of years, since I first did my fire lookout training, and I frown at it.

"You're on your own with that thing," Hunter says.

"Shouldn't you be better at this than me?" I ask, spinning it. It's got a vertical column with a narrow sight mounted on both sides of the circle, and I squint through them, lining up the column of smoke in the crosshairs.

"I don't *find* fires," he says.

"Yeah, I know, you put fires *out*," I finish for him.

Even if I'm not using it quite right, it looks like the fire is over in the direction of the Spires, a series of sharp granite peaks a good twenty miles off. The Spires themselves are impossible to scale unless you're an *advanced* rock climber, but they're also nearly impossible to get to, in the middle of a maze of steep mountains and sharp canyons.

I've never even been to the foot of the Spires. There's one trail in, and it's steep, rocky, treacherous, and the first fifteen miles of it doesn't have a single place where you could possibly camp. More than one person has died, falling off a ledge or something, after getting stuck on Spinside Trail after dark.

"You figure out where it is?" Hunter asks, coming up behind me. He blows on his coffee in one hand, peeking over my shoulder, his other hand casually on my hip.

"Not exactly," I say. "But it might be in the Spires. It's at least in that direction."

We both look at the map for a moment, Hunter studying it over my shoulder.

"You ever been there?" he asks.

I shake my head.

"You?"

"I took the trail in once," he says. "When I got back from the Marines, my parents *suggested* I join this local veterans' support group that did a lot of wilderness shit since it was supposed to help us *center ourselves* and readjust to society."

He takes a sip.

"Though they never really discussed how being with a couple of other guys in the middle of nowhere for a week was supposed to help me readjust to regular life," he says dryly.

"Spineside Trail," I say, trying to steer him back on track.

He's stroking my hip with one thumb, distractedly. I don't think he knows he's doing it, but it feels so familiar and *tender* that I'm having a hard time thinking about anything else, because *this* is what I want it to be like with us.

I went eight years without admitting it even to myself, but the good stuff was *really* good. Even though we were dumb teenagers. It took me years to realize how rare that is.

"We hiked in, and I climbed the first three routes, but after that it got way too advanced," he says, and laughs. "Not even a whole bunch of guys watching me could get me to climb a sheer cliff wall two hundred feet off the ground."

"Did anyone climb it?" I ask.

Hunter shakes his head.

"Me and another guy were the only ones who did the second route," he says like he's bragging.

It's working. I'm impressed. I've seen photos of the routes in the Spires, and they're no fucking joke.

"Let me guess," I say, teasing him. "You didn't really want to do that second climb, but you couldn't let some other guy do *one* more climb than you did."

Hunter grins, then kisses me.

"It's like you already know me," he says.

―――――

I CALL in the column of smoke. Mike is the one who answers the radio, and he runs through a detailed series of questions. I can hear him typing on the other end. He's probably filling out a report, and as we keep going, he sounds more and more worried.

"I think it might be in the Spires," I say, leaning against the fire finder and looking out toward the thin column of smoke.

"Well, that does lead me to my next question," he says. "How are you at using that spinning contraption?"

I spin it.

"I could use a refresher," I say.

Mike sighs.

"I was afraid of that," he says. "I'm not gonna lie, it's been years since I used one of those things, Clementine. If you can hold on, I'll go get Randy."

The radio goes silent. Hunter looks at me, sitting in a chair at the tiny table, eating instant oatmeal from a mug.

"Getting Randy sounds like some serious shit," he says.

"Randy is basically the Gandalf of the Copper Creek Ranger Division," I explain.

Hunter raises one eyebrow.

"You know, the wise old wizard who's been around so long that he can show demons what's what?" I say.

Hunter just kind of shrugs.

"From *Lord of the Rings*," I go on, even though I know it's pointless.

He just shakes his head. I'm starting to get incredulous.

"Did you not even see the movies?" I ask. "Didn't you ever watch them at my house?"

"If we did I was probably too busy trying to cop a feel to pay attention," he says.

He has a point there, actually.

"You seriously don't know Gandalf, though?" I ask.

Hunter shrugs, a wicked gleam in his eye as he scrapes oatmeal out of his mug.

"I don't know your nerd shit," he says, barely able to keep himself from smiling.

I roll my eyes, even though I'm smiling too, because I know he's just winding me up.

"*Lord of the Rings* is not *nerd shit* anymore," I say. "The movies were huge hits, and the books have really informed all fantasy—"

The radio crackles, cutting me off.

"Spruce Mountain Lookout, come in," a gnarled voice says. It sounds like an ent.

Not that *Hunter* would know what that is, but he's laughing at me from the kitchen table.

"This is Spruce Mountain, over," I say.

"You got the firefinder in front of you?" Randy asks.

"Roger."

"Okay then. What you wanna do first is make sure that you're facing the fire. Make sure you don't lock your knees, since you're at altitude, that can be dangerous. Get real light-headed. I knew this guy one time, Brian I think his name was, and he locked his knees trying to locate a fire and smacked his head real good when he fainted..."

"Does Gandalf tell a lot of people not to lock their knees?" Hunter whispers at me.

I flip him off and keep listening to Randy.

———

RANDY IS A VERY, very patient man, and as I listen to a long digression about how they just don't make rubber gaskets like they *used* to, I do my best to be as patient as him.

Hunter, on the other hand, couldn't take listening to Randy for this long. He went down from the lookout tower to explore around a little, though I don't think there's much to explore besides the outhouse and some rocks.

He's always been a little twitchy, though. Not the kind of person who can sit still for more than a couple minutes, which is why an exciting job with plenty of physical labor suits him. I can't imagine Hunter in an office, wearing a suit or something, calmly meeting with clients or whatever people with office jobs do.

I'm looking through both sights of the firefinder at the column of smoke, following Randy's instructions for the second time. He wanted to double-check my numbers, and I don't blame him.

"All right, that ought to do 'er," he says. "Read me the damage."

By *the damage* he means *the heading you calculated for the fire.* I rattle off coordinates into the radio.

There's a brief pause.

"They're a degree off from each other, but that's to be expected," he says. I can hear him tapping a pencil against a piece of paper, probably on a desk. "Congratulations, Clementine, you've found a lightning strike in the Spires."

"Thanks?" I say.

I walk to the windows facing the smoke. It hasn't changed at all in the past couple of hours, ever since I woke up, so I'm not exactly sure what we're going to do about it.

Randy laughs into the radio, a dry sound.

"Mike had to go to a meeting, but he left me in charge of you for the time being," he says, and I can hear the sound of a chair creaking, like Randy's leaning back and putting his feet on the desk.

"I know how much you like being in charge," I say.

Randy just sighs, because he *hates* being responsible for other people.

"How do you feel about staying at that lookout another night or so?" he asks.

I spot Hunter down below, climbing a stack of boulders. He's got his shirt off, and even though he's far away, I can see his back muscles rippling and bulging in the sunlight.

"I can do that," I say, hoping my voice sounds normal.

"In all likelihood, that fire's gonna burn itself out and it won't be a problem," he says. "Besides, that area hasn't burned in a good fifty years, so it needs to be cleared out. This'll save us having to send in a crew to do a controlled burn, which they never want to do in the Spires, because *yowza*, that hike."

That's the tricky thing about forest fires: as far as nature is concerned, they're not actually *bad*. The wildlands of the western United States are supposed to catch fire every so often, because that's how they evolved. Most of the adult trees are more than hardy enough to survive a fire, and they help clear away the underbrush, keeping the forest from getting too choked with bushes and weeds.

Basically, occasional fires from lightning strikes are part of the ecosystem. But then humans came along and fucked it up, by building houses in fire-prone places, and also by starting way, *way* more fires than there are supposed to be.

Right now, about ten percent of wildfires are started by lightning. Those are the fires that the ecosystem can handle. The other ninety percent are people leaving campfires burning, or shooting off fireworks, or dropping cigarettes, or just doing dumb, dangerous shit.

"But it *might* catch, and if it does, it's gonna flare up those steep slopes faster than a cat with its tail on fire?" I say.

Talking to Randy makes all my colorful phrases come out.

"You got it," he says, chair creaking. "We can't risk sending anyone in on foot because of that, and we can't call in the cavalry for a lightning strike that's almost definitely gonna burn itself out in twenty-four hours."

"Which is why I'm staying here and keeping an eye on it," I say.

I look at the column of smoke again, but then I look down at Hunter, almost at the top of the boulders.

Staying here another night is *completely* fine with me.

"You got it," Randy says. "If you're feeling up to it, there's a nice hike to a waterfall nearby, up high enough that you should be able to keep an eye on the smoke from there. Good swimming hole on a hot day, never anyone around. Just take the trail out of the lookout meadow and head north a ways..."

He gives me directions to the waterfall, and I trace the route on my map. The lookout cabin is already getting stuffy and hot inside, even though I've got the windows open as far as they'll go.

Randy rambles a little more before finally signing off the

radio. I put it down on top of the spinning firefinder map and take a deep breath, reveling in the silence for a moment, because that man can *talk*.

I look down at the spot on my map where the lightning strike is: twenty-five miles away, basically inaccessible. I want to believe Randy that it'll burn itself out, because he's been doing this for thirty-five years, so he's probably right. The Spires are mostly rock, and lightning strikes rarely turn into raging fires anyway.

But I still have a weird, bad, gnawing feeling in the pit of my stomach, and I don't know why. It's not as if I know more about fires than anyone else, and none of *them* are worried.

It's your first time spotting a fire, I tell myself. *It's normal to be nervous.*

I shake my head, slug down the rest of my cold instant coffee, put on my boots, and head down to suggest a waterfall hike to Hunter.

EIGHTEEN

HUNTER

"I thought Randy said this was an *easy* hike," I say.

I look up at a long stretch of boulders, leading to a plateau. I can hear the waterfall, and there's a creek winding down the other side of the rise, but it's too choked with underbrush to even consider getting up that way.

"Randy's got a different definition of *easy* than... well, humans," Clementine says, her hazel eyes flicking over the gray rocks. "Why, are you tired already?"

She glances at me, her eyes dancing. I cross my arms.

"I eat climbs like this for breakfast," I say. "But I'm not the one with a half-busted ankle."

"It's not half-busted," she says. "I've been totally fine this whole way."

She hops up and down a couple of times on her right foot, like that's gonna prove that she's fine to scramble up a bunch of boulders.

I don't like letting her do this, but I'm fully aware that I don't *let* Clementine do anything. I can have opinions, but the minute I suggest that I might not *let* her do something, look the fuck out.

"Can I talk you out of this?" I ask.

She stands on her tiptoes and kisses me.

"I'll be fine," she says. "I'm not made of glass."

I want to point out that she *did* turn her ankle yesterday while all she was just walking, but she's not gonna change her mind, so I don't. Instead I climb about ten feet behind her, close enough that if she slips, I can catch her.

I can also watch her ass, which looks surprisingly good in her hiking pants, which aren't generally very flattering.

About halfway up, her foot slips a little, sending a small shower of debris my way. My heart just about stops, but she finds her footing again half a second later and keeps climbing.

"Sorry," she calls.

"It's fine," I call back.

I don't remember *this* from before, this intense, powerful need to *protect* her. When she turned her ankle yesterday, I felt like the ground had fallen away from under me, even though she's pretty much fine now.

It's a primal, bone-deep drive to keep her safe that I've never felt before. Not even with her.

I just hope we don't run into any aggressive bears on this hike, because I swear to God, I'll fight a bear for Clementine. I'll fight two bears, and I'll lose, because I don't have claws or teeth.

She gets to the top without slipping again. I follow her, and then we both stand there, staring.

It looks like it could be in a *Visit Montana!* brochure or something, because it's picture-perfect. The waterfall isn't big, especially right now with the drought, but it's about fifty feet high, falling from a semi-circular outcropping of rock above, overhung with moss and some kind of climbing plant.

In front of us, the basin is the sort of deep, perfect blue you can only see in the middle of nowhere. It's surrounded by flat gray stones, and the whole place feels perfect, secluded, so totally out of the way that it's hard to believe *we* even found it.

"Damn, Randy," Clementine breathes.

Then she glances up. The column of smoke is still visible above the trees, and we both examine it for a moment. It hasn't changed since this morning. If anything, it's gotten smaller.

That's good. Usually, around this time of year, fire season is wrapping up. I'm ready for it to end, and to make sleeping in a regular bed and taking regular showers a fixture in my life again.

"Think this is where Randy takes *the ladies*?" I ask, walking toward one of the flat gray rocks.

"I think the only *lady* in Randy's life is Mother Nature," Clementine says.

"If this is one of his favorite spots, I see why," I say.

Clementine takes off the hiking fanny pack she *insisted* on wearing instead of a backpack and puts it on a rock. It's a hot day, in the mid-eighties at least, and we've hiked a couple of miles, so there's a big dark splotch of sweat over her lower back.

I take off my backpack, and even if I can't see it, I can *feel* the matching sweat spot on my back, so I take my shirt off too and lay it out on a rock.

Then I glance around, just to make *sure* there's no one else around, and take off my pants and boxers too. Barefoot, I gingerly walk over to where Clementine is, just watching the waterfall, and put one hand on her back.

She looks over at me and yelps.

Then she starts laughing, and I raise my eyebrows.

"You see something funny?" I ask.

"Sorry," she says, gasping. "I wasn't expecting you to be naked. I'm just surprised."

"I didn't exactly bring a swimsuit, so I don't see what other option we've got," I say, grinning.

"*Naked?*" she says. "*Here?*"

"It's hot as hell out here and I bet that water feels *good*," I say, dragging one finger down her spine. "Right now, you're hot and sweaty, but you *could* go for a quick, refreshing swim."

Clementine just laughs at me.

"I was teasing," she says. "You'd be surprised how much time I spend naked in the woods."

I lift one eyebrow as she shrugs off the button-down shirt she was wearing over a tank top. She tosses it on a rock, then gives me a sly look.

"There's no one around and it's hot," she says, shrugging. "Why not be naked?"

"I wish I'd known that there were hot, naked forest rangers out fixing trails when I was thirteen," I say. "I'd have done *nothing* but hike."

She laughs again and pulls off her tank top. Now all she's wearing is a sports bra, the underside dark with sweat.

"Turn around," she says.

"Seriously?"

"You don't need to watch me get a sports bra off," she says. "I promise it's not sexy."

"I'll be the judge of that."

She just shrugs, then grabs the band of her bra, takes a deep breath, and yanks up on it. It comes up a little, just enough to trap her upper arms, and then both her breasts suddenly bounce free.

Not sexy my *ass*. I'm at half-mast already, and things are looking *up*.

Clementine sort of wriggles back and forth, both arms still over her head, the bra awkwardly around her shoulder and upper arms. She hops a little, then takes another deep breath.

"You need—"

Suddenly the thing pops off, over her head, and she shakes out her hair, tossing it next to her other clothes before glancing over at me.

"Yeah, I don't think I can have sex with you after seeing *that*," I tease. "I especially hated the part where you hopped up and down."

"Hunter, get in the water," she says, unbuttoning her pants and pulling them down, kicking her boots off.

"Ladies first," I say.

She walks over to me, at the edge of the perfectly clear, blue pool, and sticks one foot into the water.

Then she pulls her foot back with a gasp.

"*Fuck* that's cold!"

"Are you wimping out?" I ask, taking a step into the water.

It's fucking *cold*, so cold I instantly can't feel my feet, but I force myself not to react in front of Clementine.

"No," she says. "I'm just taking it slow."

"That's gonna make it worse," I say.

She scrunches up her face and dips the toes of one foot in. I force myself to wade deeper, up to my knees, hands on hips.

I'm *not* looking forward to my balls going in. They're already clenching at the thought, but I can't back out now.

"You want help?" I ask.

She looks at me like I suggested murdering Trout, and I laugh.

"Just do it," I say, wading a little deeper. My balls clench tighter.

"How about *you* just fucking do it," she mutters. Now she's up to her ankles in cold water, her fists clenched at her sides.

I look at the center of the pool. I can see the gravel bottom from here, it's so clear, and it's four, maybe five feet deep.

Deep enough. I start wading back out, toward Clementine. She looks at me and laughs.

"Who's wimping out now?" she teases.

"Me," I say, coming to stand next to her. "Definitely me."

Clementine frowns for a split second, but it's too late. I grab her under the shoulders and behind the knees and lift her off the ground. Her arms go around my neck automatically, but she kicks her feet as I walk her further into the pool.

"No no no no no no no," she squeals. "Hunter. No. No no no, I swear to *God*—"

"What's that? Put you down?" I ask, grinning.

"I'm going to *kill* you when I get out of here," she says.

I take a deep breath. Clementine screws up her face.

I plunge us both into the deepest part of the pond, and Jesus pogo-sticking Christ it's cold. So cold it knocks the wind out of me and for a moment I *actually* panic.

Then I stand up, because it's four feet deep.

We surface at the same time, and Clementine is already shouting, but it's just a string of curse words, mostly directed at me. I think my balls have retreated *inside my body*, but I grin at her anyway, trying to look like I don't mind.

"I am actually going to kill you," she says, gasping for air as she shoves her hair off her face. "Jesus, it's so cold I can't even think. I think my brain went numb. I think you killed my brain cells."

She takes a step toward the edge, but I grab her around the waist.

"NOOOooooooo — oh," she says, as I pull her in, her head against my chest. She puts her arms around me, her nipples hard as diamonds against my chest.

I just kiss her on top of her head, laughing into her hair.

"You're the world's worst boyfriend," she mutters.

That word, *boyfriend*, makes my heart skip a beat. Or maybe it's the cold.

"There's no way that's true," I say.

"You're not even warm," she says, burrowing harder into me.

"Just give it a minute, it starts to feel warmer," I say.

"That's because your skin is going numb."

"Still feels warmer, though," I say. "I'm gonna go in again."

Clementine lets me go and backs away quickly, like she's afraid I'm going to grab her and take her with me, but I don't this time. Dunking her once was all I wanted.

After a few minutes we both warm up a little, though I think she's right and our skin is just going numb. We splash around for a while, dare each other to go through the trickle of the waterfall. Clementine tries to dunk me but it doesn't work until I finally let her, and then we float on our backs for a few minutes, just looking up at the sky.

"Okay, I'm getting cold again now," she says, and looks at one hand. "And my fingernails are turning blue."

She walks out and I watch her as she wrings water out of her hair, then lays back on a big, flat, gray rock in the sun. I wait until I think her eyes are closed to follow, because I've been in barely-melted ice water and I think my dick is the size of a gummi worm right now.

"I didn't bring a towel," she murmurs as I sit next to her. "We'll have to lay here in the sun until we dry off."

She's got her arms over her head and her eyes closed, her whole naked body stretched out on a rock. I swear it looks like a pinup calendar one of my buddies had in Afghanistan, except it's *real*. And spectacular.

I glance over at the column of smoke. It looks the same. *Maybe* a little bigger, but it's hard to tell.

"I hope that fire stays *exactly* the same size for another couple of days and then goes out," Clementine says. "There's plenty of supplies in the lookout, and I could use a vacation."

"They'd call me back before that," I say, lying down on the rock next to her. "Utah's on fire, and if we're not needed here we're going down there."

She opens her eyes and looks over at me, her expression unreadable, like she'd forgotten I was going to have to leave.

"When's fire season usually over for you guys?" she asks.

I slide one arm around her shoulders. She's still cold, but drying quickly in the heat, and she wriggles toward me on the rock.

"About now," I say. "That is, unless there are still big fires in the southwest. Then we get called down to help with those, like we did last year. In that case, late September, early October."

"That's a long season," she says.

"Six months," I say.

She just gives me a *yeah, I can do math* look.

"...Which is a long time to sleep in a tent," I finish.

"And then the other six months is a long time to live with your parents," she says.

"Only when you say it like that," I point out. "I prefer to tell people that I'm a part-time fireman, part-time cowboy."

"If you get a friend who's half cop and half construction worker, you could have your very own male strip show," she teases.

"I *did* always want to wear a thong so strange women could stick dollar bills in it," I say.

"It's usually briefs," Clementine says.

I raise myself up on one elbow and look at her.

"What?" she says, her eyes crinkling with laughter.

"Apparently you're an expert on male strippers," I say.

"I'm not an *expert*," she says, rolling over and resting her chin on my chest. "But if you wanted to give me a show, I'd be happy to offer some pointers."

My dick is warming up *much* faster now.

"Well, I've got one move where I dig fire breaks for fourteen hours a day, sleep, then get up and do it again," I say.

"And another one where I shovel horse shit out of stables for a couple of months. Am I ready for Vegas?"

Clementine slides her leg over my thighs so she's straddling me, her face above mine, and I put my hands on her still-cold hips.

Cold water be damned, I'm rock hard in seconds.

"Maybe," she says. "But then strange women would be staring at you all day, and shoving money into your underwear, and trying to cop a feel, and I'd probably get pretty jealous."

"Shoveling shit it is, then," I say, grinning.

She leans down and kisses me, a slow, lazy kiss as I stroke her back. She's still on her knees over me, and as we kiss, I open my eyes to check out her ass in the air.

Yeah, it's nice.

Clementine bites my lip as she pulls away, her eyes dark like she's up to something. I have the urge to pull her hips down and sink myself into her in one long, hard stroke, but I don't. I didn't even *bring* condoms on this hike.

"This is more like what I'm used to," I say, my voice coming out in a growl. "Getting naked somewhere we could get caught."

She laughs and leans over again, and this time she bites my earlobe, then trails her lips down my neck to my collarbone. Past my collarbone.

"You're still cold," she murmurs, her lips moving against my skin.

I realize what's happening as she takes my cock in one hand, and I swear I think my skin might split, I get so hard.

"Your cock's warm, though," she says, her lips on my stomach, her hand stroking me.

She looks up at me, her hazel eyes teasing as her head moves down until I feel her teeth on my hip, and I gasp. Clementine laughs, but I don't even breathe, my whole body rigid with anticipation.

She strokes me again, straddling my knees, looking at me.

"Relax, Hunter," she teases.

I don't, but I watch as Clementine bends her head. She licks the underside of my shaft and I exhale explosively, groaning as she folds her tongue over the tip and then swirls it around the head of my cock.

I know she's just teasing me, but I already feel like I might explode. I put my arms behind my head so I don't grab her hair, because I know that's rude, and I watch her as she lowers her warm, wet mouth onto the head of my cock and swirls her tongue around it.

I groan again and she pulls back, looking up at me, her lips still on the tip.

It's *beyond* hot, and she keeps looking at me as she lowers her mouth onto my cock, her lips sliding further down my shaft, her tongue flat against the underside.

"Jesus, Clem," I say, my breath coming in gasps.

She goes slow, taking me deeper little by little, driving me absolutely fucking crazy. I'm pretty sure the forest could burn down around me right now, and as long as Clem didn't take my cock out of her mouth, I wouldn't care or even *notice*.

Finally, I can feel myself hit the back of her mouth, and it's tight and wet as she swallows, the muscles moving against the tip. I'm still watching her, and she looks up at me again.

"You're so fucking sexy with my cock in your mouth," I say, the words spilling out of me without my brain's permission. She bobs again, and I gasp, right at the edge of coming.

Then Clementine pulls her mouth off me for a moment and swallows, her hand still stroking me.

"Good," she says, her eyes sparking. "Because I like making you come this way."

She sucks the head back into her mouth, and I nearly shout as she swirls her tongue around, and then she's moving up and down again, her lips going down my shaft until I hit the back of her mouth.

I've got one hand gently on her head, because I can't fucking stop myself. I'm panting for breath, up on one elbow so I can watch as my cock disappears into her mouth, over and over until I'm at the brink again.

"Clem, I'm gonna come," I gasp, warning her because I'm a goddamn gentleman. "Oh *fuck* I'm gonna come."

She pushes her mouth down one more time and I just fucking *explode*. Her tongue presses against my shaft as she swallows, again and again, and my entire body jolts with the sheer pleasure of it. I'm completely and utterly at her mercy, coming my brains out in the middle of the forest, and I wouldn't fucking trade it for anything.

I flop back onto the rock and Clementine takes her mouth off me, then sits back on her heels and wipes her mouth with one hand.

"Holy fuck," I say, trying to catch my breath, and Clementine laughs.

"Talking about male strippers got me all riled up," she says.

I take a deep breath and sit up, grabbing her around the waist as I pull her to me, kissing her hard. She's still straddling my legs, and I swear to God I can *smell* how turned on she is right now.

"Really?" I ask.

"Nah," she says, wrapping her fingers around the back of my head. "It was because you were naked and I like your dick."

I slide my hand between her legs and she makes a noise into my mouth, because even if I can't get it up right now — and I can*not* — I still fucking love to touch her.

NINETEEN

CLEMENTINE

Now I *really* feel eighteen again, because I'm naked in public and horny as *hell*. Hunter's kissing me so hard that he's pushing me backward, his tongue deep in my mouth as he slides his fingers around my clit, pinching it gently.

"I probably taste like jizz," I whisper when I pull back.

"Yup," he says. "And when you kiss me in a few minutes I'm gonna taste like pussy."

I laugh and he kisses me again, one arm around my waist, his other hand rubbing me in slow circles. He's the only person I've *ever* talked to like this, in this perfectly candid, honest, I-like-your-dick way.

I *think* it's because we did a lot of experimenting without a lot of time when we were teenagers, so any shyness about saying things like, "a little to the left and lick faster," was pushed aside in favor of more orgasms.

It doesn't even feel dirty. It's hot, and it turns me on like crazy, but it just feels honest and normal.

He pulls his hand out from between my legs, and then before I know it, he's rolling both of us over onto the rock and

I'm on my back, facing the sky, Hunter between my legs as he kisses the hollow of my throat.

He sucks one nipple into his mouth and flicks his tongue across it. I groan in appreciation, and he does it again, to the other one. He keeps pinching them as his lips move to my stomach, and he looks up at me.

I try not to giggle, because it tickles, and he pushes my thighs apart, running his fingers along the sensitive inside as I squirm. Then I feel his face there, too, sucking gently on the soft skin.

"Hey," I say, laughing. "No hickies."

"How am I supposed to keep track of how many times I've eaten you out?" he says, his voice buzzing, his lips *almost* brushing up against me.

I suck in a breath.

"Day planner?" I say.

He used to give me a hickey on my inner thigh every time he ate me out, and sometimes I would have seven or eight at once. I thought it was hot until I went to a waterpark with my family.

Hunter laughs, and then his tongue swipes hard across my clit.

I make a noise somewhere between a grunt and a moan, clenching my fists at my sides. He licks me hard again, his tongue flat but curling and really, I don't know what he's doing exactly but *Jesus* he's good at it.

He keeps going, moving his tongue fast and hard and *exactly* the right way to make me moan my face off, and I'm moments from coming when suddenly his tongue stops. He pauses. I'm holding my breath.

Then he licks me in a slow circle, *around* my clit, pushing his tongue between my lips and back up. He licks me everywhere but my clit, and I want to scream in frustration.

"Tease," I gasp.

His tongue makes another slow circle, and I swear I whimper, *willing* my body to climax somehow, even if he refuses to touch me right, but then he's licking me again slow and hard.

"God yes," I whisper, and then I come like I'm falling over a cliff, moaning, my eyes closed and my back arching.

Hunter doesn't stop. Even when each lap of his tongue makes my whole body jolt, he doesn't stop, and I put my hands in his hair, breathless.

"That was it," I say.

"You mean that was *one*," he says, grinning.

Then he shifts position slightly and his fingers slide inside me, bending at *exactly* the right spot.

I think I *grunt*, but then Hunter has his mouth back on me and I *think* he's sucking gently on my clit, just barely caressing it with his tongue as he does. His fingers rub the spot inside me, and God, he's *relentless*.

In no time at all I'm coming again and I'm whispering *fuck, Hunter, fuck* over and over again because my mind's pretty much gone blank.

This time he stops, and it's a good thing because I don't know how much more I can handle. He rests his head on my hip and I run my hand through his hair, taking a deep breath, because I feel like the shock of my climax is still rattling through me.

"I think I could eat you out all day," he says, his thumb stroking my lower belly. He almost sounds sleepy, and I wonder what would happen if we just fell asleep here.

Probably sunburn and bears, but it's a nice thought.

"Your jaw would get sore," I say.

"I'd have to work up to it," he says. "Like a marathon. You don't just run a marathon, first you run two miles, then five, then twenty."

I sit up, cross-legged, and he pushes himself up to kiss me.

"Told you I'd taste like pussy," he says.

"Gross," I say, and kiss him again, this time with tongue.

After a while we quit making out and just lie there, on the rock, like giant satiated lizards or something. I keep having the urge to say dumb things to him, like *I love you* or *move to Lodgepole* or *let's get married* or *how many kids do you want?*

I know it's just because of those chemicals the brain releases after sex, but it surprises me how *solid* those dumb things feel.

Try waiting until you've dated for a whole week before you start naming your kids, maybe?

Ridiculous.

I'm still lying there, my head on Hunter's chest, when he suddenly jerks to half-sitting, and I slide off. He's looking upward, and after a second, I follow his gaze to the column of smoke.

We both stare for a long, long time.

"It's bigger," I finally say.

"Yeah," he says.

Another pause.

"*Shit*," he says, and stands.

For the first time since we got to the waterfall I *feel* naked, and I look around, wondering if someone else arrived while we were half-dozing, but there's no one around. It's just us and the column of smoke above, not *much* bigger but definitely bigger.

Neither of us says anything as we get dressed again, put on our packs and our shoes, and head away from the waterfall. Before we leave, I take a pebble from the side of the pool, then look back over my shoulder as we leave, wishing I'd brought a camera. It really *is* a beautiful place.

Hunter goes first down the boulder scramble, saying that if I fall he can probably catch me while the reverse isn't true. I think he's right, and even though I go on boulder scrambles all the time and don't fall, I don't argue with him.

For now, at least, his protective concern is sweet, though it'll probably get on my nerves in a couple months.

I hope this lasts long enough for me to get annoyed, I think, just as my foot sends a shower of pebbles down the slope.

Hunter stops and looks back at me.

"I'm *fine*," I say, and he nods.

———

IT's late afternoon by the time we get back to the lookout, and we're mostly quiet the whole way back, glancing at the smoke every so often. My brain has started blossoming with worry, from *what if it gets to the lookout before we can leave* to *what if Hunter has to hike in there to fight it?*

It's a tricky hike on a sunny day, in perfect conditions. Forget carrying heavy equipment in a smoke-filled canyon.

The moment we get back, I call it in to Mike. We talk for a while. Then Randy's in his office, and they're trying to share a radio, and it's kind of a shit show but the three of us discuss the fire for a while.

Randy's still sure it'll burn itself out, even though he admits that he can see the column now, though only if he uses binoculars. Mike's found a map of towns and settlements in the area, and after a while, the conversation devolves into Randy insisting that it's nothing to get excited about, and Mike just repeating how far various points of civilization are from the fire.

I think they're driving Hunter crazy, so he goes outside for a while. Hell, they're driving me crazy, but this is my job so I can't leave. When he gets back, they're still doing the exact same thing, but it's not like I can hang up on my boss so I've just got my head down on the kitchen table, listening to Mike tell Randy that Eaglevale is *only* fifty miles from the current fire, and with the right conditions and bad luck, it could be there *tomorrow*.

"But it's *not* the right conditions," Randy is saying.

Hunter comes up behind me and puts his hands on my shoulders, massaging the tense muscles there. I let Mike and Randy argue as I lean back into him, his thumbs rubbing small, hard circles up and down my neck.

"They still at it?" he murmurs into my ear.

"Yeah," I say, sighing. "I just want to know whether we need to leave *now*, or in the morning, and whether..."

I stop talking, because I'm about to say *whether you're gonna have to go fight this thing*, but even if he doesn't go to *this* one, he's going somewhere, and I get to worry about *that*.

"Whether what?" he asks.

I swallow.

"Whether you're gonna have to hike in there and fight this thing," I say. "It's dangerous."

"It's always dangerous," he points out.

I want to say *yes, I know, but I never had a say in this and I don't have to like it*, but I don't. Hunter chose this, and he knew what he was getting himself into, and that decision had *nothing* to do with me. I can take it or leave it, but I can't start a fight about it.

I close my eyes and take a deep breath.

Take it, I think.

"I know," I say, and look up at him. "Sorry."

He leans down and kisses the top of my head.

"I practically pitched a fit when you climbed on some rocks today," he says. "It's okay if you worry about me."

"McKinnon, come *in*," Mike's annoyed voice is saying. I grab the radio and press the button.

"Yes?" I say.

There's a long, dramatic sigh.

"Hike back tomorrow," he says. "We've requested air

surveillance for this thing, so we'll have eyes a lot closer in case it breaks bad."

Hunter and I look at each other. I was secretly hoping for another day here, just hanging out and fucking a lot, but this extra day was pretty good.

"Roger that, boss," I say.

"Great. See you then. Over and out."

"Over and out," I say, then put the radio on the table and tilt my head up at Hunter.

"The professionals are coming—"

The radio sounds again, and Mike's voice comes through.

"McKinnon, are you there? I forgot something."

"What is it?" I ask.

"If this fire becomes a problem, tradition dictates that you get to name it," he says.

"I do?"

"You found it," he says. "I recommend *not* naming it after yourself, in case it kills someone."

A quick shudder runs down my spine.

"Thanks," I say.

"Think about it," he says. "And hope you don't get to name it."

"Roger *that*," I say.

TWENTY

HUNTER

We make dinner, more freeze-dried backpacking meals in bags, and eat at the tiny table. We talk, but not about anything important: whether the winter's going to be cold or mild, what the best and cheapest place to go skiing is. I ask about Trout, and Clementine ends up telling me funny dog stories for fifteen minutes, until she clears away the dishes.

I go look at the fire as twilight gathers. Last night we couldn't see the smoke after dark, but tonight, there's a distinctive *glow*, bouncing off the granite Spires, giving them a hellish glimmer.

But I'm not thinking about the fire. I'm thinking about earlier today, at the waterfall, and I'm thinking about how she called me her boyfriend. I'm thinking about whether it's too late to get a ranch job in Lodgepole for the winter, because having three hours between us feels like too much.

You might be rushing things, I think, but I'm honestly not sure.

Since we broke up I've had a couple dozen one night stands and a few casual girlfriends, and they were nice enough, but I never felt the magnetic pull that Clementine exerts on me. I never wanted to move in and adopt their dogs or argue over which couch to buy or fall asleep listening to them breathe.

I don't know what normal *is*. I used to blame Clementine for that, like she'd broken my heart so hard it ruined me, but if I couldn't get over her in *eight years* I think it was my problem, not hers.

The fire's an afterthought. She's worried, but this is pretty routine for me. We go out, we dig some breaks, we do some controlled burns. If things get *really* crazy we might be fighting some actual flames, but they rarely do.

"There's a couple board games up here when I finish the dishes," Clementine suggests from the sink. "Want to play Monopoly with half the pieces missing?"

"How about cards?" I ask.

She laughs.

"What, are we retirees?" she asks, looking at me over her shoulder.

"Your suggestion was *Monopoly*," I point out, leaning against a table. "No one has ever had fun playing that game. Ever. In the history of the world."

"Maybe we could just sit *in* the dark and stare at each other," she teases.

I walk over and smack her lightly on the ass. She's got the leggings back on, so it makes a satisfying noise and I get to watch it jiggle *just* a little.

I want to do it again, but I'm wearing the comfy lounge pants, and these pants keep *no* secrets. Clementine seems stressed about the fire, and I can be better than hey-you're-having-feelings-whoops-here's-my-dick guy. Especially because that itch already got scratched once today.

"That's not a response," she says.

"Sure it is," I tell her. "It's the best response."

She rolls her eyes and I grin.

I volunteer to take the wash basin down and dump it out.

When I get back to the lookout, Clementine is standing on the wraparound balcony, leaning against the rail, looking at the glow of the fire.

"This isn't Monopoly," I say, leaning against the railing next to her.

"It's not?" she says, glancing at me sideways.

"I know they're easy to confuse," I say.

We stand there another moment. The night has just started to cool down, and there's a nice, refreshing breeze coming in across the tops of the trees. Really, it's just a bonus that it makes Clementine's nipples stiffen through her shirt even more.

"Sorry," she finally says, and looks over at me. "I always get antsy the last day of a trip."

"A work trip, you mean?"

She shrugs.

"Vacation too, actually," she admits. "I start thinking about all the stuff I need to do that I haven't done because I've been gone, and then all the stuff that I didn't finish before I left, and..."

She looks over at me and laughs.

"You get the idea," she says. "If this spreads east, toward the valley, it'll be a logistical nightmare at the *very* least."

I put one hand on her back and rub in slow circles. She arches a little as I do, and I glance at her ass in the leggings.

Then I try to will my dick back down as I wonder why the fuck I brought *these* pants on *this* trip.

"You can't do anything about that right now, though," I point out.

She just smiles.

"Like knowing *that* helps," she says, then moves over, bumping her side against mine. "Don't worry, I know I can't do anything about it right now."

She pauses.

"And I keep worrying about you," she admits. "And I keep remembering being in college, with air conditioning and a real bed and parties and beer and knowing that you were out in the desert, probably miserable, and just wondering if you were *okay*."

"Only for me to call and pick a fight with you because I was afraid you could do better?" I ask.

Clementine laughs.

"Obviously, I couldn't," she says.

"I'm flattered," I say. Her eyes flick over my face, and I wrap one arm around her, pulling her further in front of me. "And I'll be fine."

We kiss, and when we separate, she looks at the fire again, and I wrap both arms around her, holding her close, my chin resting on top of her head.

"What should I name it?" she asks, leaning against me.

"You mean what should *we* name it?"

"I *did* see it first," she points out. "Mike said I get naming rights."

One time, the summer after we graduated, Clementine's parents went on vacation without her and Jane. We convinced Jane to spend the night with a friend, which wasn't hard since she was sixteen, knew *exactly* what we were up to, and wanted no part of it. I forget what I told my parents, but it worked.

Then we got drunk on her parents' whiskey and had sex on her couch. Afterward, lying there, we started talking about what we should name our kids, because we were both still completely moonstruck and totally certain that we'd be married by twenty-three.

This feels a little like that. It's a fire, not kids, but the memory still tickles at my brain.

"George," I say.

Clementine laughs.

"I can't name a fire *George*," she says.

"Gertrude."

"I know a dog named Gertrude," she says. "She's a panty-stealing terror."

"And you haven't told me about her yet?" I ask.

"I forgot," Clementine says, snuggling against me, my only-a-little-erect dick right between the globes of her ass. I think desperately about Trout, her cute dog, trying to *keep* it only a little erect.

"You'll meet her. I think you'll get along," Clementine goes on.

"Because I'm also a panty-stealing terror?"

"Do you *steal* them?" she asks, turning to look at me. "Don't tell me I'm gonna find a drawer full of used under-pants from all your conquests."

Her ass rubs against me as she turns my head, and I can't think of a good response very fast.

"Um," I say, then swallow. "Conquests?"

"Silas *happened* to casually mention that you get a lot of tail," she says. "I think he was trying to suggest that he was a better match for me."

My heart freezes, because I knew we were gonna talk about this sooner or later, but I was hoping I'd be better prepared. Clementine just looks at my face and then laughs.

"I haven't exactly been a nun," she says. "I kind of went on a tear after we broke up, actually."

"A sex tear?" I ask, then frown.

"Please don't ever use that phrase again."

"Sorry."

"It was more of a make-out-with-guys-in-bars-and-get-fingered... *phase*," she says deliberately. "I didn't actually fuck all that many."

"I did," I say.

At least the thought of nineteen-year-old Clementine

making out with some bro in a dark bar is making my erection fade.

"You know, it's weird," she says, leaning against me again.

"That I got laid?" I tease. "I'd think you would understand."

"I used to think about that *all the time*, after we broke up, and get really upset," she says. "I'd be studying or something, and just think, *I'm in this library at midnight and I bet Hunter has two girls on his dick at the same time*."

"Only once," I say.

Then I pause.

"No, twice."

She looks at me, eyebrows raised.

"The first time was okay, just confusing, and the second was going better until they casually mentioned that they were sisters," I say. "And... no."

She just starts laughing, and I pull her in, my nose in her hair.

"Confusing?" she says.

"I didn't know where my dick went," I say into her hair.

She laughs even harder.

"Poor thing," she says, and turns her head, kissing my shoulder.

"I didn't think you'd react like this when I finally told you what I've been up to," I say.

"Me either," she says. "It's weird, right? That I spent so long getting upset about it, but now that I *actually know* I don't care?"

"That's 'cause it's over and I know *exactly* where my dick goes," I say.

"Romantic," Clementine murmurs.

She moves against me, just a little, and it gives my dick a renewed sense of purpose.

"You know I didn't cheat on you, right?" I say, looking at the fire. "That was all after we broke up."

"I didn't cheat on you either," she says. "I think you were worried I did."

"I haven't been for a long time," I say.

She wiggles again, and this time she arches her back *just* a little, sliding my dick along her ass.

I can *tell* it's deliberate, and I'm hard in seconds. Clementine puts her hands on the railing, then leans forward a few degrees and does it again.

I put my hands on her hips and lean in.

"I could *swear* you're getting me hard on purpose," I say into her ear.

Clementine just wraps one hand around the back of my head and pulls me down, half-turning to kiss me, *still* moving her hips.

She must do yoga or something, because *damn*.

"So male strippers and talking about the time I had a threesome are what get you going," I tease.

"If you'd rather believe that than the truth, go ahead," she says.

Now I'm grabbing her hips, holding her spandex-covered ass tight against me, just watching it move against my shaft. I'm visual. Sue me.

"What's the truth?" I ask, because I just want to hear her say it.

"I like your dick," she says, looking at me over her shoulder.

I could hear her say that a million times and it wouldn't get old.

"And the rest of you, I guess," she teases.

I push myself against her and slide my hands up her shirt, cupping both breasts in my hands, rubbing her nipples against my palms. Clementine moans softly, her hand tightening on the rail, and I kiss the back of her neck.

Suddenly she stands up straight, leaning against my shoulder, looking up at me. I push her shirt over her breasts and tweak her nipples, looking down so I can watch. Clementine sighs and wriggles again.

"Hey," she says softly.

"Yeah?"

She swallows.

"Do you wrap it up with conquests?" she says.

It takes me a minute to remember what she means by *conquests*.

"Of course," I finally say.

"Always? Every single time?"

"I don't have any secret kids," I say.

"Condoms ever break?" she asks.

Her eyes are closed, and I'm still rubbing her nipples, her breasts filling my hands.

"Once, a few years ago," I say, and kiss her neck again, slowly, because I think I've figured out where she's going with this. "But there's a mandatory physical at the start of every fire season, and they're *very* thorough."

She bites her lip, eyes closed, and nuzzles the top of her head against my chin.

"I'm on the pill," she says. "And I'm clean."

I pinch her nipples, and she moans. I feel like my whole body is buzzing with sheer desire as she kisses me under the chin, the only spot she can really reach.

"You want me to fuck you bare?" I ask. My voice comes out a low growl.

Clementine looks up at me, her hazel eyes wide, her lips slightly parted, her chest heaving.

"Please?" she says.

It's so fucking hot that it knocks the wind out of my lungs, and I forget to breathe for a moment. Clementine lifts her eyebrows.

"Yes," I say, kissing her hard.

She reaches one hand into my pants and grabs my dick behind her back, holding it tight and stroking it hard. I hook my thumbs under the waist of her leggings, pull them halfway down her thighs, and Clementine parts her legs as I reach between them from behind.

She's wet as hell, her lips and clit a little swollen, and she moans again when I touch her, arching her back, grabbing the railing again with the hand that's not on my dick. I run my thumb over her soaking wet lips and down to her clit, my other hand squeezing her ass, and Clementine gasps, stroking me one more time.

Then she puts her other hand on the railing, leaning a little forward. I push my pants down and they puddle at my feet.

"I thought you didn't really like it from behind," I say into her ear. "You used to always want to do it face-to-face."

I grab her hips with one hand and press the tip of my cock against her clit, the slight pressure making a tremor run through my body. She looks over her shoulder at me and rocks back.

"Sometimes a girl just wants to get bent over and fucked hard," she murmurs, smiling.

I kiss her on the shoulder blade and move my cock until the tip is at her slippery, swollen entrance, and then I slide *just* the head inside her. She gasps softly, and a shock of pleasure runs through my body. I *want* to sink my whole cock into her right then, so bad I can barely stop myself, but I grab her shoulder and pull out.

We've never fucked bare before, but we're not teenagers any more, and we've got all the time in the world. I want to do this *right*, fuck her slow, memorize every skin-to-skin millimeter. I slide a little deeper with each thrust, and soon Clementine is gasping, panting for breath, moving her hips back like she wants *more* but I don't give it to her.

Not yet, anyway.

"You don't have to go slow," she says, looking at me over her shoulder.

"I know," I say, and kiss the back of her neck, her lower lips halfway up my shaft. I pull out.

She reaches back and puts one hand around my neck.

"C'mon," she whispers.

I push into her again, her tight muscles gripping me. She moans, and I pull back.

"I only get to fuck you bare for the first time once," I murmur. I thrust again, deeper. "I want to feel every inch."

Out, in. I'm going faster because I can't help it, and Clementine's eyes are closed and her head is back.

"And I like making *you* feel every inch," I say.

I'm moving even faster now, almost all the way in, and I think I'm slowly losing my mind.

"I think you like that too," I murmur.

"I do," she whispers.

"It doesn't get much better than when you're moaning with my cock inside you," I say.

Out, in. Out, and then suddenly I'm there, buried balls deep. Clementine is panting for breath, both hands white-knuckled on the railing. She turns her head and I kiss her savagely, rocking our hips together as she moans quietly into my mouth.

"Thank you," she murmurs when we pull apart.

Fuck, it's hot. I nuzzle her ear, half laughing as I start thrusting.

"What?" she gasps.

"You've never thanked me before," I say.

"You've never fucked me like that before," she says.

I mean to go slow, because I want to bring her to the brink

and drive her crazy until she *begs* me to make her come, but I can't help myself. I manage slow and sensual for a few seconds before a wild, primal *urge* takes me over and I push Clementine against the railing, gripping her shoulder from the front, driving my cock into her as hard as I can.

She's just *moaning*, and every so often a couple words make it through, something like *fuck yes Hunter God yes*.

"This what you wanted?" I growl in her ear, her pussy gripping me so tight that I bite her shoulder.

"Jesus yes," she whispers, turning her head. "Hunter, I'm—"

Suddenly her hand flies off the railing and for a split second, Clementine lurches forward.

I pull her back instantly, away from the railing, until my back hits the glass of the lookout windows and they rattle.

"Shit, ow," she says, shaking her right hand, still panting for breath.

"Are you okay?" I ask, holding her tight against me. I thought the railing had broken, but it's still there, perfectly solid.

"I'm fine, my hand slipped," she says. She grabs my hair and pulls my face to hers, kissing me hungrily.

"Don't stop," she murmurs.

I spin her around, push her against the window as she laughs, then pull her down until we're both on our knees on the wooden plank floor of the balcony. Somehow, she tugs her leggings the rest of the way off and braces herself against the wall as I kneel behind her, cock in hand.

I don't tease her this time. I don't have the willpower, I just thrust into her as hard as I can and listen to her guttural moan echo off the wall in front of her.

Before I know it we're back where we were and I'm driving into her as hard as I can, her forearms against the wall, her palms flat against it, her head against her arms. I've got one arm against the wall, my hand over hers, one hand on her hip.

"God, I like fucking you this way," I growl. "Clem, I'm gonna come soon if —"

"Don't stop," she gasps, interrupting me. "Please don't stop, Hunter, *please.*"

I don't. I wrap my arm around her waist and slam into her harder, my knees grinding against the wooden floor.

"*Fuck!*" Clem shouts, her eyes closed, her mouth open. "Fuck, Hunter, make me come," she whispers.

Her muscles are gripping and fluttering around me, and she feels so intoxicating that if I lost control right now I'd come my brains out.

I don't. I force myself not to come as I slow down and fuck her hard and *deep*, leaning my head against hers.

"You feel so fucking good," she whispers, locking her hand in my hair. "Don't stop, don't you fucking dare stop."

"Jesus, Clem," I say into her ear.

"I'm gonna come," she gasps, her muscles clenching.

Then she opens her eyes halfway and looks at me.

"I come so fucking hard when you're inside me," she whispers.

Then she comes and I can *feel* how hard she comes, her muscles clamping down around me, her hand clenching my hair as she moans *oh fuck yes* over and over.

I've seen her come a *lot* but I've never seen her lose control like this. I've never felt her come this hard, or look at me like *that.*

I'd walk across the fucking Sahara to make it happen again.

I want to say *you're so fucking beautiful* but she pulls my mouth to hers and kisses me, long and hard, and as she does she rocks back against me and then pulls forward, her muscles squeezing me tight.

She lets me go and does it again, so I put one hand against the wall and let her fuck me fast and hard and in moments I'm at the edge.

"Jesus, Clem, you feel good," I gasp.

Clementine looks over her shoulder, her lips parted, the wickedest look I've ever seen on her face.

"I want you to come inside me," she says.

It's barely out of her mouth before I do, practically exploding deep in her as she keeps moving back and forth, and it's all I can do to stay upright as I release myself into her again and again.

When I finally stop coming I think I'm shaking, and I bend forward gently, kissing Clementine on the shoulder and then on the lips when she turns her head toward me. I wrap my arm around her waist, and I never, ever want to move again.

This is better than it was, I think.

We're covered in sweat and we still haven't moved, still kneeling and leaning against the wall of the lookout, fifty feet off the ground. The thought just comes to me, out of nowhere, but I know it's true.

I put my hand over Hunter's, on my waist, and slide my fingers between his. He kisses the back of my neck, and I wonder if it can be this good off the mountain, down in the real world, where he leaves to go fight fires and I stay in Lodgepole and wonder if he's okay.

You have to try, I think. *You know this is worth it.*

Hunter finally slides out and then sits with his back against the wall, pulling me to his chest. It's a long time before I look at him, then look down at myself, then start laughing.

He just looks at me quizzically.

"We're still both wearing shirts," I say.

He looks down, then starts laughing.

"It's not a good look," I say.

"You weren't complaining," he says, tilting his head back.

I put my hand on the floor to shift my weight, and something pinches in my palm. I look closer in the dying sunlight, holding it up in front of my face, and Hunter takes it in his other hand.

"I think I got a nasty splinter," I say.

"Looks like it," he says. "That from the railing?"

"Yeah, they're old and my hand slipped," I say, poking at the splinter with my other hand.

"I seriously thought you were falling over for a second," he says. "Scared the shit out of me."

"Good thing I didn't," I say. "For one thing, there's no way you *don't* get charged with murder."

"For another thing, I'm glad you're not dead," he teases. "That was my first thought, actually."

I tilt my face toward him and he kisses me.

"Aren't you sweet," I say.

"Come on, let's go fix your splinter," he says. "And maybe tomorrow there will be a whole day where you don't hurt yourself."

"Don't get too excited about that," I say. "I'm a magnet for minor injuries."

I COULD GET the splinter out pretty easily myself, but I let Hunter do it at the tiny table, under the light of a Coleman camping lantern. Then we sit on the cot and watch the glow of the fire, a map in front of us. When the wind blows the right way, I can smell the smoke.

An hour after nightfall, there's a helicopter. It circles the glow a couple of times, then flies away again.

"I guess our work here is done," I say.

"Think they can give us a ride out?" Hunter asks.

It takes me a long time to fall asleep. The cot's uncomfortable, it's too hot with my sleeping bag on and too cold with it off. There's a fire. I'm worrying, stupidly, that Hunter and I can only be together in pieces at a time, as teenagers or in lookout cabins, that going out into the world is what wrecked us before and it's what will wreck us again.

I know I'm being over-dramatic, but that doesn't necessarily help. I think too much, all the time, about everything, and sometimes it leads me here.

Hunter, on the other hand, is dead asleep, one arm dangling off the too-short, too-narrow cot.

———

"Clem."

I blink. It's still dark.

"*Clem.*"

I roll over, Hunter's on one knee next to my cot, his face right in front of mine.

"Are you sleepwalking?" I ask him.

"Someone's coming up the stairs," he says, his voice so low it's barely audible.

We stare at each other for a moment. I wonder again if he's sleepwalking, since I know that happens a lot to people who were in the military.

"Hunter, there's no—"

I hear a tiny, faint creak from outside. In a moment I'm bolt upright in bed, my heart pounding.

"Is there an axe in here?" he asks.

I point at a corner.

"Probably in the crate," I whisper.

There's another creak, so soft it *could* be my imagination.

Hunter pads to the crate, opens it, rummages around for a moment. Then he pulls out a long axe and holds it up, examining it.

There's a creak, closer to the top of the stairs.

It's a serial killer, I think. *Probably dressed like a clown.*

I stand up, heart pounding.

There's a creak at the very top of the stairs, but I don't see anything. Hunter grips the axe tighter. It's completely, perfectly, *totally* silent so it's easy to hear the way the creaks move along the balcony toward the door.

I still don't see anything.

"What is it?" I whisper.

Hunter just shakes his head.

"Get behind me," he says, his voice still low.

It's a ghost, I think wildly. *I'm having a nightmare. Something.*

Then a furry head pops up outside a window.

I shout and jump back. Hunter raises the axe and takes a step forward.

Then we both stop and stare. The mountain lion puts its nose to the glass and sniffs, almost like it's judging a fine wine, and I start laughing. Hunter exhales and lets the axe drop to his side.

"Shit," he says.

"Oh my God," I say, taking a deep breath. "Oh God. I thought it was gonna be a serial killer dressed like a clown."

"Is the door locked?" he asks.

"It's a cat, it can't turn doorknobs," I say.

Hunter checks it anyway. It's locked. The lion stops sniffing the window and sits back on its haunches, staring at us. We stare back.

"I've never seen one up close before," I say.

"That's a good thing," he points out.

Big Sky National Forest has two large predatory mammals: black bears and mountain lions. Black bears are basically over-grown raccoons — they dig through trash, they forage for food, and if you make noise, they run away. They're dangerous if you sneak up on them or get between a mother and cubs, but I've seen dozens of them and I'm fine.

Mountain lions, on the other hand, you *don't* want to see. They're nocturnal, sneaky, quiet, and don't like being around humans. I'm sure dozens of them have seen *me*, but I've only seen a lion once, from across a canyon.

If a mountain lion is letting you see it, you're probably in for a bad time.

I'm pretty happy for the glass right now.

"So..." I start. Hunter looks at me. "What do we do about this guy?"

"This is your department," he says. "If it's not a fire or an enemy combatant, I don't know shit."

The lion shakes its head, then starts walking again. We turn in place as it paces around the lookout to the other side, facing the fire. Then it looks at us again, and I swear it looks *offended*.

"I think we might be in its spot," I say. "It doesn't really seem *worried*."

Hunter crosses his arms in front of his chest and keeps watching it. After a moment, the lion yawns, then lays down, sprawling out on the balcony like a lazy house cat, facing the distant glow of the fire.

"They *do* like being up high," I say. "It makes sense that this guy would come to the lookout to check on his territory."

Hunter takes a step forward and puts one knee on the cot by the windows. The lion tilts its head and looks back at him.

"Hey, this is for people, not cats," he says.

The lion blinks.

"I can't believe that didn't work," I say.

"How do we get it down?" he asks, still looking at the lion.

"I think we wait for it to leave," I say. "I'm sure he'll be gone when we wake up."

He just looks at me incredulously.

"I'm not sure I can sleep with a literal lion at my literal door," he says.

I start laughing.

"What?" he mutters.

"You were in a war zone with *enemy combatants*, and now you fight wildfires, and you don't want to sleep with a kitty cat outside?" I tease.

"It's a *lion*," he says.

"It still can't get in."

He sighs.

"Really, this is amazing," I say. "Most people never see one up close like this, especially in the wild. And I don't think it wants to eat us. I think it's annoyed that we're here, fucking up its sweet lookout spot."

He glances at the lion again and sighs.

"Okay," he says. "But if you get mauled, I told you so."

I step in and kiss him.

"I'm not gonna get mauled," I say.

He leans over the cot again, toward the windows where the lion's hanging out.

"Don't try anything," he says. "I've got an axe and I'll fuck you up."

The lion licks a paw, not even looking at him.

"*And* it's a jerk," he says as I get back in my sleeping bag.

"I'm sorry the mountain lion doesn't respect you," I say.

He gets back onto his cot and looks up at me. I scoot over and kiss his forehead, then ruffle his hair.

"Just enjoy the majesty of nature and go to sleep," I murmur.

———

WHEN I WAKE up in the morning, the lion is gone but the fire is bigger. I can tell before I even open my eyes, because the moment I'm awake I can smell the faint aroma of smoke in the air. I roll over onto my stomach and stare out at it.

The fire's still far away, plenty far enough that we'll hike out in time, even if the wind is blowing it our way, which the wind sock outside tells me it's not. But it's big enough now that I can see the dull orange glow even in the daytime, and it gives me a bad feeling in the pit of my stomach, like a coffee grinder is chewing through my insides.

Hunter's still asleep. I think he was kind of nervous about the whole mountain lion thing, which is fair. They have lots of teeth and they're notoriously dangerous. I didn't even mention the thing that scared me the most, which is that animals will often swarm out of an area before the fire hits it.

I wonder if our lion friend was running and stopped here to keep an eye on things.

I get out of bed quietly and start making instant coffee as Hunter stirs, then finally wakes up and looks at me.

"Is that cat gone?" he asks, sounding groggy.

"Yeah, but the fire's bigger," I say.

He glances over at it, considers it for a moment, then looks back.

"It's not that big," he says. "C'mere."

I put down my coffee, then sit on the side of his cot. He grabs me by the waist and pulls me down.

"Hey!" I say, giggling. "I'd lay down if you *asked*."

"I like dragging you around, though," he says, trying to scoot backwards on the cot because I'm falling off this side.

"Caveman," I say, and try to wriggle in, but that's not happening either.

"These things are tiny," Hunter mutters.

"Yeah," I say.

He frowns at me, his hand in the curve of my waist. He's stroking me with his thumb, absentmindedly.

"You okay?" he asks.

"I'm fine," I say, trying to deflect.

Be fucking honest, I think, and I take a deep breath.

"I'm worried about the fire," I say.

"It's just a fire," he says.

"I know, but…" I trail off, closing my eyes. "I don't know, I have a weird bad feeling about it, and I'm worried for you, even though I know you've been doing this for a while and you're fine."

And I don't know what's going to happen once we're down there, and fire season is over, because having a lot of sex in a fire lookout isn't the same as arguing over whose turn it is to do the dishes.

I decide to save that batch of feelings for *after* the fire is dealt with.

As of yesterday, it was about 95% certain that, if this fire got bigger, the Canyon Country Hotshots would be on the front lines. They're already here and they're the best, so of *course* they're going.

Well, it got bigger, and I can put two and two together.

Hunter pulls me close and I tuck my head under his chin.

"I'll dig ditches for a few days," he says. "And if I get really lucky, I'll get to start a controlled burn. Those are the most fun."

"I know, I know," I say.

"I'm coming back to you," he says.

I sigh.

"Once fire season is over, I mean," he says. "It's probably time to move out of my parents' guest house."

"That was fast," I say.

Hunter just laughs. He's playing with my hair behind my back, gently tugging at my scalp.

"We first sat next to each other in chemistry class almost a decade ago," he says. "How long do I have to know you before I get to decide I want to make it work this time?"

I squirm.

"It's not gonna get *worse* than me saying I never loved you," he points out.

"It could," I say. "You could have a long affair with a coworker and then tell everyone that I'm the one who's been sleeping around."

Hunter frowns.

"My parents," I say quietly. "Sorry."

"I'm not gonna sleep with a coworker," he says. "They're all hairy, they smell bad, and you've got a much nicer rack."

I laugh.

"You were saying we've already dramatically screamed at each other over video chat, so it probably won't get worse?" I say.

"Right. So I'm moving to Lodgepole and keeping your bed warm until you decide it's been long enough that we can be seen together in public," he teases.

"Is *that* the plan?" I ask.

"Winning my way into your heart via orgasm?" he says, grinning. "There are worse avenues."

Now his hand is pressing into the small of my back, suddenly *much* more deliberate.

"I could just start now, if you wanted," he says.

"We're supposed to be hiking down," I point out.

Hunter rolls over on top of me, pushing me toward the center of the very narrow bed, and I wrap my legs around his hips.

"We'll hike fast," he says.

We don't leave the lookout for another hour.

TWENTY-TWO

HUNTER

The hike down *does* go faster than the hike up, even if we leave later than we meant to. Clementine says her ankle is fine, or at least *almost* completely better, so even though I can't help but keep an eye on her as we make our way down, nothing terrible happens.

She's quiet, but I am too. I'm ticking off equipment in my head, thinking about what the plan's going to be. Trying to take mental notes of anything in particular I might have seen or heard while I was up there, anything I know because I grew up in the area.

I'm probably the only one who's hiked into the Spires, I realize.

Suddenly, I feel a lot more useful. As one of the newest guys on the hotshot team with only two seasons done, I do a lot more learning than teaching. Some of the guys who've been doing it for ten, fifteen years seem to have vast encyclopedias of knowledge stored away in their heads, and I never feel like I have anything to offer.

But this time, I might.

With about a mile left to go, Clem's portable radio suddenly crackles. The batteries on those things are shit, so they don't use them much, but she looks surprised and answers.

"McKinnon," she says.

"What'd you name the fire?" Mike asks.

Clementine doesn't respond right away. She just looks at me for a long moment.

"*Harold*," I whisper.

"The Saturn Fire," she says.

"All right, thanks," Mike says. "Over and out."

"Harold's a much better name," I say.

"I'm not naming a wildfire Harold," she says, and pokes me in the stomach. I grab her wrist, pull her toward me, and kiss her just because I can.

I don't know when I decided I was moving to be with her. I just woke up and knew I was going to, even though I think she's a little more cautious about this than I am.

It's not that I don't have doubts, or that I think it'll magically be perfect. I stayed in a war zone just to avoid her because she broke my heart so hard, for fuck's sake.

But some things are worth the effort.

"Oh good, it's still here," Clementine says when we see the Forest Service truck parked at the end of the fire road.

"Do these get stolen?" I ask, slinging my pack into the back.

"I'm sure it's happened," she says, turning the key. The AC comes on full blast, still hot, and Clementine cranks it down. "But can you imagine what a pain in the ass it would be if we got down here and there was no truck? I'm kind of relieved every time."

On the drive back, we talk about mountain lions and her favorite trees. We talk about the best route to Yellowstone, and about how to sneak into Canada if you *really* need to. I try to explain the appeal of the *Fast and Furious* movies, though Clementine remains skeptical.

We don't talk about *us*, or what's going to happen, or whether any of this is a good idea. It's all I've been thinking about for nearly a week, and I can't think about it anymore. It's happening, full steam ahead, and I don't give a shit about the rest.

When she parks at the ranger station, the place is already hopping. We grab our packs and go inside, where Mandy is sitting behind a reception desk with a taxidermied raccoon on it.

"There you are!" she says, her perky voice sounding just a little *too* chipper.

"It was a nine-mile hike," Clementine says.

Mandy's eyes dart from me to Clementine, and I think she blushes, just a little.

"Oh, I know," she says quickly. "I just meant it's great that you're back and all. Trout misses you."

Clementine puts her pack on the floor and leans her elbows against the counter.

"Where are we with everything?" she asks.

Mandy starts clicking away on the computer, and Clementine leans over.

"We've started clearing out the backcountry campgrounds," Mandy says, pointing to her computer screens. "There's a couple of old structures out there that we also checked, because sometimes people decide they're going to live there without telling anyone…"

I look at the taxidermied raccoon. Whoever did it did a pretty good job. Looks real natural.

"That's Sebastién," Mandy says, and I look up when I realize she's talking to me.

"The raccoon?"

She nods.

"Fancy," I say, looking back down at him.

"Your crew is in the amphitheater," Mandy says. "Down that hall and then out the door that says *No Exit*. Ignore the sign, we should change that."

"Of course," I say.

"I'll see you later?" Clementine says.

"For sure," I say, lifting my pack again.

I want to kiss her goodbye, but suddenly it seems strange and unprofessional, and like maybe I should let Clementine tell her coworkers what's going on before just laying one on her in the workplace.

"Have a good meeting," she says, and smiles.

"Enjoy your campground evacuations," I say, heading to the amphitheater through the No Exit door.

———

PORTER'S STANDING in front of the small amphitheater with a map tacked to a rolling whiteboard, the other guys all seated around on wooden benches. It's hot out, but at least there's a sunshade.

I take a seat on a bench next to Silas and put my pack down. He looks over and nods at me.

"What'd I miss?" I mutter.

"The Saturn fire jumped Gold Canyon and now it's burning up the other side pretty fast," he says. "There are some local guys doing controlled burns and digging fire breaks to the south, but the fire's got a hundred or so miles before it gets to anything in that direction."

I look at the laminated topo map up on the board. Porter's drawn a red shape around the chunk of national forest that includes the Spires. There's nothing much to the south of the red splotch, but to the east are a couple of small towns leading down out of the canyon. Then Ashlake, my hometown, at the mouth.

The towns to the east of the fire aren't as far away. Just looking at the map, I can tell they're in that uncertain gray zone that we all hate so much.

If the Saturn Fire keeps moving in the direction it's going, Eaglevale, Coldwater, and the other tiny towns that dot the river along the canyon will be totally untouched. But if the wind changes direction, they'll be right in the fire's path, and whatever fire team gets sent there is gonna have a hell of a time with that terrain.

I lean forward and crack the knuckles on my right hand, studying the map. I know why we're not digging fire breaks and doing controlled burns with the local guys.

It's because, if the wind *does* change, we're the unlucky bastards who'll be keeping Eaglevale and Coldwater from burning down, and I'd be lying if I said I'm not a little excited about it.

"We're cooling our heels until this thing gets hot?" I ask Silas.

He looks over at me and grins.

"You got it," he says, still keeping his voice low. "The minute the wind changes, we're on our way up."

A thrill goes through me. It's not that I hope the towns burn down, or that people have to be evacuated, or that, God forbid, anyone dies. Hell, I'm gonna do everything in my power to keep all that from happening. But it's been a long fire season, and most of it's been boring and backbreaking: digging, controlled burns, sleep, do it again.

If the Saturn Fire burns east, it'll be a *challenge*. An incredibly dangerous challenge, but I've never let that stop me, and right now I'm itching for something like this.

Porter is pointing at a column of numbers along the side of the whiteboard: temperature, wind speed, dew point, and humidity. I force myself to pay attention. It's hard, though, because my mind is elsewhere, flying all over the place.

To Spineside Trail, the only way into the Spires. To Eaglevale and Coldwater, both perched on low peaks in the middle of a dense forest with only one road out. To how hard it is to predict where a fire will go even on open prairie, never mind terrain like that.

To Clementine this morning, her body against mine on that tiny cot in the fire lookout. I think about how I wanted to stop the world for that moment and stay there, alone with her, in that perfect stillness.

"Casden," Porter says. I realize everyone is looking at me, and I'm staring off into space.

"Yes," I say.

Now there are two men up front: Porter, and an older, gray-haired, wiry forest ranger.

"You're familiar with the area, right?"

"Grew up in Ashlake, still live there when I'm not with you all," I say.

I look at the map again. Now Spineside Trail is highlighted, a winding, switchback-filled green line into the canyon.

"And I've hiked into the Spires," I say.

"Good man," the ranger says, nodding like he approves. "Useful to be sending someone who knows the territory at least a little. Get your pants on straight and your shoes tied right."

This *must* be Randy.

The other hotshots all look politely baffled, like they're not quite sure whether that was a compliment or not.

"Thanks," I say.

"Come sit down here by me," Randy says, pointing at a wooden bench. "You can help me out when my memory starts to go a little blurry."

It's weird, but I just do as he asks. He seems like a charming weirdo, and I try to humor charming weirdos.

"All right," Randy begins. "The first problem with Spineside is it's gonna be about two feet wide. Sometimes less. Sometimes a little more, but expect to get real up close and personal with some rock face when you get in there. Not too personal, mind you."

Confused laughter ripples through the crowd, and I try not to smile.

TWENTY-THREE

CLEMENTINE

The moment the door closes behind Hunter, Mandy looks around furtively, then leans over the counter toward me.

"Clementine, can we *please* talk?" she stage-whispers.

Fuck. I wish I'd answered the door when she knocked, because now that's another thing I have to explain. For a moment I consider telling her that I've got *really* important work to get done and maybe we can discuss this later, but I don't have anything that can't wait five minutes.

Plus, I'm dealing with things like an adult now, remember?

I put my elbows on the counter and lean down.

"About Hunter?" I ask.

The door opens behind me, and I straighten up. Two other rangers walk past us, and when they're gone, Mandy gives a small, impatient sigh.

"Not here," she says, still whispering. "Come on."

Now I'm nervous, because I have no idea what she's gonna say. Did she hook up with Hunter before the spaghetti dinner or something? Did she see him kick Trout?

He didn't do something with her after the night with the telescopes, did he? He seemed upset that I was gone and didn't even text...

We walk down a hallway and Mandy pulls open a door, looks around again, and steps inside, turning on the light.

I stop short.

"That's the supply closet," I say, assuming she opened the wrong door.

"Come *on*," she says, so I shrug and step inside. She pulls the door shut.

"Why are we in a closet?" I say, keeping my voice low in case someone walks by.

"I need to talk to you *privately*," she says. She's a little shorter than me, and the closet's not very big, so I feel like her wide brown eyes are filling my entire field of vision.

"About Hunter?"

"What's up with you guys?" she asks, blinking.

"We're... dating," I say, and take a deep breath, getting ready to tell the whole long story.

"Since when?" Mandy asks. "When did you *start* dating?"

I almost laugh at the question, because it seems so strange, but Mandy looks so serious that I don't.

"Two nights ago, I guess," I say, slowly. "But we were..."

Mandy heaves a huge sigh of relief, cutting me off again. She's not usually this weird and impatient, but I think between whatever she's going to tell me about Hunter and the Saturn Fire, she's kind of stressed right now.

"So you weren't dating yet the day there was that big thunderstorm?" she asks.

I cross my arms in front of myself.

"You *have* to get to the point," I say.

"I would *never* flirt with someone else's boyfriend," she says, her eyes still wide and completely serious. "I just don't want you to think that I'm someone who would *do* that."

Oh my God, just tell me whatever you're going to tell me, I think. Now I'm seriously annoyed, because I have a million things to do and dragging something out of Mandy isn't on that list.

"Did you and Hunter do something or not?" I say, irritated.

She gasps.

"No!" she breathes.

My stomach unclenches.

"I didn't realize that you were interested in him, because I wouldn't have started flirting with him," she says. "Clementine, *please* don't think that I was trying to steal your boyfriend, or that I'm some kind of floozy, because it would break my heart if you thought I was that kind of person."

There it is. She just wants to stop feeling guilty, and she wants to make sure everyone knows she didn't do anything wrong. It's not *quite* the same as a heartfelt apology, but she didn't know about Hunter and I, so it's not like she owes me one.

"Of course not," I say. "I didn't tell you."

"You just seemed so upset," she goes on.

"It's a long story," I say, because now that this is over, I just want to get out of that closet.

"You weren't mad with me?"

For a moment I feel bad, because she really *is* sweet, the kind of person who can't bear the thought that someone might be angry with her.

"Not at all," I reassure her, then open the door back into the office.

Jennifer gives us a weird look but doesn't say anything.

———

LATE THAT AFTERNOON, I'm staring at my computer monitor between my fingers, resting my chin on the palms of my hands. All the map symbols have stopped making sense, and my to-do list is two haphazard sheets of printer paper, but most of the things on it are crossed off.

Emergency phone calls: made. Emergency shelter in case the fire turns: available, with volunteers on notice. I've made sure the hospital in Ashlake is alerted to the situation. I've arranged for all broadcast media on the east side of the Spires to warn people, I've sent hundreds of emails with the evacuation checklist, and I've made dozens of phone calls.

At this point, I almost *hope* the wind changes, because I worked hard, dammit. If the fire keeps going the way it is right now — and it probably will — then I spent a day doing useless preparation.

Well, not useless. Completely vital, even if the fire doesn't turn. And I don't *really* want it to, obviously. Towns could burn down.

Plus, Hunter's crew is still here. They haven't been sent to help contain the fire to the south, and no one can say what they *will* be doing. I have a bad feeling they're being held in reserve in case things get really hairy.

"Okay," I say out loud, and stand. I've been sitting for hours, and my butt is starting to feel like it might *actually* be part of the chair.

I stretch a few times, still standing in my cubicle, reaching way over my head and then touching my toes. I jump up and down a few times, do some arm circles, then run in place a little, all with my eyes closed because I've been staring at a screen all day.

"Okay, okay," I mutter again, stretching my hands against each other. "Time to tackle some fuckin' road closures."

I open my eyes, and then I jump a mile in the air because Hunter is leaning against one wall of my cube, grinning at me like an asshole.

"Jesus!" I hiss.

"Hey there," he says.

"Shit, how long were you standing there?"

I put my hand over my chest, my heart still pounding with the surprise. He just shrugs.

"Not that long," he says.

"I've been sitting all day," I explain, glancing around the room full of cubicles. No one else can see us from where we're standing, so I lean in and give him a quick, chaste, quiet kiss.

Hunter puts one hand on my hip, drums his fingers for a moment, then removes it. I laugh a little.

"Yeah, I haven't really mentioned this to anyone besides Mandy yet," I say, keeping my voice low even though most people are out of the office right now. "I don't tend to keep my coworkers updated on my romance situation, and I also haven't gotten the chance because there's this fire..."

"And here I thought it was because you were ashamed of me," he teases.

"*So* ashamed," I say. "Can you imagine my reputation if they found out I was involved with one of the hotshot crew?"

"You may as well shave your head and move into a cave in the mountains," he agrees, somberly.

"I'll get on that as soon as I send out these road closure bulletins," I say. "What's going on with you guys?"

"Nothing yet," he says, his deep blue eyes looking at me steadily. "If the fire keeps burning south, we'll head out sometime tomorrow."

I nod, because I can read between the lines of his half-answer.

"And if it turns east you're the ones they'll call?"

"Clem, I'll be fine."

"I know."

"Lorenzo's is bringing over a truck full of free Italian food in an hour," he says. "You and Mandy and Lucy want to come by?"

"Hey, Clementine," Jennifer's voice shouts from across the room.

I stand on my toes and look over the wall. I guess no one else is around.

"Yeah?" I call.

"Did you talk to that guy who had all the turkeys in his freezer and was really concerned—"

She pops her head over her own cubicle wall, sees Hunter standing there, and stops.

"Sorry, I thought we were alone in here," she says, coming out of her cube. She walks around to where we're standing, laughing a little to herself. "Hi, I'm Jennifer, the ranger coordinator."

"Hunter," he says. "I'm with the hotshots."

"You guys like your plaque?" Jennifer asks. "I was supposed to give it out but then there was this raccoon in my house, and you know how *that* goes."

She waves one hand in the air, like everyone gets raccoons in their houses sometimes.

"The plaque is great," Hunter says, putting his hands in his pockets. "How'd the raccoon get in?"

"Dog door," she sighs. "We're both gone all day, and if she can't get out she'll just pee on the rug right *by* the door. We tried those pee pads, but..."

Jennifer shakes her head.

"Gertrude isn't the sharpest knife in the drawer," I say gently.

Hunter's eyebrows raise at the name Gertrude.

"Except when it comes to stealing underpants," I go on.

"I see her reputation precedes her," Jennifer says.

"You know, it wouldn't be hard to rig up an RFID-activated lock on the dog door," Hunter says. "Put something on Gertrude's collar, and it'd unlock if she was within a couple feet, but the raccoons couldn't get in."

Jennifer crosses her arms and leans against the wall of my cubicle.

"Go on," she says.

"Jen, turkeys," I say.

She points at Hunter.

"I want to hear more about this dog door, but I gotta talk to Clementine," she says. "How do I find you?"

"Take my number," he says. "I'll be back in town when fire season's over."

I just sit there and watch my boyfriend and my boss exchange information. I'm a little jealous, but I'm jealous that he can just *talk* to people like this and make friends so easily, not that he's talking to Jennifer.

If that were me I'd probably still be fumbling over *RFID-activated*.

Hunter puts his phone back in his pocket, then looks at me.

"See you at dinner?" he asks.

"For sure," I say.

Then we nod at each other, because I'm not sure how else to say goodbye in front of Jennifer. We both watch him go, and then she looks at me, one eyebrow raised.

"*That's* certainly none of my business," she says.

"Nope," I agree.

"And I'd never ask unprofessional questions," she goes on.

I laugh.

"Good," I say.

"But you could do a *lot* worse than a cute firefighter with a nice butt," she finishes.

I blush, even though I'm still laughing.

"Thanks," I say. "Turkeys?"

"Right," she says. "This guy is really freaking out that all his turkeys are gonna thaw, and he wants to know if there will be freezing facilities if he gets evacuated..."

———

WE SORT OUT THE guy with the turkey problem. I update the road closures. I keep all the other ranger stations abreast of what's happening, and then *finally*, ninety minutes later, I get to leave work and head home.

I take the world's fastest shower, because I haven't bathed in three days, and then I frown at myself in the mirror. I feel like some kind of bedraggled rodent, because I've got circles under my eyes, my hair is wet, and I just *look* stressed.

I'm worried about Hunter fighting a dangerous fire, but of course I'm worried about that. I *should* be worried about that. If I weren't a little worried I'd be some kind of monster.

But beneath that, I can feel a familiar cold, raw sensation gnawing at me, and I hate it. It's the tiny voice that whispers *he likes doing things that take him away from you*, the voice that whispers *he's only here until he figures out you're not very exciting*.

I try not to listen to it, but it won't *fucking* shut up.

Still, it used to be much, much louder. It used to shout at me when he was in the Marines, and thank God, it's not nearly that loud now. I wish it would shut up entirely, but no matter how wrong I know it is, it won't.

I take a deep breath, then point at myself in the mirror.

"Quit it," I say to my reflection. Then I swipe on some mascara so I don't look so tired, get dressed, and head next door.

———

AFTER THREE DAYS in the woods eating granola bars, oatmeal, and freeze-dried spaghetti, I eat two servings of lasagna, chicken cacciatore, meatballs, and then have cannoli for dessert. It's delicious, and all the guys are in high spirits, laughing and shouting and eating an *incredible* amount of pasta.

After dinner, a bunch of us sit around the couches in the living room and bullshit for a while. Hunter puts his arm around me, and no one blinks an eye, so I lean against him a little and listen to the guys talk about which dive bars in the western states have the strongest, cheapest drinks.

"What was that place in Deadwood called?" one guy is saying. He's slouched on a love seat, his feet on the coffee table. "Something saloon, probably."

"The Scarlet Lady Saloon?" someone else suggests.

"Nah, that's in Idaho. Outside Moscow, maybe?"

"Maybe it was just the Deadwood Saloon," the first guy says. "I just remember I got tanked there off of Jack and Coke. That cute redhead bartender practically had to pull me back to that shitty motel that put us up."

Silas, the guy I played baggo with last Saturday, laughs.

"She wasn't that cute," he says.

"She wasn't that redheaded," Hunter says.

The guy who was talking about the saloon just grins and shrugs.

"She did drag my sorry ass home," he says. "That's what counts, right?"

"Yeah, that's true love," Silas says, leaning back in an easy chair.

"For my money it's the Wildcat's Lair," says Daniel, the only other guy whose name I can remember. They keep introducing themselves, and I keep forgetting. "In beautiful Elko, Nevada."

At least three of the guys, Hunter included, just groan.

"I've been there," I pipe up.

The conversation stops awkwardly for a moment, like they're not quite sure what to do with a new member, and I immediately feel like there's a spotlight pointing directly on my face.

"What were you doing in Elko?" Daniel finally asks. "And what were you being punished for?"

I laugh, even though I can feel my face turning bright pink, because they were having a nice conversation about getting drunk and I interrupted.

"I had a conference for work," I say.

"You're the forest ranger, right?" a guy whose name I don't know asks.

"I'm one of them," I say.

"And there was a conference in Elko?"

I pull one foot onto the couch in front of me, still *very* aware that everyone's looking at me. I kind of wish I hadn't said anything.

"It was on, um, the microbiomes particular to the high desert region," I say.

"That's the crust, right?" Daniel asks.

"Yeah," I say, a little surprised that he knows about this. "Cryptobiotic crust. There's a lot of it near Elko, so we'd look at crusts during the day and drink at the Wildcat's Lair at night."

"You don't have to look *that* surprised that I know about desert crust," Daniel says, lifting his eyebrows.

I turn a deeper shade of pink.

"I wasn't surprised," I say.

"Mhm," he says.

"I mean, I'm surprised whenever *anyone* knows about it because most people don't really know a lot about desert bacteria? I only know because of my job. Otherwise I'd be clueless as a babe in the woods. Or a babe in the desert, I guess."

I can't believe I opened my mouth just to call Daniel dumb, I think. *Shit.*

Shit shit shit.

"Daniel, quit being an asshole, she's new," Hunter says.

Daniel just laughs.

"He's not *being* an asshole, it's just his shitty personality," Silas says, also grinning.

"Yeah, I can't help it," Daniel says, then looks back at me. "Sorry, I have a shitty personality."

"At least you know what desert crust is," I say. I'm still blushing, but I'm relieved that at least I wasn't being the asshole.

"And thank God for *that*," Silas says.

Hunter strokes my shoulder with his thumb, and I feel some of my anxiety dissipate. He's acting so *normal* about this, like of course he's got a girlfriend over at the house, and none of the other guys seem to even notice.

I, on the other hand, had a weird conversation in a supply closet at work, and then completely clammed up when my very nice boss tried to ask about Hunter. I'm doing *spectacularly* on the "not making it weird" front.

"Did the Wildcat's Lair get out the moonshine for the rangers?" Silas asks me.

"Not that I know of," I say.

"Maybe it's the desert crust that made that stuff so lethal," Hunter offers.

"Everybody listen up," says a voice from the door. We all turn, but no one stands.

Hunter's boss is standing there, a dark-haired guy in his forties who's just starting to go gray. The living room goes silent, and I hold my breath, because I have a feeling the announcement isn't "There are cupcakes in the kitchen."

"I just got the call that a cold front is moving through," he says. "And there's likely to be a pretty big shift in weather patterns over the next few days, so we're heading up north to Eaglevale an hour before dawn tomorrow. Briefing in twenty."

Then he walks off, and the pit of my stomach goes cold.

The guys in the room all exhale at the same time, like they've got one set of lungs. Hunter rubs one hand over his head and starts laughing, and then so do the rest.

"God, I thought we were gonna be stuck here forever," Silas says.

"No kidding," says Hunter. "Send us or don't, just fucking decide. I can't stand the sitting around."

"I know it," Daniel says, standing. "See you guys in twenty."

"I should get going," I say, uncurling my legs, standing, and sliding my shoes back on. Hunter gets off the couch too, but I can't bring myself to look him in the eye right now.

"It was nice meeting you guys, maybe I'll see you around again?" I say.

They both stand, and weirdly, we all shake hands.

"Have a good one, Clementine," Silas says, and then I walk for the door, Hunter following me.

"Walk me home?" I ask him, trying to smile, but it feels mechanical.

"Of course," he says, but he looks puzzled.

We head through the foyer. I wave goodbye to some of the other guys, and then I'm outside in the cool night air.

"Clem," Hunter says, the moment the door is shut.

I walk down the porch stairs and onto the sidewalk before I answer.

He's happy about it, I think, over and over. *He didn't like being here, sitting around. With me.*

"Yeah?"

He grabs my arm and stops me.

"Say something, you can't just go quiet and walk away."

I want to wrench my arm away and shout *watch me* but instead I take a deep breath.

"I'm worried about you guys, because the Saturn Fire seems pretty bad," I say. At least it's *part* of the truth.

"I'll be *fine*," he says. "I'm always fine."

"Yeah," I mutter.

"*What*," he says.

I just shake my head.

"And if I'm not, you can find someone who knows about desert crust," he says.

"What the hell?" I say, my voice starting to rise. I swallow hard, trying to keep it down.

We stare at each other for a moment, and I can sense that we're on the knife's edge, one more word away from a stupid fight that I don't actually want to have.

"Nothing," he says, crossing his arms over his chest, looking away. "Sorry. Just forget it."

I close my eyes and breathe deep.

It's not about you, I remind myself. *Almost nothing is about you, really, so chill the fuck out.*

"I'm sorry," I say, though the words come out stiffly. "You're leaving and I don't know when I'm going to see you again."

"I know," he says. "That was an asshole thing to say, I'm sorry."

We stand there, awkwardly, on the sidewalk for another moment.

"I'll see you in a couple weeks, okay?" he says.

I just nod.

We kiss, but it's not quite right, too stiff and strange and mechanical. It's almost worse than if we hadn't had a goodbye kiss at all.

"Stay safe," I say, and climb the steps to my porch.

"See you soon," he says, and I go inside my house.

Then I close the door, put my forehead against the wall, and think: *fuck. Fuck. FUCK.*

TWENTY-FOUR

HUNTER

I can't fucking believe I said the thing about desert crust. Now I'm not gonna see Clementine for weeks, and the last conversation we had was an almost-argument because I'm goddamn *jealous*.

This is familiar, too, in the worst kind of way, because I feel like I can't give her what she needs. She goes to conferences about bacteria and I dig holes in dirt for a living, and sometimes, it feels like there's no way she won't get bored with me sooner or later.

And I fucking *know* picking fights with her won't help. Especially not now, but then I went and almost did it anyway, out of some terrible self-sabotaging instinct.

I head back inside, into the kitchen, where Porter's got everyone assembled, two guys holding up the laminated map like a makeshift bulletin board. On it, the towns of Eaglevale and Coldwater are big black squares, and Porter points at them.

"These fire breaks are gonna be our first priority," he says. "Emergency personnel have already started evacuations, but we need to save as many homes as we can..."

———

It feels like it takes me hours to finally fall asleep. I'm thinking about the time that I hiked into the Spires, and how hard it was even without equipment. I'm thinking about building fire breaks on rocky, steep terrain like that.

I'm thinking that maybe I should go to Clementine's house before we leave, even though it'll be 5:15 in the morning, and apologize, because I hate the thought of saying goodbye like *this*, the weight of things unsaid hanging in the air like an axe over my head.

By 4:45 a.m., nearly everyone is awake and out of bed. I'm not the only one who could barely sleep, and even though we all get dressed and prep our equipment without talking too much, the air feels charged, electric, like a spark could make everything explode.

I haul stuff outside to where the trucks are waiting. We load them, as quietly as we can, so we don't wake anyone up. I keep looking at the house next door where Clementine lives, hoping to see a lighted window that I can take as a sign.

Her house stays dark. I load more stuff, then start checking that it's all secured, that we've got everything. Everyone mills around a little. None of us are very good at *waiting*, and once everything is loaded and checked and triple-checked, we stand around, kicking the sidewalk, hands in our pockets.

I look at her windows again and again. I think that maybe I should let sleeping dogs lie, and when I get back it'll be better. We'll talk it over then, like adults.

But then I remember our uncomfortable, stiff kiss. The way she couldn't look at me, the way I lashed out at her for no reason, and I *know* I can't say goodbye to her like that.

I turn to Silas, who's standing next to me, lost in his own thoughts.

"I'll be back in five minutes," I say.

He just nods tensely. It's hard to be *about* to head into a fire zone. Almost easier to just be there.

I mount Clementine's porch steps as my phone dials her number, because I don't want to wake her roommates if I don't have to. The call takes a few moments to go through, and as it starts ringing, I stand on her porch, my stomach in knots, hoping she answers.

It feels like an eternity, but then the ringing stops.

"Hey," she says softly, and her voice comes through the phone and also through the front door.

Before I can answer, it swings open, and she's standing there, her phone up to her ear.

"Oh," she says, still talking into the phone.

"Surprise," I say into mine, and she smiles, closing her door behind her.

"I was about to come say goodbye," she says, keeping her voice low, clicking her phone off.

She looks away, at the trucks with the guys standing around.

"I didn't want to leave things like we did," she starts, then pauses.

"I'm sorry I was an asshole," I blurt out. "It's the same bullshit. I can do better."

Clementine just looks surprised. She pushes her bangs off her forehead.

"Me too," she finally says. "I can be petty and jealous and insecure, and…"

She shuffles her feet against the porch floor.

"And I don't really like that about myself," she finishes.

"I don't *want* to be away from you," I say. "I wish there was a third option, to have this job but come home at night."

She smiles faintly.

"I don't care if you don't know what cryptobiotic crust is," she says. "You've never bored me, which is more than I can say for most people."

I step forward and put my arms around her.

"This was stupid," I say.

"Yeah," she agrees. "I promise to never have stupid feelings again."

I just laugh, and so does she.

"Same," I say.

Behind me, I hear a truck start, and I turn my head. The guys are milling around with slightly more purpose, and even though a few of them glance over, they look away quickly, like they're faintly embarrassed.

"You should go," Clementine says.

I kiss her, and this time it feels normal, her lips firm but yielding under mine, her arms tight around me. A *proper* goodbye kiss.

We separate and I kiss her forehead.

"I'll call you when I can," I say.

"Wait," she says, and reaches into her pocket. She holds up a small, smooth, gray rock.

"We've already got plenty of ways to start a fire," I say. "We're not *actual* cavemen."

Clementine rolls her eyes, but she's smiling.

"It's from the waterfall," she says. "Just fucking take it and think nice thoughts about me once in a while."

She puts it in my hand, small and heavy, warm from being in her pocket.

"Can I think nice thoughts about you a lot?" I ask.

"Don't go overboard," she teases.

"Like when I'm alone in my tent, and I'm dead tired but still too wired to sleep—"

Another truck starts behind me, and we both turn to look at it.

"*Yes*, you can jerk off thinking about me," Clementine laughs, then kisses me before I can respond.

"Did that anyway," I say.

"*Go*," she says, pushing me toward the porch steps. "I don't wanna hear that Eaglevale burned down because one of the fire crew wouldn't quit talking to his girlfriend."

I grin, kiss her hand, and head down the steps.

Minutes later we're driving out of Lodgepole, the sky just barely starting to lighten at the eastern edge, the truck silent. Daniel and I are in the back seat, Silas in the front as we head north.

Daniel turns to me.

"Clementine's nice," he says.

"Yeah, she seemed cool," Silas says from the front.

"Thanks," I say.

We fall quiet again.

THE WHOLE WAY UP, we listen to reports from the people already in Eaglevale — a few forest rangers, the Ashlake Volunteer Fire Department. They're bad, the Saturn Fire's bigger and faster than anyone predicted.

We should have left earlier, maybe even yesterday, and the feeling that I was in Lodgepole eating Italian food and laughing with Clementine gnaws at me. Logically, I know that fires are nearly impossible to predict, and that everyone always does their best, but deep down, the thought that someone might lose their home because I wasn't fast enough is hard to shake.

We all ride along in tense silence, listening to slightly staticky voices talk about the Saturn Fire making its way down the canyon, watching the smoke billow out of the forest north of us.

The air gets a little thicker, and the mountains in the distance have a dull haze in front of them, the sickly yellow color of wood putty. Bits of ash collect on the ground. When the sun comes up it's a dull, glowing, nuclear orange, and as it rises it becomes a blood-red ball in the sky.

Heading toward a fire always feels apocalyptic, almost like I'm in a movie where society has broken down and everyone lives in cars in the desert or something. The light is always the color of sunset, even if it's seven o'clock in the morning, and it makes the primal, instinctual part of my brain whisper *it's nearly dark, it's nearly dark* all day.

I thought I'd get used to it after the first few times, but I never did. I guess humans aren't wired that way.

As we get close, helicopter and drop planes start buzzing overhead, more and more often. The flame retardant powder they drop combines with the smoke and turns everything a little redder. It feels a little more like the end of the world. It feels like that every time, but the end hasn't come yet.

The truck doesn't even stop in Eaglevale. A ranger wearing a big hat and an orange safety vest just waves us past some sort of checkpoint, and we head down a rough road and into the canyon. We drive until the road runs out, and then we park behind the other Canyon Country Hotshot trucks.

No one talks much as we load up with our gear. I think we all feel the same way right now, the buzz and excitement of last night gone, traded in for a grim determination about the task ahead.

The *first* thing we have to do is hike down a tricky trail, carrying seventy pounds of equipment: drip torches, rhinos, chainsaws, plus food and water. Once we get there, then we get to actually start work.

Another truck pulls up behind us. Guys pile out. I double check that I've got everything, that it's all firmly strapped to my back.

I run my fingertips over the rock Clementine gave me, safe in a small zippered pocket, and for a moment I let myself think about tossing her into the pool, about lying with her on a warm rock in the sun and teasing her about male strippers.

Then we get moving.

TWENTY-FIVE

CLEMENTINE

I watch Hunter drive off, and surprisingly, it feels okay. Sure, it could feel better. We could be asleep in my bed right now, snuggled together, but that's not what's happening.

This is. And, honestly: it's okay.

The land line starts ringing almost the moment I walk back into the house, and I rush to grab the receiver since Lucy and Mandy are still asleep. I don't even have to answer to know it's not going to be a good phone call.

"Get your rangin' hat on," Randy says.

I glare out the window at the darkness for a full two seconds before I respond, because I'm tired and it's early and I'm stressed on several fronts, and all of that isn't putting me in the mood for Randy's weird shit right now.

"My ranging hat?" I finally ask. "Are we evacuating?"

"You got it," he says. "This here sheet says you're to report to the Eaglevale checkpoint and then receive further instructions, which I assume are gonna be, 'tell people to leave because there's a fire.'"

"Where's the checkpoint?" I ask, my stomach tightening.

I've only had to evacuate people once, when there was a big fire in the Lolo National Forest, a few hundred miles to the west, and the Forest Service over there needed all the help they could get.

I hated having to do it. I became a ranger because I like being outdoors, because I think plants and fungi are interesting, and because I don't mind going for stretches without seeing another human.

Telling people that they need to leave their homes, *now*, and that I don't know if they'll ever be able to come back isn't really my strong suit. Even the people who are well-prepared, packed, and ready to leave are pretty emotional about it.

When I have to convince someone that they need to go or they might die? It doesn't get much worse.

"There's only the one road into Eaglevale," Randy says. "You're not gonna miss the checkpoint, I promise."

"Right," I say.

"Grab Lucy and get a move on," he suggests, and then hangs up without saying goodbye.

He's also stressed and worried, I remind myself. *Everyone is today. Be nice. Just be nice.*

We'll see.

It's a long drive. A couple hours to Ashlake, where I grew up, then down a twisting, winding mountain road until we finally climb into Eaglevale. The fire's gotten bigger and moved faster than anyone thought it might, and with the wind blowing east the sky is an unsettling yellow color, the sun an angry red ball in the middle.

It creeps me out. I always feel like I'm in some horror movie when there are fires around. The light looks wrong, the air smells wrong, and everything just feels *strange*.

I've got Lucy and another ranger in the car, but we don't say much on the drive. I know none of us are looking forward to this, and talking about how much it's going to suck isn't going to make it better.

"They sent the hotshots in this morning, right?" Lucy asks suddenly.

"Yeah," I say. "I think they're headed into the canyon. Last I heard, anyway."

"I hope they're okay," she says, looking straight ahead out the windshield. "This is a shitty thing to happen, especially right at the end of fire season. I bet they'd rather go home."

I swallow, then nod.

"I bet so," I say, and then we keep driving in silence, each thinking our own thoughts.

At the checkpoint we pull over, and we're herded to a card table manned by a no-nonsense woman wearing a traffic-cone-orange shirt. At least she's visible.

"All right. You all done this before?" she asks, like she's the one in charge and we're the volunteers. Already, it grates on my nerves a little, but I remind myself that *every single person here* is having a terrible day, and maybe I should get over it.

Or, at the very least, not let on.

"Yes," the three of us chorus.

"Good," she says, and begins handing out clipboards and stacks of paper. "You're doing the streets north of Main Street. This is a list of items they should bring with them, official records, birth certificates, things like that. If they've got someone out of town they can stay with, family or friends or whatever, they should go there. If not, Ashlake High is the current evacuation center, and this is the map to it."

I look at the documents she's given us. They're clearly photocopies of photocopies, the black lines a little unsteady, a little crooked on the page.

When this is over I should make better evacuation handouts, I think. *These look like the directions to a church barbecue, not official documents.*

"And remember, this is a *mandatory* evacuation," says Mike's voice from behind us, and we turn.

He looks tired, deep circles under his eyes, his uniform rumpled.

"We aren't likely to drag anyone out of here in handcuffs, but don't give people the choice to stay in their homes," he goes on. "Knock on every door. If there's no answer, go to the back door. Be a nuisance, but try to be compassionate. If anyone still refuses, alert us."

"What about pets?" Lucy asks.

"The Ponderosa Ranch down Route Forty-Two is taking on stock animals for now," Mike says, then looks questioningly at the volunteer woman in the orange shirt. "And household pets...?"

"They should take all pets with them and ask when they get to Ashlake," she says. "The Humane Society was working on something last I checked."

Sometimes, during evacuations, people just let their dogs and cats go free. As if a house cat or a Schnauzer can somehow escape a forest fire on its own.

I look down at the materials, mentally steeling myself.

"Anything else we should know?" I ask.

Mike sighs.

"This is the kind of area where a ranger knocking on a door will occasionally be greeted with a firearm," he says reluctantly. "There's never been a shooting incident, but if that happens, back away, don't engage. If that asshole wants to burn to death, let 'em."

I almost smile at the dark joke.

"Got it," I say.

Mike nods at the three of us, his hands on his hips.

"Thanks, guys," he says.

———

We quickly split up our side of the small town. The roads on the north side of Main Street wind further up the mountain, and they're full of potholes and patches. The houses are spread out, and there's no real rhyme or reason to them: some are pristine log cabins, probably some rich person's vacation getaway. Some are little more than ramshackle plywood buildings with two busted cars out front and a porch sagging off the back.

But most are just regular houses, a regular size, regular cars in the driveway, a swing set in the back yard.

The first few houses are obviously empty, but I have to knock on all the doors, just to make sure, before I can stick the EVACUATED sign on the front door and check it off my list. We spend a lot of time worrying about the holdouts, the people who'll refuse to leave for one reason or another, but they're a tiny percentage of the population.

Most people, when they learn that there's a mandatory fire evacuation in place, leave right away, because most people are pretty reasonable.

When I get to the fourth house, there's a loaded sedan in the driveway and a little girl, maybe two years old, wearing a harness shaped like a monkey. The harness is attached to a leash that's tied to the inside of the fence around the front yard.

Some alarms start going off in my head, and I walk a little faster toward the kid on the leash, then crouch down on the other side of the fence.

"Hey," I say.

The little girl frowns at me, then stands, grabs her stuffed dog, and backs a couple of feet away. She doesn't say anything.

Well, at least she knows stranger danger.

"Are your parents here?" I ask, glancing at the car. All four doors are open, so they're probably around somewhere, but I still don't like this, even though I know it's probably the result of panicked parenting and not malicious.

"Can I help you?" a woman's voice says from the door, sharply.

I stand up.

"I'm doing evacuation rounds with the Forest Service," I say, glancing from the kid to her.

She's young, probably not much older than me, and there's an infant in a carrier on her back, her lips puffy, her eyes red, like she's been crying.

We look at each other for a moment, and she shifts the big tupperware box that she's holding in front of herself.

"Please don't report me to CPS," she says, her eyes filling with tears. "I'm sorry, my husband is out of town and I've been up all night and I just needed to keep her out of the way without running off for five minutes while I loaded the car."

The kid looks over at me, quizzically, the stuffed dog dangling by one leg.

"Don't worry about it," I say, because the kid seems perfectly fine and happy, playing in the front yard, and because I can't imagine I'd do a whole lot better in the same circumstances. "Want me to keep her company?"

She sags with relief.

"That would be so nice of you," she says. "I swear I'll just be five more minutes, I need to grab a couple more things from inside and then we're heading to my sister's in Bozeman."

"No problem," I say. The baby on her back starts fussing, and she walks toward the car, jiggling it a little until it quiets down. "You look like you've got your hands full."

"Thank you," she says. "I swear, I'm never letting Chuck go on another business trip."

I come into the front yard and sit on the grass near the kid.

"Hi, I'm Clementine," I say. "What's your name?"

The kid looks over at her mom, loading the box into the trunk.

"She's okay, sweetheart," the mom calls.

The kid just looks at me, silent.

I point to the stuffed dog.

"What's the dog's name?" I ask.

She looks from me, to the dog, back to me, and then grins.

"Kee-tah," she says.

"Kita?"

"Kee-TAHHH."

"Cheetah?"

"Gee. TAWWW."

I blink at the kid for a minute, my mind racing, because I don't really speak toddler.

"Guitar?" I finally say.

She nods and laughs.

"That's a really good name," I say. "I have a dog named Trout."

———

I SEE the little family off a few minutes later and watch them drive away. Then I put the sticker on their door and check their house off my list, hoping that a perfectly fine toddler with a frazzled mom is the worst thing I see today.

It's not, but nothing awful happens. There's a couple fighting in their front yard over whether they're gonna go to her mom's house or his buddy Wayne's house, and when I calmly try to inform them of evacuation procedures, the woman just screams "We're trying, you goddamn forest bitch!" at me.

I don't shout back, even though I want to, and make a mental note that *goddamn forest bitch* would be a pretty funny insult in a different context.

There are more families, more kids with stuffed animals. I wake one guy up when I knock on his door, and he answers in his boxers, scratching his beer gut, and seems surprised that there's a fire.

I give him the rundown: where to go, what to take, be sure to shut off your AC to keep as much smoke as possible out of the house, all that. He just looks at me as I talk, like he's hearing me but not necessarily listening.

I leave his house, walk to the next one, and as I'm about to knock on that door, I see him driving away in a pickup truck, still not wearing a shirt. I'm guessing he didn't grab his important documents, either.

I tried, I think.

I knock on doors all day. A volunteer gives me a tuna fish sandwich for lunch, and I scarf it down, then help Lucy with her section, since she managed to get the problem houses this time. Afternoon comes, then evening, and after darkness falls I'm still knocking on doors of empty houses, making sure everyone is out.

My radio crackles every so often with updates: the hotshot crew is doing a controlled burn to the south and the west, though the heat and the winds are making even that dangerous. I try not to think about Hunter, out there in the middle of all that, but I can't help it.

I wish I'd give him something better than a dumb rock, but I don't have anything, and I definitely don't have anything that can do what I want, which is keep him safe.

When we finish, it's almost two o'clock in the morning, but every house in Eaglevale is empty, the stores closed, hardly any cars on the street. It's eerie, a town with almost no one in it. A ghost town.

"You're staying in Ashlake?" Mike asks as we walk to the Forest Service vehicles.

"Yeah, Lucy and I are staying with my sister," I say. "I'll be at the high school to help out first thing tomorrow."

He nods.

"Thanks, Clementine," he says.

TWENTY-SIX

HUNTER

I t's a long walk, and there isn't all that much to talk about. Plus, we're walking single file, so it's hard to hear or be heard. It's not long before we all just lapse into silence.

Eaglevale is in the saddle of a hill. The Quartzite river runs to the south of the mountain, right below the steep, rocky slopes. Right now, the fire is burning hard to the west, on the north side of the river, and to the south, across the river from Eaglevale.

If it weren't for the river, Eaglevale would already be fucked, but all that water makes a perfect, natural firebreak. We find a wide, gravel beach on the north side and set up our base station. It'll be uncomfortable for sleeping, but the gravel makes it a relatively safe zone. Rock doesn't burn.

Across the river, the blackened spikes of former pine trees poke up into the smoky sky like they're trying to point upward. Every time the wind runs through the valley, ash swirls up from the burned area across the river from us.

We call that area *the black*, for obvious reasons. It's ugly and unsettling, but it's the safest place to be, since there's no more fuel to burn. The lush, overgrown forest, full of trees and undergrowth is the most dangerous. That's the sort of terrain that goes up in seconds.

Once we're set up, Porter gathers us along the riverbank.

"Everyone good?" he asks.

"Hell yeah!" we all shout, because we're all crazy people who can't wait to get to work.

You have to be a *little* crazy to take this job in the first place.

Porter allows himself one smile.

"Good, because I'm gonna work the shit out of you guys," he says.

We cheer again.

"Our primary goal here is to keep Eaglevale from burning to the ground," he says, pointing vaguely in the direction of the town, somewhere up the hill. "Right now, the fire to the west of here on the north side of the Quartzite is our main objective while we keep an eye on the area across the river."

The Saturn Fire is big, hot, and incredibly dangerous. Most fires move along at the ground level, because that's where most of the dry, dead material is: leaves, fallen trees and branches, undergrowth, et cetera. But this fire is large enough and hot enough that it's spreading through the crowns of trees — the living top part.

Crown fires are even more unpredictable and therefore even more dangerous than a normal fire. Every so often we can hear a faraway *crack* as a living tree gets so hot that its sap boils instantly and the whole tree explodes.

Porter's still got a big laminated map of the area, and he lays it out on the ground, holding it down with river rocks. Because this fire is off the ground, we need to fell a wide swath of trees *before* we can start the back burn.

And because fire travels uphill almost unimaginably fast, the burn needs to be on flat land, before the Saturn fire gets there. That means we start *now*.

"Any questions?" Porter shouts.

No one has any.

"Then it's time to move out," he says.

———

WE TAKE turns at all the jobs. Taking down full-size trees, even though we've got chainsaws, is exhausting, backbreaking work, and it's even more so because I started the day with a three-hour fully loaded hike.

I chainsaw for a while, then Silas takes over, handing me a GPS and a can of orange paint. Then I mark trees for removal, making sure we're keeping the break the right shape and width, and he cuts them down.

Around lunch, we go on lookout for an hour and watch the fire from a high, rocky outcropping. We report in every fifteen minutes, but miraculously, the Saturn Fire seems like it may have stalled, or at least, like it might have slowed, both to the west and across the river.

The dry, hot winds from the west have stopped blowing, so the fire doesn't have that force driving it forward any more. It's still destructive and dangerous, and we can still hear trees exploding every once in a while.

But it seems like we might be getting the upper hand, like Eaglevale and Coldwater are being evacuated for nothing.

At least, I hope so.

———

"CASDEN, DEWAR, TAKE A BREAK," Porter says. We're standing on either side of the fire break, carefully lighting fallen trees and tree stumps on fire, then watching the fire as it burns itself out, making sure there are no embers remaining.

It's hot, hard work, but everything here is hot, hard work.

"I'm fine," I say, and Silas agrees with me, nodding assent from across a blackened, charred log.

"Guys, I said go take a dinner break," Porter repeats, jerking his thumb over his shoulder.

I look down and stomp out an ember, my heavy boot crushing it into the charred black earth.

Fucking asshole, I think. *Giving orders all day while I sweat my balls off.*

Silas shrugs.

"Okay," he says, and gives me a look.

I glare at Porter, but he doesn't take the bait.

Fuck it. I'm hungry anyway. We eat more MREs, because that's all the food that's here, and talk a little about what we're doing when fire season ends. I mention that I'm moving to Lodgepole, where my girlfriend lives, and he says again that Clementine is cool. That's about it.

We go back to the fire break, and we burn until it's past dark, when Porter comes back and orders us to take the first four-hour sleep shift.

I don't bother setting up a tent, just lay out my foam pad on the gravel beach by the river and crawl into my sleeping bag with my clothes in a pile next to me. Even though there's something poking into my back, I fall asleep almost instantly, thinking *I wonder what Clementine is doing.*

TWENTY-SEVEN

CLEMENTINE

I wake up in the dark to a horrible, rattling, buzzing sound, and it takes me a second to realize that it's my phone, on the floor, in vibrate mode. I dangle one hand off of Jane's couch and grab it, answering without even looking at who it is.

"Yeah?" I say.

"There's a guy in a cabin," Jennifer says.

The gears in my head have to turn for a few moments as I look around the room, trying to figure out where I am and what I'm doing there.

Then I remember what's going on, and what *there's a guy in a cabin* means.

"Shit," I say.

"Can you go?"

I sit up on the couch and look at the inflatable mattress where Lucy was sleeping. It's empty, so she must have left, or she's in the shower, or something.

"What kind of guy in a cabin?"

"He's a crotchety old goddamn lunatic who's probably got three dogs, a shotgun, and some very strong ideas about private property rights as if a fire gives a flying fuck about the constitution," Jennifer says, sounding more than a little irritated. "The usual kind of guy in a cabin, Clementine."

"Jesus, it was just a question," I say, rubbing my eyes with one hand.

Jennifer takes a deep breath. So do I.

"Sorry—"

"—No, I shouldn't have—"

"—Just haven't slept—"

"—You're fine, it's fine, don't worry about it—"

We go quiet again.

"I'll go see if I can get him out," I say.

"Thanks," she says. "Everyone else I either can't reach or they're already at the high school."

She gives me directions to the crotchety lunatic's cabin, and we hang up. It's five a.m. I get off Jane's couch, pull my uniform back on, pee, and put my shoes on. As I'm heading out, I see a note from Lucy.

Jane - Thanks so much for the bed. I owe you one.

Clementine - Couldn't sleep so I went to the high school to help out there. See you soon.

I lock Jane's front door behind myself, and remind myself that I probably also owe her one.

———

THE UPDATES on the fire are constant now, but it sounds like it slowed down yesterday afternoon and overnight. Still, driving into Eaglevale is unsettling at best and feels like the end of a zombie movie at worst. The smoke swirls and thickens, the headlights of my Forest Service truck reflecting back at me in the dark.

I turn off the highway and down a dirt road, and when I go around the shoulder of the mountain, suddenly I can see the bright orange glow in the distance. I can't see flames over the trees, but it looks like there's an opening to Hell west of me.

Hunter's there, I think, and my heart beats a little faster. I haven't heard from him at all, but it's not like he's got a cell signal, and the radios are for official business only. It isn't like he just *hasn't called.*

The cabin with the guy is a long way away, down this dirt road. It's further than I realized, and I start getting nervous before long. I don't think Jennifer or Mike would send me here if I were in immediate danger, and there's a clear escape path, but I'm still not crazy about being even closer to a giant forest fire.

At last, the cabin comes into view. The sun's just come up, and I'm surprised at how pleasant it is. I was expecting something more along the lines of what Jennifer was describing: a plywood shack, a couple dogs chained in the yard, probably several NO TRESPASSING signs scattered around.

But this is a surprisingly cute house, small and cozy, well-tended, pine slats with a shake roof and an old but well-cared-for pickup truck in front. It's actually kind of... nice.

It gives me hope. Maybe I'm about to have a reasonable conversation with the guy inside.

I cut the engine, get out, and walk to the front porch. I straighten my rumpled uniform a little, because I'm pretty sure I look like a mess, and I have a feeling I don't smell fantastic either. Good thing that's not exactly my number one priority right now.

As soon as I knock on the door, I hear someone thumping around inside. It doesn't sound like happy, *thank God the Forest Service is here* thumping, but I stand there, hands folded in front of myself, and try to figure out what I'm going to say.

Leave so I don't have to be the last person to see you alive seems like an okay place to start.

The door jerks open six inches.

A shotgun barrel and a face poke out.

"Shit!" I yell. I jump back, putting my hands up in front of me in the universal sign of *don't fucking shoot me.* I'm pretty sure they're shaking.

"I'm from the Forest Service," I yell from across the porch. My heart's going a million miles a minute, and I can't tear my eyes away from the twin black holes pointed right at me.

I want to run, but I know I can't run fast enough if this goddamn lunatic actually shoots.

There's a moment of silence. Then the gun barrels lower, and I put my hands down slowly, *definitely* shaking.

"Sorry," a man's voice says, creaky with age. "I didn't know they were gonna send a girl."

Not what I was expecting to hear.

"Were you gonna shoot a man?" I ask, still flabbergasted that a shotgun was his first move.

"Nah," he says, and then he sighs, pushing the door open wider. "I just wouldn't feel so bad."

I don't have a response for *that*, because I'm pretty opposed to pointing a gun at anyone, but I don't particularly want to have that argument right now. He leans the shotgun against the wall, and I finally get a good look at him.

He's wearing brown canvas pants and a blue flannel shirt, along with reading glasses and slippers. I can't tell how old he is, but he's up there — in his seventies at least, probably eight-ies, his face deeply lined, his short hair steel gray.

"It's not even loaded," he says. "You here to tell me to get out?"

"Pretty much," I say, because there's no point in sugar-coating this to someone who just pointed a gun at me, loaded or not.

"I ain't leaving," he says, and pushes the door all the way open. Then he turns, slowly, and walks further into his house like he's expecting me to follow him.

He moves carefully and stiffly, but he seems pretty in control of all his faculties. I step to the threshold and stand there, peering into the darker inside of the cabin.

"You're under mandatory evacuation, you know," I call after him.

"I fought in Korea," he calls back. "Try to take me."

I sigh and lean against the door jamb. I hear the sink run for a moment, and then he comes back, still walking carefully and carrying two glasses of water. He hands me one, and I take a sip.

"Thanks," I say. "The smoke bothers my throat."

"Mine too," he admits.

"It's much less smoky in Ashlake," I say, lifting my eyebrows.

He smiles at me and shakes his head a little.

"I'm not leaving," he says again. "But you can come in. I need to sit."

He doesn't wait for my response, just walks back into a front room, puts his glass of water down, and then lowers himself carefully into a plaid easy chair. I lean in through the front door, watching, not quite sure how to proceed.

On one hand, I don't go into strange houses, as a general rule. It's too easy to imagine a horror story.

On the other hand, I can out run this guy if I need to. I walk inside gingerly, looking around at the pine interior.

"Sit," he says. "I don't bite."

I sit gingerly on a plaid couch that *almost* matches the chair, glass of water in hand, and I wonder how to talk a guy sixty years older than me into doing something he doesn't want to do.

"Look, you should really leave," I say, because that seems like a good place to start. He watches me. "There's a fire crew working down below, and they're doing their best, but..."

I trail off for a minute, because I don't know what the *but* is going to be.

"But fires are unpredictable and beyond all human control," he says.

I push my greasy, gross bangs off my face.

"Yeah. That," I say.

"What's your name?" he asks.

"Clementine," I say.

He laughs a little, a dry laugh.

"That's a pretty name," he says. "Like the song. *Oh my darlin', oh my darlin'...*"

"I hate that song," I say, laughing.

"It's a nice song," he says.

"Clementine stubs her toe, falls into a river, and drowns," I say. "It's not a good way to go."

Better than burning to death in your own home, I think, but I don't say it.

He just shrugs.

"What's your name?" I ask, because I have to say something. I've got my radio on my belt, and if I need to leave, someone will tell me.

"Harold," he says.

Whatever I was about to say just dies on my lips.

"It's not as pretty," he says.

"My boyfriend wanted to name the fire Harold," I say, the words just tumbling out of my mouth. "He was joking, but... weird, huh?"

He thinks about it for a moment, and I can't help but thinking about Hunter and I, standing on the path, on the way out of the forest. A perfect, sunny day, him suggesting I name the fire something stupid.

"*The Harold Fire* does lack a certain gravitas," he says.

"That doesn't mean it won't burn your house down with you inside it," I point out.

He takes a long drink of the water, just looking at me. Then he holds his water glass on his lap and takes a long, slow look around the room, like he's remembering something, and like he's deciding whether to tell me something.

"Think you can humor a silly old man for a moment?" he asks, his voice even softer than it was.

I lean my elbows on my knees, both hands around my water glass, and hope that Harold doesn't suddenly say something perverted.

"Okay," I say.

"I don't want to leave the house where Mildred died," he says softly.

I look down into my water glass, my mind going blank for a moment. That's not what I was prepared for.

"Who's Mildred?" I ask, even though I think I already know.

"My wife," he says simply. "We were married for fifty-three years. Forty-five right here. She built this cabin with me."

Suddenly there's a lump in my throat, and I'm pressing my lips together, trying to keep my breathing normal.

I want that, I think, unbidden.

"That's a long time," I say.

"People don't stay married that long any more," he says.

"No, they don't," I say, my voice sounding a little hollow.

I think about the cuckoo clock missing from my parents' house – my mom's house, I guess. I think about the bad, weird kiss I gave Hunter last night, about waking up at four in the morning and finding that rock just so he would have *something* to take with him.

I stare at the coffee table, because I'm pretty sure if I look at Harold, I'll lose it.

Fifty-three years, and now she's gone. I can't even imagine.

"I'm sorry," I say, even though I know it's dumb. I swallow.

I swallow again. The lump won't go. "How long... when did...?"

As hard as I'm trying to sound normal, my voice trails off into a desperate squeak as pressure builds behind my eyes.

Harold looks over at me, and his face changes.

"Three years ago," he says. "And you know something funny? I still don't sleep on her side of the bed."

I just nod, staring stonily at the coffee table. I hold my breath, because I feel like a pile of poorly stacked bricks, like the slightest thing will send me tumbling into a pile.

"I guess it's habit," I say, and my voice comes out as a choked whisper.

I don't know why I'm suddenly losing it like this. I've heard sad things before, for fuck's sake, and I don't usually dissolve into a pathetic puddle of forest ranger.

Harold's still staring off into the distance, and if he's noticed that I'm an inch from bursting into tears in his living room, he hasn't let on.

"Sometimes when I wake up, before I open my eyes, there's this moment where I still think she's there," he says. "Makes it hard to get out of bed. And strange as it probably sounds, I like being here, where everything reminds me of her. I feel a little like she's still with me."

I bite my lip so hard I taste blood, just so I don't cry, but it doesn't work. My eyes are full to the brim, and when I finally blink, tears rush down my cheeks faster than I can rub them away.

"Oh, honey," Harold says.

"I'm fine," I say, but it comes out a squeak-whisper. "Sorry, sorry, I'm fine."

There's a long, slow creaking sound as he gets out of his chair, then walks carefully to the couch where I am. He leans on the arm and lowers himself slowly, then one gnarled hand pats me on the shoulder.

"I didn't mean to make you cry," he says, sounding embarrassed.

"I didn't mean to cry," I say miserably, then take a deep breath.

"Is everything all right?" he asks.

I pinch the bridge of my nose, sniffle, and then laugh.

"No, Harold, everything is not okay," I say. "There's a huge fire bearing down on us right now, and I'm supposed to be talking you into leaving for your own sake, but instead I'm crying in your living room while you comfort me."

"It's not as bad as all that," he says mildly.

"It's exactly as bad as all that," I say.

Harold just chuckles, and I take a couple of deep breaths, looking out the picture windows that look over the valley. It's yellow-gray with smoke, ash swirling between us and the trees. I wipe under my eyes and reflect for a moment that, actually, it's eerily pretty.

I look over at Harold. I'm certain I look like a wreck, but I've got one more idea.

"If I were a ghost, and my husband of fifty-three years tried to stay in a house in the path of a forest fire just to be closer to my stuff, I'd be *pissed*," I say. "I never met Mildred, but I bet she doesn't want you to die here just because she did."

There's a long, long pause.

That's the best I've got, I think.

"You're right, you didn't know Mildred," he says.

I raise my eyebrows.

"Just kidding," he says, looking around again. Then he sighs. "I think she'd be pretty pissed off, too. She had a hell of a temper."

"I can give you a ride," I offer.

Harold doesn't say anything.

"I've got the truck out there," he says, and begins the

process of standing again, leaning hard on the arm of the couch.

I just look up at him, questioningly, and I try again to swallow the lump in my throat.

"I don't know if I can leave," he says, looking around again. "But I'll try. You should go ahead."

"If you need to pack, I can help," I offer.

Harold shakes his head firmly.

"There's an evacuation center in—"

"Clementine, I got it from here," he says. "Go on. You probably have things to do besides talk to an old man. I got a daughter outside Missoula."

"Are you sure?" I ask.

"*Go*," he says, and I walk for the door, then out onto the porch. He leans out of his front door after me.

"Clementine," he says.

I turn around.

"Thanks," he says.

TWENTY-EIGHT

HUNTER

The guys wake me up when it's still dark. Something this intense, we take four-hour shifts sleeping. It can be tempting to stay awake for forty-eight hours straight, but that's a good way to burn down the wrong part of the forest or fell a tree onto someone by accident.

As soon as I get out of my sleeping bag and stuff it away, I can tell that something's up. The wind is slightly different, and strangely, it's cooler. I can feel the breeze coming off the river for the first time, even though we're fifty feet away from it, like something's drawing it toward our encampment.

Hard to tell what exactly it is. It's too early in the day for a thunderstorm, but there could be one building somewhere close by. The air feels charged, even though it's cool, and the guys are a little quieter than usual.

We're all a little uneasy, a little on edge. I grab my gear, shove an MRE into my mouth, and get back to work.

Silas and I switch off again for a couple of hours, and strange as the weather feels, nothing changes. Not yet, anyway.

After a couple hours, Dashiell, Porter's second-in-command, comes up to us. I cut the chainsaw and Silas walks over. His hair is covered in ash, and his face is smeared with black except for where his sweat has cut tracks through it.

I probably look the same.

"Take a break," he says. "It's your turn for lookout."

A helicopter whirls overhead, and all three of us look up at it until it flies behind the dense forest, out of sight.

"How's it going?" I ask. We haven't gotten an update in a little while, but we've been lost in the rhythm of our work, the noise of the chainsaw.

"Not too bad," he says, shouting over the noise of the other chainsaws. "Fire's slowed down pretty good."

Silas and I grab our lunch MREs, then make our way up a steep, rocky slope until we get to a patch of boulders at the top with a panoramic view of almost the whole valley. We radio down that we made it, report on the fire, the wind direction, the air temperature.

Right away, I see it: fluffy white cumulus clouds to the west starting to gather together and darken. That's it, the thunderstorm building. I report it to Porter, down the hill, and he goes quiet for a moment.

"Well, maybe we'll get some rain," he says after a moment. "Hopefully it stays to the west and doesn't fuck us up too much."

By the time our lookout is over, the clouds have gathered more, just this side of the Spires. They're bright white on top but a deep, flat gray along the bottom, the color of molten lead.

Thunderstorms are bad news for fires. The rain is welcome, but not at the expensive of the huge updraft the pressure changes create, not to mention the hard, unpredictable winds. That's why it feels like the air is trying to lift me up.

This could get ugly, and I have a bad feeling that it might. My stomach tightens, and even though I can't see Eaglevale, I look over my shoulder in its direction.

We went there sometimes when I was growing up. That's where my Boy Scout camp was, where I learned to shoot a bow and arrow, to start a fire, and to patch my own tent. If I was good, sometimes I'd get an ice cream cone from Popsy's, the old-fashioned shop on Main Street.

I hate the thought that maybe we can't save it. I hate the thought of the Boy Scout cabins going up in flames, of Main Street burning, of houses with kids' toys in the yard turning into ash.

Every time we can't stop a fire in time, it feels like a kick in the balls, like we've failed at the one task we had to do. Logically, I know that sometimes fires get too big, too hot, too out of control, and no one can do anything. That's just how it works.

It just feels *wrong*.

When the hour's over, we head back down and get to work, but as hard as I try, I can't stop thinking about Eaglevale burning.

TWENTY-NINE

CLEMENTINE

I pull into the lot of Ashlake High School, cut the engine, and stare out the windshield for a few more moments. I feel like I've been doing this a lot lately, driving in silence before parking somewhere and sitting in *more* silence, but my brain is starting to feel fried. Like a frayed knot.

Isn't that the punch line to some joke? A rope walks into a bar, and the bartender says...

Before I can drift completely off course, my radio buzzes at me.

"Clementine, come in," Jennifer's voice says.

"I'm here," I say.

"Are you coming back to the high school?"

"I just pulled up," I say.

"Good. Can you come inside?" she says, sounding distracted.

I almost tell her *no, I was thinking I'd just sit in the parking lot while the rest of you worked all day*, but that's not even a little bit helpful.

Instead I get out of the truck and walk into the high school, looking at the sky to the west. It's still sunny here, for now, but a cool wind is just starting to pick up, and I can see the near-black clouds on the horizon, blocking our view of the Spires.

It's gotten bigger and darker since I left Harold's cabin. I've been watching it in my rear view mirror all morning, hoping that it runs to the north or south of us instead of right over top. Doesn't look likely.

Maybe the rain will help, I think.

INSIDE, Jennifer gives me the rundown: The Red Cross is here, organizing donations and cots and people and everything imaginable. Ashlake General Hospital is close to capacity, mostly people having smoke-related breathing trouble.

"Old people and asthmatics, you know," Jennifer says. "And the people who panicked and got into car wrecks when they were evacuating."

"That's a way to make your day worse," I say.

"Right?" Jennifer says, shaking her head. "I can't imagine. Anyway, anyone here has a medical problem, take them over there. There's a couple nurses here doing the rounds, but they can't do much beyond the basics. Otherwise, distribute food and blankets, calm people down, give them emergency numbers. That kind of thing."

"How's the fire?" I ask.

"I haven't really heard details," Jennifer says, picking up a stack of papers and looking through them. It looks like numbers to call in case of some specific emergency. "It might be shifting with the thunderstorm, so who knows how fucked things even are."

I just nod, then Jennifer looks up at me.

"The hotshot crew is fine, though," she says, her voice a little gentler now. "Working like animals, but fine."

I smile, and a warm wave of relief washes over my whole body. I hadn't even realized how worried I was until right now.

"Thanks," I say.

"And Robbie over at the checkpoint into Eaglevale reported an old guy in a pickup truck driving out about fifteen minutes ago," she says. "Dunno what you said, but it worked."

"I invoked the ghost of his dead wife is all," I mutter.

Jennifer shrugs.

"Well, now he's not dead in a cabin," she says. "Go hand out blankets and wet wipes. Nice butt will be fine."

I stick my tongue out at her, and she laughs.

THIRTY

HUNTER

Into the afternoon, the storm picks up speed. The winds get faster and sharper, and I can feel the updraft while I'm just standing still, watching the forest.

Worse, smoke is billowing upward as the wind sucks it skyward, yellow wood smoke against blue-black storm clouds.

We take a quick break, and I turn on my phone to snap a few pictures, because it's striking, almost beautiful. There's no service, or I'd send them to Clementine, just to let her know I'm okay, still here, taking photos.

That I'm thinking about her, even if I didn't get to follow through with my promise to jerk off while I'm doing it. The rock she gave me is still safe, in a pocket that zips shut so it won't fall out. I wish I'd given her something, but it just didn't occur to me.

Next time.

Silas and I are taking a quick break when the radio crackles, and he answers it.

"Briefing on the beach," says Porter's voice. "Report immediately."

Silas and I look at each other, then practically swallow the rest of our granola bars whole, grab our gear, and head back. We can both tell this isn't good, even if we were both expecting the storm to change things around.

When we get there, there's a dozen guys from the crew geared up and heading off. Everyone is busy, with the frantic energy that always accompanies a change in plans.

Porter looks tired. His skin is nearly gray, his eyes look sunken, and he's even grouchier than normal.

In that moment, I don't envy the guy his job. Even if I think he's an asshole sometimes, he's responsible for making sure a whole crew does their job and doesn't die in the process, not to mention the well-being of the people whose houses we're trying to save.

Making the wrong decision is *easy* when you're faced with steep mountains and raging wildfires and storms that seem to come out of nowhere, and it's easy for that decision to be deadly. For once I'm glad that I only have to follow orders.

"Casden, Dewar, there you are," he says.

I want to point out that we were nearly a mile and a half away, but I know it's not the time.

"We're gonna leave the Eaglevale firebreak where it is," he says to us. "Air support thinks that between what we've already done and water drops, we've got it handled."

As if on cue, a tanker plane flies overhead, and Porter gives it a few moments until he can be heard again. There's another dozen guys readying equipment on the beach, handing tools, packages of food, ponchos, and water bottles back and forth.

Porter points at them.

"Dewar, you're with them," he says to Silas. "There's a place a mile up you can cross the river. We can't let the fire burn over the ridges to the south of here. Thomas can fill you in."

We both turn and look at the tall, steep peaks in the distance. Once the fire gets there, it'll be hard to keep contained, since fighting it on nearly-vertical terrain is pretty much impossible. Plus, with winds like this, fire travels downhill almost as fast as it travels uphill.

"Got it," Silas says, nodding. He claps me on the shoulder and then walks to the group.

"And me?" I ask, since I'm still the only person who isn't busy, and I'm *itching* to get back to work, nearly crawling in my own skin.

"You're with me," Porter says. "I need eyes on this thing. I'm working blind. I don't know where it's going or what it's doing, and you're the one who knows the area best. You up for that?"

"Shit yes," I say, just glad to know what I'm going to be doing.

"Good," Porter says, nearly cracking a smile. He folds a map into a small square, puts it in his pocket, and lifts his own pack. "Let's do this thing, then."

———

WE HEAD FOR A SMALL, rocky outcropping right on the shoulder of the mountain. It's hard as hell to get to, but it looks like it's going to offer a near-perfect view of most of the valley, so that's where we go.

In addition to all the other problems with forest fires, it's surprisingly hard to know where exactly they *are*. They can move incredibly fast, especially one this big and hot, and since they're vast and in the wilderness, it isn't like someone's reporting where the edges are at all times. Even with air support, it can be hard to get a good picture.

And you wouldn't think it, but a fire can sneak up on you. In a dense forest, when you can't see over the tops of the trees, it's easy not to realize how close one is until you feel that incredible wall of heat, and a fire can outrun a person, especially in the deep forest on tricky terrain. That's why you need a lookout.

The spot Porter's chosen is only about two miles away, but there's no trail. For the first mile we have to shove our way through branches and undergrowth, continually checking that we're on the right path. Then we get to a long, steep boulder scramble, and though we look for an easier way up, everything else is nearly vertical.

As we climb, the sky gets darker and darker, even though it's still early afternoon. The wind picks up around us, and I can hear it whistling through the trees, even through the small spaces between the rocks I'm climbing over.

Halfway up, Porter leans against a rock. He's breathing hard, has his jacket open, and his t-shirt is soaked with sweat. I stop as well, and we both take a drink of water. We'll be useless if we pass out from dehydration.

"Shit," he says, when he finishes drinking. "I was hoping we'd be up there before the wind really hit."

"We couldn't see this slide from the beach," I say. "It's harder and longer than it looks."

"Ain't that always how it is," Porter says, almost reflectively, and I just nod.

He's not so bad all the time, I think. *I could stand to remember that.*

"You recovered?" he asks, hooking his water back onto his pack.

"Never been readier," I say, and then both of us laugh, because it's beyond untrue.

By the time we get to the ridge, every muscle in my body is screaming. They've all been screaming for at least twelve hours, so I just ignore it. We take another moment to drink, catch our breath, and get our bearings. The wind is nearly howling now, so strong that I can feel it trying to knock me over, and the sky is an unholy gray-black-yellow color, half wood smoke from the fire and half the oncoming underbelly of a nasty thunderstorm.

Don't get burned alive and don't get struck by lightning, I think to myself. *Piece of cake.*

At least we're in the mountains and there won't be any tornadoes. Once we were out fighting a prairie fire in one of the Dakotas, and during an incredible thunderstorm, I got to watch a tornado twist across the landscape only a couple of miles away. We all just stood there and watched it, because what else were we going to do? It's not like there are basements in the middle of nowhere.

As soon as we can, we keep moving to the lookout point. The trees thin out, and between their tops, I can see the vast swath of black, brown, and gray burned areas. It's an uneven line going back toward the Spires, and from here, it's easy to see how random wildfires are. In some spots the burned area is narrow, nearly cut off completely by lush green foliage. In other spots, it's wide, almost the entire area between the river and the ridge line to the north.

Then, closer to us, I can see the spot where the fire jumped the Quartzite River. It's narrower where that happened, not nearly as solid and wide a fire break as it is here.

At last, we reach the point, and both of us just look around for a moment. It's beautiful, wild, and *dangerous*. We're in the middle of an enormous U, made by the fire: one leg across the river from us, to the southeast, the main body of the fire still to the west. Through the smoke, I can see the bright orange line flickering only a few miles from the firebreak we made, a big black swath that cuts along the base of the hill.

I hope it works. Dear *God* I hope it works. Too late to do anything else about it.

"It's going up the ridge," Porter mutters, looking to the northwest. There's another bright orange line, and this one is moving up a mountain, so quickly we can actually see it moving. The storm is closer to that side of the fire, and even from here I can see the wind whipping it in every direction.

As we watch, an updraft sweeps the mountain, and where it meets the flames the fire spins upward, into a loose cylinder of orange and yellow.

Porter and I both hold our breath, because fire whorls are dangerous and almost impossible to predict, even in a place where *everything* feels dangerous and impossible to predict, mostly because it is.

An involuntary shiver goes down my back, and I pull out my GPS and compass.

Porter and I take measurements quickly: wind direction and speed, temperature. We mark where the fire is right now on a map, where it might be heading soon, though with the updraft and the wind changing direction every few minutes, we may as well be throwing darts at a map.

Still, I was afraid it would be worse. The firebreak protecting Eaglevale is as good as we could make it, and that's air support's first priority, though the thunderstorm is making flying dangerous for them. The fire working its way up the ridge, far to the northwest, *could* be a big problem, but not for a few more hours, and there's no point in worrying about it until this storm blows over.

Most of the crew heads downriver, to the east, and they're protected from the fire by the wide, rushing waters of the Quartzite. Porter radios air support while I radio the guys down below, but for once, it seems like the situation might be under control.

Well, relatively speaking. By wildlands firefighting standards.

"We should head back down before this storm blows us off the ridge," Porter says, facing the fire to the northwest. "You said you've hiked into the Spires?"

"Two years ago," I confirm, and I tell him the story about

how my mom thought it might help me re-integrate into society.

He almost cracks a smile.

"What's the terrain over there? Rough, rocky?"

"And steep," I say. "Especially those ridges where the fire's heading now. If they burn and then get rain, it'll be rockslide central with all the plant matter gone."

Porter just shakes his head.

"Too risky to send anyone," he says, then points at another long, low valley. "What about that way in?"

He's already thinking about next steps, about where to contain the fire on the other sides, and together, we start planning a strategy. We talk for a good ten minutes, checking the wind and the weather and the maps every so often. It starts to rain, big, fat drops, and I think *we should leave before the rocks get too slippery.*

We're wrapping it up when the radio crackles.

"Captain, *come in,*" says a staticky voice, and even those three words are shot through with panic.

Porter frowns and takes the radio off his belt.

"Porter," he says.

"It's jumped the river," the voice says. "Just east of the camp by about a quarter mile, when the winds picked up."

We both turn around in silent horror and look to the southeast. As we do, a hot, dry, smoky wind blows up the slope and into our faces, stinging my eyes.

Down below there's a bright orange spot, muted by the smoke pouring off of it. It's crawling along the river bank, on this side of the river, toward our camp.

It's also starting up the slope, and even from here, I can see the base of each tree smoke, then catch, and then the fast *whoosh* of flame as it consumes the whole trunk, leaving the whole tree a hundred-foot torch.

"Go," Porter says, and points at the boulder scramble.

THIRTY-ONE

CLEMENTINE

People are pouring into the high school now. Not just from Eaglevale, but anyone who didn't have somewhere else to go in Coldwater or the other small, surrounding towns. They're sitting in small groups in the gymnasium, in the cafeteria, collecting in the high school auditorium.

For the most part, people are calm and orderly. They mostly know each other, which isn't surprising, and for much of the day, Ashlake High operates like a commercial for the best of humanity.

Outside, it gets darker. Trees are shaking in the wind, and when I glance out the windows that face west, I can see that the sky over there is nearly black.

He's fine, I tell myself. *The rain will help. He's with two dozen other guys, all of whom will be perfectly fine.*

I still wish I could hear from him, but the radios are for official business only.

I walk into the classroom where they've stored piles of blankets and grab an armful. There's a woman with a week-old baby who had to evacuate, and while I don't have most of what she needs, I can at least make myself useful somehow.

Outside the thick-paned school window, the wind starts to *howl*, and despite everything, the sound raises goosebumps on the back of my neck.

If something happened to the fire crew, they'd tell you, I remind myself, then head to deliver blankets.

———

THE NEW MOM looks tired and stressed, but she smiles and thanks me for the blankets and her husband takes them from me, even as the baby cries.

"If it helps, you're taking this better than plenty of people who don't have newborns," I tell them.

They both look at the baby, who's wrapped in a blanket, kicking her feet, wailing away. The mom pulls her blanket a little tighter, then looks at me and shrugs, a half-smile coming onto her face.

"We were in pure survival mode anyway," she says. "I've barely noticed we're not at our house."

Yikes, I think, looking at the baby's tiny, angry face.

"Well, good luck," I say to them. "It can only get better from here."

I close the door gently and leave.

Turning the corner, I nearly run head-on into another woman.

"Sorry!" I say, holding out my hands.

"Do you work here?" she asks, taking my shoulder firmly in her hand.

"I'm with the Forest Service," I say.

She takes a deep breath, and my stomach tightens, because this woman is obviously just *barely* keeping it together.

"I can't find my daughter," she says.

I nod, and strangely, a sense of calm washes over me, now

that I have a task, something to *do* besides trying to be useful and thinking about Hunter.

"What's her name?" I ask.

"Delilah Clark," the woman says. "I'm Kim Clark. She was spending the night at a friend's house, and, you know, I've been so busy lately with the kids and work and school that I wasn't watching the news or listening to the radio, and I didn't know we were being evacuated…"

"Kim, I'm gonna take you to the gym, where we can sort this out," I say, even as a flutter of anxiety ripples through my stomach for Delilah. "She's gotta be somewhere, and we can sort of it out there."

Kim just nods, her eyes lowering. She's clearly about ten seconds away from total meltdown, and I lead her toward the gym where my bosses and the Red Cross volunteers are gathered.

The short version is that Kim didn't realize they were under evacuation orders, and let Delilah spend the night at a friend's house in Coldwater. The moment she realized, she tried to call Delilah, the friend, the friend's parents, but couldn't find *any* of them.

She drove over, but the house was empty, a red EVACU-ATED sticker on the front door.

"That means Delilah is safe," I say, pushing open the door to the gym.

"From the fire," Kim says. "I hope, anyway."

I'd be willing to bet fifty bucks that Delilah is safe and sound somewhere, and hasn't been kidnapped into an international sex trafficking ring.

I know better than to say the words *international sex trafficking ring* to Kim right now, though, even if I were trying to reassure her. We walk toward the knot of people gathered around folding tables in the corner.

"Jen, Mike," I say. "This is…."

They both turn around and look at me, their faces so pale and *stricken* that the words die on my lips.

"Clementine," Jennifer says, her voice a scratchy whisper. "There you are."

Suddenly I feel like there's a clamp on my chest, metal teeth bearing down. I forget all about Kim and Delilah, and I look from Jennifer to Mike and back.

"What?" I ask.

THIRTY-TWO

HUNTER

I don't question Porter, I just make for the boulder scramble as fast as I can. I know he's right. If we can get down and around the shoulder of the hill before the fire reaches that point, we might make it back into the black.

It's our only chance, because there's absolutely no way we can outrun a fire moving uphill. Even this is going to be very, *very* close, and it's going to depend on moving as fast as we can, in the howling wind and rain, wearing heavy packs.

We're five feet down the scramble when my foot slips on a wet rock and I go down on one knee, *hard*. Pain flashes through my leg and I gasp, stars in front of my eyes. Porter stops and turns, just staring at me, waiting.

After a few seconds, I force myself to stand. I put my weight on it, and it hurts like hell, but the leg holds. I bend it, and same thing: painful as hell, still functional. I nod at Porter, and he nods back.

"Careful," he says.

"Thanks," I say, and we start moving again, each glancing back at the fire every few moments.

"We might have to deploy," Porter says, panting for breath, his voice ragged.

He means deploy our fire shelters, the silicon-and-aluminum bags that resist heat.

They're an absolute last resort, and a bolt of terror shoots through me at the thought: trapped, face-down on the ground, nothing but a thin layer between me and unimaginable heat.

Earlier this year, a dozen men in Arizona died after deploying in the Kaibab fire. They lost sight of it, only to find it below them on a slope, and they were left with no choice.

Kind of like we might be right now. I lower myself, knee a throb of pain, and hope that we get a choice.

This is fucking unfair, I think, even though I know that *fair* doesn't matter. *It was across the river. There was a one in a thousand chance...*

"There's a gravel fan at the bottom of the scramble that would be the best place to do it," he goes on. "No flammable materials, up against a rock wall where—"

Mid-sentence, he slips. I hear rocks clatter down the slope and turn just in time to see Porter go over sideways, his heavy pack making him go off-balance.

Just before he hits the ground, I hear a dull *crack*.

Porter's leg bends the wrong way.

For a moment, there's total silence. I stand perfectly still, praying that it's some kind of optical illusion, that Porter's ankle is just sprained or something. That he can still get down.

Then he *screams*, a horrifying, gut-wrenching noise, coming from one of the toughest men I've ever met. Porter was in the Army before spending ten years in the hotshots, and I've never heard him *scream* before.

It jolts me back into action, and I cross the jagged granite toward him as fast as I can, careful not to fall myself. Porter's just lying on his back, his face almost gray, his breathing shallow. He's dripping with sweat, and I grab the bottom of his pants and pull the leg up.

I have to close my eyes for a moment and collect myself, because no matter how much ugly, gory shit I've seen, a bone poking through the skin will always make my stomach turn.

"It's bad," Porter whispers, his breathing still fast and shallow.

"Breathe," I tell him. He keeps panting. "Deep breaths," I command.

He takes one, long and shaky. His hands are still splayed out to the sides, and I can see them shaking. I can't even imagine how much this must hurt.

I sling my pack off my back, unzip a pocket, and pull out my field first aid kit, unrolling the gauze. There's not that much of it, but it's gonna have to do.

"Casden, don't," Porter says, his voice thick and dull. "Go."

"This is gonna hurt," I say, and stretch the gauze over his shin.

"Just fucking —"

He screams again, and I grit my teeth together, wrapping his lower leg as tight and fast as I can. It's a pretty shitty job, but given the circumstances, I just want to keep him from damaging it more if I can. He's panting for breath again, but as I finish wrapping his leg he catches himself and I hear another long, deep breath.

Good.

Something about emergencies always snaps my mind into perfect, crystal clear focus, and I know exactly what I'm going to do, like it's already been written down for me. I put my gear on my back again, strap it on, and glance at the fire.

It's coming, fast, The heat and smoke buffeting my face. Sparks and embers float up toward the sky, conveyed on a river of gray-yellow wood smoke.

But the sound. Jesus, the sound. Fires roar and *howl* as they make their own wind systems, and this one sounds like demons shrieking out of hell.

"I'm gonna need you to stand," I tell Porter.

"You can't get both of us down," he says, his teeth clenched tightly. Sweat is running off his face and onto the rock below his head, and I can see every vein in his forehead standing out.

I kneel on my good knee next to him and offer one hand.

"Casden, *go*. That's a direct order," he says. It's a last resort and he knows it, saying *direct order* like it'll trigger some latent military switch in my brain and I'll suddenly just leave him there.

Instead, I laugh.

"Fuck orders," I tell him. "I don't leave men behind."

Reluctantly, he takes my hand. I pull him into a sitting position, and then he uses my knee to push himself up on his good leg until we're both standing. He's unsteady, but he's still got his pack.

"This is gonna hurt," I say, bending at the waist.

"No shit," he mutters, but he still gasps when I drape him over my shoulders and stand.

Fucking hell, he's heavy, but there's so much adrenaline in my system right now that it doesn't matter. I think I could lift a car if I needed to.

I pick my way down the rock slope slowly, carefully, smoke and rain blowing over us, the fire raging nearby. My eyes sting and my lungs already hurt, but I keep fucking moving.

I remember hauling Clementine up the stairs to the fire lookout. She was a lot lighter.

Hunter, I like your muscles, I think, and in the smoke and the rain and the heat, I smile.

Next to me there's a crackle, and then Porter's talking

quietly and urgently into his radio. He doesn't mention that he's on my back, just that we've got no choice but to deploy.

The radio goes quiet.

"Godspeed," the man's voice on the other end says.

When we reach the gravel fan at the bottom of the slide, it's almost unbearably hot, wind whipping against my clothes and face. I put Porter down as gently as I can, and he balances on his good leg and tears into his pack, bringing out the silver tent.

I'm so utterly spent that I'm shaking as I get my pack off. Porter shouts something but I can't hear him over the roar and the *howl* of the fire, the hot wind pushing us both against the rock wall. I swear I can almost feel my skin brighten and blister in the heat, but I don't stop. I don't even look at the fire.

I grab my shelter and shake out the long half-cylinder. Porter does the same, leaning against the rock wall, unsteady on one leg, and I glance at the fire one last time, heat and smoke rolling toward us. An ember lands on the sleeve of my jacket and goes out, singeing it.

Then, suddenly, everything seems very matter-of-fact, like there's no more point in being afraid because I've got only one option left, and this is it.

"Get in," Porter shouts, and I pull the shelter over myself. I lie face-down on the gravel, my hands and feet anchoring it to the ground as best I can, and I press my face into the rocks, getting as low as I can.

Now the fire is even closer, closer than I've ever been to a fire. It sounds like there's a freight train bearing down on me, and I do the last thing I learned in training.

I turn my radio off, just in case, and now I'm alone in this flimsy tube, holding it down as tightly as I can. Superheated air and smoke rushes through the gaps, no matter how small I try to make them, and the temperature is already sweltering, my skin starting to feel like it's on fire.

I press my face into the gravel harder and try to breathe, but even the stone below me is hot.

I shift, trying to get a better angle, and I feel the lump in my pocket. Clementine's rock, from the waterfall. I remember tossing her into the ice-cold water, her stretched out naked on that rock, and I grab the handles on my shelter and I press them down into the earth as hard as I can.

I look at the radio on the table, everyone standing around it. There's a staticky, hard-to-understand voice coming out of it. He's talking to Mike and Mike is talking back, but all I know is I heard the words *have to deploy* and everyone around the table went silent, even Kim.

Hunter's there, and he has to deploy, and I don't even know what that fucking *means* but I can tell it's very, very bad and the gym feels like it's flickering in and out of reality.

I clear my throat.

"Deploy what?" I ask, my voice still a weird, foggy whisper.

"Fire shelters," Mike says.

We're all just staring at the radio.

"Oh," I say. No one answers.

"Deployed," the voice says after a few more moments. "Cutting communication."

Then the thing goes quiet. I look up at Mike, frantic, and he just shakes his head.

"When they deploy they turn their radios off as a courtesy," he explains.

"Courtesy?" I ask, because my brain may as well be filled

with sand right now. All I can think of is Hunter, face down on the ground, in a long tinfoil tube. Like a burrito.

"So whoever's on the other end doesn't have to listen," Mike says gently. "Just in case."

Then I get it, all at once.

It's so no one has to listen to a man possibly burn to death.

I don't respond. I just turn around and walk blindly. I push open a door and walk into a hallway and I walk through another door and down a set of stairs. It's dark at the bottom, the lights out, and when I get there I go under the stairs and slide down the wall until I'm sitting on the cold, dirty tile floor.

I'm coming back to you, I think.

Hunter and I on that tiny cot, the morning we left the lookout.

I'm coming back to you, once fire season is over.

I sit very, very still. I keep breathing, and I don't move, because I feel like if I move the dark around me might shatter, and the thick, inky blackness is the only thing that's keeping me from screaming.

You said you never loved me in the first place.

I didn't mean it.

I inhale, I exhale.

Please come back to me, I think. *Please.*

THIRTY-FOUR

"CASDEN!" Porter's voice shouts, barely audible over the screaming roar of the fire.

I take a breath, my face crushed against the gravel, dirt between my teeth, and force myself not to cough.

"WHAT?"

"Who was your first grade teacher?"

My skin feels like it's boiling off, every nerve ending pulsing with pure, seething *pain*. It's all I can do to stay still, because every last instinct I've got is screaming *it hurts here, run!*

I can feel Clementine's rock in my pocket, though, a small hard uncomfortable lump between my thigh and the ground. It presses into my leg, and I think about her, lying on my chest in the lookout, pointing at Saturn, and I stay down.

"Mrs. Thomason," I shout back.

"Who was your best friend?"

"I don't know!" I shout.

"Try!"

I force my mind back. John G. Matthews Elementary school, the big white doors to the outside, the brick facade, the playground with the wood chips where I seemed to get a splinter a week.

"Wayne," I shout back. "I got that poor bastard in a *lot* of trouble, too."

"What kind?"

I take another breath, skin burning, fire roaring. I inhale dirt and cough a little, but I try to remember the shit that Wayne and I got up to, even if I have no fucking clue why Porter wants to know all of a sudden.

"One time I stole horse shit from my parents' barn and put it on the principal's windshield," I shout. "And Wayne didn't do anything, but he was standing there when I got caught, so he got into just as much trouble as me."

"Horse shit?" Porter shouts back. "When you were in first grade?"

"Grew up on a ranch, had more access to it than eggs," I shout.

"How'd you get it to his car?"

Suddenly, it dawns on me what Porter's doing. He's keeping me talking, keeping me as distracted as he can, even though he's got a hell of a broken leg and is in the exact same position as me.

"Used grocery bag," I shout. "But once I got busted I had to clean it with my bare hands."

There's a sound, and I think Porter is *laughing.* Everything still hurts like hell, but it's working, even if only a little.

"What was your first car?" I shout back.

"A piece-of-shit Ford from the seventies," he shouts. "But I could get it up to ninety-five on the interstate."

He tells me about cars. I tell him about horses and guns and schools, digging deep to remember details, *anything* to keep my mind off the fire, the pain, and most of all, the horror that I might burn to death.

Clementine's rock is still there, solid. As Porter and I shout back and forth, telling each other the inanities of our lives, I'm thinking of her, the little funny things she says: *I feel like a noble-woman. I'm sorry the mountain lion doesn't respect you.*

I think of her naked in the moonlight, of her lips around my cock, but mostly I think about just *being* with her, hiking or driving or just sitting around. God, I just like it when she's around.

I can't give up without *talking* to her again. I can't.

Gradually, I realize the intense heat is lessening, the air that seeps in through the tiny cracks no longer quite as super-heated. The roar has died down, and even though it's still hot and loud, I realize: the worst is over.

It might be a long time before we can get out, since the protocol is not to leave until someone outside gives the all-clear, but we're going to make it.

Holy fuck, we're going to make it.

THIRTY-FIVE

CLEMENTINE

I don't know how long I sit there. It feels like time has stopped, like I somehow escaped reality and this dark, cold stairwell is the only place where none of this is happening. My eyes adjust and the darkness sharpens into shadows.

I count my breaths and force my mind blank. I have the feeling that I'm supposed to be upstairs, gathered around the radio, letting my coworkers and strangers hug me and reassure me that everything is going to be fine, that Hunter's going to be fine, but I can't.

I *can't*. If I could find a smaller, darker place I'd be in it.

After five minutes or five hours, I hear voices above, echoing through the hall. Slowly, they separate, two people calling to each other.

One is Jennifer.

No: one is Jennifer, talking about me.

"Have *you* seen Clementine?" she asks. "The truck is still here, so she hasn't left, but I can't find her and I'm getting worried."

"Sorry," calls the other voice, one I don't recognize.

I clear my throat and take a shaky breath.

"Jen," I call.

Silence, then footsteps on the stairs. She rounds the landing in a whirl, calling my name, and then the lights go on and I squeeze my eyes shut, shielding them with my hand.

"There you are," she says.

I open one eye and look up at her, afraid to speak. Jennifer holds out one hand.

"They made it," she says softly.

I lean my head back against the wall and take a deep breath.

It's okay, I think over and over. *It's okay it's okay it's okay. It's okay.*

"C'mon," Jennifer says. "They're in a helicopter, heading to Ashlake General."

I grab her hand and let her pull me up, and before I can stop her she's pulling me in, wrapping her arms around me.

"There's a football trophy with Cute Butt's name on it by the principal's office," she says softly. "You never said you'd known each other since high school."

That does it.

The dam breaks and I start *sobbing* into Jennifer's shoulder, and it's a loud, messy, snot-filled *ugly* cry but I don't care because I feel limp and spent like a rubber band that's been stretched too far and snapped back. Jennifer just strokes my hair and makes soothing noises as I babble, shit like *I thought he was gonna die* and *I couldn't fucking do anything* and *Jesus I'm a mess I'm sorry.*

Eventually, the waterworks are over and I've just got the hiccups. Jennifer reaches into a pocket and hands me half a brown paper towel from one of the school bathrooms.

I clear my throat and blow my nose, then wish I'd dried my eyes before blowing my nose, and Jennifer guides me upstairs to the girl's bathroom where there are as many paper towels as

I need. I splash my face, and as I dry it on more scratchy paper towels, Jennifer's radio says her name.

"Yeah," she says.

"Did you find Clementine?"

She looks at me.

"Yeah, I got her," she says.

"Can she talk?"

I nod.

"Sure," she says, and hands me the radio.

There's another lump in my throat, and I try to clear it. The radio is quiet for a long time, and I just watch it, waiting.

Then there's a quick burst of static.

"Clem?" Hunter's voice says.

"Hey," I say, and I grin despite myself, my eyes filling up again.

Jennifer turns and leaves the girls' bathroom.

"I told you I'd be fine," he says.

"I believed you," I say, my voice a little shaky.

"I've still got your rock," he says. "I had to fight the paramedics for it when they cut my pants off, though."

"You could have replaced it with another one and I'd never have figured it out," I say.

"Yeah, but I'd have known," he says.

I look at myself in the mirror. I'm a mess, but I'm grinning like an idiot.

"Are you really okay?" I ask.

"I will be," he says, and then the radio goes quiet for a moment. "Listen, Clem, they gotta do some hospital stuff because I guess I inhaled a lot of smoke. And I'm not really supposed to be using the radio for personal shit, anyway, but they said I could."

"Hunter, I think you could ask for a pony right now and get it," I say.

"That's not a bad idea," he says.

"When can I come see you?"

More silence. Then a sigh. Then a deep, wracking cough, and I cringe.

"They said tomorrow," he says, his voice raspy.

"Tomorrow?" I ask, my heart sinking.

"I guess they don't want visitors for the first couple of hours because of, uh, stuff, and then visiting hours are gonna be over..."

Visiting hours? Fuck *visiting hours*.

"I gotta go," he says. "But Clem, I, uh..."

He trails off, my heart suddenly in my throat.

"I'll see you soon?" he finishes.

"I'll see you soon," I say.

The radio clicks off, and I put it down on a sink. I grab the ugly, hard water-stained porcelain in both hands and lean my forehead against the scratched mirror.

He's okay, I tell myself. *He's okay, he's okay.*

It still takes me a little while to pull myself together. I feel like an asshole that he called me after nearly dying and what I said was *you could ask for a pony*. A good girlfriend would have said *oh my God, I'm so glad you're okay, I was so scared, I don't know what I'd do without you.*

And I am, I was, and I don't. But somehow it came out of my mouth as *are you really okay?*

I quit thinking about it. I stand up straight, wipe the smudge off the mirror with another paper towel, compose myself, and leave the bathroom.

Right away, someone needs something: blankets, cots, food, phone numbers. Someone else is finding Delilah for her mother, but I get yanked in a hundred directions instantly.

The second I can sneak off again, I call my mother.

"Minty!" she says. "I was just about to call you, because you heard that two of the hotshots had to deploy their fire shelters? I mean, my God, I can't imagine."

"I did hear," I say. "And—"

"You're *never* going to guess who one of them was," she goes on.

"My high school boyfriend Hunter Casden?"

She laughs.

"Darn it, Minty, I thought I was the first one with the news for once," she says. "He's fine, but I couldn't *believe* it when I saw his name on the charts as I was leaving. You know, I had to throw out that couch in the basement after you two broke up."

I push my bangs off my forehead, thinking *I may as well tell her*.

"Actually, mom, I—"

I pause, frowning.

"Why'd you have to throw out the couch?"

"It was disgusting," she says, matter-of-factly. "Minty, there was practically a *crust* on it."

I can feel myself turn *beet red*, and I take a deep breath.

"Hunter and I are dating again and I need your help busting in to see him after visiting hours are over," I say, the words rocketing out of my mouth.

There's a pause.

"Hunter *Casden*?" she says, sounding a little incredulous.

"What? Yes," I say. It's not like we were talking about a *different* Hunter.

There's a long pause on the other end.

"Please?" I say.

My mom sighs.

"All right," she says.

THIRTY-SIX

HUNTER

On the upside, I get to watch this thunderstorm from indoors, behind the thick glass of my hospital room. The rain lashes against it, the sky almost black, the flashes of lightning intermittent shocks of white daylight.

It's quite a show.

As it's happening, I get an honest-to-God sponge bath. I try to convince the two kindly, middle-aged nurses that I could take a shower, but they fuss at me that I have second-degree burns over a sizable chunk of my body, and until I heal up a little, running water isn't a good idea.

Honestly, I just want them to hurry up, because I'm secretly hoping I can see Clementine before visiting hours end. I know it's not very likely, and I know that, at *worst*, she'll come see me in the morning

They have to go through ten buckets of water before it stops turning black with soot, and then they can finally bandage me up. I'm not quite sure that my burns warranted all *that*, but after my day, I don't mind letting other people bathe me while I lie there.

At least I'm not Porter, who got rushed into surgery the

second we were in the hospital. The guys in the helicopter, who rescued us, could barely look at his leg either. I heard one of them muttering to the other *hope he doesn't lose that*, but I was too busy sucking in oxygen from a mask to really listen.

I do hope he doesn't lose it, though.

After they treat my burns with a sponge bath and gauze, I get to see the pulmonologist. She listens to my chest very seriously, asks me lots of questions, listens to my chest again, then frowns.

"I'm going to keep you overnight," she says. "In the morning we can see if you're going to need a pulmonary CT scan or not, because you likely breathed in some superheated air and it could have caused permanent scarring."

I swallow and breathe in. All I know is my lungs kinda hurt.

"How much?" I ask her.

She shakes her head.

"No way to tell just yet," she says, but pats my shoulder. "But you're here, so you're out of the woods."

Then she laughs.

"Literally!" she says, and laughs again. "But seriously, there could be permanent damage. We'll know more soon."

"Thanks," I say.

I get a mask to wear. I get an IV, because I'm dehydrated, but at least they don't give me a catheter since I'm still perfectly capable of getting up to pee.

They do let my parents see me, but not for long. My mom cries and talks a lot about Jesus. My dad makes me pray with the two of them for a good ten minutes, even though I run out of stuff to say to God after about forty-five seconds. I'm just not very religious.

Around ten that night, after hours of waiting and prodding and wrapping and more waiting and poking and *more waiting*, I get moved to a regular room at last, walking along with my oxygen mask and IV. At least my hospital gown closes all the way up the back.

When I open the door to my room, it's absolutely fucking *stuffed* with flowers. There are arrangements on every horizontal surface, so many that they're overflowing onto the floor. There are roses, sunflowers, carnations, lilies, and that's all the flowers I can really name but I swear there's a hundred kinds of flowers in here.

"I swear, every other phone call to the nurse's station was someone delivering flowers for the fireman," the nurse who escorted me says.

I look up at the ceiling. It's choked with *GET WELL* balloons, plus one that says *Happy Birthday.*

"I don't know what to say," I tell her. "People are always nice, but... wow."

"You earned it," she says. "Hope you're not allergic."

———

AFTER I GET into the bed, another nurse seems to visit every ten minutes. I wish they'd let me sleep, but they're coming in offering more pillows, chamomile tea, warmer socks, a white noise machine. They're all so nice and sweet that I can't even get annoyed.

None of it's what I really *want*, but I know I just need patience. Tomorrow morning. I'll wake up, eat breakfast, and she'll be here.

I've just drifted off to sleep again when the door opens.

Please don't give me anything else to make me more comfortable, I think. *Just let me sleep.*

Then whoever opened the door pauses, like they're uncertain. I open my eyes, but I can't see them yet because of how the room's laid out.

After a moment the bar of light cast by the open door

disappears, and the door clicks shut. Quiet, tentative footsteps enter the room, and then a dark shape comes around the corner.

My heart leaps.

"Hey," I whisper.

"You awake?" Clementine whispers back.

"No, I'm talking in my sleep," I say, keeping my voice low, since she obviously sneaked in somehow.

She comes up to my bed, leans over, and kisses me gently on the forehead. I slide one of my hands into hers, and she squeezes.

"You missed," I murmur. "The proper hello kiss is down here."

She kisses me on the mouth hesitantly, like I'm made of glass, so I put my other hand on the back of her head and pull her in, harder. *Then* she kisses me so fiercely I can feel the sharpness of her teeth against my lips, our mouths open, my tongue reaching for hers.

I'm *beyond* glad I held on and didn't run out of the shelter, because now she's making soft little noises, her hand's in my hair, and she's practically pushing me back into my pillows.

When Clementine finally pulls away, she leans her forehead against mine, eyes closed.

"I'm glad you're okay," she whispers.

"Me too," I say.

I'm glad I got to see you again, I think. *This is what I hung on for.*

I don't say it out loud. It's too cheesy, sounds too much like it's from a bad made-for-TV movie.

Clementine sits on my bed, then looks around at the room like she's seeing it for the first time.

"This is a *fuckton* of flowers," she says, still keeping her voice low.

I grin and rub the back of her hand with my thumb.

"Well, I'm a hero," I say, putting my other arm behind my head.

Clementine laughs.

"You get to use that for a week," she says. "Two, tops."

"I *saved* Eaglevale," I go on, teasing her. "Singlehandedly. I think."

Then I pause, because I realize I don't actually know what happened to Eaglevale. I'm just assuming if it burned down, someone would have said something.

"How... *is* Eaglevale?" I ask.

She laughs in the dark.

"Unburnt," she says. "But that doesn't mean six months from now, you get to play the hero card to get out of doing the dishes."

Then she stops, my room's quiet again, because we both realize what she just said. Six months from now, she thinks we'll be arguing over the dishes.

I *like* it, and I like that she said it so casually. She didn't even have to think about it.

"After the ordeal I went through, I'm still gonna have to wash dishes?" I say. "I don't get even *one* servant?"

"You *do* have a gaggle of nurses attending to your every whim and desire," she teases me. "My mom had to lure them away from their station so I could sneak in."

"I got a sponge bath from *two* nurses earlier," I say. "Consider that a fantasy come true."

"I thought you weren't crazy about two women at once," she says, laughing. "Or did you figure out where to put your dick?"

"Front, center, and flaccid," I say. "I think they got off from it more than I did."

Clementine rolls her eyes at me.

"Clem," I whisper.

She raises one eyebrow, so I hold up my arm and flex my bicep.

"Is that how you got them to sponge bathe you?" she says.

"You can touch it if you want," I say, and wink at her.

Before Clementine can either touch my muscle or tease me again, the door opens brusquely and the lights flash on. We both wince, squinting.

One of the nurses is standing just inside my room, looking stern. I lower my arm and act like I wasn't trying to impress a cute girl with my muscles.

Which is, of course, exactly what I was doing.

"Visiting hours are *over*," she says.

"Sorry, I was just going," Clementine says, though she doesn't move from where she's sitting, next to me on the bed.

"Mhm," says the nurse.

"It's my fault," I say, and rub my thumb across the back of her hand. "I just needed to see her after today."

The nurse softens a little bit, her face less stern.

"Look, they start again at eight tomorrow morning," she says. "But I do have to kick you out now."

Clementine nods. The nurse turns and leaves.

"When are you getting out of here?" she asks.

"Tomorrow, day after that at the latest," I say. "They might have to do a CT scan of my lungs, but I should be out soon."

"Okay," Clementine says, then kisses me again, not as deep or hard as before but not quite gently either.

"Get some sleep," she says when she pulls back.

I lift her hand to my mouth and kiss the back of it softly, her hazel eyes dark and serious.

"I'm glad you're okay," she whispers. "I was really scared."

I look at her face, so open and serious and *vulnerable*, and I decide to tell the truth.

"You know what I kept thinking of?" I ask.

"What?"

"When that mountain lion was on the tower, and he wouldn't get down, and you said *I'm sorry the mountain lion doesn't respect you.* For some reason, I just thought that over and over, and I got through it."

She smiles and looks down, but I think her eyes are bright with tears.

"*That's* the thing you thought?" she says.

The nurse pops her head back in and clears her throat.

"I gotta go," Clementine says, and kisses me quickly. I squeeze her hand, and then, just like that, she's out of my hospital room and it's dark again.

I fall asleep slowly, the scent of flowers in my nostrils. I hope I dream of Clementine but I don't dream of anything at all.

THIRTY-SEVEN

CLEMENTINE

The next morning, I scan the rows of donuts in their glass cases, behind the counter.

"Two more," says the bored teenager, snapping a pair of metal tongs together.

"How about those... round ones with the icing and the bits of stuff on top?" I say, pointing.

She looks.

"Those are maple walnut," she says, like I should really *know* that already.

"I'll take them," I say, because I don't really care what they are. I've already got the single old-fashioned donut I'm interested in eating, and the rest are a "please like me, and sorry for sneaking in last night" offering.

"Twelve-oh-nine," she says. I hand her a twenty, she gives me change, and then I head back to the Forest Service vehicle in the parking lot.

It's a beautiful, sunny day, and even though smoke still hangs in the air, it doesn't feel nearly as dire as it has the past few days. Even better, I actually took a shower and put on clean clothes this morning, so for the first time in a couple of days I'm not wearing my dirty forest ranger uniform.

I'm wearing Jane's clothes, actually. I *might* have borrowed them while she was in the shower and then left a gushing note on her table about how she's the world's greatest sister. She *might* be annoyed with me right now.

Life's just full of possibilities. I drive to the hospital and get there at five 'til eight, fully determined to stare down some nurses until they let me see Hunter.

When you walk through a hospital with a large box of donuts, heads turn. People watch you.

Perfect, I think, hitting the fourth floor button in the elevator. *Operation 'please like me' is already going great.* Sure, Hunter has one of those charming personalities that wins people over in minutes, but I've got *donuts*.

I push through the double doors to his wing, expecting the nurses to be crowded around their station, but there's only one woman there, and she looks up at me through half-moon reading glasses. I smile at her anyway and put the box on the counter, opening it.

"Who are you here to see?" she asks, her expression not changing.

"Hunter Casden," I say. "And I brought donuts for all the nurses, as a thank you for working so hard..."

It seems like there should be more to say, but I can't think of it.

She looks at me. She looks at the box.

"Where are they from?" she asks.

Come the fuck on, they're donuts, I think.

"Aunt Mae's," I say, trying to keep up the forced cheer. "I'd never bring you donuts from anywhere else."

She considers this for a moment, then stands, slowly, her hands on the desk, and peers into the open box. I swear she's *examining* the donuts like she's a jeweler and they're cut diamonds.

"Ooh, maple nut," she says at last. "My favorite. No one ever brings these."

The nurse grabs one and finally cracks a smile.

"Thanks, sweetheart," she says. "Hunter's in his room."

Practically on cue, I hear a burst of female laughter come from his door. The nurse and I share a look.

"I hope you're his sister, because otherwise you're not gonna be too popular around here," she says. "I've never seen a group of women so interested in checking a patient's vitals."

I look down at the box.

"Well, that's why I brought these," I say.

"Good thinking," she says, and takes a bite of hers.

I swallow, smile, and walk into Hunter's room with the box of donuts.

"Hi," I say.

Three women in scrubs and Hunter all turn toward me. They're standing and he's sitting up on the bed. When he sees me, he smiles, and the nurses all pause for a moment.

I hold up the box, almost like a shield.

"Donuts?" I ask.

The nurses swarm me, ooh-ing, and I lift the lid off the box. Behind them, Hunter swings his legs off the bed and stands, a little more slowly than normal.

"Guys, this is Clementine," he says, walking toward me a little gingerly.

All three nurses stop and look at me, donuts in hand. They're clearly not thrilled, but the one on the right, wearing floral scrubs, manages to smile first.

"We've been hearing *all* about you," she says.

"We heard Monica kicked you out last night," says the one wearing green scrubs.

The final one, wearing pink scrubs, laughs. She looks like she's in her forties, smile lines around her eyes.

"Damn, I was hoping you were his sister," she says.

Hunter skirts around them, wearing an under shirt and pajama pants, and puts a hand on my hip. Then he leans down and kisses me.

It's a slightly longer kiss than it needs to be.

"Donut?" I ask.

He takes one and I set the box down on the bed, grabbing the last old-fashioned for myself. Hunter puts his arm around me as we lean against the sink.

"How's he doing?" I ask the nurses.

"I'm right here," Hunter says.

"Yeah, but you'll just tell me you're fine," I tease. "I want the truth."

"That *is* the truth," he says, taking a bite of donut. "C'mon, Clem, I'm practically good as new."

"His lungs are damaged, and it's hard to tell how much," says Pink Scrubs.

"I inhaled some smoke," Hunter admits, taking another bite.

"He inhaled some *very hot* smoke," Pink Scrubs says.

"They're doing a CT scan on me today because I haven't impressed the doctor," he says. "They might want to keep me another night."

Shit. I was secretly hoping I'd get to... well, not take him home to Lodgepole, but at least take him out of *here*.

"We just can't get enough of him," says Floral Scrubs.

I laugh, even though it's not that funny.

A few minutes later, Pink Scrubs more or less herds the other two nurses out of Hunter's room, waving to him.

The second they're gone, he moves around in front of me, his hands on my hips.

"I thought they were never gonna leave," he murmurs.

"Maybe I should call in sick so I can stay here and make sure none of the nurses are putting the moves on you," I tease.

"They are *definitely* putting the moves on me," he says. "It's only eight in the morning and I'm half-expecting one of them to come in here salaciously sucking on a popsicle."

I laugh, and I let my hands alight on his shoulders, because I'm not quite sure where he's burned. He still smells like smoke and fire, the scent probably imprinted on his skin, and he leans down and kisses me slowly, his hips pressing mine into the sink behind me.

Desire unfurls through me like a ribbon uncoiling, and before I know it I've got both hands in his hair, pressing his face to mine. Hunter lifts me up onto the edge of the sink and I arch my back as he presses between my legs.

He pulls back for a moment, and I realize he's breathing hard, harder than normal.

"You okay?" I whisper.

Hunter puts one hand on my jaw and runs his thumb along the edge of my bottom lip, smiling at me like we've got a secret.

"Yeah," he says.

I know for a *fact* that I can't have him right now, in his hospital room, while the staff is doing morning rounds, but holy shit do I *want* him.

I'm desperately relieved that he's fine, but no matter how much we kiss or hold hands I can feel the wild, primal urge to really get *close* to him, to get him inside me, like that's what will prove once and for all that he's really here and really okay.

He's still running his thumb along my lip, and without thinking I suck it into my mouth to the first knuckle and run my tongue along the salty pad, looking up into his deep blue eyes.

Hunter *growls*, his other hand grabbing my ass even harder, and he presses his hips against me, his cock a hard steel rod.

"You're beautiful and I want to fuck you right here on this sink," he whispers.

There's a knock on the door, and before either of us can say anything, a woman breezes into the room, looking down at a clipboard.

"Good morning, Mr. Casden," she says.

I spit out his thumb as she looks up at us, but there's no way I can pretend we were doing anything but making out on the counter. For a moment, the three of us just stare at each other.

"I'll give you a moment," she says, her tone surprisingly professional.

"Thanks," Hunter and I chorus.

She walks back out, and we just start laughing.

"Maybe that'll keep the nurses off me," Hunter says.

"That was my plan all along," I tease.

I kiss him again quickly, then hop off the counter, adjusting Jane's jeans. Hunter reaches into his pajama pants and rearranges his dick, making a face.

"I'll see you tonight, Casanova," I say, and give him *one* more kiss.

"I can't help it if everybody wants me," he says.

Then he smacks my ass as I leave.

The doctor is standing right outside the door. I nod at her quickly, pretty sure she's laughing.

"Thanks!" I say.

"Not a problem," she says. She's young, maybe in her thirties, and looks Southeast Asian. "Don't worry, it happens more than you'd think."

"Sorry," I say.

She laughs again, and I head to the elevators, then out of the hospital.

THIRTY-EIGHT

HUNTER

I stare up at the ceiling as the cot starts to move, slowly, into the giant white tube. Some thoughtful person taped photos up there: autumn leaves, Yosemite Valley, a river, some penguins.

They tried, I think, and I close my eyes. I'm not really claustrophobic, but does anyone *enjoy* being trapped in a narrow tube?

I'm not supposed to move during the CT scan, but the second I'm in there, I swear my entire body starts itching. My foot keeps twitching for no reason. I've *never* been able to hold still, so why start now?

Think about something else, I tell myself.

I think about getting a job in Lodgepole. I think about the rest of the crew, still fighting the Saturn fire, though it's off in the middle of nowhere again.

I think about Clementine that morning. Sitting on the sink, her legs around me. The look in her eyes as she sucked on my thumb that sent a bolt of pure need through me, like I'm not *really* okay until I have her again.

My mind wanders, and now I'm just fantasizing, nothing much else to do in this big tube. Yanking off her jeans. Leaning her back against the mirror, her knees on my shoulders, her thighs against my face.

The sound she makes when I lick her, when I slide my tongue between her lips and—

"Excuse me, Mr. Casden?" a voice says. "Could you please not... move?"

I come back down to earth, and instantly realize that my dick is sticking *straight* up like the goddamn Washington Monument.

"Sorry," I say, clearing my throat. "I... fell asleep."

"No problem," the voice says.

I take a deep breath and think about what the rest of the Canyon Country Hotshots are doing right now. I think about it very, very hard.

———

THAT AFTERNOON, they finally let me go visit Porter. I walk there on my own, though the nurses make me take a tank of oxygen and a mask, just in case I get winded walking from one side to the hospital to the other.

I actually do, just a little. I don't use the tank though.

Porter's got even more flowers than me. They're stacked on the sink, on the bedside table, and when I peek into the bathroom, there are a couple bouquets in the shower.

His leg is in traction, and he's got a cast plus some kind of metal framework on the thing.

"Casden," he says as I walk in, rolling my oxygen tank behind me.

"How's it going?" I ask, sitting in the armchair next to the bed.

"Better than it was," he says. His words are slow and a little blurry, and he's blinking hard at me, like he's trying to clear a film from his eyes. "But hell, crawling through a pit of live snakes is better than yesterday was."

"I'd take it," I say.

He blinks again, then rubs his eyes with one hand.

"They put me on morphine and I'm high as a fucking kite," he says. "God, why do people like this?"

I couldn't be less surprised that Porter doesn't like being high. The man might have some control issues.

"I couldn't tell you," I say.

He looks at his hands, then shakes his head. He clears his throat.

"Thanks for not leaving me behind," he says, still looking at his hands, clenching them slowly, then unclenching. He shakes his head again and looks at me.

"You could have gone on and no one would have blamed you," he says.

I lean forward, my elbows on my knees, and look at the tile floor.

"I wasn't the best Marine and you can probably guess why," I start.

"Cocky, impatient, problems with authority?" he says.

I didn't mean for him to actually guess, but I go on.

"But I don't leave men behind to burn to death," I finish.

"I had my knife," Porter says. "I wasn't gonna burn to death."

It's not a nice thought, but it's comforting in a strange way.

"What I'm trying to say, here, is that I know we don't get along too well sometimes, but you're one of the best men I've got and I'm going to spend the rest of my life glad you were on that lookout with me," he says.

I open my mouth to say that none of us would have left him, but he holds up a hand.

"Don't get talkative about it," he orders. "Am I gonna see you next year?"

I stand up, sensing that this is over.

"Hell yes," I say.

"Good," he says, and I leave.

THIRTY-NINE

CLEMENTINE

I'm on livestock duty at the Ponderosa Ranch. It's mostly horses with a couple of goats and llamas thrown in. Or maybe they're alpacas. I can never tell.

Anyway, I spend half the day telling people where their animals are. Then I spend the other half looking at animals and trying to figure out where their owners are.

The animals and the people are about equally helpful, to be honest.

When it's over, it's already evening. I wolf down a sandwich that the Red Cross gives me and head to Jane's for a quick shower, because I smell like animals and B.O., and it's gross.

Jane's already there when I unlock her door with my key, standing at the counter and eating a bowl of cereal. She gives me a long look up and down, spoon in mouth, and looks irritated.

"You know you have an entire stash of your *own* clothes here, right?" she says.

"Sorry," I say, looking down at myself. Then I look back up. "Wait, I do?"

"Yeah, you leave something here practically every time you visit, dumbass," she says, and walks out of the kitchen and into her bedroom.

Jane rummages through a couple of drawers before finally pulling out a couple of t-shirts, an old pair of corduroys I'd completely forgotten I had, a knee-length jersey skirt, and several pairs of socks.

"Pants-stealing jerk," she says, and walks back into the living room.

"Thanks!" I call after her. "Can I use your shower?"

"Knock yourself out," she calls.

I shower fast, and I'm pulling on the pants I found, wishing that my stash included underwear, when I have a thought.

It's Hunter, pressing me against the sink this morning, me sucking on his thumb.

I pause for a second, heart pounding, heat gathering below.

Then I take the pants off, grab the skirt, and pull it on, sans underwear.

I hesitate again.

Really? I think.

An old memory: Hunter and I, eighteen, at the county fair. I'm saying something but he's just staring at my chest, not hearing a word I say.

I skip a bra and pull on a t-shirt. My heart's going a mile a minute.

This is trashy as hell, I think. *Who the fuck waltzes into the hospital without panties so they can get laid easier?*

Besides the hooker in that one episode of the Sopranos. It's you and her, Clementine.

I stuff the rest of my clothes into a bag, then grab my jacket and put it on, hiding my nipples at least. I'm not going in there *completely* slutty.

"I'm gonna go visit Hunter again before I head home," I say, walking back into the kitchen.

"I can't believe you're dating Hunter Casden again," Jane says. "You guys were *so* gross. Did Mom tell you she had to throw out that couch because it was practically—"

"Yeah, she told me," I say.

"You know you have to tell me how the hell you got back together someday, right?" she says. "Like, I get that now isn't the best time, but *damn*, Minty."

I shrug my bag over my shoulder and think.

"He was staying next door with the hotshot crew, we made out, then we had a bunch of sex in a lookout cabin, and voila!" I say, waving my hands in the air.

"Definitely not good enough," she says.

"Bye," I say, laughing.

———

I WALK THROUGH THE HOSPITAL, and somehow, no one looks at me. No one stares, open-mouthed, as I walk by, even though I feel like there's a big neon sign over my head that says SKANK, and the knowledge of what I'm doing has me wildly, insanely, *incredibly* turned on.

I take the elevator up. I head for the nurses' station and wave at them. They wave back. I keep pretending that I have underpants on and walk into Hunter's room, shutting the door behind myself. The lights are half-off, and he's propped up in the bed, watching TV, looking bored, and he grins when he sees me.

"I get out tomorrow," he says.

I put my purse on a chair, my heart thumping, and lean over the bed to give him a kiss.

"What then?" I ask.

"I'm gonna stay with my parents for a few days, but my fire

season's over for this year," he says. "I can just start looking in Lodgepole, because for some reason they don't want guys with burns and fucked up lungs tagging along."

He grabs my jacket and tugs me closer. He's got the bed tilted a little higher than forty-five degrees, so he's basically upright.

"*And* I can take up residence in your bed and start convincing you this is a good idea," he teases.

I kiss him again, then sit on the bed, one hand on his chest.

"I don't need convincing," I say quietly. "I think it might work this time."

"I want it to work," he says, and puts his hand top of mine.

"I want it to work too," I say, and squeeze our fingers together.

"I think I'd have fallen for you even if I just met you last week," he says, his voice still quiet and serious.

Then he grins.

"I mean, your ass looked *great* in that skirt at the spaghetti dinner," he says. "I got at least thirty percent hard watching you walk up to that microphone."

"Only thirty?" I ask.

"It was a fast walk," he says. "And your ass looks good in this skirt, too."

"Should I walk around and see what percentage you come up with?" I ask.

Hunter grins and puts his hands behind his head, so I stand up and shrug off my jacket. My nipples point outward like arrows, and Hunter laughs, pushing the sheets off himself and sitting up.

"Clem, I swear to God——"

I put one hand on his chest and push him slightly backward, even as he cups one breast in his hand, his palm rough on my nipple through my shirt.

"Aren't you supposed to be resting?" I ask, grinning.

"I can rest later," he says.

I push harder, and he lets me move him backward.

"You're an invalid, you know," I say. "You've got an oxygen tank and everything. I wouldn't want you to have an *episode*."

I push him back onto the bed, and I pull the covers over his legs. He's pitching a *massive* tent already, and just looking at it makes me a little wetter.

Hunter sees me looking, so he gathers the blankets around his cock in one hand and then just holds it there, leaning back on the hospital bed, grinning at me, and it's fucking sexy as *hell*.

"Okay, I'm an invalid," he says, his voice deep and raspy. "Let's watch your ass in that skirt."

I slide my shoes off, then turn my back on Hunter and walk slowly to the foot of the bed, swinging my hips. It's not very tight or very short, but I can still feel the soft fabric whispering across my ass as I move, and besides that, I swear I can *feel* Hunter's eyes.

When I get to the foot of the bed I put one hand on the railing there and look over my shoulder, sticking my ass out a little.

Hunter's pushed the blankets off himself, and when I look back he grabs his dick through his pajama pants, grinning. For a second, I'm breathless with desire, and *all* I want to do is crawl onto the bed and jump on top of it.

"Eighty-seven percent," he says.

I blow my bangs off my forehead.

"That's it?" I tease. "What's a girl gotta do?"

"That was a pretty good start," he says, stroking himself slowly, through his clothes.

I swallow, because as much as I want him, I also have the wild urge to show off for him. Hunter makes me feel like the bad girl sexpot in an old movie, and dear *God* do I like it.

The sink is across from the foot of the bed, so I walk to it, grab the edge, and arch my back, pushing my ass back. I look over my shoulder at Hunter, wiggling slowly from side to side.

"How about this?" I ask, lowering myself to my elbows on the sink.

He's got his cock out and he's stroking it slowly.

"You're not wearing panties, either," he says, his voice low.

"Oops," I say, grinning.

I move one hand to my ass, and rub it, like I'm checking for panty lines.

"Guess I forgot," I say.

Hunter growls.

I pull the hem of my skirt up the back of my legs, slowly, dragging it with one finger just to tease him. I'm so turned on it almost hurts, and his eyes following the hem of my skirt as I raise it are only making it worse.

"Keep going," he says.

I bite my lip and pull my skirt the rest of the way up so it's around my hips and I'm bent over at the waist, totally exposed and vulnerable and desperately, *desperately* horny.

"Touch yourself," he says.

Something's changed, just slightly, and this has gone from me asking him what percentage hard he is to him telling me what to do, half-naked in his hospital room. It's new, but I think I like it.

I reach behind myself, look over my shoulder at him, and slide my fingers over my lips, just barely parting them before I circle my clit with them. It's a little strange to do it backwards — it's not like I ever reach over my butt to masturbate — but the strangeness of it feels good, too.

"Like this?" I whisper.

I'm so slippery that my fingers slide over my clit by accident. My eyes close and I make a soft *grunt*.

"Just like that," Hunter murmurs.

I keep going, my slippery fingers sliding over my clit. I'm

beyond turned on and so sensitive that I have to bite my lip to keep myself from making too much noise, because it's a strange new angle, and because I know Hunter is watching, hard cock in hand.

"Don't come," he growls.

I *want* to. I'm surprisingly close, and I want him to *watch* what he does to me without even having to touch me.

"You don't want to watch?" I say.

"I want to make you come myself," he says.

Reluctantly, I move my fingers off my clit and back over my lips. Hunter's still watching, so I push one finger inside, then two.

I gasp and move my hips, trying to find the right spot, but my own hand is a bad substitute.

"Jesus, Clem," Hunter says.

I bite my lip and look back at him, pushing my fingers deeper as I gasp.

"Like the show?" I ask.

Before he can answer, the doorknob turns.

I spin around so fast I nearly fall over, and before the door's fully open, I'm leaning against the sink, arms crossed over my chest, in the most affectedly casual pose I've ever managed.

"Hello," says the nurse. "Sorry, I just need to check his chart real quick."

"No problem," I say.

Hunter's yanked his pants and blanket back up, and the two of us don't say a word. I try to act like I wasn't just putting on a sex show for my boyfriend, or that I'm still *throbbing* with desire.

"How are you feeling?" she asks, looking at something up by his head.

She's facing away from me. Slowly, I uncross my arms and I rub my *very* visible nipples through my shirt, looking at Hunter the whole time.

He clears his throat, staring at me.

"I'm on the mend," he says distantly.

"That's good," she says. "Getting out of here tomorrow?"

"Sure am," he says.

I re-cross my arms just as she turns around and looks at something else.

"All right, everything looks fine," she says. "Do you guys want this door closed?"

"Yeah, we were having a private conversation," Hunter says. "Thanks."

"Sure thing!" she says brightly, then leaves, the door clicking behind her.

I can't stop myself anymore, and before I know it, I've crossed the room to Hunter's bedside. He's already got the blankets off, his cock pointing skyward. I lean over and kiss him hard and he pulls my shirt up, over my breasts, and pinches both nipples between his fingers until I moan into his mouth.

Then he pinches a little harder, and I bite his lower lip, my hands curling around the rails of his hospital bed. I pull myself up and straddle him, the underside of his cock against my slit, and I move my hips so I rub against him.

Hunter *growls*. He pushes himself up with one arm so we're face-to-face and reaches around me with the other. I push my fingers through his hair, and kiss him again. Then we separate, our faces together, his cock in his fist, the tip right at my entrance.

I don't move for a second because I want to mark this moment in my memory: Hunter's body against mine, so close I can feel his heartbeat, just about to enter me and give me what I *need*, and even though everything about this is carnal as fuck, there's something beautiful and simple and pure about it. Something I couldn't dream of ever having with anyone else.

Then I slide onto Hunter's cock and *moan* as he fills me up, my eyes shutting as he hits *that spot* instantly and we start moving together. I try to start slow, control myself, make it last, but my brain's not in charge any more. This is urgent and needy, hard and fast.

And Jesus, it feels good. I lean back a little, hanging onto Hunter's shoulder, and every time his cock hits that spot a bolt of white shoots across my vision. I'm gasping with every thrust and trying not to moan as he wraps his arms around me and presses his lips to my neck.

I'm gonna come if we don't slow down, but I don't want to, not just yet. It feels so fucking *good* that I want to just do this a little longer, riding Hunter deep, my mind slowly blinking out with pleasure.

"Slower," I whisper. "I want this to last."

"Do you know how hard that is?" he whispers back, even though we slow together.

"I just need *this*," I say. "I need to be close to you."

He pulls me down by the hips, pressing our bodies together as hard as they'll go, and I sigh.

"Close enough?" he whispers.

I just kiss him again, the two of us intertwined on this hospital bed. I have this urgent, driving impulse to *possess* him, to hold him close and never let him go, and it's so strong I don't think I can possibly explain it with words.

I move my hips against him, just enough for his cock to move inside me as I bite my lip. Hunter exhales and his fingers dig into my hips, one hand reaching around me to grip my shoulder from the back.

"You're fucking beautiful," he murmurs. "I can't believe I get to do this with you."

Even though we're going slow I feel myself losing it a little. I push him backward until he's almost upright against the tilted hospital bed, his breathing heavy, his hands still on my hips. I put one hand on his shoulder to steady myself, and he turns to kiss it, his lips surprisingly soft against my skin.

"It didn't work," I murmur, my eyes half-closed, my hand on his shoulder.

Hunter's watching me with a look of pure concentration as I flex my hips back and forth again, taking him deep with every stroke.

"What didn't work?"

"Going slow so I wouldn't come," I say.

Hunter growls at me, his hands tight on my hips, and he brings he down hard again. This time I moan out loud, my hand tightening against his shoulder.

"Then don't go slow," he says, a wicked grin on his face. "I missed you and this was *all* I thought about today."

I kiss him again, already moving faster.

"What did you think about?" I ask.

Hunter's breathing is ragged, and he clears his throat before he answers.

"I *thought* about bending you over the sink and watching your face in the mirror," he says.

He reaches one hand up and pinches a nipple.

"But I'll take watching you ride my cock until you come," he growls.

I sink onto him again and this time we *both* groan, so I lean backward, grabbing his leg in one hand. The other drifts off his shoulder and he grabs it. I ride him faster, leaning back, back arched, and *Jesus* it feels good.

"You feel fucking perfect, Clem," he says.

I keep going and I can feel Hunter's eyes raking over me, and even though it's his fault I'm about to come *hard*, I fucking love that he's watching me like that. I like showing him how *good* he makes me feel.

His hand is in mine and I press it against my face. I'm whispering his name, over and over again and then suddenly he pulls me forward until my face is against his, my elbows on the pillow next to his head, his hands on my hips again.

"Yes," I whisper, and he pushes my hips down onto him *hard*. I'm about to come, at the edge of a cliff, about to dive over. "God, Hunter, yes."

He does it again and I explode, white light flashing through my vision and heat rippling through my body. I press my mouth to Hunter's shoulder so I don't scream but I *moan*, still riding him as wave after wave rolls over me.

"I love how hard you make me come," I whimper.

"I love making you come this hard," he gasps back. "Oh, *fuck*, Clementine."

He growls and curls his fingers into my hips and I can *feel* him come inside me, his thick cock jerking as he breathes hard. I keep moving until he's stopped and is starting to go limp inside me, and he wraps one hand around my head and pulls me down. We kiss slowly, for a long time, our bodies touching. I pull my shirt back down over myself but I stay there, him still inside me, for longer than I should because it feels warm and good and right, and even though we're on a hospital bed I just want this to *last*.

Finally, I roll off, pulling my skirt down, and Hunter scoots over and then his arms are around me, my head on his chest, the scent of smoke still in his skin. He doesn't say anything, but he plays with my hands, holding them up against his bigger ones, fingers splayed, palms together. Then he laces them together and kisses them slowly, pulling my arms over my shoulders.

I don't know what he's doing, and I don't care. For the first time in days I'm exactly where I want to be. There's nothing else I'm thinking about. Just this.

FORTY

HUNTER

I'm playing with Clementine's hands, the two of us nestled together on the hospital bed. I've never been able to sit still so I'm running the tips of my fingers over her soft, bony knuckles, over the tendons in her hands, again and again. Sliding my fingers between hers, squeezing them, letting them go.

Visiting hours are nearly over, and I know at 8:55 on the dot one of the nurses is going to come in here and tell her to leave, but we've got another ten minutes before that happens and I just want to lie here with her in my arms.

"I've got something to get excited about," she says at last, her voice slow and lazy.

"What?" I ask.

She flexes her hand as I stroke over her knuckles again, her fingers twisting against mine.

"I've got a double bed," she says. "It's *actually* big enough for two adults to sleep in."

I smile into her hair, because I feel a little like a kid on the first day of school, excited and nervous.

"I think we've done an admirable job with the available tools," I say.

She laughs softly, then kisses the knuckles on one of my hands.

"I guess I should tell people about you," she says. "They're gonna be confused when I show up places holding hands with a tall buff guy they've never met."

"I can't *believe* you haven't told anyone we're together," I tease.

"*When* was I gonna tell anyone?" she asks, laughing. "Hunter, I thought you'd fallen off the face of the earth until what, last week?"

"Is it because I embarrass you?"

"Yeah, it's really horrible having to introduce my charming, former-Marine current-firefighter boyfriend to people," she says. "I can just *tell* they're thinking I could do better."

"You forgot cowboy," I point out.

"I should just tell people I'm lonely and I've hired a male prostitute," she says. "Spare myself the shame."

"No one would believe you," I say, laughing into her hair. "I'd be way out of a forest ranger's price range if I were a hooker."

We're both quiet for another moment.

"I wish you didn't have to leave," I say.

"I wish you were leaving with me," she says quietly. "The real bed's at my place."

For a moment, she threads her fingers through mine looking thoughtful. I let her do it and watch.

"I've never done that," I say, thoughtfully.

"Done what?"

"Woken up with you next to me."

She stops for a moment, looks at our hands, and then starts again.

"The lookout was close," she says.

"It wasn't the same, though," I say.

Before Clementine can answer, the door swings open and a column of light falls into the room.

It's followed by my mother.

The moment she sees me and Clementine on the bed, she stops short. Her mouth comes open and for a second, she just *stares*.

Then she clears her throat.

"Clementine," she says, her tone almost aggressively neutral.

Clementine's frozen, my arms still around her, but when my mom says her name she pushes me off her and sits up.

"Hi, Mrs. Casden," she says, and stands.

She's still not wearing a bra. I get out of the bed behind her and put one hand on her lower back.

"I didn't know you'd reconnected," my mom says, giving me a *look*.

"My ranger division hosted Hunter's hotshot crew in Lodgepole between assignments," Clementine says, and grabs her jacket off the chair, shrugging it on.

"I see," my mom says. She's still standing just inside the entryway, wearing jeans, a turquoise belt, and a button-down white shirt, the picture of Western no-nonsense.

"She presented us with a plaque for containing the Elkhorn fire," I say, fingertips rubbing a small circle on Clementine's back. "We got dinner later, and..."

I shrug.

My mom nods once, brusquely. She's being polite, but she's never liked Clementine. Eight years ago, she was certain that Clementine was ruining me, a perfectly good, church-going, all-American teenager. And *then* we broke up while I was overseas, and I don't think my mom's forgiven her for making me go back to Afghanistan.

I get it. If someone broke my kid's heart as hard as she broke mine, I'd have trouble welcoming them back.

"It's nice to see you," Clementine says, a forced smile on her face. "I should get going, though."

"Lovely to see you again as well," my mom says, and even though her tone is perfectly polite, not one person in this room thinks she's telling the truth.

Clementine turns toward me, my hand still on her back.

"Call me?"

"I'll walk you to the elevator," I say, because I want to say goodbye to her *without* my mom watching.

We leave the room silently, and we're a good fifty feet away, out of earshot, before Clementine just starts giggling.

"*That* felt familiar," she says.

"I might get to their house to find all my stuff in the front yard," I say. "That, or every single twenty-something from their church is gonna be in my living room."

"It's almost like there are *downsides* to living with your parents in your mid-twenties," Clementine says as I push open the double door out of my wing.

I hold it for her, then grab her ass as she walks through. A guy on the other side gives me a very judgy look.

"I don't *live with my parents*," I say. "I work on their dude ranch for six months of the year, and like everyone else who works there, room and board is provided."

"And you're not allowed to have guests."

"I *choose* to entertain guests elsewhere in order to keep the peace," I say, turning the corner toward the elevator bank. "For example, in your bed."

She stands on her toes and I kiss her.

"If I don't hear from you within forty-eight hours, I'll assume you've been forced into a re-education camp and report you missing," she says.

"Thanks," I say.

She gets on the elevator and I walk back to my room. I'm not looking forward to this. I knew it had to happen sometime, but I was *planning* on telling my parents tomorrow, with words, instead of just letting my mom find Clementine half-naked, in my bed, and probably reeking of sex.

My mom's sitting in the armchair, her hands clasped on her crossed knees, staring distantly at a wall. I take a deep breath and lean against the sink.

"I'm not working at the dude ranch this winter," I say. "I'm moving to Lodgepole."

"Do you have a job there?"

"Not yet."

I decided this three days ago, I think, but I don't say it out loud.

"A place to stay?"

Here we go.

"I'm staying with Clementine until I get my own place," I say, crossing my arms over my chest.

My mom looks at me for a long, long time. Then she stands slowly and puts her purse on her shoulder.

"I know you think I don't like her because she led you into sin," she says.

"Mom, you know that—"

She holds up one hand and goes on, talking over me.

"That girl used you and then tossed you aside the moment things got a little difficult," she says.

"That's not what happened."

"Well, that's sure what it looked like," she says. "Hunter, you're grown, and I can't stop you, but I can tell you to think twice before making the exact same mistakes that you did before."

"I'm not."

The expression on her face says that she doesn't believe me, even a little bit, but I know when arguing is pointless. When we broke up before, it's not like I gave them a detailed account of everything that went down. They just know that I joined the military, she went to college, and six months later I told them she dumped me.

"Call when you're getting discharged," she says. "I brought you some clothes, and I'll come pick you up."

She points to a chair, where there's a neat stack.

"Thanks, Mom," I say.

She steps forward and kisses me on the cheek, then leaves without saying anything else.

———

THREE DAYS LATER, I park my shitty, old truck outside Clementine's house, grab my duffel bag, and walk up her porch steps. She pulls the door open before I can even knock and for a moment we both stand there, grinning like idiots.

Then a ball of yellow-and-white fur shoves past Clementine, nearly knocking her over, and jumps up, both paws right on my stomach.

"Oof!" I say, caught by surprise.

"Trout, get *down*," Clementine says.

Trout gets off me and starts hopping up and down on her front paws.

"Trout, sit," Clementine says.

Trout looks back at her, then at me again. Then she sits, slowly, her tail thumping the porch, staring at me like she has to tell me something *really urgent*.

Clementine waits about three seconds. Trout picks up one front paw at a time and moves them, like she's fidgeting.

"Okay!" Clementine says, and Trout jumps to her feet and rams herself against my legs.

"Atta girl," I say, bending down and thumping Trout hard. She wags her tail and throws her head back, clearly enjoying this.

"Do I get a greeting?" Clementine asks, leaning against the door frame. "I promise I'm wagging my tail on the inside."

I laugh, leaning over Trout, and give Clementine a long hello kiss.

"Welcome to your temporary lodgings," she says.

I step around Trout and walk inside, the dog close on my heels. I look around, realizing I've never actually been in Clementine's house before.

"Mandy, Lucy, and I had a house meeting about you," she says, keeping her voice low. "You get your own shelf in the fridge and we're charging you rent after two weeks."

"Fair," I say.

She stops, then glances toward the living room, craning her neck around the corner. Then she pulls me back, out of sight, and whispers.

"Literally half the meeting was about the toilet seat," she says. "For the love of *God*, please put it down. Please. They'll murder you in your sleep."

I laugh quietly and kiss her, lowering my duffel bag to the floor. I grab her hips and pull her against me, her body soft and yielding.

"I'm serious," she says.

"I'm looking at a couple places this weekend," I say. "And I promise not to horrify your roommates while I'm here. I wasn't raised by wolves."

She kisses me again, her body pressed against mine, and I'm glad I'm wearing jeans.

I'm just staying with Clementine and her roommates until I find a place. It's not like I can just move in with her and her roommates, and even though I thought about suggesting we look for a place together, I know she doesn't want to move quite that fast.

"I'll give you a tour in a few minutes," she says, pulling

away. "There's rules about which soap you can use in the shower."

"Am I gonna have to take notes?" I ask.

Clementine laughs.

"Probably," she says, and tugs on a belt loop with one finger. "But I'll try to make it worth your while."

"You could start now," I murmur.

"Mandy and Lucy are in the living room," she says. "Probably wondering what the *fuck* is taking us so long."

"We could take longer."

She doesn't answer, just kisses me one more time, then grabs my hand and pulls me along.

"C'mon," she says.

FORTY-ONE

CLEMENTINE

Six Weeks Later

"Wait, no," I say, glancing around. "I think it's this way."

I take off without waiting for Hunter to answer, mostly because I know he's going to disagree.

"It's not," he says, but he follows me anyway.

I round the corner and stop. It's just another row of ugly, half-dead cornstalks. A dead end.

"Goddamn *motherfucker*," I mutter, clenching my fists in the pockets of my fleece.

"It's back there," Hunter says, pointing.

"We went that way already," I say.

"We went this way too."

"Well, we did *now*," I say.

"You could try believing me," Hunter says.

A breeze blows through the corn maze, shaking the stalks and rattling the leaves, and I realize that we're about to get into a fight over a Halloween attraction for children.

I think Hunter realizes it too, because for a moment, we just look at each other.

"Want to be that couple who gets into a fight in the Great Maize Maze?" I ask.

"Only if we can air our dirty laundry at the top of our lungs," he says, and pushes his hands into his pockets, relaxing a little.

"I was thinking we could argue about our sex life in detail near a group of children," I say.

Now Hunter laughs.

"C'mere," he says, walking toward me. He puts one arm around me and points with the other toward the wooden tower in the middle of the maze.

The wooden tower we *cannot fucking seem* to find, by the way.

"Didn't that kid enter the maze with us?" he says.

I blow my bangs out of my eyes, because I need a haircut.

"Magenta jacket?" I ask. "Yeah, I think she did."

We stand there for a moment, and I'm pretty sure we're thinking the same thing: we *both* navigate the wilderness as part of our jobs. How the hell are we so bad at this?

"I bet she cheated," he says. "It's not like these are real walls, she's probably small enough to just run between the cornstalks."

"Probably," I agree. "Kids are cheating jerks."

Hunter kisses me on the cheek, the tip of his nose cold against my face.

"Want to go try your way?" I ask.

———

WE FIND the tower without getting into a fight. Turns out neither of us was right, and the turnoff was further back than either of us thought.

From twenty feet in the air, the corn maze is *embarrassingly* small. We both look at it for a while, considering the best exit strategy.

"Looks like we start by going north," I say, pulling out my compass.

"I can't believe you brought a compass to a corn maze," he says.

"I like being prepared," I say.

"*Then* what heading do we proceed along?" he teases.

"The heading is *shut up or I'm leaving you to fend for yourself*," I say. "It's getting dark and someone told me that they release wolves into the maze at sundown, so be nice to me."

"I could fight a wolf," Hunter says, grinning.

"You could fight *one* wolf," I say. "Not a pack of wolves."

"I'd retreat up here," he says, looking around the tower. "They'd be forced to come at me one at a time, like henchmen in a bad action movie."

"Sure, no problem," I say.

A magenta jacket catches my eye. It's running out of the maze. Hunter sees it too, and we both sigh.

"Cheater," I mutter.

———

WHEN WE FINALLY GET OUT OF the maze, it's nearly sunset, so we skip the pumpkin patch, get hot apple cider, and go sit by the bonfire. I sit against a haystack, Hunter leans against me, and I drape one arm over his chest.

We're *surrounded* by teenagers making out. It's pretty obvious that the Ladies Auxiliary didn't quite think the bonfire through, because several of them are just walking the bonfire in circles, frowning at teens and reprimanding their inappropriate behavior.

"Hey," says Hunter.

"Are you gonna ask me to make out?" I say.

"I was gonna ask if you wanted to get *inappropriate*," he says.

"Maybe if you put your jacket over your lap I can give you a hand job without anyone noticing," I say, laughing.

I'm *slightly* more tempted by the idea than I should be.

"Or you could sit on my dick and pretend you're just sitting on my lap," he suggests, grinning up at me.

"Solid plan," I tease. "It'll fool everyone."

Another Lady of the Auxiliary walks by, glaring. Hunter and I wave slightly, and she nods at us. We both go quiet for a little while, watching the fire. After a few minutes he sits up and puts his arm around me and I lean against him, our positions reversed, his thumb slowly stroking my shoulder.

"I really like this," he says quietly.

"The bonfire?"

"Everything," he says, slowly. "I like the festival, I like living in Lodgepole. I like being with *you*."

I snuggle into him a little more.

"I like it too," I say. "We didn't even get into that fight in the corn maze."

He considers the fire for a moment.

"What about our sex life would we be *arguing* about?" he says, mostly teasing.

I laugh.

"That was a joke," I say. "Though I was really annoyed two weeks ago when you had a cold and wouldn't have sex with me."

"I was afraid I'd sneeze and cover you in a layer of snot," he says.

"Ew," I say.

"Exactly," Hunter says.

Another pause.

"So my plan worked," he says. "I had sex with you until you decided this was an okay idea."

"It sounds *really* terrible when you put it that way," I say.

"I need one of those *Orgasm Donor* t-shirts," he says.

"If you got that shirt this relationship would be a less okay idea," I say, and Hunter laughs.

It took him all of a week to find a job as the Lift Operations Supervisor at a nearby ski resort. The words "veteran" and "firefighter" came out of his mouth, and he got hired because *of course* he did.

Once he had a job, it was another five days before he found a studio apartment above a clothing boutique on Lodgepole's tiny Main Street. Technically, he was living with me for fifteen days, but we had another house meeting and decided not to charge him rent for that last twenty-four hours.

"You know, I thought it would be harder," he says. "Not just the job and the apartment, but with us. And it hasn't been hard."

"Hunter, are you calling me easy?" I ask.

"You did offer to give me a public hand job five minutes ago," he says into my hair.

I laugh.

"I *am* spectacularly bad at turning you down," I say. "I was twenty minutes late for work the other day."

"I misread the clock and thought it said five-thirty," he says. "That was an accident."

"Every time you don't want me going somewhere, you just whip your dick out and I climb right on," I tease.

An Auxiliary Lady walks past and *glares* at me. I smile innocently.

"That's not true," Hunter says. "I would never use my dick for nefarious purposes, only for good."

"Well, that's the problem," I say. "If it weren't good, it wouldn't make me late for things."

"Maybe you just need willpower," Hunter teases.

I laugh. He pulls me a little closer, and I can feel him swallow, then take a deep breath.

"What I'm *trying* to say is I love you," he says. "You probably think it's too soon, and it's okay if—"

I put my hand over his mouth and sit up straighter, looking right into his face, my heart beating wildly.

I suddenly feel reckless, almost like this is dangerous to say out loud. But it's true, so fuck it.

"I love you too," I say.

He smiles under my hand, so I take it off his mouth.

"I promise not to take it back this time," he says, his forehead against mine.

I don't know what to say, so I kiss him, and even though there are teenagers making weird noises all around us, it feels secret and intimate, just us and this bonfire and the chilly October air. He sneaks his hand up under my shirt and I wind my fingers through his hair, my tongue in his mouth, and then we're *definitely* making out.

Hunter pulls back a little.

"There's a chaperone," he says.

I'm half on top of him and not too far from suggesting that we sneak back into the corn maze, where at least it's dark.

"It's okay, we're in love," I say, and Hunter grins.

The chaperone walks on past. We don't stop making out.

CHRISTMAS EVE

Jennifer looks up and down the long table, biting her lip, looking very serious.

"I want the tiara," she finally says.

"You can't *have* the tiara," Lucy says, her words just a little mushy-sounding. "It's already been traded twice. I am the *final owner* of the tiara."

Her face is perfectly straight as she places the tiara on her head, staring down Jennifer.

Jennifer sighs, her shoulders slumping. Her husband Carl pats her on the back.

"Okay, what's actually available?" she asks for at least the third time.

"Not this," Lucy says, pointing at her head.

"I *know*," Jennifer says.

"Don't confuse the situation any more than it's already done been confused," says Mike, who's drunk enough to get folksy.

Since it's nine o'clock the night before Christmas, the

Rusty Beaver is empty except for us. Actually, I think they might have intended to close at eight, but the bartender and the single waitress seem like they're enjoying this show.

We were supposed to have our office holiday party a week ago, but a black bear went rogue in the National Forest and we had to deal with it. The bear is fine, just relocated, and now we're doing this on Christmas Eve.

"This is available," Mandy says, holding up a twelve-pack of toilet paper. "It's available. And useful."

"It's utilitarian as fuck," I say.

"Jennifer," Hunter says. "Jennifer. *Jennifer.*"

"*What,*" she says.

"Have you ever played with these," he says, holding up a package of what looks like multi-colored pills. "When you put them in water, they *turn into dinosaurs*, and I'm not even kidding."

Jennifer just rolls her eyes and keeps looking.

"This is all bullshit," she says after a minute. "I want a new one."

She reaches for the pile and grabs a hastily-wrapped present from the pile, as allowed by the somewhat-complicated rules of our annual workplace gift exchange.

There are two easy rules, though: one, the gift cannot cost more than ten dollars, and two, the exchange *must* take place at the Rusty Beaver.

She rips the paper off, revealing a metal sign, and starts laughing hysterically. We shout at her to turn it around, so the whole table can see.

There's a moment of silence, and then *we* start laughing.

On the metal sign is a cartoon bear, skiing down a mountain, its front paws over its genital region, and the bear looks either sultry or embarrassed. It's surprisingly hard to tell.

Across the bottom, the sign reads BEAR NAKED SKIING.

"But *why?*" Mandy gasps.

"It's beautiful," Mike says.

"Bears are always naked," says Mandy. "Why's it embarrassed?"

"Maybe it's embarrassed that it's skiing," Lucy says, tiara still on her head.

I turn to Hunter, laughing so hard I can barely talk.

"Did you steal this from the ski resort gift store?" I ask.

"*No*, I bought it from the ski resort gift store with my employee discount, *thank you very much*," he says.

"Hunter," Jennifer says, pointing. "You're my new favorite. Did I tell you guys about the dog door? Gertrude can get in and out but *not the raccoons*."

"Babe, I'm right here," Carl says dryly.

Jennifer kisses him quickly, and we all *aww* because of alcohol.

"Babe, I know you're the father of my children, but you didn't fix the dog door," Jennifer explains.

"Good to know what the hierarchy is," Carl says.

"Whose turn is it?" Mike asks.

Carl holds up his slip of paper with the number five on it.

"I'd take the sign but it's coming home with me anyway," he says.

Mandy holds up the toilet paper, and Hunter holds up the sponges that turn into dinosaurs. Carl considers them for a moment.

"I'll take my chances with the pile," he says.

———

AN HOUR LATER, we all leave the Rusty Beaver. It's not snowing now, but there's a light dusting on the ground, and we're all bundled up as we leave.

"You're driving, right?" I call to the sober-seeming Carl as Jennifer looks at the bear sign again and laughs.

"Definitely," Carl says, looking at her. "Don't worry."

"I'm not *drunk*, I'm tipsy and excitable," Jennifer says.

Carl puts a hand on her back and they walk toward the only car on the street.

"Merry Christmas!" Jennifer calls over her shoulder.

"Us or him?" Lucy asks.

"You make it sound so *dire*," I say.

"Choose wisely," Lucy says.

"*That's* from *Lord of Rings*, right?" Hunter says.

I put one hand on his arm.

"That's from *Indiana Jones*," I say, petting his arm. "You tried."

He sticks his tongue out at me.

"Lucy, she's not gonna pick us," Mandy says.

"It's okay, we've got Trout to give us kisses," Lucy says.

"Sorry, guys," I say, laughing. "Merry Christmas?"

We all hug, then I put my hand in Hunter's and we head off in the opposite direction from Lucy and Mandy.

"I like them," he says.

"Which ones?"

"All of them," he says. "Even Mandy, once she stopped being afraid to talk to me."

I laugh.

"I *should* go with them and pack for visiting your parents," I say.

"It's one night. Pack in the morning," Hunter says.

Lodgepole is quiet, and even though it's not that late, even the streetlights are off and everything is lit by the moon. The whole town has an old western feel already, made older-feeling by the night.

"There's *no one* around," I say.

"It's Christmas Eve," Hunter says.

"It's still weird," I say.

He pulls me into the middle of the street and we walk down the dotted yellow line, looking into dark store windows. It's only a couple of blocks to his apartment, where we hang layers and layers of cold weather gear in his entryway before we walk inside.

I walk into the kitchen, grab a glass of water, and lean against the counter. Hunter does the same, standing next to me, and I lean against him.

"I haven't packed at *all*," I say, and sigh. "Every time I go on a trip I promise myself I'm gonna pack ahead of time, and then I never do."

"Make sure you take your *Minion of Satan* t-shirt," he says.

"Not funny," I say. "They're either gonna eat me alive or not speak to me at *all*."

"I think they're getting better," Hunter says, slowly. "And if it's really awful, we don't have to spend the night."

"I know," I say. "I just hate feeling like I'm coming between you and your parents."

We saw my parents for Thanksgiving: my dad and his brother the day of, and then we went to my mom's house a week later. I've still never told my mom that I know what really happened, but she's finally started talking about something besides my dad.

The thing she's really into now is birdwatching, but my God, I'll take anything.

"As long as you're *coming*," he teases, his voice low and slow.

"Ew," I say.

He puts his arm around my waist, and I lean my head into his shoulder.

"There's something I should tell you," he says.

"They've converted to Wicca," I guess.

"I told them we were engaged to kind of smooth things over," he says.

I drink some water and consider this for a moment.

"Did they buy it?" I ask.

To my surprise, I'm not even a little nervous that his parents think we're gonna get married. The two of us have talked about it and agreed that we like the idea of marriage sometime in the future, but this is the first time we've mentioned it to anyone else.

I guess that's a thing now, I think.

"I couldn't tell," he says. "They seemed skeptical."

"Should I talk incessantly about what wedding flowers I want?" I ask, my head still against his shoulder.

"Nah, then they'll *know* it's fake," he says. "But hold on, I had an idea about that."

He leaves the kitchen and walks into his bedroom, the only other room in the apartment.

"About wedding flowers?" I call.

That's kind of putting the cart before the horse, I think. I hear a drawer open and close, and I yawn.

"About them believing us," he says, walking back into the kitchen and putting his arm around me again. "Wear this, it'll be more convincing."

He holds up a small black box with a diamond ring in it.

I freeze, my water glass halfway to my mouth, and stare at it. For a second I think *he even got fake jewelry to lie to his parents with*, but then I look at his face.

"Marry me?" he says.

"Wait, what?" I ask, because I'm just astonished.

He starts laughing.

"Is this for real?" I ask.

I'm trying not to laugh, but I can't help it.

"Yeah, and I fucked it up," Hunter says, grinning. "Stay there, I'm gonna try again."

He walks out of the kitchen. I put my water glass on the counter, head still spinning.

I definitely wasn't expecting this, and that's a fucking understatement. I figured we'd move in together in a couple months, and *maybe* get engaged six months after that.

But I like this, too. I *want* to marry Hunter and spend the rest of my life with him. Hell, I was planning on doing that anyway, whether we got engaged now or never.

In the next room, I can hear him clear his throat, and I sort of want to shout *hurry up and get back in here already* but I manage to stay quiet.

The floor creaks a little. Hunter appears in the doorway, his face *very* serious. He walks up to me and gets down on one knee, holding up the ring.

I start giggling, not because it's funny, but from sheer *giddiness*.

"Clementine," he says, cracking a smile.

I start laughing harder, and now Hunter's trying not to laugh.

"Quit it, I'm trying to propose," he says.

"Sorry," I say, and bite my lip so I stop.

"I love you and I think I'm always going to love you, so will you marry me?" he says.

He looks up at me, his eyes deep pools in his dark kitchen, and something about it takes my breath away.

I nod.

"Yes," I finally manage to whisper. "Yes, fucking *of course*."

Then I'm on my knees too, his face in my hands as I kiss him and laugh at the same time and so does he. We get tangled up and nearly fall over, still on the floor, until he's sitting with his back against the cabinets, both arms around me.

"Give me your hand," he says.

I hold up my right hand.

"Seriously?" he teases.

Duh, Clementine.

I laugh and give him my left hand.

"Shut up," I say and lean against his chest.

He slides the ring onto my finger, and for a moment, we both just look at it, sparkling dimly in the light coming from his kitchen window.

"I love you too," I finally say, and he pulls me closer. "And I'm glad I found you again."

"Sorry for botching the proposal," he says, lacing his fingers through mine, still looking at the ring on my finger. "I picked it up from the jeweler yesterday, and I meant to wait and take you on a picnic or something, but I got too excited."

I nuzzle my nose against his cheek, grinning.

"*You* got impatient?" I tease.

"This was an impulse," he says. There's a gentle tug on my scalp as he plays with my hair. "As you can tell by our romantic surroundings."

"I *am* surprised," I say.

"Well, you said the words every man's hoping to hear when he proposes," he says. "'*Wait, what?*'"

"That was your own fault," I say.

He kisses me again.

"I got it the second try," he says.

"Thanks for not waiting eight years to give it another shot," I say.

"Clem, I couldn't wait twenty-four hours to propose the first time," he says. "I *almost* drove to your office so I could propose in your cubicle."

"Thanks for not doing that either," I say, and kiss him again, longer and harder. Our tongues twine together and he moves his hand down my back, then under my shirt. "And I think I'll always love you too."

We kiss again, and now I'm sliding one hand up his thigh and he's grabbing my ass, pulling me toward him until I'm straddling him, one hand gripping the waistband of his jeans and the other on his chest.

"Engagement sex right here, or...?" he says, grinning.

"This floor is freezing," I say, and nuzzle his ear. "Carry me to your bed?"

"Just toss you over my shoulder?" he teases.

"Carry me *romantically*," I say, and he squeezes my ass.

Hunter stands, pulls me up, and then grabs me. I wrap my arms around his neck and kiss him, trying not to kick anything in his kitchen.

Then he walks me into his bedroom, tosses me onto his bed, and crawls on top of me.

"I'd love you even if you weren't amazing at sex," he murmurs into my ear, and I laugh.

"I'd love you anyway, too," I say, and pull him harder against me, wrapping my legs around his hips.

We kiss slowly, and I pull his shirt off, his skin warm against me.

"Let's do this for another fifty years," I say.

"Only fifty?"

"Fifty's a good start," I say.

Hunter kisses me again and I hold him as close as I can, just the two of us together in the dark of his tiny apartment.

"It's a start," he says.

THE END

ABOUT ROXIE

Roxie is a romance author by day, and also a romance author by night. She lives in Los Angeles with her husband, cat, child, and a stack of used notebooks.

Want to be the first to hear about new releases and free extras? Sign up for her newsletter with the QR code below!

www.roxienoir.com
roxie@roxienoir.com

www.ingramcontent.com/pod-product-compliance
Lightning Source LLC
Chambersburg PA
CBHW020907060726
47591CB00004B/1131